MAKING A MARK

THE TRISKELION SERIES
BOOK 2

JODI PAYNE

BA TORTUGA

MAKING A MARK

When Troy and Saul became lovers, they worried about a lot of things. There was their age gap, their younger Dom-older sub relationship, and Troy's health, which was made worse by job stress. They managed all that and more with a deep commitment, and with a lot of help from Troy's longtime best friends, fellow Dom and sub couple Carter and Geoff.

In fact, Saul seems to be what all three of the other men need to see what's been there all along, and to provide the balance they need to deepen their relationship in a very meaningful way. They've already made their marks on each other's hearts. Now it's time to start living the life they've all been dreaming of.

Nothing is ever perfect or easy, though, and they all have to shift their perceptions. Geoff has to come to terms with his need for submission and desire to dominate Troy, and Carter must redefine the two most important relationships in his life. Troy struggles to understand why Geoff and Carter want this with him now, after years of watching from the outside. And Saul has to create a whole new definition of family. Can they all break the rules again and become something more special than they can even imagine?

Making a Mark, The Triskelion Series, Book Two
Copyright © 2021 by Jodi Payne & BA Tortuga

Edited by LC Hinson

Cover illustration by AJ Corza
http://www.seeingstatic.com/
Cover content is for illustrative purposes only and any person depicted on the cover is a model.

ISBN: 978-1-951011-60-4

Published by Tygerseye Publishing, LLC, October 2021
Printed in the USA

As always, to our wives.

1

"You want something to eat, or do you want to go straight home and sit in the hot tub, baby?" Carter Lee didn't care, to be honest. He just wanted to get his ass somewhere and process what the fuck had just happened.

More than that, he wanted to see what his husband had to say.

Twenty-five years he and Geoff had been together, Dom and sub from minute one, and while they had experimented together more than once, they'd never acknowledged that Geoff was a switch.

"I'm not hungry. Take me home?" Geoff leaned into him and massaged one palm thoughtfully, bangs still damp from his long tattoo session with Troy.

"You got it." Home wasn't too far up the mountain, but it wasn't the first time he wondered if they shouldn't have bought down in Boulder like their best friend Troy. They'd chosen to renovate an old house they found away from their businesses so that they could leave Geoff's tattoo parlor and his diner behind when they weren't working.

"Mmm. Good to me." Geoff kissed his neck. "I'll lock up."

The ride home was nearly silent. He assumed Geoff was processing the session as much as he was. That was fine; they'd climb into their hot tub and talk there. But instead of heading straight out to the deck when they got home, Geoff headed for the kitchen.

"Smoothie? I'm thinking peach. Want one?"

"Sure. I'll start the water bubbling. I'll meet you out there." It wasn't a request. They needed to chat, process, decompress.

"Yes, sir."

Geoff accepted the order as it was intended, and a few minutes later, he appeared with two smoothies, garnished with lime and raspberries and fat, colorful straws.

"Look at that. They look amazing." Carter had to grin. Geoff made him happy—always had, always would. "You sure you don't want to open a smoothie bar, babe? Yours are the best."

"These are only for you, love." Geoff winked and set the smoothies down, grabbed a couple of towels out of an outdoor storage bin, stripped quickly and then stepped into the tub to get out of the cold air.

Carter made sure their robes were in the outdoor warmer and turned the lights down before he climbed into the water. Oh, this was the best thing they'd invested in for forever.

When they were settled, with hardly a hair between them, Geoff handed him a smoothie. "Cheers."

"Cheers." He took a sip, the peach bright and sweet. He waited for Geoff to finish his sip and then he grabbed his boy, dragging him close for a kiss.

"Mmm." Geoff set his drink down hard on the edge of

the tub and opened to his kiss with a sweet moan, molding into him, hands fluttering against his shoulders.

Carter managed to put his smoothie down so he could grab his boy and take what he needed. Watching Geoff ink Troy had been hot, and making out with Troy's Master? That had revved him up.

Geoff managed a loud, surprised sound against his lips, and practiced fingers dove into the warm water, wrapping around his stiff prick.

Hell yes. He wrapped his hand in Geoff's hair, keeping his boy where he wanted him so he could plunder the sweet mouth.

His boy's hand sped, nothing subtle about the way Geoff worked to get him off, thumb sweeping heavily on every upward stroke.

"Fuck." Carter grunted, his fingers curling into fists. "More."

Show me what you have, boy.

"I watched you kissing Saul, Master," Geoff whispered in his ear, pressure and friction relentless. "You were beautiful together."

"It was time." And soon it would be Geoff's turn to kiss Troy. It had been on Geoff's mind for years.

"And this? Is it time now?" Geoff's thumb burrowed through his slit. "Will you stand up, Master? So I can taste you? Please?"

"Fuck, boy, you beg so pretty." Carter took another kiss, intending to make Geoff wild and hungry before he pulled himself up out of the water, the cold air slapping his wet skin.

Geoff clearly didn't intend to leave him in the cold long; the boy knelt in the water, that hungry mouth taking him in, heat and suction just right. His boy's fingers dug into his ass, keeping him close and making it hard to move. He put one hand on Geoff's head—not holding on but keeping them connected. The hot water licked at his thighs, the steam filling the air and making it look otherworldly.

He knew he was everything in Geoff's world right now. The boy's focus was completely on him, his need. Whatever he wanted. Geoff could get completely lost if he allowed it, and right now, as his nipples grew hard in the cold air and everything below the belt was on fire, it was tempting. But Geoff took him in deep and swallowed, the sensation rippling up his shaft as his body went tight.

"Boy!" he barked out a warning, because after watching Geoff with Troy and kissing Saul, he'd already been close to the edge. His boy knew him, knew what he liked, and Carter arched, pressed deep, and shot down Geoff's willing throat.

His boy's sounds were muffled and muted as Geoff sucked down everything he had to offer. "Master." Then Geoff lapped at him, licked and sucked along his spent shaft, sending aftershocks through him, making his knees weak.

"Damn, boy." He blinked for a second, trying to clear his head. "I may have to keep you."

"If you must. I guess that would be okay." Geoff coaxed him back down into the warm water and snuggled in. "You're not going to ask me to sit by your feet while you work all day again, though, are you? Not. Happening."

He pinched one little nipple, laughing softly. "Don't make me put you over my knee, boy."

Because he would, as soon as his bones solidified again, anyway.

"Ow. Don't fuss, sir," his boy teased. "You'll lose your buzz."

"Mmm. I don't want that." He wrapped his boy in his

arms. He'd get Geoff off, but he could take it slow now. "You did good work tonight."

"Oh!" Geoff beamed at him proudly. "Did you like it? I spent a lot of time thinking about how to make it work. I think Troy was happy."

"I think so too. He floated out the door."

Geoff reached for their smoothies and handed his over. "It gets to be this really intimate thing. The first few minutes, it's just like any other session, but then the way that Troy..." Geoff sighed and sipped his drink thoughtfully. "I don't even know how to explain it. He has this energy, and it is about the pain but it's also about the ink. It has a purpose, you know? And he craves that connection. It's not him or me anymore; it's us. We're in it together. That's what makes it addicting, and that's what gets me high. He just turns his body over to me. He trusts me. He's... for a little while, he's mine."

His boy blinked the faraway stare out of his eyes and glanced at him. "Wow. Sorry. I kind of babbled there."

"Good. Your honesty honors me, and I want us to share your experience together." He reached up, cupped Geoff's jaw, thumb rubbing his boy's bottom lip.

"I'm just relieved that you're a part of it again. It was too hard to think about giving it up, but I always felt guilty the day after. I never wanted to make you jealous or think..." Geoff bit that lip, still swollen from his kisses. "I love you."

"Boy." Carter waited patiently for Geoff to look at him, easing that bottom lip from between his teeth. "I have never doubted you. You are my boy, balls to bones."

"I am. Thank you, sir." Geoff swallowed and nuzzled into his neck. His boy's anxiety was something they still dealt with to some extent, but he'd learned over the years how to handle it. What to say and how to say it.

He held on, loving the contrast between hot water, cold peach, bubbling liquid, and smooth skin.

"Did you like having Saul there?"

Carter chuckled—softly at first, but the sound grew into a warm, full laugh. "Oh, babe. That was fun. I haven't played with another Dom since...was it Rick and Tony we played with on the cruise?"

"Yeah, remember that? That was a while ago. But kissing is tame compared to that cruise." Geoff sat back and sipped his smoothie, giggling. "And I still want to know how you and Rick figured out which of you outranked who."

Shit, so did he. Making out with Rick had been like having a fight with a rabid grizzly bear.

"Dom secrets, of course."

"Oh. Of course." Geoff laughed harder. "Dom secrets. I wonder if Saul knows the same secrets? I can't say that Troy and I do. But then we haven't talked about that yet. We will though. I'm happy with this whole thing."

"Good. Troy really was floating." He put his drink down and reached beneath the water to cup Geoff's prick. "So were you."

Geoff gasped softly and gingerly set his own drink down too. "I was. I am still, sir. Some."

"Yes. Was it hard not to touch Troy? To kiss him?" He knew how much Geoff was affected by his words, by his voice.

Geoff nodded slowly, prick filling fully in his fingers. "It's always a temptation, sir. I've never told him that though."

"You can now." He rubbed their cheeks together as he wrapped his fingers around Geoff's shaft. He was still getting his head around their new relationship with Saul and Troy. He knew that Geoff and Troy already had a power-play arrangement between them that was intrinsic to the tattoo sessions, but he'd never imagined himself agreeing to such a thing in the past. Saul had changed all of them. "What do you want to do first, boy?"

"I..." Geoff sighed in his ear, hips arching into his hand. "I want to kiss him, sir. Just lightly, something... sweet. I want to give him something that doesn't hurt." His boy's words were so sincere.

"You've given him pain and beauty, hmm? Now it's time for pleasure? Such a thoughtful boy." Carter kept his touches light, steady—not teasing, but not at all frantic.

"And I—" His boy flicked his eyes away. Oh, that blush was something. Deep pink and the color ran long, right over the boy's throat.

He followed the line of throat with his lips, threatening with his teeth. "And you?"

"I... Oh, sir." Geoff arched to his mouth. "That. I want to taste him. Taste his ink."

"Your mouth is magical. You'll make him lose his mind, boy." He nibbled his way down to Geoff's shoulder. "And what do you want from him, boy? Do you want him on his knees?"

Geoff groaned. "God. I've never let myself think about that, but... I think I do."

"Mmm..." He thought he did too. While he was laying down stripes, maybe, or while Saul was fucking Troy. "You get to play with him once a month, boy. Plenty of time to plan a scene."

He bit down on the ball of Geoff's shoulder, making his boy whimper and buck into his hand. "Together," Geoff said, panting, that soft voice tight. "We'll plan it together."

"Together. My favorite word." He tightened his hand, driving Geoff that much higher. "I'd love to fuck you while you fuck his mouth, boy."

"Oh!" Geoff rocked against him, that pretty mouth going slack as his boy shot for him. "Fuck! Sir!"

"Mmhmm." *Oh, very nice.* Carter loosened his grip, encouraging the aftershocks to go on and on.

"Sir. Thank you, sir." Geoff found his mouth and kissed him between the panting and soft moans. When his boy finally relaxed, they sank back against the side of the tub together.

"I love you, boy." He kissed Geoff's temple and handed his boy one of the smoothies.

"I love you too." Geoff took a long sip. "Do you think they'll go for it?"

"I have no doubt." He grinned over. "Also, that's one more swat for cursing."

2

C arter had kissed Saul.

Not a peck on the cheek.

Not a hey-there smooch.

It had been a draped over the arm, grinding together, full-on tongue kiss.

Troy didn't know what to say.

Well, okay, he knew that it had been blistering hot, and he knew he wanted to watch it again. Possibly without being so focused on Geoff that he couldn't see.

Saul hadn't said a word about it yet. His Master was concentrating on him, fussing, making sure he was comfortable, giving him all of that aftercare that he was never really able to get from Geoff when he got up from his friend's tattoo table. He knew it was important, knew that Saul needed it as much as he did. His Master's hands were loving, affectionate. But he really wished Saul would bring it up. Say something. Ask a question. Anything.

Troy was soaring—it hadn't been a brutal session, and the ink covering the scar from his heart attack was gorgeous.

More triskelia to go with the ones that covered the rest of his body.

"Geoff does such beautiful work." Saul put the aftercare kit back in the nightstand and stretched out in bed beside him. "How do you feel, boy?"

Curious. Horny. Buzzed. "I'm good, Master."

"You are." Saul rolled against him, a hard prick pressing into his thigh. "That was something to watch, boy. You and Geoff."

"It wasn't the only thing to watch, sir." Not even a little bit. Carter and Saul had been devouring each other.

Saul laughed softly. "No, I guess not. That was something too. He's... it took us a minute to work out, but then it was... he..." His Master laughed again. "I don't know how to explain it. Curious? Patient. It felt almost like an important conversation. And of course, he's sexy as fuck."

"Patient is Carter to the bone, yes." And sexy, but he wasn't going to admit that.

"Yes. I see why he is so perfect for Geoff." Saul reached a hand down and cupped Troy's balls, one finger stretching to play with his guiche piercings. "It was fun. Hot. But really it was like foreplay. It just made me want you."

"Oh, thank God." He grinned at Saul and dragged one hand down his body. "Yes, please. I need you."

"My boy." Saul moved over him, avoiding the new ink across his sternum, and took a kiss. "Mine." The next kiss was deeper, heavier, and Saul rubbed their cocks together, making them both moan.

Yours. He cupped Saul's ass, squeezing hard. Saul's kisses were sharp enough to steal his breath and make him dizzy.

Saul moved to Troy's nipples, licking and biting at the studs there. "Want you." There was a flash of lube and foil and then Saul was back at him, tugging on his piercing with pinching teeth until they stung.

"Oh fuck." He held Saul there, arching up into Saul's mouth.

Saul hissed, rolling on the rubber and then fingers breached him, slicked him up. "Not gonna wait long, boy. Tell me you're ready."

"Fuck me, Master. I'm yours. Ready."

"Mine." The fingers disappeared just that quickly, and Saul pushed in; the slow, gentle thrusts sinking deeper and deeper until his ass pressed against Saul's body. He could feel Saul tremble, knew what coiled inside his Master. "You feel so good."

Troy forced himself to stay still, at least where Saul could see. His inner muscles squeezed and rippled, working Saul's cock. Saul grunted and those hips started to move, thrusting deep and hard, taking him, claiming him. Reminding them both where he belonged and to whom. Troy fought to hold it together, but his Master was driving into him, demanding his control, his need, his everything, and he was going to give it.

"Don't hold back, boy. I want to feel you." His Master's fingers curled around his cock, pumping steadily in time with the thrusts as they evened out, still deep but purposeful, angling just right.

Troy grabbed his knees and pulled, grunting as that lit him up, making him sob in pure need.

"Gorgeous. Fuck, you're so beautiful." He could feel Saul's eyes on him, burning into his skin like Geoff's tattoo needle.

"Please don't stop, lover. Master. Sir." *Need*. He needed.

Saul was breathing heavy, hips working, thick cock nudging him in all the right places. "Right here, baby. Do you feel good? I want you to come for me. I want to see your face. I want you to fly."

"Sir." His body tightened, and he arched, squeezing his Master with all his strength as his body fought to come. Saul thrust again, Troy's cock slapping on his own belly, that little tiny sting enough to push him over the edge.

"Fuck, Troy." Saul shook and grunted, face taking on a lovely wide-mouthed grimace and several frantic thrusts later, his Master shot with a long, low moan, cock pumping inside him. "Oh fuck. Love you."

"Love you." Troy watched as his Master relaxed, working through the aftershocks.

"Mmm." Saul bent to kiss him, gently teasing his cock with light strokes. "My own. You're amazing. Beautiful."

"God, it's so good. Us. Together." Saul made him a little bit stupid.

"Nothing better." Saul shifted and stretched out next to him again. "I'll watch you and Geoff together any time. But that isn't this."

"No. This is magic." He reached down, holding Saul's hand. "This is beautiful."

"It is." He got a kiss on his neck and then Saul laughed quietly. "Listen to us. We're like lovesick puppies."

"You're the puppy. I'm an old dog."

"Bullshit." Saul cupped his cheek. "Just an old soul."

"I wish that was true, Master, but I'm going to be your old soul forever."

"I love you. Your age isn't important to me. You're beautiful, and you're more than I ever imagined I could have. More than I thought I deserved."

Lord have mercy, he did love this fine, hot, committed man. "You want to go for a long ride tomorrow? It's going to be too cold soon."

Saul smiled happily at him. His Master did love that bike. "I'd love it. You sure your chest will be up for it?"

"I'll manage." Given the things his chest had been through, the ink seemed anticlimactic.

His Master hopped up and ducked into the bathroom. "We could pack a lunch, make a whole day of it if it's nice and not too chilly."

"Mmhmm. I'll run into the diner and do some paperwork early and grab us something to lunch on."

"Sounds perfect. I can check the bikes over and the tires and everything." His lover climbed back into bed. "But right now, you need sleep, baby. Lots of sleep."

"Yeah?" He loved that, how Saul thought about him, took care of him instead of leaving him alone.

"Yeah." Saul grinned at him. "You're floating right now, but you look pretty wrecked. Like you've been very, very well used today." He got a kiss before Saul poked him on the nose. "Like really well."

"It's hard work, keeping all y'all satisfied." Good work. Amazing work. But hard.

"Ha." Saul laughed at him. "Then you better go to sleep because now you have even more work to do, don't you?"

"Yes, Master. Love you." He blinked over and squeezed Saul's fingers.

More work. Lord help him.

3

S aul had guilt.

He pulled out his tire gauge and checked the bikes while he thought about that.

He wasn't feeling guilty for the reasons he should have expected. It wasn't about kissing Carter, or even about how much he enjoyed kissing Carter.

And, damn. He really enjoyed kissing Carter.

It wasn't because he was already thinking about the next time, about maybe a scene or even better an overnight. It wasn't even about seeming greedy or unfaithful when he had an amazing, hot, devoted sub and lover of his own.

He certainly could have felt guilty about any of those things, but he didn't.

What he actually felt guilty about was his gut reaction as soon as Geoff's needle had touched Troy's skin. It was weirdly possessive, and not at all how he felt—or how he thought he felt—about polyamory, about shifting their relationship from just each other to include Carter and Geoff.

All he wanted after Geoff was done was to get his boy

back. The aftercare, the sex... that's what he'd be focusing on. Reminding Troy who he belonged to.

He put Troy's bike up on a stand and checked the chain, the gears, gave everything a little lube.

So. This was a thing. And not a discuss-with-Troy thing.

He needed a Dom. One that would get it. He pulled out his cell phone and called Carter.

"Hey." Carter sounded like he was damn pleased to hear from him, voice warm, low. "How goes?"

"Good. Good. How are you?" *How are things with you and Geoff? Did you feel like you needed to take him back last night, or was that just me?*

"Good. Tired. Me and Geoff were up a long while last night."

"Yeah, us too. Troy was flying, and I was pretty wound up. It was... amazing. But also a little..." He didn't finish the thought. He wasn't exactly sure how.

"Possessive as fuck?"

"Yes. God. Thank you." Oh, thank God. He wasn't a creep. "You too?"

"Some, yeah, and I can't imagine how bad it is for you, man. My boy wasn't the one getting topped by someone else." Carter chuckled softly. "Tell me you enjoyed the aftermath, at least."

"I did. Fuck, Carter, I enjoyed all of it. The whole thing. Possessive is part of being a Dom, right? I just don't like that it crept up on me." He didn't like being surprised in scene.

"Now you know how it affects you. My boy was lit up, wild."

"Troy was... focused. Needy, you know? And really turned on." They'd shared something more, too, a conversation more intimate than sex that he wasn't going to tell Carter about.

"I hear you. Geoff's going to call Troy and invite you both to supper and celebrate the first snowfall. It's supposed to hit Saturday night."

"Hey, that sounds great. Troy and I are getting in a last ride before the snow today, in fact." He had his snow bike, but it would be a couple of weeks before the trails were ready for him. "Man, I'm really glad I called you. I was feeling—well, honestly, I was feeling pretty guilty."

"Shit, none of this—no matter what *this* is—will work if we don't talk, especially you and me. We need open lines of communication."

Carter was right. Troy and Geoff would look to them for cues, and he and Carter needed to be on the same page about things. "Yeah, I agree. I'm looking forward to figuring out what *this* is, by the way. I enjoyed that kiss." It felt a little weird to say that, but hadn't Carter just said to stay open? He wanted this to be good for all of them.

"Yes." Carter's voice dropped, went husky. "I came home hard as nails."

Well, that voice warmed him right up, didn't it? He liked knowing he did that for Carter. "Right? Me too. And I don't have any guilt about that. At all."

"No. Not even a bit." Carter chuckled softly. "Troy says to tell you he's headed home with lunch."

"Sounds like my cue to finish up with the bikes. Thanks for listening. I guess we'll see you this weekend in the snow." In the snow, yay. He loved the snow. "You gonna light up that big fireplace?"

"You know it. You two are welcome to plan to spend the night, if you'd like to. That way no one has to stress having a couple cocktails."

He laughed. "Will I sound overeager if I say yes?"

"Of course not. Bring a bag. I'll make sure there are doughnuts."

"Looking forward to it. Thanks again. Bye." He hung up the phone, grinning. Okay. So they were cool and he was normal and it was all good. He appreciated Carter even more now.

He finished up the once-over on his bike while he waited for Troy. He had to smile when he heard the truck, country music blaring from the open window. Oh, someone was in a good mood this morning.

He pulled his bike off the rack and set it down, squinting from the garage out into the sunshine. "Hey, you. Did you get your work done?"

"Yes, Sir. Turkey and provolone sandwiches and apple hand pies sound good?"

"Sounds perfect." He pulled Troy in and kissed his boy. "You smell good. Did you shower while you were letting me sleep in?"

"Yes, Master. I needed to rinse my ink."

He nodded. "How does it feel? You good to ride?" Troy was almost as aggressive on the mountain as Saul was, and they had a blast riding together. Just pure fun and adrenaline.

"Yes, Sir. It's tender, but not bad. I'll grab the backpacks and the waters and ice packs after I change into something more comfortable."

"Right on. I'll load the bikes up." He took another quick kiss and let Troy go, smiling at the little spring in his boy's step.

Screw the guilt. Look at his boy. His lover. Look at how happy Troy was.

He was doing something right.

4

"Look at this. It's really coming down, love." Geoff stood by the big wall of windows that looked out over their deck, watching the snow pile up on the railing and the way the clouds completely obscured their view of the mountain. It looked like they had six or seven inches already, with no sign of stopping any time soon. It was absolutely beautiful. "We're going to wake up to a winter wonderland."

A sudden pang of worry exploded in his chest, and he looked back at Carter. "God. I hope Saul and Troy are okay driving. You think we should tell them not to come? I don't want them to get stuck. You know how our driveway disappears in the snow and—" He caught the look in Carter's eyes and pressed his lips together, stopping the flow of words.

Right. He knew what that look meant. "Breathe?"

"Breathe. Troy has been driving in this for twenty years, and you know it. Why are you really nervous?"

Well, what if they got stuck in the snow? What if Saul was driving? What if a meteor hit and killed them? It would be safer if they stayed home, right? He blinked at Carter, cheeks blazing. "Because I want to kiss Troy tonight."

"Good boy." Carter nodded and reached for him, cupped his cheek with a heated hand. "Honesty, right? Total honesty."

He leaned into his Master's touch and sighed. "What if he doesn't want to?"

"Then he'll say no." Carter's smile was knowing, warm. "You have two Doms here to help read clues. Two other men that care about you both."

"I know. It's just that I haven't... been Toppy in a long time. I'm not worried, I'm just... anxious. But like, happy-anxious." He got butterflies thinking about Saul and Carter watching him and Troy. And a little turned on. Wow.

"Happy-anxious? I like that. Happy turned-on too?" Carter cupped his cock, teasing him madly.

He hissed, eyes crossing. *Dammit*. His half-hard cock liked the attention. Stupid thing betrayed him with Carter all the time. "Sir! They're going to be here any minute!"

"Because Troy's never seen your sweet prick needing." Still, his Master backed off, giving him one last squeeze.

He snorted at Carter and looked back out the window. "You're not nervous at all? You're the one that asked them to stay the night. I was just planning on dinner."

"I'm not nervous. I'm excited, I'm looking forward to having chili and visiting with our friends, and I'm curious to see what will happen tonight."

"Curious." Carter and Saul nearly swallowed each other whole in his shop the other day, but his Master was just curious? God, that was so Carter. "That could mean anything, you know. How do you do that?" He leaned in for a quick kiss.

"I'm the Master." Carter cupped the back of his head, encouraging the kiss to go from quick to heady.

Cheating.

Carter was so cheating.

"Mmm." Not fair but so good anyway. Carter's kisses were everything. Geoff was just getting lost when the doorbell rang.

"Your company is here, boy." Carter looked like the cat that got the cream.

Right. Company. He licked his lips and took a deep breath, then slid a hand over Carter's fly before heading for the door. "Thank you, Sir."

"I love you, too, boy." Carter's smile was warm as hell, and it heated him to the bone.

Saul and Troy were all smiles, looking happy as hell when he opened the door. "Hey! Oh my God, you guys, it's cold out there. Come in. Come on."

Saul and Troy laughed at each other as they tried to squeeze through the door together. "Where do you want snowy stuff?"

"I'll take it. Leave your boots by the door. Sir? Would you grab the chili from Troy so he can get his stuff off, please?"

"Totally. Oh Crock-Pot. Good choice." Carter grinned at Troy. "This is the special stuff, huh? Not the stuff for the diner?"

"You got it. Real homemade chili. You make cornbread?" Troy beamed, all flushed, obviously pleased.

"I did!" He called as he hung up their coats. "And slaw." He got back just in time to see Saul kiss Carter square on the lips. Just a quick hello and then Saul headed his way.

"Troy was talking about your cornbread all the way here." Saul cupped his cheek, then kissed him on the other one, and he couldn't help blushing.

"He's a fan. I got this, Sir." He lifted the pot from his Master's hands and set it down on the kitchen counter, hoping Saul hadn't noticed the blush.

"What can I do to help?" Troy came in, offering him a warm, sweet smile. "The cornbread smells like heaven."

"Hang on. I know where to start." Geoff plugged the crockpot in and then gave Troy a hug. "It's good to see you."

Troy hugged him back, leaning hard—and didn't that feel good? "Hey. I've been looking forward to tonight all week."

"Me too." He let Troy go, smiling. "Did you heal up? Let me see."

Troy pulled his sweater and T-shirt up, exposing the lean chest and tight little nipples. The ink was healing, well cared for, and made Troy's scar seem like a natural addition to the design.

He knew Troy's body well; he'd spent a lot of time with it. He wanted to touch the new ink, but it was probably still tender so he held back. "Hey, it turned out pretty good, huh?" Of all the work he'd done on Troy's body, this one had become his favorite. It wasn't all that unique in design, but it had so much meaning—covering the scar with Carter and Saul watching. It wasn't something he'd ever forget.

"It's gorgeous. Thank you. You made it right. I hated having it there."

He held Troy's eyes, and the green seemed brighter in the kitchen lighting. "It was good to turn it into something beautiful."

"You always turn me into something beautiful."

"Oh, honey. You've always been beautiful." He took Troy's hand and squeezed it. "Always."

Troy beamed at him. "Thank you."

"Did you two get lost in here?" Carter's voice seemed so loud that he jumped.

He fought the urge to let go of Troy's hand and took a breath. Total honesty. There wasn't any reason to be embarrassed. "No, we were just catching up. Troy showed me his new ink."

"Can I see?"

Oh. Oh whoa. Carter was asking *his* permission, not Troy's.

He blinked at Carter. How should he balance his Dom on one hand and Troy on the other? "Uh. Sure. Yes." He looked at Troy. "Show Master Carter your ink, please."

Troy lifted his shirt easily. "Isn't it beautiful, Sir?"

God.

Had he handled that right? Should he have said, "Yes, Sir?" to Carter? Should he have—

Stop.

He wiggled his fingers and took a deep breath, trying to just relax. This was new for all of them. He could make mistakes. He could almost hear Carter's voice in his head.

Breathe and just be honest.

If it was a mistake, Carter would tell him, right? And they'd talk about it, and next time he'd know.

"Yes, boy. It's perfect." Carter grinned at Troy, then at him. "Absolutely perfect."

Those words warmed him right up, and he leaned toward Carter. He felt so proud. "Thank you, Sir."

"You guys, this view with the snow!" Saul called from the living room. "It's amazing!"

He gave Carter a quick kiss on the cheek. "We better head out there."

"Should I get everyone a drink, or..." Troy looked so

unsure, so worried for a second that it almost broke his heart.

"I'll help." He took Troy's hand, squeezed it gently, and looked at Carter. "What can I get you to drink, Sir?"

"I'd like a beer, thank you."

Troy squeezed his fingers. "That'll be two of those, for sure."

"Go on out, Sir. We'll bring out some snacks too." He waited for Carter to head back out to Saul and then turned to Troy. "I'm a little nervous too. It's hard having to relearn things."

"Right? I feel ramped up as anything. Can I have another hug? Please?"

"I'd like that too." He pulled Troy in and held him. "Carter says if we stay totally honest, it will all be fine. And it's not like we flipped a switch, and everything has to change at once."

Troy rested hard, cheek on his shoulder. "I feel a little stupid, you know? Like everyone knew something I didn't."

"I understand that. But honestly, it doesn't matter what we knew or didn't know, honey. We didn't have the courage to even talk about it until Saul came along." It had come up once, and he and Carter danced around it and never brought it up again.

"Yeah. He's a little magical, isn't he?"

He laughed softly. "He's a surprise, for sure. That first date you had with him? We laughed about it. Saul was too young. He couldn't possibly be good for you."

Saul was perfect for Troy. And good for all of them. The kid was young, sure, but Saul breathed new energy into all of them by falling for Troy. Good energy.

"I didn't laugh. He was so sweet to me. We watched the

sunset." Troy smiled against him and began to relax. "It was romantic."

"You deserve that. It makes me happy that you have someone like that finally. I used to worry so much about you, and I just... don't anymore. Not that way. Saul's a good man." He chuckled. "Even if he is twelve."

"Possibly twelve and a half."

"I heard that, boy!" Saul called, and they both cracked up.

"The Masters will want their beers." But he didn't let go of Troy right away; he wanted to wait for Troy to be ready. "I made some guac, and we could put out chips?"

"Sounds perfect. You want a beer too?" Troy straightened up and kissed his cheek. "Thank you."

He touched Troy's forehead, slipping a curly red lock of hair to one side. "You're welcome. Honest, right? We'll get this."

"Honest. Right. Chips, guacamole, beer." Troy nodded, and suddenly Geoff could see Troy when he first showed up.

"That's better." He pulled the guac out of the fridge and handed it to Troy along with the bag of chips. Then opened up four cold beers and balanced them in his fingers. "After you."

Troy led the way to where Carter had the fireplace roaring, the curtains pulled open to watch the snow piling up.

It was getting dark, but Saul was watching the snow fall in the light that flooded the deck. Geoff handed out beers and hovered close to the food, trying to decide where he should sit.

He took a sip and then ended up joining Saul to look out the window. "The first real snowfall of the season is always an event, isn't it? It makes me feel like a kid."

"Right? And it came in a rush this year. Boom." Saul clinked their bottles together. "Thanks for the invite."

"We wanted—" Geoff stopped himself. "Honestly I needed to see you both. Troy especially after the session the other day, you know?"

Saul turned and looked at him, really looked, right into his eyes. "I do. Completely. And thanks for just putting that out there."

"Oh." He blushed and covered it with a sip of his beer. "Master told me—"

"I know." Saul reached over and took his hand. "He told me too."

"He did?" He glanced quickly over at Carter who shot him a wink and a grin.

Saul looked out the window again. "I am so going out to play in this tomorrow."

"Can I come?" The question popped out of Geoff's mouth without any hesitation, shocking the hell out of him.

That got him a laugh, happy enough that it echoed off the high ceiling. "Please do. Anyone else? Snowman? Sledding? Good old-fashioned Doms versus subs snowball fight?"

"As long as we get to soak in the hot tub afterward, I'm up for anything." Troy was curled up on the sofa, in his spot where he could watch everything.

Saul squeezed his hand and let it go, moving to the sofa and settling down with Troy. "That sounds like a plan."

"Hell, we could jump in the hot tub tonight. I love it in the snow." Geoff dipped a chip in the guac and handed it to Carter before sitting beside his Master. "Couldn't we?"

"Of course. I have it all fired up and towels in the warmer." Clever man.

Geoff leaned against Carter and kissed his Master's shoulder. "So maybe after dinner if you guys are up for it."

"I don't know. Hot water, good company? Sounds awful, doesn't it, Troy?" He grinned at the tease and watched as Saul chuckled against Troy's neck.

"Terrible. Torture. I'm so in." Troy's voice was full of laughter.

"Mmm. That's what I thought." Saul looked over at Carter. "This fire is gorgeous too. I love your house."

"Thank you. We knew exactly what we wanted." Carter smiled at Geoff as he said that, sharing the pride with him.

"Troy's view is amazing also. The windows in the bedroom? It's the best place to wake up."

"Our view," Troy corrected gently.

"Our view. Sorry, boy. I know that must drive you crazy. I'm still getting used to things."

Geoff shrugged. "I used to do that. Everything was Carter's at first, you know? It took a while."

Saul looked at Geoff with shrug. "Yeah? I'll get used to it."

Carter's arm hooked around his shoulders, and he leaned in. A silence fell as they sipped their beer and watched the fire or the snow, but it wasn't uncomfortable. It was nice. Troy and Saul looked so relaxed, like they belonged right where they were.

Eventually Troy sat up and grinned at Saul, and Saul laughed. "Okay, so when did you want to serve the chili?"

"Someone's belly is trying to gnaw through his backbone." Troy rolled up and stood, so graceful. "The chili is ready. Let's eat."

Geoff laughed and kissed Sir's cheek. "You guys sit at the table, and we'll get dinner." He hopped up and followed Troy back into the kitchen.

"Such service." Saul called after him. "You'd think we were Doms or something."

"Ha." Geoff caught a quick glimpse of Saul offering Carter a hand up as he disappeared into the kitchen. "It smells so good. This is such a treat, Troy."

"I'm glad you like it. I've never made it for Saul before. I hope he likes it." Troy knew their kitchen as well as his own and pulled out bowls and spoons.

"If he doesn't, I'm making him walk home." He laughed and found a ladle for Troy.

"Now that's love." Troy pinched his butt and started serving up.

"Ow." It didn't hurt, it was just what you said when someone goosed you. He pulled the cornbread out of the oven where he'd left it on real low just to stay warm. "I'll set this out and come back for the other stuff."

Carter and Saul were seated adjacent to each other and talking quietly. "Anyone need another beer?" He set the cornbread down in the center of the table.

Saul nodded. "I'll take one. Thank you."

"Sir?" Carter looked so relaxed. He couldn't really be that relaxed, could he?

"Please. It all smells amazing." He loved the way Carter smiled at him.

"Be right back, gentlemen." Geoff gave a little bow and hurried back to the kitchen. "The guys want beers. You in?" He opened the fridge and started pulling out the fixings and beer.

"Sure. Nothing goes better with chili, right?" Troy gathered up the bowls. "I'll be right back to help."

"Look at you, juggling all those bowls. You'd think you worked in a diner." He followed along with four beers.

"Oh, wow." Saul sat up straighter in his chair as they

came out. "I can't wait to try this. I've been smelling it all day, and this naughty boy wouldn't let his Master have even a taste."

"You're in for a treat. Troy's chili is special." Carter's smile was playful, wicked. "It's not the stuff he serves at the diner, of course. I'm not sure why..."

"This is an expression of love, not work."

"I can't think of a better reason. It is extra special now." Saul smiled at Troy and patted the chair across from Carter.

"See? Best chili ever. You sit, honey. I'll get the fixings." He gave Troy a quick kiss on the cheek and went to get the rest of the food. Chopped onions, cheddar cheese, and some sour cream for those of them with tender bellies.

"Does this mean I can try this finally?" Saul joked as he set everything out and sat down.

"Don't wait on little ol' me." Geoff laughed and picked up his spoon.

Troy sat there, watching Saul without even breathing. Hell, Saul had better like the chili or Troy was going to shatter.

Saul nodded through the first bite and was making yummy noises by the second. "Oh man. This is amazing." *Oh, thank God.* Even Geoff had been holding his breath.

Troy visibly relaxed, took a deep breath, and looked around. "Who all is having onions? If y'all aren't, I won't."

Geoff snorted and picked up the bowl, scattering a spoonful across his chili. "Please, I didn't dice them up for them to sit there on the table and look pretty." He handed the bowl to Troy.

"Well, I don't want to have dragon breath." Troy did the same and added some cheese.

"It's chili. We're all going to have dragon breath anyway."

Saul helped himself and went for the cheese and a dollop of sour cream too. "The spice is just perfect, Troy. So good."

"We'd get a name if he'd just make it for the diner." Carter grinned around his beer.

"It's for people I love. That's it. Not for sale." Troy stuck his tongue out at Carter. "And we have a name."

"You do. You have amazing coffee. You used to have the best French toast, but I don't know if you do anymore." Saul winked at Carter.

"No, that's saved for you, Sir. Possibly for a few other special people..." Troy fluttered his eyelashes, flirting hard.

"Oh, look at that! Troy just volunteered to make us snow-day breakfast."

Geoff really hadn't been able to take his eyes off Troy since they'd arrived, and Troy's confidence tonight just made the man even more beautiful. Geoff took a sip of his beer and caught Carter looking at him, making him blush.

Damn. The fact that Carter *knew* was such a turn-on.

"Are you sure y'all are special?" Troy teased. "I mean, I could be cooking for people behind your back."

Saul looked at Troy, and Geoff blinked at the change of tone in the Dom's voice. "I have a flogger that says we're as special as they come."

Troy blushed and ducked his head. "You know y'all are. I'm teasing."

He didn't think Troy was as much upset as he was pleased.

Saul leaned over and whispered something in Troy's ear that only made the sub blush harder and then gave Troy a sweet kiss. "Your cornbread is really good, Geoff. Troy told me on the way over that he was looking forward to it."

He had to grin at the change of subject. "The first time I

made it, Troy told me it was as good as any he'd had. That was quite a compliment, I thought."

"Even better than my granny's." The look in Troy's eyes heated Geoff to the core. He swallowed as his mouth went dry.

"I don't see how that's possible, but thank you, honey."

"So, while we've all been blabbering, Carter has finished his chili and his beer." Saul reached out and gave Carter a little shove. "So quiet."

"Do you want another bowl?" Troy asked.

"No, I'm good. I was imagining watching Geoff kiss you."

Wait. What? Did Carter just say that out loud? He stared at Carter and then looked at Troy. He thought for a second that maybe he should go with polite; deflect, laugh it off. But given the way Troy was staring back at him, that wasn't going to happen.

He started to say something, but Saul spoke up first, reaching for Carter and tangling their fingers. "Oh, I'd like to see that."

"You don't have to, honey," Troy murmured, holding his gaze for a second before looking back at the table. "It won't hurt my feelings."

"Don't tell me that. I've been thinking about kissing you all day." He pushed his chair back and stood up, holding a hand out to Troy.

Troy took his hand, standing up and ending right next to him. "So have I."

He reached for Troy, curling his fingers around Troy's nape. "Thank God for that." He leaned close, letting his lips hover over Troy's. He loved this moment and wanted to hold onto it a second longer. They'd both been waiting for it for so long, and it wasn't one they'd ever get back.

"You smell good." He breathed in Troy's scent, stronger

and closer than he ever had before, and finally brought their lips together.

Troy sighed softly, one hand coming to light on his waist, so warm and solid. When Geoff opened his eyes, Troy was watching him, those bright green eyes focused on him.

He let that first connection simmer between them and smiled at Troy, knowing it was his move and Troy was waiting on him. He licked his lips, tightened his grip and took the kiss he really wanted this time, tongue teasing Troy's mouth open. Troy tasted spicy, and his lips tingled where they touched his, but the thing that made him burn was the tiny sound, the swallowed moan that he'd never heard before.

To be truthful, he'd been thinking about this kiss for years and had even dared to fantasize beyond kissing, but he'd never believed for one second that it would happen. Every nerve was on fire now that he had Troy this close, it was overwhelming. He moaned and looped an arm around Troy's waist, pulling their bodies together.

Troy gasped, opening wider, tongue sliding against his. Troy was erect in his jeans, belly taut, and Geoff could feel the muscles rippling against him.

"Gorgeous." That was Saul's voice, husky and low. "Hot as the sun."

He'd forgotten there was anyone else in the room; almost forgotten there was anyone else in the world for a minute.

Troy moaned and arched against him, and Geoff was a little shocked to find that Saul was standing behind Troy, right up close, lips devouring Troy's neck. He hadn't even heard the man move.

Troy whimpered and begged for another kiss, from him, and damn wasn't that heady?

"Mmm...you're like a wet dream come to life, boys." Carter's voice was raw.

Geoff took the kiss happily, hungrily, fingers working Troy's shirt out of his jeans again. Not to see this time, but to touch. Finally, to touch Troy in a different way, to make all that pain he'd given Troy mean more. "I want to touch you."

"Please." Troy blinked at him, lips swollen, eyes dazed. "You've marked me everywhere."

"Not everywhere." He lifted Troy's shirt and sweater up, and Saul helped wordlessly, the two of them baring Troy's inked skin together. He caught Saul's eye over Troy's shoulder—he'd never noticed just how blue those eyes were before—and Saul winked at him and nodded.

That was all he needed, not so much Saul's permission, but Saul's approval. He dropped his mouth to Troy's collarbone, any anxiety he might have had left now gone.

"Oh God." Troy gasped, eyes flying open wide. Saul had his back, supporting him, and when Geoff looked down, he could see Saul working Troy's pierced nipples.

"Just watching, Carter?" Saul had a teasing tone in his voice. "Our boys are on fire."

"Yeah." Troy rocked against him, fly to fly and he gasped with how hard he was wanting. "Oh, fuck."

"I want to... Can I touch?"

Geoff swallowed and nodded, not trusting whatever sound was going to come out instead of words.

"Couch. We're not going to do this over dirty dishes, boys." Carter was husky, turned on, but his order brooked no argument.

Geoff rocked on his heels, his Master's voice cutting through the tension between him and Troy.

Saul stepped back, giving them room. "You heard the man. Dinner will wait."

"Yes, Sir." He didn't take his eyes off Troy though. He tangled their fingers and moved backward, pulling Troy along by the hand.

"This is real, right? I'm not dreaming?" Troy never glanced away from him. "We're here together?"

"We're together. Here. And you're beautiful, Troy. You know what this means to me, don't you?" He lifted Troy's hand and kissed it.

Troy shivered. "Oh God."

He loved that, that Troy wanted him.

"Almost there, boys. We're waiting." Carter didn't have to sound so damned smug. Saul laughed softly and said something to Carter that he couldn't hear.

This wasn't a show for the Doms as far as he was concerned. He was focused on Troy. But nobody would judge if he happened to like the idea that they were watching.

He flopped onto the couch and pulled Troy down with him.

"Hey, you." Troy sat hard, bouncing into him, and on the second one, he snuggled in.

"Hey." Geoff looked over at Carter, expectantly. Sir had moved them for a reason; he didn't want to make assumptions.

Carter cupped his jaw and drew him into a hard, needy kiss that burned him to the ground.

He blinked at his Master and tried to get a breath. He was sure he should say something sweet, but he couldn't think. He was still holding Troy's hand, but in this second, Carter was everything. "Sir."

"Mmm. Yes, boy. Go on, back to showing me the prettiest thing I've seen in a long time."

Geoff smiled and gave Carter another quick peck, then

turned back to Troy. "My Master thinks you're beautiful too." Geoff unbuttoned his shirt and pulled it out of his trousers, then took Troy's hand and pressed it against his chest.

Troy blushed, fingers curling against his skin, fingertips stroking featherlight. "Will you kiss me again?"

"Oh, honey. Any time." He tangled his fingers in Troy's red hair, so soft and strange after years of seeing his friend bald, and did as Troy asked, passing on the heat that Carter had left him with.

Troy yielded beautifully, simply melting against him. One hand crept around his waist, thumb rubbing the small of his back in steady circles.

He hardly knew what to do with someone like Troy anymore. He wasn't used to being the one making the moves. That was Carter, always so sure of himself, so knowing. He just stayed in the moment and tried not to think too far ahead.

Geoff drew a thumb over Troy's piercings, remembering the day he put them there and how much Troy had liked them. He remembered the other ones, too, though he hadn't seen those since the day he did them.

Troy grunted into his lips, that tiny nip drawing up so hard.

Saul's fingers, which knew something he didn't, covered Geoff's and gave the hardware a little twist, making Troy moan. The sound made his balls ache, and suddenly he knew exactly what he wanted. Geoff pushed Troy's hand from his chest, over his abs, and right up against the straining bulge in his pants.

"Yes." Troy blinked up at him, hand rubbing, sliding on his jeans. "I want to suck you. I want to know how you taste."

The words burned on the air, hot enough Geoff swore he could see them.

"Yeah. Yes." He nodded, kissing Troy between his words. He got to work, opening his pants and slipping out of them. He'd been naked in front of this fire many times, but this was all different.

Saul took Troy's place on the couch as Troy shifted to the floor. "I'm the only one that hasn't kissed you yet."

"I—yes, Sir." Geoff barely got the words out when Saul took his mouth. It wasn't like Carter's kiss at all. It wasn't the kiss of a Dom that knew him. Saul's was exploring, curious, as sweet as it was hot.

Geoff's world stopped as he learned this new touch, this new kiss. Saul kissed him like he wanted to learn him, like—

Troy's mouth wrapped around his cock and his eyes flew open, a short scream escaping him. "Oh God. Troy."

Yeah, that was Troy's mouth on him, Troy making his eyes cross and his toes curl and everything in between burn.

Saul hummed to him and pulled away. "God, these two."

"I always thought your boy was born to suck, Saul." Carter's voice was like another touch, all on its own.

"Mmm. If you play your cards right, you might find out soon yourself."

"Troy." That was all he had. Jesus, Geoff was about ready to short out. He plunged one hand into Troy's hair, and the other flailed out, looking for Carter.

Suddenly Carter had him, kissed him until he stopped worrying about breathing. He relaxed in Carter's arms and let Troy take him higher, feeling the need start to settle into the pit of his stomach. His thighs began to tremble, and his hips rocked, and as much as he wanted to pretend he had control here, he knew he had none.

"Make him come, boy." Saul's husky voice vibrated at the

base of his skull.

Troy took him down to the root, swallowing over and over, throat closing around the tip of his prick.

"Fuck!" Geoff gasped and clung to Carter, his need so sudden and strong it was on the edge of painful. His heart pounded, blood roared in his ears, and his vision was useless. He cried out and shot hard, balls aching and every involuntary shudder making him moan.

Troy eased that excruciating pressure, and for a second, Geoff could breathe. He leaned forward, bending over Troy. "Kiss me," he rasped. "Please, honey. Kiss me."

Troy lifted his face, lips fuck-swollen and red. "God yes. Please."

Geoff brought their lips together and they both made needy sounds pulling on each other until Troy was on the couch, half in his lap. Saul moved out of their way, settling on the arm of the couch behind Carter, one arm resting on Carter's shoulder.

"They look magical together," Carter murmured.

"I can't imagine what it's been like for them all these years with that just barely under the surface." Saul leaned down and stage-whispered in Carter's ear. "And Troy is still so hard he might cream his jeans."

"And I haven't even gotten my kiss yet." Carter chuckled softly, and the sound was joined by Saul's laughter.

"Well, it looks like you're going to have to wait a bit. Troy's busy." Geoff caught the grin, though, as Saul slid off the arm of the couch and bent over Carter. "Will you settle for me?"

"For now, I suppose." Carter grabbed Saul and dragged him down into a hungry kiss. They both watched their Masters devour each other, Troy panting against his shoulder.

"Oh. Damn." For a minute, it looked a little like wrestling. He saw a flash of Saul's teeth, Carter's fingers tugged hard on Saul's sweater, tongues tangling and sparring. They finally settled, though the kiss was no less heated, and he looked back at Troy. "You need, honey?" He pressed a hand gently against the little damp spot staining Troy's jeans.

Troy's answer was a stunning, wide-eyed stare, a cry, and then Troy humped against his hand.

"Yeah. Okay, hang on." He returned the stare with a smoldering look and opened Troy's jeans. He reached for Troy's cock, admiring the Prince Albert piercing he hadn't seen since the day he did the work. "I got you."

"Do you like it?" Troy pushed up into his hand, sliding that heavy prick over his palm.

"It's stunning. The piercing is hot too." Saul winked at Troy.

Geoff rolled the little ball under his thumb, fingers stretching down his length.

"You don't have to be shy with it, Geoff. He likes a little pressure," Saul said.

Troy's eyes shot to Saul. "Master!"

"Oh nice. Thank you, Sir." He pushed down on the piercing, letting his thumb settle in Troy's damp slit and rocked his hand back and forth. "Better, honey?"

"Uhn." He was fairly sure that was a yes, especially when he added the sound to the rolled eyes and blush.

"Look at you." He closed his fist around Troy's shaft and alternated heavy strokes with firm pressure across that piercing. A couple pumps and a roll of his palm, over and over, Geoff's focus pinned on Troy's face. "So pretty."

Bright green eyes searched his face, and he got a dazed look before they went unfocused. "Make me ache."

"That's it. Ache so good, right?" He licked his lips. "I want a taste, honey. You want my mouth? I know you're close but... just a taste." He didn't wait for an answer. Troy wasn't going to say no. He slid to his knees, tugged Troy's jeans down and off, and then circled that piercing with his tongue. "Mmm. Sweet."

"Is this real? Tell me this is real." Troy reached down to him with trembling hands, even as his gaze searched for Saul's. "Master?"

"It's *still* real. And it's good. It feels right. Enjoy Geoff, boy. He wants you to feel good."

Geoff moaned and nodded, taking Troy into his mouth. He wanted to make Troy fly.

Troy curled over Geoff's head, hands dragging across his shoulders. "I do. It feels so good."

"I bet it does." He caught movement out of one eye and Troy's next moan was long and low, muffled by a kiss. He blinked up, a deep groan escaping him as he saw his Master, taking Troy's mouth.

Captivated, he let himself watch just another second, but then Saul's fingers tangled in his hair. "Back to work, boy."

Geoff groaned again, Saul's touch and that order making him tingle. "Yes, Sir." He took a breath and drew Troy in deep, humming around the pretty prick.

He slid his hand under Troy's pierced balls, playing and tugging, making Troy's prick throb. It took another hard suck to make Troy shoot, the hot seed pouring into him.

Carter swallowed Troy's cry in their kiss, Saul twirled and tugged on his hair, and he gladly took everything Troy had and made sure Troy knew he liked it.

Afterward, he climbed over Troy, sliding their bodies together, skin against skin, and stole the kiss from Carter, nudging his Master gently out of the way so he could claim Troy's mouth for himself. He heard Saul chuckle behind him.

Geoff wondered if Troy felt as changed as he did right now. He'd held this back from Troy for so many years it had become habit, sheer reflex, to the point where he didn't even notice he was doing it anymore. He felt so much more aware now. So much more awake.

Troy moaned and cuddled into him, trembling. A blanket landed on them, cocooning them.

"You two take your time. We're going to the tub and get it warmed up for us." Carter stroked Geoff's temple. "Please don't rush. We'll see you out there later."

He caught Carter's fingers and kissed them, giving him a smile. "Thank you, love."

Saul bent and kissed Troy's temple, whispering, "I love you," before following Carter.

Geoff took a breath and looked around the room. Saul was leaving Troy to him, and that was a wild concept. He got more comfortable and tucked the heavy blanket under one arm so he could hold Troy close. He was a little shocked that he was so... good. He wasn't anxious at all. Carter loved him, and Troy was in his arms, and it really was everything he wanted.

He wanted to know what Troy was thinking, but he wasn't going to ask questions right now. Still, so many were swirling around in his head. *Are you okay? Do you feel safe? Do you love me?*

Troy held him like he might disappear, like he'd go poof. Slowly—so slowly—the tremors started to ease, Troy melting into him, and by that time, he didn't need to ask those questions anymore. He knew the answers.

"This is nice, holding you." He ran his fingers through

Troy's hair. "They left for a reason, you know. So we could be ourselves, be honest." So they wouldn't feel like they had to be careful how they said something or worry. Carter and Saul were good men; he and Troy were so lucky.

Troy stayed close, silent, but Geoff knew that Troy needed more time to process. That cowboy moved slow, like tectonic-plate slow. So he waited.

"I used to feel so guilty, thinking about you. Having wishes."

Oh man. God, that hurt to hear and made him feel a little mean and selfish. Not that he was, not that Troy meant it that way. But he'd mostly been holding back desire. Troy had been holding back so much more, and watching him and Carter together the whole time.

"I didn't have the guilt, but I wanted. I wanted you every time you left my studio. I never dreamed we'd...I mean never." Geoff sighed and kissed Troy's forehead. "One more reason to be grateful for Saul." He thought they all were, really. Even Carter. Maybe especially Carter.

"Yes. He's not mad about this. He's just so relaxed." Troy lifted his chin for another kiss. "Is Carter okay?"

"Yeah. He's good. Trust me he enjoyed watching. Also? I think he's going to find a real friend in Saul, if he lets himself." Carter's fantasies were a little more hardcore than blow jobs, but he wasn't going to put that in Troy's head right now. "You know how he is."

"I do." Troy dragged his hand over Geoff's belly, the touch warm, more comforting than sexual. "You taste good."

He felt himself blush. It was amazing they could say that sort of thing to each other now. "Your kiss makes me feel like I'm the only person left in the universe." So focused.

"You're my best friend." Troy kissed the corner of his mouth, humming softly, lips buzzing against his skin.

"I am. We are. Whatever." He laughed and returned the kisses, so affectionate and sweet. "I feel pretty fucking good." Maybe a little emotionally raw, but really good. Good enough to earn stripes for swearing so it was lucky for him Carter wasn't in earshot. "Is it weird now if I say I love you? I do. Every bit of you." He had before; he just didn't get to show it this way.

"We loved each other before. It's just—" Troy shrugged, pinked, and smiled. "—fuller now."

"Fuller. An appropriate word on many... fronts." God, he was a dork. "So, are you okay?"

"I think so. We're all together in this. No one's cheating, right?"

"No one is cheating, no one's jealous that they've let on, and we've all promised to be honest so... I know we'll respect whatever boundaries come up, if they come up, and otherwise, we're working on becoming a legit quad, I think. Don't you?" If they weren't already, because the four of them had love and intimacy now. So maybe they were there already.

"Listen to you—legit quad. You sound like Saul." Troy hugged him. "I pay attention. I'll be honest."

Geoff laughed. In fact, those were probably Saul's exact words that he was repeating. How about that? He hugged Troy back and gave an extra tight squeeze before letting go. "Me too. You want a soak?"

"I do. Totally. My bones are finally solidified. You melted me." Troy rolled up, and it was a sight to behold, his ink in motion.

Geoff grinned. "You shut my brain down."

His ink, my work. And now he'd finally gotten to give Troy the pleasure that went with it.

5

Carter poured himself a cup of coffee and sat to watch the sunrise. He'd spent too many years waking up early to be able to sleep in, so he let himself enjoy the ritual of coffee-crossword-solitaire, even with Troy and Saul sleeping in the guest room upstairs.

Geoff had woken up worrying—about him, about breakfast, about whether the guest bed was comfortable—so his morning ritual had actually begun with a nice warming of his sub's backside. That was satisfying, and seemed to have done the trick, because the boy was settled now, sipping coffee and puttering around doing the laundry from their soak in the hot tub the night before.

They hadn't needed to reconcile the day's punishments in a long time. But maybe it would settle Geoff in a wildly changing climate.

"Warm up, Sir?" Geoff appeared with the coffee pot, filled his mug without waiting for a reply, and then kissed him without waiting for permission.

"Keep track, boy. Your number of swats tonight and mine had better match." He had counted three.

Geoff blinked at him, looking surprised. "I—yes, Sir. I'm sorry, I don't know—uh—how many was that, Sir?"

Now he got to decide how he wanted to play this. What would serve his boy best? He didn't want Geoff uncomfortable, but focused, aware, and paying attention. "Three, boy. We'll count tonight, and give us something to look forward to."

Geoff smiled at him. "Thank you, Sir."

"Good morning." Saul and Troy made their way over from the stairs, hand in hand, looking adorable with their mussed hair, bare feet, and loose sweats.

"May I, Sir?"

"Yes, boy." He winked at Saul, who grinned right back at him. They were going to have so much fun together.

"Good morning!" Geoff set the coffee pot down and trotted over, kissed Saul on the cheek, and threw his arms around Troy. "Did you sleep okay?"

"Like the dead. No lie. Between the chilly air, that big fat comforter, and this guy? I was comfy and happy."

"I always sleep well here. It's like being home." Troy knew how to make his boy beam.

"It is home, honey. Even more now." Geoff kissed Troy square on the lips. "I was just thinking about breakfast. Do you want to make something with me?"

"I'd love to. I'll make French toast, hmm? Coffee, Sir?" Troy asked Saul.

"Yes please, boy." Saul sank into the couch next to Carter. "Gorgeous morning."

"Just grab a mug. I already have the pot out here." Geoff scooped it back up off the magazine he'd set it down on.

"I'm on it."

Carter grinned at Saul, at the snow glinting outside, at the fire. "It is a gorgeous morning. I think you got enough snow to play out in it today. I vote we tell the boys to make snow sex toys."

"Frosty the butt plug?" Saul grinned right back. "Jolly Old St. Dick?"

"Ho ho ho, Ice Giant Dick," he sang.

Troy came over with Saul's coffee, one bright red eyebrow arching. "I don't want to know."

Saul cracked up and took the coffee with a thank-you nod. "This is a private conversation, boy. Run along."

"With pleasure. Ice giant dick..."

Carter managed to hold in his laughter until Troy was back in the kitchen. Then he damn near howled with it.

"Naughty!" Saul called after Troy, then looked at Carter, giggling. "He forgot to say *Sir*."

"That's one, hmm?" he teased. "Geoff's already on three."

"We don't do that. Troy didn't take to it very well, and with his history, punishment is... a bad call. We're still working out what atonement looks like for us." Saul shrugged. "We're still working out a lot of things like that."

"I'm just giving you shit, man. You do what works for you. It keeps Geoff happy, when we're both not too busy to remember." He wasn't sure what to say, to be honest. Troy's ex had been his best friend, but he hadn't known until afterward how utterly fucked the situation had been.

Saul rested a hand on his thigh. "He's happy. Today, he happens to be extra happy. We're going to have to start thinking about what works for all of us, I guess."

"Of course. Do you want that, Saul? For there to be an us?" He thought it was important to ask.

"Can I be dead honest?" Saul looked at him. "I figured out quickly that if I wanted Troy, I had to accept you guys and everything you are to him, you know?" Saul sat back and looked out at the snow-covered deck thoughtfully. "I don't have twenty years history like all of you yet, but I do feel welcome. Every bit of me is invested in Troy; in making him happy, keeping him safe, meeting his needs. I'm... humbled, I guess, that you'd want me to be a part of this. That you'd let me in."

Damn, he hadn't been that articulate at twenty-five. Hell, he was still apt to reduce to grunts and clicks now. He was fucking grateful as shit that Troy had Saul—that they all did —and Carter was totally willing to take the credit for setting it up. After their bikes crashed, it could have gone so wrong.

"Troy did good, choosing you. You're a good man."

"I hope so." Saul was quiet for a while, and still as a stone. "I try. I have to try, right?"

"Trying is all we can do." He knew it might not be welcome, but he opened his arms to Saul anyway. Everyone needed a friend.

Saul nodded at him, then smiled and accepted the hug. "Thanks. I guess you probably know what I mean. I can't just be... a thug, or whatever." Saul exhaled heavily.

"You really don't read thug to me, Saul." What was he missing? "But then I want to know all about you."

Saul leaned back in the couch again. "Well... what do you call your need? I mean, I worry sometimes what I'd be if I hadn't met the right people, if I hadn't found this... community. What if I hadn't found someone to teach me what to do with it? Normal people—I don't mean—I mean regular people don't—" Saul shook his head looking... worried? Ashamed? "I've thought about this a lot, and I don't have an answer. I don't think there is one."

Ah. So that's why Saul was so articulate about this. Because he'd spent time worrying about it. Because he'd clearly listened carefully to the people that taught him how to be who he was. What it meant to be a Dom. But it sounded like somebody forgot to teach him that it was okay.

"I hear you. When I started trying to understand what I was feeling, I lucked out and found my way home. You know, I hear that from almost every Dom I know? That somehow they found their tribe, their nest, their family." Dom didn't equal asshole. He refused to believe that.

"You do?" Saul seemed interested in that and sat up like it was important. "That often, really?"

"Seriously. I doubt all of us find home, but a lot of us do. I think people find out what they need earlier than they used to, but we're drawn together."

"I think you're right about that because I've had people say really ageist things like it's impossible that I could know myself at twenty-five. Or, well I knew... man, maybe forever in a way. I didn't know what to do about it at first or how everything worked, but I knew sure as I knew I was gay."

"Fuck, me too. I knew that I was queer as a three-dollar bill when I was a kid, and I knew that I was a Dom when I was nineteen and saw the right kind of porn. Man, it opened my eyes." Opened his eyes, hardened his prick, tightened his balls.

"God, I wish I'd seen that at nineteen. That would have been way easier. Or harder. Probably way harder." Saul laughed and drained the last of the coffee in his mug. "Oh, hey, random, but did Geoff tell you we'd like to spend Thanksgiving with you guys? He says you do a big thing."

"Everyone comes. We do that on Saturday evening, to avoid messing with family plans." He wasn't sure what Geoff expected for Thursday, so he saved back his invitation for actual Turkey Day. "Geoff does the lion's share of the cooking because Troy and I will be swamped Friday and Saturday at the diner."

"The shop closes for the week so I'll help him. I'm not a great cook, but I'm extra hands. Or company at least. I usually go home so I'll be looking for something to do."

"He would love that. Honestly. You can chop and visit." And no matter what weird-assed, awful, crazy side dishes his boy came up with, they'd pretend to love it.

"And then we'll all go home for Christmas?" Saul smiled at him, the invitation so genuine.

"Well, Geoff and I don't have extended family. We just have us. Troy says you are heading to meet your mom. He's excited as hell."

"No, I meant come home with me. You have extended family now, right?"

"Oh!" He blinked in surprise, and then he smiled. "Seriously? Your folks would be cool with that?"

"Just Mom, and she's always been cool with me bringing lovers and subs home. I'll just have to make sure I tell her how many people." Saul laughed. "She's very easy. She won't get it, but she isn't one of those people who feel like they need to, you know? She'll be fine. Now, my siblings? I have no idea how they'll feel about a quad, but it's Mom's house."

"Let's all discuss it then. Thank you for the invitation—I haven't had a family Christmas in decades." He needed to make sure that Troy would welcome company on his first Christmas with Saul, that Geoff was interested in traveling.

"Yeah. Good." Saul looked into his empty coffee mug and then toward the kitchen. "Boy! I need some more coffee, please."

Geoff appeared instead of Troy, his boy looking so pretty, so fine in the sunlight. "Sorry, Troy's up to his armpits in French toast. He asked me to help you out."

"You'll do. You answer to 'boy', right?" Saul caught Geoff

by the collar and kissed Carter's boy's cheek once the mug was full. "Thank you."

"Yes, Sir. Most of the time. All the time for special people." Geoff looked so pleased with himself. "You're welcome, Sir."

Saul gave Geoff a wink and a smile. "I'm looking forward to the snowball fight."

"Am I on your team?"

Oh, his boy was flirting madly. Also taking one hell of a chance, because he'd played baseball with Troy on a league for years. He knew Troy could peg someone hard.

"Yes. Please. You and me against Carter and Troy." Saul took Geoff's hand and nodded like that was that.

Carter didn't remember agreeing to a snowball fight. He wasn't going to warn Saul though. If his boy wanted to play, they could so play.

"I don't suppose you guys have sleds, do you? We could drive over to Scott Carpenter Park. You guys ever done that? And then get cocoa." Saul looked about twelve years old talking about sledding and cocoa.

"Weirdly enough, we have about a dozen in the shed. Geoff is addicted to them." He shook his head, grinning at the memory of Geoff coming in just a few weeks ago with a bright red disc, a youthful light in his eyes.

Saul let Geoff's hand go. "No way! Oh, we're going to have fun."

"It's not an addiction, Sir. It's an obsession." Geoff laughed and headed back toward the kitchen. "I'll show you after breakfast."

"Can't wait." Saul leaned closer to him, grinning. "He didn't ask to be excused."

"Oh, very nice. That's four." Possibly five, if he counted letting Troy ignore his Master's request for coffee...

"Fun fun. It's been wild living with Troy. I've never done 24/7 and it took some figuring out."

"What was the hardest part for you? Mine was feeling like an asshole sometimes. Sometimes I just wanted to be two dudes fucking."

"I guess that was the hardest part, yeah. I want a sub, but I also want a lover. Taking care is Troy's strength, and sometimes I don't have to be a Dom to get that, you know? We have date night on Fridays, and mostly on those nights we're just... on a date. You should try it. It's amazing."

"We spend a lot of time not focused on the lifestyle, believe it or not." Carter knew how it looked, and there was no denying that he could be...incredibly sure of himself all the time, but they didn't worry about it. "I just trust my instincts, and I listen. So does he. He knows when I need his submission."

"That's beautiful. Troy is better at that than I am, maybe because he's watched you guys for so long. This is the first time for me that my sub and my lover were the same person, never mind living together... he's very understanding, and we just keep talking. I'm starting to anticipate him better."

Geoff appeared with syrup and butter and a plate of scrambled eggs and sat it all out on the table. "If Sirs would like to come have a seat, breakfast is ready."

Troy brought in a big plate of French toast and set it down with a smile, looking pretty pleased with himself. Both boys stood by the chairs, ready to pull them out for their Masters.

"Our boys look sharp. Should we worry they're scheming?" Saul bumped shoulders with Carter, got up off the couch, and offered him a hand up. "Come on, old man."

"I'll show you old man." Carter grabbed Saul's hand and

tugged, the kid landing in his lap. He took a hard kiss, making sure the boys saw it, then let Saul go.

He felt more than a little smug when Saul blinked at him, looking stunned. "Well." Saul grinned at him. "Just don't expect me to call you Daddy."

"Not my kink. For that, you have to talk to Doc and Ben." He managed to keep a straight face.

"Wow." Saul slid off his knees. "Good to know."

"Lord. Those two. Happy as anything." Geoff snorted. "Come eat, guys, the food's getting cold."

"And you'll regret it, Sir. It's your favorite." Troy had a wicked look in his eyes that Carter hadn't ever seen. Fascinating.

Saul lit up at that look and went right to Troy for a kiss. "It is. I've been looking forward to it since I got up."

"Thank you, Sir." Troy reached for Saul, fingers tracing along his cheeks as they embraced.

Pretty pretty.

He looked at his boy, winked, and sat.

"You ready for a snowball fight?" Saul rubbed a hand over Troy's chest and then took a seat. "Smells so good."

"Are we having a snowball fight?" Troy asked, and Carter nodded.

"Your Master and Geoff are going to be a team, so you're stuck with me." Which was nothing new. God knew he and Troy had spent more time together than he'd spent with anyone, ever.

Man, what a thought.

Saul loaded up his plate with French toast and reached for the bacon. "Geoff is taking a chance on the newbie. Plus, how often do you get to throw snowballs at your Masters?"

"I have faith." Geoff handed the plate of bacon over, practically batting his eyelashes at Saul.

Carter caught Troy's attention, and he seemed calm, assured, and Carter knew that they were going to take the guys *down*.

Geoff served him a scoop of eggs, a piece of French toast, and four strips of bacon. "There's more bacon in the kitchen."

Saul handed him the pitcher of syrup. "You like a little bacon, huh?"

"Bacon is proof that there's a God and He loves us, man." He made himself limit to three times a week because he wasn't a kid anymore, and saturated fat was bad, but bacon was magical.

"Troy, you have to make turkey bacon for Sir one day. I bet you could make it edible."

Saul laughed. "It's not that bad."

"Yes, it is."

He had to laugh at the look on Saul's face as everyone else at the table corrected the kid at once.

"Okay, then." Saul dug into the French toast, chewing and making happy noises. "So good, baby."

"Thank you, Sir." Troy reached over, stroking Saul's leg under the table, and Carter found himself admiring, watching.

"So... anyone want to say anything about last night? Is everybody good?" Saul looked around the table and then dug back into breakfast.

Geoff looked at Carter with wide eyes. "We're supposed to say something?"

"Do you want to say something?" he shot back.

"Do you?" Saul interrupted, looking at Carter.

"Absolutely. Watching the boys touch, need, was hot as hell. I'm interested in a second round."

Geoff's cheeks caught on fire.

"I was thinking the same thing. The level of trust was kind of a turn-on too, right? Not everyone could be that honest in company."

"Yes. We're lucky that Troy is willing to share so much with us, and that Geoff is exploring new parts of himself and letting us in." He was so proud of them both that he could barely breathe.

"I was telling Troy last night that we were proud of them." Saul brushed the back of one hand across Troy's cheek. "That it wasn't self-serving, but a gift."

"I'm liking the new parts." Geoff winked at Troy.

Troy blushed so dark that Carter imagined he could feel the heat from across the table. "I still feel like I'm living in a dream."

"Gotta love falling for one guy and getting three." Saul reached for more French toast, chuckling. "Three hot guys who know more about everything than I do."

"I'm the one that didn't know anything, Master, not you," Troy murmured, focus on his plate.

Carter looked at Saul, who was putting his fork down slowly, and knew Saul was giving himself a second to think about his answer. Then Saul reached over and took Troy's hands in his. "If you're talking about submission, boy, that's different with every Dom. If you're talking about love, I learned everything I know from you."

Oh, good job. He kept eating, letting Saul offer Troy what he needed first. He and Geoff had some apologies to make eventually—to each other, but mainly to Troy.

Saul and Troy shared a look, a kiss, and not very many words. Not surprisingly, Carter's boy was absolutely in tune with him and tangled their fingers, leaning closer. "Would you like some more coffee, Sir?"

His answer was to pull Geoff close and take a soft kiss of his own.

"I knew the second I saw your ink you were someone I wanted to get to know, but I didn't know how much we'd learn from each other. I'm still learning. And now we have this, the four of us are new, and we need to learn about that to. It's not about what we know. It's about our willingness to learn." Saul smiled at Troy. "I guess it's really more about what we don't know."

Geoff grinned against his lips. "That's my ink, hmm? So I can take the credit for the original attraction?"

"Nope. I'm the one he crashed into. I introduced them."

Troy gave Carter a wide-eyed glare. "Because you let the food die in the window!"

"And I am addicted to Troy's French toast." Saul took a big bite and grinned. "Kismet."

"Yes. We're lucky." Troy relaxed visibly, like some tension deflated in him.

God, Carter wanted to know what was going on in Troy's head.

"So... we have today, and then everyone has to go back to work tomorrow, huh? I guess we lucked out, being able to get at least one day off all at the same time. And the snow was helpful in cooperating."

Saul seemed to be indicating that they should move past this moment with Troy for now. At least someone had an idea what was in the boy's mind.

"Yeah. Carter and I have to plan for our holiday specials, make orders, all that mess..." Troy started.

"Tomorrow, guys. Tomorrow. Today the diner is running itself." Geoff rolled his eyes. "Help, Saul! Given a chance, they'll be all about the diner, and we'll never get their attention back!"

"I'll show you attention, boy." Carter growled a little, letting Geoff hear it, enjoy it.

"Ooh. Okay, that's on tonight's agenda." Saul leaned back in his chair, one hand on a full stomach. "No work talk today; we have a full day planned. Snowball fight, sledding, soak in the hot tub, maybe a scene or something to send us all off into the work week settled?" Saul blinked at Carter. "Or... sorry, I guess I should... um. We should probably head home to sleep, huh? It's an early morning for you guys I know."

Carter chuckled. Someone was eager, and he understood, and Saul got points for politeness. "I think, even with that, we can all be in bed by ten."

He'd have to confer with Saul on a scene. They hadn't worked together and, to be honest, he wasn't sure what Saul and Troy needed. Playing it by ear wasn't his deal.

Geoff got up and started clearing dishes. "Everybody full? More coffee?"

Saul groaned. "I am stuffed. Thank you both. That was a great breakfast."

Geoff smiled at him. "Troy's cooking is kind of like a hug, right?"

"Just like that." Saul winked at Troy.

"Thanks. It's just what it is."

Troy moved to take his plate, and Carter wrapped his fingers around the man's wrist. "It's love, and we all know it. Buck up. You're my friend, my partner, and a hell of a lot more. No more bullshit."

None of them had the time or the energy for that.

Saul didn't make a move to interfere. The kid didn't even twitch. "Answer Master Carter, please, boy."

"No more bullshit." Troy eased away from him and gathered more dishes.

He needed to speak to Saul, discuss what their boundaries were, because right now, everything inside him was telling him to pull Troy down and swat his ass, then take a kiss.

Saul watched as Troy left the table and raised an eyebrow at Carter. "Are you going to go after him, or do I need to?"

"I will." That was all he needed to hear, to be honest. He stood and headed to the kitchen, not even hesitating as he muscled into Troy's space.

"What's up?" God, he loved how green Troy's eyes got when he was like this. Now Carter wanted to know exactly what *this* was—Anger? Guilt? Desire? Confusion?

"You know what's up, boy. I want to know what's on your mind."

"I'm fine."

He gave into his instincts, spun Troy around, and popped him on his ass. "Don't lie to me, boy."

Troy balked at that but didn't try to turn back around. "I need to clean up breakfast. Master wants to get out and play in the snow."

Oh, nice try. Clever, too, bringing Saul into this. But he had that trump card. He had all of them. "I have Saul's blessing. Talk."

"What do you want to hear?" Troy rumbled at him. "I'm fine."

"Troy."

"Do you know how big of an idiot I feel? You knew, Geoff knew. I've been here for twenty years. Twenty years and Saul shows up and suddenly y'all want me? Suddenly I'm not a cook, but part owner? Did I suddenly get worth because somebody else wanted me or something?" Troy turned around, met his eyes. "Please don't answer that. I don't want to know the answer."

There were reasons. There were very good reasons twenty, even fifteen years ago. Troy should find a new lover, a new Dom. Troy would meet someone.

And then, when Troy hadn't and he and Geoff talked about it, when they'd finally asked the question out loud, he'd made the decision. No matter the guilt, no matter how much he understood that Troy deserved more—and no matter what Geoff wanted—his boy needed everything he had. Geoff was his priority.

He reached out and pulled Troy in hard, holding on. "I'm sorry. It's never been you. It was me. I couldn't. I just wasn't enough."

"I shouldn't have asked." Troy kissed his temple, the touch light as a feather, the sensation left behind like butterfly wings. "Let me do the dishes, and we'll go beat their asses with snowballs."

He owed Troy more of an explanation. He owed Geoff an apology. But now he had questions too. He took Troy's face in his hands and kissed him. "I love you. We love you. But do you really want this? If you don't, now's the time to say so. Saul's young, idealistic. Don't do this just because he thinks you should."

"I haven't done anything because someone else thinks I should in twenty years. Well, I eat more than one meal a day and I stopped smoking." Troy sighed softly. "I have loved y'all a long, long time. I never thought...I never let myself think, and I feel like a fool, but I'm not stupid. I know what I'm doing."

"It's hard, but I'm glad you asked. We have to ask the hard questions, clear the air. It's important so we can trust each other when we need to most. Saul is changing things for all of us. He's the Dom you should have had years ago, the Dom I was never going to be able to be for you. We want you both. I'm not asking you to forgive me. I just need to know you're okay."

Troy nodded, the look just as firm as if he was starting a ride. "I've got this. You go get ready to play. Everyone's waiting."

It didn't feel like they were done; it felt like Troy was shutting the conversation down. "Yeah. I'll see you out there." He looked at Geoff when he got back to the table. "Go help him. Please."

"Yes, Sir. You and Master Saul help each other, please?" Geoff smiled at him like it was going to be okay.

He looked at Saul, totally unsure about what to say. That wasn't something he was used to.

He didn't intend to get used to it either.

"I think I fucked up, man."

"With Troy?" Saul got up and moved them both toward the couch. "Just now?"

"Yeah, with Troy, just now. He asked why I hadn't come to him before you. My answer wasn't satisfactory." It had been the truth, but not satisfactory.

Saul was quiet for a second, then rested a hand on his knee. "Was it the truth?"

He covered Saul's hand with his. "It was. Geoff needed me, full-time. I couldn't be the full-time Dom to two subs." That was more than any man that had his own business whose sub had his own business could do, right?

"I couldn't either," Saul said easily. "No way. From what I know of Geoff, he seems like he can be handful. It wouldn't be right to try to split your time."

"He can, and it's amazing. I'm so looking forward to all of us exploring our dynamic, but Troy's upset, understandably." And Troy was trying to hide it instead of deal with it.

"Geoff should be able to get him settled enough for today, and I guess I know what we're working on this week. You know Troy; he'll come around. He just needs time. Sometimes a lot of time."

"I do." He grinned over, the tension easing a bit, his shoulders coming down from his ears. "I've always been the last person he listens to."

"He listens. He might ignore you, but he listens. He doesn't miss anything. You told him the truth, so it's on him to decide what to do with it." Saul stood up. "I can't have a snowball fight in pajamas."

"No? I might pay to see that, man." Okay, that felt good to hear. Saul had Troy's number, all the way.

"I'm going to grab Troy from the kitchen and take him up to change. Back in a few." Saul gave him a smile and headed for the kitchen, and barely a minute later, he was leading the boy up the stairs.

Carter went to check on his boy. The kitchen was cleaned up, and Geoff was wiping down the counters.

"You good, boy?"

"Yes, Sir. We got the dishes done and put the leftovers away. There's enough for us to share tomorrow morning."

He looked at Geoff, waiting.

"He seemed glad I was here... like, he wanted the company, but he didn't talk. He said he was fine."

"You know him, boy. He needs his time." He didn't feel the slightest bit of regret, repeating Saul's words. "Are you looking forward to our day?"

Geoff's grin was wicked. "I am. I get to watch Troy pelt Saul with snowballs!" His boy moved into his arms. "Mmm. It's been good having them here."

"It has. I think getting out of the house will be good for us. We can play." Exercise. Blow off some steam.

"You ready to go get dressed?" Geoff looked at him through narrowed eyes. "I like this side of you. I don't see it that often."

"Which side is that, boy?" He started leading Geoff upstairs toward their room.

"The let's-go-play side. It's been a while since you wanted to play with me outside the house." Geoff emphasized *outside*, and although there wasn't any stress in the boy's tone, the point was clear enough.

The guest room door was closed when they passed by, and he could hear voices; Saul giggling like a kid and Troy's soft laughter. That was a good sign.

"We get caught up in busy, don't we?" He cupped Geoff's ass, making him squeak. Oh, he loved that happy little sound.

"We do. We have to make time. More time now, right?" Geoff followed him into the bedroom and ducked into their walk-in closet. "I'm going to dig out my flannel-lined jeans, you want me to find yours, Sir?"

"Sounds good, boy. Where are those good socks?"

"The wool ones? Bottom center drawer in the big dresser. Oh, our boots are in the garage, so they're going to be cold. You want me to go grab them and stick them by the fire?" Geoff sat their jeans down on the bed.

Every so often, Geoff would do something—something simple and genuine and dear—and Carter would fall in love again in a rush so big it made him dizzy. He grabbed Geoff and kissed him hard.

Geoff blinked and made that little squeak sound again, but the way his boy accepted his kiss, the boy's whole body surrendering at once, made everything sweeter.

"Mmm." He let the kiss end easily, naturally. "I love you."

His boy smiled at him curiously. "I know, Sir. I love you too."

"Good deal." Carter settled Geoff on his feet again and moved to get dressed.

"I'll get the boots." Geoff ducked out the door and closed it behind him.

He sat on the end of the bed and grabbed his socks. Sledding and snowballs and time to reconnect. They all needed this. Equal footing.

They needed to play.

6

Troy finished the order, the scheduling, and then made sure everything was ready to open tomorrow. Then he sat and waited for Saul to come pick him up. It was snowing hard and bitter cold, too cold to walk back to the condo.

The place was dark, quiet, and he played stupid games on his phone and tried to decide if he wanted to get bundled up and walk over to the coffee shop.

Sorry, Emma had to leave early so I closed up alone. OMW. The text from Saul came in, interrupting his game. It was just a few minutes from the shop to the diner, maybe a few extra to get the snow off the truck and drive in the weather.

No worries. Be careful. He grabbed his coat and started bundling up. He'd just ask Saul if he wanted coffee.

The truck pulled up and honked, and he trudged across the snowy sidewalk to get in, surprised by how much had fallen already.

"Hey, you." Saul was blasting the heat and the truck was warm, but the smile he got was even warmer. His lover looked adorable in a knit cap, gray fleece scarf, and a big, red, fluffy down jacket. "Good day?"

"Long, but good. You want coffee out or at home?" Troy crawled in the truck and tugged on his seat belt.

"You want to hit up Big Bean, Little Bean? I'm in." The shop was technically walking distance. It took them about five minutes to get there and park, and they were both pretty snow-covered when they went inside, but they were by no means alone. The place was busy, toasty, and smelled great as usual.

"Hey! Look who's out in the weather." Sue smiled at them from behind the counter. "Caramel hazelnut latte for the kid, right? And I have something special for you, Troy."

"Uh-oh." Saul winked at him. "The man is cold, Sue. No pranks from Geoff tonight, huh?"

Sue just rolled her eyes. "You're no fun, sweetheart. What can I make you, Troy?"

"I'll have a white chocolate hazelnut with an extra shot of espresso, please." He shot Saul a smile in thanks.

Saul paid, and Sue slid a plate with a couple of biscotti on it over to them. "These are on the house. Grab a seat; we'll bring your drinks over."

"Thanks, Sue." He looked around and caught two people getting up from a small sofa over by the fireplace and led Saul over.

"Hey, this is great." Saul set the biscotti down on the little table and sat with him. "Good catch."

"Thank you. How's it going?" *I love you. You were on my mind all day.*

"Good. The shop was dead. We'll be closing soon for the winter. Emma and I spent part of the day getting ready to close up and the rest looking at those seasonal jobs I told you about. There are a lot available, but they'll be gone fast so I need to make a decision." Saul took his hand, held it on one knee.

"Did you find anything that turned you on?" He was looking forward to them having a lazy, quiet winter.

"I worked at a resort last year, renting and servicing equipment. I'll probably do that again. But Emma says I should see if I can get work in the business department. I don't know. I like the hands-on stuff."

"You can take the truck, if you need to. I can always walk." Or Carter or Geoff could pick him up, take him to the diner.

"Actually, I want to buy a truck of my own. I was hoping you'd help me pick it out. I want a new one with some fancy stuff in it like nav and heated seats and Bluetooth for my phone. What do you think?"

"I think it sounds stunning. Seriously. We could go to spend a day in Denver, maybe spend the night somewhere nice and have a few drinks."

"Yeah? You could get away from the diner? I'd love that." Saul squeezed his fingers. "I really would."

"I'll talk to Carter, but yeah, I can. I'd love to." They were beginning to figure things out again. Troy's part-time job was more full-time, because he was needed there at the diner, so he kept looking for time to spend together.

"Cool. I'd like to get a truck before the real winter hits. Save our night with Carter and Geoff though; we don't want to be gone the one day we all have off together."

"Sounds good. It'll be Thanksgiving soon. Maybe we should go before." After Thanksgiving, he'd be swamped, especially if Carter was going to work right around Christmas.

"Yeah. Definitely before. Then I can show it off to the guys at the Thanksgiving party." Saul laughed. "Right?"

Sue handed them each a coffee. "Here you go, guys. Enjoy."

He blew Sue a kiss of thanks and took a sip. Oh, sweet, creamy goodness. He hummed softly, pinking as he caught Saul staring at him. Oops.

Saul touched his warmed cheek. "Hey, handsome. Is it weird that I missed you today?"

"I don't think so. You've been on my mind today too." He wasn't sure why, but maybe there wasn't a why.

"Well." Saul sipped his coffee. "Maybe we need something. Maybe we need to work. I know you've been working through this thing with Carter..."

"Yeah." It wasn't just Carter. It wasn't even mostly Carter. It was mostly him. He wasn't sure it wasn't just all him. He felt so goddamn stupid, because he'd fantasized, sure, but they'd talked about it, about him. What if the Doms at the monthly gathering had talked? No one had wanted him for twenty years.

Twenty.

Now he was—not old, but he was middle-aged and worried and—

"Boy."

He looked at Saul, who was staring at him, so serious. "What?"

"I can't help if you don't tell me what you're thinking. Don't get lost in your head. Tell me." Saul's look didn't leave a lot of room for argument.

"I—everything in my head is..." Worrisome? Ridiculous? Negative? Stupid? Utter bullshit? "I'm just working shit out."

"Oh, so I should just leave you to it?" Saul lowered his volume level, and his tone was stern. "I can't spank you in a coffee shop, boy. I suggest you try. Or I can take you home."

That tone lit him up in a dozen different ways—it

relaxed him, excited him, thrilled him, but mostly it concentrated his focus. "Master. Yes, Sir. I'm..." *Come on, man. Spit it out.* "I don't like that everyone seemed to know but me. It bothers me."

"Good boy." Saul squeezed his hand and nodded. "Because Carter and Geoff talked about this, about you, and didn't include you in that conversation. Or are you including me as well? Be honest."

What? Troy was sure he'd been there, seen his Master working this out with him. "Did you talk to them before me?"

"No, no. I was worried maybe you thought I had. I'd had a feeling, but the first time I realized anything for sure was at dinner that night at our place. I just... noticed something about you guys. The connection was... more."

"That's what I thought, too, so good." Troy took a deep, cleansing breath. "I trust you, Master, and you have to know that I'm yours, at the core. I waited for you my whole life."

"I did, too, even if it was a shorter wait." Saul leaned close and kissed his cheek. "Okay. So I hear what you're saying. And I guess I can understand how that might make you feel. I think if it were me I'd feel kind of..." Saul looked thoughtful for a second. "Embarrassed? Maybe kind of dumb for not getting it myself? Maybe angry they kept it to themselves all this time..."

"Maybe all of the above." He drank another deep swig, buying himself some time. "And then there's the part where I still want to explore, to touch and see where this takes us."

Saul nodded, watching him, studying him. "I've been thinking about this too."

That was obvious. Saul had more words for what was in his head than he did.

"Carter loves you, but he's only one man, and he had a

solid commitment to Geoff. I think he made the tough decision to let you find someone that could give you everything you need. Someone you could give everything to."

Saul took a slow sip of his own latte, swallowed it thickly, and shrugged. "For what it's worth, imagine if you had been a triad. You'd have settled for sharing Carter with Geoff and you wouldn't have been looking for me."

"That would suck. I can't imagine not finding you." It actually made his stomach turn, the idea that he wouldn't have found Saul.

"Me neither. We fit. You're mine." Saul gave him one of those smiles, the ones that were so honest and so young. "So. We don't have to talk all night, but do you still want this? Have you thought about what you want from it? Or even what you don't? Boundaries, you know?"

"I hope you have things you'd rather do than talk all night with me, Sir." He winked and sat back, finally able to relax. "I'm trusting you to know when to slow things down. I have so many feelings, so many thoughts. I don't want to get lost."

"All right. I'll take that on. And we're all moving slowly, anyway. It's for the best." Saul leaned back with him, that voice dropping low again. "I'm not thinking about moving too slowly tonight though. I think we need the real deal. Not long, not a big scene, but... I need you."

"Yes, please." His cock started to fill, right there in the coffee shop, just like he was a kid, a randy teenager.

"Maybe I should make you sit here, right here in all this company, while I tell you what I plan to do to you tonight."

His mouth dropped open, and his eyes went wide. "Master!"

"What? Nobody is listening. Nobody can hear. If I speak

just like this? Tell you about how I'm going to cuff you, warm up my arm on that perfect ass of yours, and then let fly on your shoulders with my flogger? Raise stripes you won't forget for days? No one's going to hear that. Except you. And you don't have any choice but to listen." Saul sipped his coffee, acting at least like that didn't have any effect at all.

Troy groaned softly, hiding in his cup. Soon he would install the apparatus in their room—bars and places to attach chains and ropes, an adjustable padded spanking bench that folded up, everything Saul had asked for—then Saul would have more promises to make.

"So, had enough coffee? Are you ready to go?" Saul dangled the truck keys in front of his nose.

"Yes, Sir. Are you driving?" Troy almost fought his smile. He had the feeling his Master intended to drive all evening.

"I'm not driving your truck in the dark in all this snow." Saul winked and put the keys in his hand and stood up. "You can drive home."

"Yeah, yeah, yeah. Come on, Master Worrywart." He grabbed his coat and handed Saul's to him.

"I'm not worried. I'm just not going to risk denting your truck." They gave Sue a wave as they left and stepped out into the evening. The snow was still coming down hard, and it was cold enough that Saul tugged on his arm and walked close. "Back in PA, we'd probably be having a snow day tomorrow. They don't deal with snow as well there as they do here."

"Yeah, well, I'm tickled tomorrow's my day off. I can sleep in, snuggle with your pillow." Maybe even with Saul.

"Screw that. If you're home, I'll telling Emma we should close tomorrow. We didn't get a single person in the door today."

"Works for me, Master. I've got the day off and stuff for soup in the fridge." He felt like bouncing. Hell yes! It was a challenge to plan days off together. Bonus days were like magic.

"God, I'm just not ready for the cold yet. It feels like it snuck up on us this year, doesn't it?" Sir climbed into the passenger seat and finger-combed the snow out of his hair.

"We've been busy, and it's early." Troy eased out of his parking space, heading toward the house.

"I'll text her right now." Master pulled out his phone and did just that, thumbs flying. His phone chimed barely a minute later. "She was going to suggest the same thing. Looks like we officially have a snow day. Woohoo!"

"Hot cocoa, soup, a scene, and our fire. I'm so in."

His Master did bounce, like a twenty-something would with a snow day. Would, and should, even if that twenty-something was a Dom. Carter had said that Saul was changing things for all of them. His Master knew when it was time to be serious and focus, but Saul was young and owned it, and knew when it was time to play too.

"I can't wait to enjoy the view out the bedroom windows in the morning, knowing there's no hurry to go out in it. We can just sip coffee and snuggle and take it in." Saul ran a warm hand over his knee. "And I can take a little more time with you tonight."

Troy's legs spread instinctively, and he could feel the heat moving up from each fingertip, out toward his crotch. He forced himself to focus, remembering how scared he'd been that first year, learning how to drive in the snow.

"This one time when I was a kid, there was this crazy snowstorm and I was in the car with Mom. It was just the two of us, and I was so excited because I got to sit in the front seat. That never happened because one of my older brothers always got it. It wasn't dark, but it was cold, and Mom was in a great mood because it was Christmas time and 'Jingle Bells' was on the radio, and we sang the whole thing at the top of our lungs." Saul sighed, the sound happy. "I don't know why I remembered that all of a sudden. I was eight. Good times."

"Yeah? That's adorable, and not in a snide way either. I can just imagine." He tried not to remember anything before Arnie. Sometimes he tried not to remember anything before he came to Boulder. He'd sure left his entire universe behind—rodeoing, being a cowboy, everything.

"You're going to like Mom, I think. Everybody does. She's just... I don't know. She's a hippie. You'll like her." Saul grinned over at him. "Just show up hungry."

"I can probably do that. I hope she likes me." Mothers didn't, as a rule. He wasn't sure why, but it was what it was.

"I love you. She'll love you." Saul gave his knee a squeeze. "Plus, you cook! You're going to be her best friend. But—" Saul laughed. "We're not talking about my mother tonight. What a mood-killer."

Troy barked out a laugh that sounded like he'd stepped on a duck. "Right. No deep Dom action while we're talking about your momma."

"Mmm. Deep Dom action. Such a perfect phrase. I plan to be very deep tonight."

His cock jerked, and he sank his teeth into his bottom lip. *Damn*. "Listen to you, Sir."

Saul reached over, hit the button clipped to the visor, and the garage door opened. "Inside, boy." Master let him park, but as soon as they were in the door, Sir grabbed a handful of his hair and pulled him in for a hard kiss. Troy's knees buckled and he rocked against Saul, daring to push his boundaries.

Saul didn't miss a beat. His Master hooked an arm around his back and turned him, pushing him into the wall and pressing up against him.

He dove into Saul's kisses, moaning as he let his hunger grow.

Saul grunted, broke it off suddenly, and stepped away, taking deep breaths. "Upstairs, boy. Naked. Knees."

Troy groaned, almost grabbing Saul and begging for more kisses. He knew better, so he started moving toward the stairs.

"Double time. Move." Saul came up behind him and swatted him on the ass, then chased him up the stairs. He got another smack as they reached the top. "I'm more interested in what we need than what we want, boy. Naked. Now."

"I'm working on it," he grunted out as he bent to tug his damn boots off. "Swear to God." He was caught between being frustrated sexually, excited to do a scene, and breathless as hell.

"Come on, boy. Don't keep me waiting. You have a clean bill of health now, don't you?" Saul stood in front of him, arms crossed over a bare chest. He hadn't seen Sir lose the shirt.

"Last time I checked, Sir." He got his other boot off and started working on his jeans. "I was fighting not to damage my dick. I'm hard as nails."

His Master laughed darkly. "Me too. I'm hoping you'll take care of that for me shortly. You'll have to wait for my flogger. At the very least."

God, he loved that wicked, wonderful tone in Saul's voice.

"Anything you need, Master." And hopefully everything he needed too.

"Oh, good boy." Saul held out a hand to help him to his knees and then walked a slow circle around him, eyes dragging over his skin. "You naked is such a treat."

Troy's nipples went hard, his cock didn't flag a bit, and his ass clenched. He loved that—having Saul talk to him, growl, and ramp him up. "Thank you, Sir."

"You're welcome. Close your eyes, take a deep breath, and tell me how you feel." He heard Saul step away from him to dig around in that yellow toolbox where his Master kept the cuffs he knew would be coming next.

Troy closed his eyes and inhaled, the words slipping out easily. "Horny, excited. Mostly excited. I want you."

"Mmm. I want you too. And you know my plans. Basically." Master stopped in front of him, cuffs in hand and a flogger under one arm. "Hands, please. God, I can't wait for you to get this room done."

It would be soon. It was going to be a present for his Master. He already had it arranged that Carter was going to take Saul out while he and Geoff set it up.

Saul set the cuffs on him, gently as always, touching his hands and arms, soothing him as they went on and were fastened around his wrists. They felt like love, like a hug by the time his Master was done. "Not too tight?"

"Perfect." He relaxed—not that he had been tense, but this space, this *beginning* made the universe start to shrink.

"Why do you think I spend so much time on these?" His Master attached a double-headed dog clip to the cuffs, locking his hands close together.

"Because it's how we start a scene, Master." It was the way they started on the path they needed to go.

"Yes, it is. It's ritual now, and that's important so you can settle, and I can focus. We need to put everything else away and tune in. The cuffs remind you who you belong to, the touches remind me of my responsibility to you." Saul ran fingers through his hair and smiled down at him. "We could be anywhere, any time, and this would be the same, serve the same purpose, have the same result."

"Yes, Sir. This is how we start. Together." He couldn't stop smiling, and honestly, he didn't want to. He wanted to be with his Master, in this moment.

"Yes, boy. Together. I like that you said that because it's not about me, or about you. It's about us." Saul held the flogger and swung it gently, the grip graceful and relaxed. "There are things we'll share with Carter and Geoff, things we may even share at gatherings, but this connection stays between us."

"Thank God." He took another deep breath, then one more and let it out all the way. "I love when we're on the same page."

"I've thought a lot about things." Saul nodded, cupping his cheek with one hand, warm and reassuring. "We'll talk details and boundaries later, but I wanted to say that. I didn't want you worrying, and I knew you would."

"You know me well, Master. Seriously. You know what's in my heart."

His Master knelt—actually knelt right in front of him—and held his cuffed hands. "That's one of the rewards of being honest, boy. We're stronger when we don't hide things from each other. It's one of the risks, too, which is why trust is so important. I've been taught that knowing is the most important thing for a Dom. Intellectually, I got it. But I never really understood it until I met you." Saul kissed him, gentle and slow, all that honesty pouring into him. "I'm so proud of you. I'm proud of us. No matter what other relationships, friendships, family we choose, we're at the core of it. That's where we're grounded. In each other."

"Yes, exactly. I'm your boy, you're my Master, and that's our center." Troy got this. He really got this.

"That's it." He got another light kiss and then Master stood up. "Good boy. Safewords, please."

"Red and yellow, Master." He let himself spend a nice, long, lazy minute admiring his Sir, the tight belly.

"Yellow and red. Thank you." Sir seemed to appreciate the attention and turned to give him a view from the back before swinging the flogger in the air with more purpose.

"Gorgeous." The word slipped from him. He felt like he couldn't stop staring, like he couldn't help his praise.

Saul looked over his shoulder and winked at him. "Thank you, boy." Sir swung harder, the flogger singing through the air, back muscles rippling. "Are you ready for me?"

"I think I was made to be ready for you." The words made him a little shivery, because it was true. He came to Saul well-trained and still curious to know more. He'd been making himself ready for Saul for years.

He heard the groan, but his attention was on Saul's fingers, adjusting that cock through worn blue jeans. "Pretty words." Saul drew the handle of the flogger along his cheek and hooked it under his chin. "Stand up. Ask for help if you need it."

Thank God for yoga. He stood easily, humming with the motion. "Yes, Sir."

Saul made him feel so strong.

Saul glanced around the room. He knew his Master was considering areas of open wall—the floor-to-ceiling windows were privacy glass and had an incredible view of the mountains, but they'd learned that the smooth surface got slippery under his fingers.

"I've got your hands bound close together so... let's try

the doorframe. Go see if you can be comfortable there. I've got room enough to swing." Saul swatted him playfully on the ass with the flogger when he turned around.

"Arms up toward the top, Master?" He squeaked and jumped a little, playing right along.

"No, more like shoulder height. You're going to be there a while, and I don't want your hands to fall asleep." Saul walked up close behind him, his voice raspy. "And you might need to brace yourself."

"Yes, Master." He tried to find his center, his balance, but he wasn't there yet. He was buzzing, so awake, so alive.

"Good boy." Saul started swinging underhand, the falls of the flogger lightly brushing his calves, his knees, the back of his thighs. A light, rhythmic touch; just enough to make his skin tingle. "Pay attention to the rhythm. Breathe. Move all you want, speak if you like, but focus on my flogger."

"Yes, Sir." Pay attention. He was good at that. Breathe into the blows, feel, focus.

He braced himself, holding still while Saul laid down more of those balanced blows.

Saul surprised him with two firmer downward strokes, one to each butt cheek, hard enough the thud was audible but not enough to sting. "Tell me something Carter taught you." The blows started to alternate, light on one leg, harder on his ass, light on the other, then harder again.

Carter. Focus. Carter had taught him to work, to be brave, to be submissive when no one was watching. "How to cook."

"You like cooking, I know." The blows kept falling in the same rhythm, though the intensity started to vary, and Saul was going for his thighs more. "It's one of the ways you take care of people. One way you take care of me and show me you love me."

He nodded and licked his lips. "I do. I was lost and needed a way to show it. Carter helped."

"He's very... in tune. I like that about him." Two blows landed on his shoulders, not hard, just that thud again. "What about Geoff. What is something he's taught you?"

"To trust." That was easy, quick, and it felt good to turn it into words. "I gave him my skin, and he made me beautiful."

"He did. Though you are beautiful for other reasons too." Two more blows to his shoulders, a little harder this time. "Trust is hard to learn. Geoff is really special."

"He is. My best friend. Does that hurt your feelings?" Troy thought it was a fair question. Maybe more than— Another blow landed, and he groaned, his toes curling.

"No, boy. Not at all. He has definitely earned that. You need friends, you need perspective. Thank you for asking though." Saul stepped away and walked past him, shaking out the swinging arm. "I have one more question for you," Saul said finally, lining up behind him again. "What is something you've taught me?"

"What?" He wasn't sure how to answer that. What had he taught Saul? Patience? How to deal with someone 24/7? "Do you mean, like, faith?"

"I do have faith in you, yes. I guess that's even a step farther than trust. It's a hard question, isn't it? But I like that answer. Maybe you'll think of others tonight. Ways that I am a better person because of you."

He heard the flogger swooping through the air behind him, once... twice... "Breathe. Shoulders."

Master's flogger came down hard, once on each shoulder, the thud heavy and loud in his ears. He groaned, letting Saul hear what those strokes did to him, for him. The burn followed after his sound, a dull heat that moved down his shoulder blades and into his back.

"Very nice, boy. Beautiful. Pay attention now. I want to work on the line between what you need and what you'll take because I ask you to. I know you have a lot of depth, but I want to see if we can learn where that transition is."

Saul paced behind him. "Breathe. Tell me when you're ready."

Oh. He blinked and nodded. The line between what he needed and what he could take. God, he wasn't sure if that was worrisome or just exciting as fuck. "I'm ready, Master."

He hoped.

"Good boy. Shoulders, backside, legs...all fair game. Breathe." He didn't get much time to process that. The first blow came up from below, catching one ass cheek and the second came down on the opposite shoulder. The next set mirrored those.

"Fuck!" The shoulder blows were familiar and right, but the ones under his ass were sharp, shocking, and his abs drew up tight.

"Good boy." Saul followed that with lighter attention to the upper, larger areas on the back of each leg. "Fuck is not a safeword. Just saying."

"N-no. No, it's not." It would earn a punishment from Carter though.

"Good. More then. Spread your legs a little wider, please." He heard the flogger swoosh behind him again, but it didn't make contact.

He forced himself to spread, even if his lizard brain groaned and wanted to say no.

"That's it. Thank you. Don't forget to breathe." He heard Saul take a breath behind him before he heard his Master's arm move. Saul followed the same pattern as before, ass and shoulder, only with his legs wider, the ones to his ass felt a little more threatening.

He squeezed his eyes shut, but that made the anticipation worse, made his muscles tighter, made him clench.

"You're tensing. Talk to me." The flogger swung gently between his legs, licking at his balls.

Troy didn't want to answer. He didn't want to know the answer, so he just opened his mouth and let the words vomit out. "I closed my eyes, and everything got bigger. Too big for comfort. Part of me wants to pull away—protect myself. It makes no sense."

"That would have been a good time for a *yellow*, boy. So we could stop and talk. Do you agree? Let's hear it." Saul's tone was patient but firm.

Oh, he hated admitting he needed to safeword. Thank God he hated shorting them their work more. "Yellow, Sir. Please."

"Good boy." Saul put the flogger down where he could see it and moved in close. "Are you okay? Do you need the cuffs off? Do you need to sit?"

"I am okay, yes, Sir, and the cuffs are a comfort. I don't know if I need to sit. I don't feel dizzy, but honestly, I don't know what I need right now." Hopefully Saul didn't *hear Jesus, my boy is stupid* in what he was saying.

"Okay. Then you'll just stay here until we figure it out." Saul reached for him, though, placing a warm hand on his belly. "You're safe, and I'm listening. Let's break this down. You like the flogger, don't you?"

"God yes." That was easy, immediate, and true.

Saul looked thoughtful. His Master was trying to listen, trying to understand him. "I'm covering more of your body tonight, is that throwing you?"

"I think so. My lizard brain fights with my heart, huh?"

Part of him wanted to protect his balls, and another part wanted to see where they were heading.

Saul smiled at him and leaned on the wall next to his hands. "Your lizard brain doesn't trust me."

"I do trust you!" No one could control that instinct, right?

"Do you? You didn't safeword when you felt defensive."

"I didn't think I needed to. I didn't know what to do." He'd been trying to figure it out.

Saul looked at him, and there was nothing in his Master's eyes but concern. "You'd have let me hit you feeling that way?"

"You won't damage me. I know that." That wasn't the question. He believed in Saul, balls to bones.

"Hm." Saul looked away, then moved away, pacing across the room silently. He saw Saul's deep breath and long exhale, and then his Master scooped up the flogger and stepped around behind him again. "You're just nervous. What I'm doing is new, something we haven't done before. So we'll work through it. I know your words, and I'm listening. Take a deep breath and tell me when you're ready."

"Did I do something wrong, Sir?" He took that deep breath, letting the oxygen settle him.

"Not at all. But if you trust me and you know I won't hurt you, then whatever is happening is reflex. Reflex happens when you know something is going to happen, but you don't know how you're going to feel about it. So, I think we should find out how you feel." Saul sounded so sure of himself.

"Yes, Sir." He loved that—that Saul heard him. "I'm trying so hard."

"I know. You're doing great. Take a breath and let me know when you're ready."

He kept his eyes open this time, because he needed to focus on his Master, on them, not himself.

"That's it. You're safe, boy. You're mine. Are you ready?"

"Yes, Master. I'm ready." And it was true. One more deep breath and he settled.

"Good boy. You know what's coming." He heard Saul settle behind him and the blows started to fall, only Saul didn't stop after one set, he kept going, steady and rhythmic.

Troy began to breathe with each stroke, connecting himself with his Master, soul deep.

"Good boy. Very good." His Master sounded a little winded as the blows slowed and grew lighter. "You feel better, don't you? You're relaxed now. I'm very pleased. That's one reward for the appropriate use of your safewords. Other rewards are coming, boy." Saul leaned a shoulder against the wall next to him and wrapped a hand around his cock.

"Hot!" Jesus, Saul's hand was fiery, like a brand around his shaft, and his hips bucked wildly for a couple thrusts before he found his control again.

Saul let him move for a few strokes and then took the hand away, all the sweet heat and pressure disappearing with it. "Soon." Saul paced away toward the toolbox.

Troy found himself just standing there, smiling, floating with the buzz on his skin. His thoughts were gentle, disappearing whenever he tried to focus on anyone.

"Knees, please, keep your hands braced wherever is comfortable." Saul walked past him, swinging two floggers this time.

"Yes, Master." He hit his knees, settling back on his heels in hero pose. "Like this, Sir, or tall kneeling?"

"Hm. Let me see." The falls of the floggers landed gently on his shoulders one after the other as Saul turned them around each other like a pinwheel. "Up tall, please, boy. This is too low."

"Yes, Sir." He pulled himself up, clenching his ass cheeks and his thighs so that when he let go, everything relaxed.

"Better. Knees a little wider." Saul tested out the floggers on his back again. "Good. Breathe and tell me when you're ready."

In through the nose, out through the mouth. In. Out. In. "Ready, Master."

Saul started in on his shoulders, the tails of the floggers falling quickly and heavily in a figure eight, heavy enough he was glad he was bracing himself, but more thud and pressure than sting. Troy swayed with the blows, side to side, the world beginning to spin.

The rhythm didn't let up, not for a while. Not until he'd lost track of time and his place in it. A flogger landed next to him on the floor and Saul took a deep breath, letting it out slow. "Boy. Remember we're looking for that line. Use your words if you need them."

The swooping sound was almost jarring, and the blow of his Master's flogger bit into his already warmed and sensitive shoulder.

He jerked, his body pulling away. He didn't want to lose where he was. He felt whole here. "Master!"

"Boy." Despite the flinch, Saul didn't let up, bringing the falls down on his other shoulder just as hard.

"Master, yellow. Yellow, please. Let me stay here where I am." He forced the words out of his throat. He could bear more, but he had been in Heaven there for a bit.

The second flogger landed next to the first and Saul moved in behind him, resting hands on the tops of his shoulders. "Talk."

"It was perfect." He tried to focus, to explain himself, but it was so hard. "I was floating, Master."

Saul gave his shoulders a light squeeze. "I was, too, a little. That rhythm is entrancing, right? And you were content there? That was enough for you?"

"Heaven. I was..." *Come on, Troy. Focus. Use your words.* "I was lost in you." *And I didn't want it to end.*

"Good boy." Saul hooked a finger under his chin and tilted his head back, then kissed him upside down. "My boy."

"Yes." *God. Yours. Master.* That 'good boy' meant the world, allowing him to stay relaxed.

"I'll take you back there soon. Right now, I want your mouth on me." He heard a zipper as Master's jeans opened and then Saul turned his head, coaxing him around.

"Oh..." That was the easiest request. He opened up without hesitation, his lips parted and begged for his Master's sweet prick.

"Yeah." Saul guided just the head in, circling it in his mouth, rubbing it along the inside of one cheek. "Hungry boy."

Troy wasn't sure Saul understood how true that was, how genuinely he craved the pleasure and pressure of Saul driving into his lips, filling him. He groaned, forcing himself not to move, to simply stay open and willing, submitting completely.

"Heaven, huh? I like that flogger technique so I'm glad you do too. It's a workout, but it feels great. This is like Heaven to me, your mouth." Saul tangled fingers in his hair and slipped in deeper, starting to move in shallow strokes, talking to him softly in a soothing tone. "All this ginger hair. I never asked you whether you like it better than the bald you'd gotten used to. I'm glad you grew it for me though. I love all the curls and how soft it is."

Troy relaxed, leaning into Saul's hands, offering himself for use. It didn't matter whether he liked the hair. Saul loved it, and he loved that touch.

"What I didn't tell you at the coffee shop was that I am going to fuck you until the whole world disappears. This is just a little taste, boy. Just to keep us humming. Hm?"

Humming? He totally could do that. Troy closed his eyes and groaned, humming low so Saul felt every single inch of his prick.

"Oh, fuck." Those fingers clenched into a fist in his hair and tugged as Saul rocked toward him, prick pressing in deeper. "Naughty."

Troy refused to feel guilty about that. Trying to make his Master lose control was one of his jobs. He continued to mix humming with needy swallows.

Saul drew in a breath through his teeth and didn't seem to want to argue the point. "Heaven." He knew the choice of words was deliberate, echoing what he'd said earlier. His Master started thrusting, looking for friction, clearly taking more now than just a taste. Troy sucked suck, to pull on Master's cock, begging for each drop of salt he got.

Saul thrust deep and held him still, both of them frozen for a second before Saul put a hand on his forehead and pulled out, stepping back several steps.

"Turn back to the wall, naughty boy." Saul sounded playfully stern, rough and a little breathless. His Master reached for both floggers again. "Shame on you, distracting me."

"'M good, Master. I promise." Oh, he was on fire, testing them both, exploring his boundaries.

"Good? Well, you're good at guessing how far I'll let you

go before you're in trouble. I'll have to be more specific with my instructions next time, my *good* boy."

The floggers swooped through the air behind him as if they might come down hard, but they didn't touch him. A second later, Master started in on that thudding, rhythmic pinwheel again. One blow after another after another, a constant barrage of sensation. "Breathe, boy. Float again for me."

"Master..." It was easy to slide beneath the waves of sensation, let himself get lost knowing Saul would always find him.

"That's it. Think about this, boy. Why do you want this? Why do you need it? I don't need the answer, but the why is important for you to understand. So while you're relaxed, be honest with yourself. Do you know the answer? If not, that's your next goal." Saul's words sounded like a song, soft and musical.

It was who he was, pure and simple. He was built to belong to someone, to Saul. Troy didn't think it was— deeper wasn't the right word, because this went straight to his marrow—more complicated than that.

"Mmm. You didn't even twitch." The floggers still rained down as Saul spoke to him, though the space between them was getting longer and the contact softer little by little. "You know the answer. Good for you. I know mine as well. That truth is what makes this possible for me."

"So many words." He didn't understand how Saul could be so fucking coherent. He was just fighting to breathe.

Master chuckled behind him. "It's my scene, boy. I have to be coherent for it, make sure you get what you need." Everything went still then, and the room was quiet except for the sound of them breathing. Saul's deep inhales and rough exhales were close behind him.

He swayed, fighting hard to focus, to stay upright, but he ended slumped against the doorframe, letting it hold all of his weight as he tried to put himself back together.

Master's hands were on him, holding him. "Right here." Saul dropped down to steady him, taking his weight and removing his cuffs. "Breathe, boy. Nice deep breath in."

It took a few harsh gulps of air to get to that deep inhale because he'd forgotten to breathe, and suddenly he was utterly present, in his body, with his Master, lit up and burning.

"Yeah, that's it. Look at you. You ready?" Saul pulled him to his feet, bumping hips and chests herding him back toward the bed.

"Yes, Sir." All he knew in all the world was Master, which suited him just fine. He followed along, reminding himself how to walk.

"Sit. And be careful, because your ass is plenty pink." Saul guided him down on the edge of the bed and then knelt in front of him, pulling him into a kiss.

He groaned and leaned, his abdomen almost resting on his thighs as he folded himself.

Saul cupped his cheek, laughing gently into the kiss, then broke it off and wrapped hot fingers around his erection. "Time for a naughty boy to get a little of his own back. You don't get to come without my permission. Clear?"

Oh, dammit. Just the words ramped him up. If he was lucky, Saul wouldn't talk to him, drive him mad. "Yes, Sir."

Saul didn't talk at first. His Master leaned in and licked a line up the center of his chest, drew a wet tongue over his scar, his nipple, and slid a thumb along his slit, jostling his hardware.

Toes clenching, Troy squeezed his eyes closed, refusing to respond. Christ that was fine.

"Such restraint. That must be hard." Saul bent to him and his Master's tongue circled the head of his prick. "You know what I'm going to do next, boy, don't you? Tell me."

His lips parted, but instead of an answer, because Saul was going to take him, touch him everywhere, all that came out was a wild groan.

That must have satisfied his Master because Saul hummed for him and then swallowed him down deep, as hot fingers probed behind his balls and farther.

"Fuck. Fuck. Fuck." His hips rolled, and his whole world went electric. Don't shoot. Don't. For Master Saul. "Fuck!"

Saul pulled up and off him with a pop. "You really are delicious. Good boy." Just when he thought he could breathe, Saul took him again, letting his cock find pressure and rub.

He began to beg, pleading for permission to come, knowing that he was too close for one more sensation, one more rush.

Saul pulled up just long enough to rasp out, "Yes," before that mouth was on him again, willing and waiting for him.

He leaned back, a short, sharp scream tearing from him as he shot hard, his abs tight enough he didn't have to hold himself with his hands.

Saul was sweet with him, swallowing, nuzzling and licking, gentle fingers soothing and keeping contact. There was no hurry, Saul whispered to him and gave him time to breathe. "My beautiful boy."

"Master." He eased back onto the bed as his abs gave out with a hiss and a wince.

"Stings. You need to roll over?" Saul moved up beside him and rested a warm hand on his belly. "I need you."

"Yours." That was the best he had, the only thing. Saul

helped him roll onto his side, and he pulled his knees to his chest, offering his ass to his Sir.

"Damn, boy." Saul rummaged for a minute and then moved in behind him, a slippery and gentle but impatient cock pressing against his ass. "So fucking hard."

He moaned and arched, the movement helping the thick head of Saul's cock pop inside.

"Fuck. Oh God." Saul rocked slowly, each time pressing a little deeper, stretching him. Once Saul was buried deep, he felt a stream of cool air on his back, Saul blowing on it, just to make him buzz.

His body trembled and tightened rhythmically, and Saul grunted, hips jerking and driving in a hair deeper.

"Jesus." Saul shifted, leveraging up on his knees. His Master braced himself on the bed behind Troy's back, and started moving slow, rocking in deep and pulling back, bracing himself on Troy's hip and thigh. "Proud of you, boy. Working so hard for me."

"You. Jesus, so full." He felt like Saul was everywhere inside him.

Saul grunted in response, hands searing into his skin. He could hear his Master's breathing going shallow, ragged, feel Saul getting lost in him.

All he could do was hold on and offer himself—heart, body, and soul.

"Not... enough. Not enough of you." Saul pulled out and flopped on his back. "Come on, boy. Ride."

It took him a minute to catch up, to follow along, and he climbed up on Saul, resting their chests together for a second.

Saul caught his eyes and smiled, tracing a finger over his cheek. "That's what I needed. I needed to see you." Saul kissed him, fingers going after his hips.

Oh, didn't that feel good? He grinned, finding his focus and a surge of energy, and he straddled his Master, settling in for way longer than eight seconds.

"Yeah." Saul helped him line up and then thrust up as he was bearing down.

"I feel you." He pushed up to kneeling, hips rolling as he took Saul in to the root.

"Yeah? Fuck, I... I feel you too." Saul groaned and bucked up to meet him, their skin slapping together where their bodies met.

There was no way he could get it up again—he was forty-five fucking years old—but no one seemed to have told his body about that fact.

Saul's hands went from his hips to his abs and slid up his chest to tug at his nipples. "Fucking beautiful boy." All the while, his Master hadn't stopped moving under him, challenging him, sending that cock deep inside him.

"Yours." His eyes crossed, the zing through his rings shooting down through the metal in his cock. "Sir..."

His Master liked that. His words made Saul arch and groan, made that cock jerk and throb inside him. "Mine," Saul growled back, fighting for a deep breath.

"Jesus. Please, Master. Again?" He squeezed Saul's cock as hard as he could.

"Mine! Fuck!" The words sounded strangled. Saul gasped, eyes going wide, and that cock swelled and pumped inside him, his Master's orgasm overtaking them both.

He slumped forward, resting hard against his Sir, both of them breathing together. Troy would swear their hearts were beating in sync.

Saul's arms wrapped around his shoulders and held him, kept him still and near. "Do you know how beautiful you are to me?"

"I know how beautiful you make me feel, Master."

"Maybe that's close." Saul rolled them so he landed on his side and kissed him. "I love you. I need to take care of your back before I fall asleep."

"Love." This was something else so new, this aftercare. He'd seen it with the couples in their monthly get-together but hadn't experienced it. Master Saul took incredible care of him.

"I know, boy." Saul kissed him again and took a breath before slipping away. Master wasn't gone a minute, returning with the kit he kept in the bathroom. "You did well today, boy. I am proud of the way you stopped me and even found words to explain what was going on. Did you want to talk about that at all? That was a pretty significant boundary."

"Did I? I just felt like I was deep in us. So deep." And he hadn't been ready to come out yet. It didn't hurt that he knew Saul wanted to hear him, hear his voice.

"That's wonderful. And I wasn't working with anywhere near the force I have before with you. It's interesting. Your back is... red, your skin is hot, but there's nothing here I need to pay close attention to." Saul worked cream into his skin with more pressure than usual, fingers finding his muscle.

"It must have been the consistency? The rhythm maybe. That technique sends the blows muscle-deep instead of skin-deep, you know what I mean?"

It must be interesting because Saul was talking. Usually this time was quieter.

The massage pressed him into the mattress. "I felt like I was in deep meditation, like you were my heartbeat."

"I felt very connected. That takes concentration to keep up. It's one of the things I like about it. I have to pay attention. We'll file that one as a keeper, hm?" Saul put the kit on the nightstand and climbed into bed with him. "Not bad for a weeknight."

"It was—" He stopped short, a stray thought floating through his mind.

Saul ran a hand through his hair. "Was what, boy?"

"I—It was where I wanted to get before, during my sessions with Geoff." Oh God. Was that wrong?

Saul didn't give any sign if it was. "Where you wanted to get? Did you usually get there?"

"Never. Almost. I could get the hint, but then it turned to too much or not enough." He kept his eyes closed. That thought had been unexpected, confusing, but totally honest.

"So that's your ideal. That's where you float. It's not quite subspace; you need to be more alert for that. You couldn't serve me in that space. At least not yet. Maybe if we explore it more." Saul kissed his forehead and their fingers found each other. "All this time letting Geoff... and you—I'm sorry."

He didn't know what to say, what to do, so he just didn't. He lay there and kept his mouth shut.

They were both quiet for a while, but he knew Saul wasn't sleeping. "It's hard for me to—" Saul finally said with a sigh. "I'm sorry you didn't have someone who could have given you what you really needed all that time. I know Geoff tried, and he must have believed he could. I'm sorry for that, but I'm glad there was room for me. It really doesn't matter anymore. You have what you need now."

"I need you. I'm glad we have our friends, but I need you, Saul." And that was that.

"I need you, Troy. I love you." Saul reached out and touched his collar, warming the metal links. "I'm as much yours as you are mine."

"Thank you, Sir." He glanced out the window, smiling at the heavy flakes coming down in a blanket. "Happy snow day, Master."

Saul tucked him close. "Oh, right! I almost forgot. Happy snow day. God, I can't wait to just sleep in and wake up with you and no plans."

"Sounds like Heaven." He cuddled in with a soft sigh. "I'll make supper and a fire in a few, okay?"

"Mmm. Eventually. Relax and watch the snow. I'm happy right here. I'm not letting you go yet."

"Let's vote for ever."

7

Tuesdays were apparently the best day for both owners to be away from the diner because Troy was sleeping in, and Carter had called Saul and invited him on an adventure. Breakfast, skiing, and there was even mention of a soak in one of the resort spas.

Damn, if this was how Doms usually went out on a date, he was all over it.

Saul had loaded up on carbs and eggs for breakfast, and they'd hit the slopes early. It was a cold but gorgeously sunny day, and he was feeling pretty good, so he and Carter had made a bunch of runs. Carter was a better skier than he was for sure. By early afternoon, his legs were toast.

He groaned like an old man as he flopped onto one of the soft couches by a huge fireplace in the lodge and started stripping off his gear. "I have to work up to my skiing legs. You're tough to keep up with, old man." He tossed his goggles and gloves into his helmet and bent over to loosen his boots.

"I'll take that as a compliment. You're not bad. At all."

Carter grinned over at him, the look wicked as hell. "We'll have to have a standing date."

Not bad. Ha. Look at those eyes. Carter could be a little shit when he wanted to be, but Saul liked that about him. "Why does that sound like a challenge?"

"You'll just get better. My boy is *not* a skier." Carter rubbed his hands together. "It was a great day for it."

"It was." The fire felt good. He loved the atmosphere in ski lodges; all ages, everyone just there to have fun. He got the last buckle undone on his boots, folded the tongue out and wiggled his toes. "Ah. Better. I guess we should think about food? Or do you have a master plan that involves a sauna or something?"

"I figured we'd have a bite and a drink. I'm supposed to keep you out for the majority of the day, so I'm looking forward to just taking it easy and enjoy ourselves."

He raised an eyebrow. "Supposed to keep me out, huh?" He grinned. Someone was plotting something. And it wasn't even his birthday yet. "Taking it easy sounds great. You want to hit the lockers and change?"

"Works for me." Carter grinned suddenly, shook his head. "Assuming I can haul my ass up."

"My ass might be younger than yours, but I bet it's twice as sore." He tucked the tongues of his boots back in, got up with another groan, and offered Carter a hand up. "Troy's going to laugh his ass off."

"We're not going to tell him about this part, man." Carter took it and hauled himself up with a soft groan.

He laughed. Some things could certainly stay between them. "Nope. But I'm not sure how I'm going to hide the bruise on my hip from that wipeout. Which, I might add, was an eleven on a scale of ten for stupidest falls ever."

"Oh, I think you could have a bigger fuckup..." Carter snuck a touch to his hip, right where the bruise was.

He liked that. Carter had very deliberate touch, and it was kind of a turn-on. Not even kind of, it was, which reminded him that he and Carter had things to talk about. Handy they had some time to themselves.

All he had to do was survive the locker room without jumping his... what? Did they qualify as lovers yet? Boyfriends? God, labels. Some were so necessary—Dom, sub—and others were so useless. "Been a while since I used one of these." He held the door for Carter. "Damn. Do you remember where we put our stuff?"

"I have the key." Carter dangled the locker key from around his wrist, trying to look at the number on the back. "107."

He started down the aisle, looking. Eight a.m. felt like a lifetime ago for some reason. "I'm going to sleep well tonight. Oh. Down here." He led Carter to their locker, looking forward to getting his ski boots off.

"I take that to mean you don't want to do another couple runs this afternoon?" Carter sat down hard, rolling his shoulders. Yeah, he wasn't the only one that was going to sleep like the dead.

Saul laughed. A couple more runs? Carter would be lucky to get up off that bench. "No worries, man. You can use me as an excuse for why we didn't ski all afternoon." He leaned against the lockers, crossed his arms over his chest, and did his best Carter impression. "I could have gone a few more, but Saul is still working on his ski legs..."

That one so-expressive eyebrow winged up, the smile barely held at bay. "Very nice. Do you do that to scare your boy?"

"Nope." He grinned at Carter. "You don't scare him."

"No? Man, I'm disappointed. I want to inspire terror."

He cracked up and sat down next to Carter to take his boots and snow gear off. "Troy doesn't do terror. He's more about desperately wanting not to make a mistake. I don't scare him either. I worry him maybe, but I'm not scary."

"No, he really doesn't. I've only seen him pissed a handful of times, and scared? I can't think of that." Carter got one boot off, holding his foot up off the floor while he grabbed his shoe.

"He rode bulls. He's seen way scarier than us." He elbowed Carter, playing. "You could gain a couple thousand pounds; then you might even scare me."

"Oh, Geoff would be so pleased. Married to the Blob."

"Oh, man. Yeah, that's a bad idea. Poor Geoff. I bet you already scare him."

"Ha." Carter dressed quick and easy, changing out his shirt. "Did he ever tell you how we met? I was the least scary option he had."

"He did. The way he tells it you were quite the knight in shining armor. It's totally romantic—" He leaned closer and lowered his voice. "—minus the collar and the chains."

"Shit, man. He came complete with those. He had to work for weeks before I'd even contemplate a scene with him." Carter met his gaze, eyes steady, warm. "But he's right. It was total romance."

How sweet was that? Geoff was a lucky—well, he was lucky, too, he guessed. If that was really how this was going to work. He stripped off his long johns and pulled on jeans, warm socks, and comfy, waterproof hiking boots. "See? That is why you're not terrifying. You let your old softie side show." He gave Carter's bare shoulder a very bro-like squeeze, though his fingers tingled touching Carter's warm skin. He probably should have thought that move through a little more.

Oops. Only he didn't have regrets so, not really.

"Just keep it between us. I have a reputation to protect." Carter stood, and the motion let his hand drag all the way down Carter's arm.

Oh, so smooth.

He let his fingers linger in Carter's for just a second and then tugged his shirt off, switching it out for a T-shirt and flannel. The subtle flirting was making him buzz a little; it was fun. "I'm glad we have some time to talk today. I want to make sure we're on the same page before we're all in one room again, you know?"

"I do. Geoff is going to need some direction, and we'll be the ones to help with that." Carter was built like a truck— solid and firm, barrel-chested—and it was a lovely view.

"That's fair. And Troy's going to need time to adjust, but I think we should push him a little. We'll talk once we get a beer." He folded everything into his bag and hooked his boot carrier through the buckles in his boots.

"Sounds like a plan. I think we've earned fried things, too, don't you? I swear, I work out just for the ability to devour onion rings."

"I have a great metabolism. Fried everything, bring it on. And a beer." There was at least one advantage to being twenty-five in this crowd. He stuffed everything back in the locker except his boots, which he stuck against one wall with a bunch of others. "You ready? Come on."

"I was born ready, kiddo." Carter snorted and locked up before herding him to the door. "Or at least that's the rumor."

Kiddo. He snorted. Right. Nobody but Carter and his mom could get away with that.

"I bet you were." He let Carter hustle him back out to the bar, the experience of someone else taking charge of the moment odd and unfamiliar but not unwelcome. What a strange space they were in; both of them totally tops, but totally attracted to each other.

He'd thought about it. About having sex with Carter. The idea, the fantasy turned him on, but always left him hanging. His mind couldn't get beyond heavy petting.

The fact that he didn't just assume he'd be on top was very interesting, even though he didn't assume he'd be catching either.

"Where do you want to sit?"

"Let's go find a nice, quiet corner. That way we can talk freely. Fair?" At his nod, Carter steered him to the back of the bar, finding a nice sunny spot to settle. "How's this?"

"This is great. The sun feels good. No kids are listening... perfect." Saul sat and stretched, feeling every muscle he had. So much fun and such a great workout too.

"Yeah. I think we could just sit and have a couple." Carter stretched up tall, his back popping and cracking audibly.

He waved someone over who looked reasonably official. "Hey there. Do we get beer at the bar or order?"

"I can grab something for you." The server looked young, even to him. But the guy had to be twenty-one at least, right? He'd been hanging out with the forty-somethings too long.

"I'll have what he's having." He pointed to Carter.

"I think a pale ale, hmm? And a menu, please. I'm starving." Carter ordered without any hesitation.

"Yeah, that totally works. Thanks."

"You got it. Back in a sec, guys." The server headed for the bar, and he smiled at Carter.

"Onion rings. Maybe a burger to go with them." Saul pulled out his phone. "I'm sending Troy that selfie we took at the top of Splashdown. Man, that run was tough. Fun, but real work."

He sent the pic and followed it with, *Me and this hot guy I'm on a date with.*

It took about a second before the answering text came back—Geoff and Troy waving a giant purple dildo.

Jesus, where the hell did Troy get that thing? And a better question, why didn't he know the boy had a stash? He laughed out loud and handed his phone to Carter. "Looks like the boys are having fun."

"Oh, man. I remember that!" Carter barked out a laugh. "We had a white elephant party at Christmas. Troy ended up with that thing."

"He kept it, Carter. That's the real point of interest here. He kept the damn thing." He grinned and took the phone back.

Can't wait to use it on you. Thought of you skiing 'Hook 'em'. Having a couple of beers. Be good.

Good? Moi? I'm eternally good. E.T. E. R. Nally.

"We have Hoopla on tap. Hope that works." The server sat two glasses of beer down on their table. "And menus. I'll be around again. Take your time."

"Thanks." Ah, beer. He was pretty sure this conversation was going to go much smoother with a beer in him.

Ha. Love u, boy. He texted Troy and put his phone away.

"I think they're high." He laughed. With Geoff around, anything was possible. "I'm glad they're having fun."

"They don't get this too often, do they? Just goof off and be free without us around."

"No, but they should. One of several things we should

talk about, I guess. I don't really know where to start." He sipped his beer. "Not bad."

"Well..." Carter tried his beer, nodded. "I can live with that. Tell me your ideal situation with the four of us."

"Me?" That didn't seem... it felt arrogant. The three of them already had a dynamic before he'd shown up. "I'm just the new kid on the block." There were things he wanted, though, and things he wanted for Troy. And things that felt more like a fairy tale than reality. Not that he knew where that line was anymore. Not really. Maybe none of them did.

"I want everybody safe and happy. I don't want stress. I want clear boundaries so the boys don't worry. I want us to spend more time together just... hanging out. Informal time, you know?" That wasn't answering Carter's question exactly, but it was a start.

"I love the idea of hanging out, enjoying each other." Carter leaned back, eyes on him. "That will take a little time, because that new-relationship energy is such a high."

"That... and Troy's just not relaxed yet. It's just going to take him a little time to give himself permission and also to look forward and not back. But he's positive about it, overall. He wants this."

Carter pursed his lips and nodded. "Geoff's excited. Giddy enough that he's pushing me. I think—and please don't think I don't trust my boy—that he needs boundaries."

"It's not about trust. I know that. It's about taking the confusion of in-the-moment decision-making off him. Probably good for Troy too." One thing he knew about Geoff; that boy wanted Troy. Pretty desperately. "So let's set some. You want to stop them at blow jobs? Make sure they ask permission? Tell me what Geoff needs."

"I think, for right now, I'd like us to be present when the boys explore their relationship. Geoff is excited by the idea of topping Troy, but I am not comfortable without you being able to assure me that Troy is willing, not just submitting."

He nodded, thinking that over. He couldn't begin to guess where Troy was on that score, but just submitting was a real risk where Geoff was concerned. He couldn't even be sure, just sitting here with Carter and not in the moment, that Troy wouldn't do it thinking it would please him.

"That's... yes. Let's do that. Thank you. I honestly hadn't thought about it from that angle."

"You're welcome. I've watched Troy for a long time. He's built to submit, but he needs to learn to use his words instead of taking whatever is handed out."

He felt a little surge of pride remembering the other night and the way Troy had done just that. "We've made some progress there, I think." It was a harder lesson than either of them had expected. Emotionally at least.

"Yeah? That is important, but I know it has to be a challenge. Good job." The praise felt damn good, especially from Carter's lips.

"Thanks. It is. He's so worried about disappointing me or... well I don't have to tell you. You know. But along those lines, I think it's important to make it clear that, in a room full of Doms, if there's any question, he should look to me. Understanding that ultimately using safewords and looking after himself is about my expectations of him. If he can't make the call, I'll make it for him."

"I'm pleased to hear you say that. Geoff will respond to me, no question. I don't doubt him."

Saul figured Carter hadn't doubted anything in a while.

"Sure, I trust him. I trust both of you." The bottom line was that they both loved Troy. He really didn't need more assurance than that. "So, what about you and Troy? What do you want?" He trusted Carter to be honest too. What good would it do any of them to hold back?

"My main goal is to...protect him?" Carter met his gaze. "I don't want to hurt him in any way."

"Spoken like a Dom." He held Carter's look easily. "We're good, then. You've looked after him forever. He loves you, you know."

Carter hadn't addressed the physical issue, and Saul wondered if he should push a little, but something about the look in the Dom's eyes told him that Carter wasn't sure yet. That was fine. They weren't making forever rules, just starting boundaries.

"If it helps, I don't think Troy knows what he wants, physically. I'm working right now on making sure he knows that the two of us are rock solid and that he understands he has my permission—or, not even just that, more like my blessing. He's struggling with the way he was raised and his own integrity. That's what I mean when I say we should push him. He's not going to come to the trough on his own. We have to make him want what he's missing if he doesn't."

He knew he was monologuing, thinking out loud. Carter was watching him curiously with those intense eyes, but the Dom was listening too.

"He does so well when you ask him to step up just a little at a time. He... we really celebrate every little victory."

"So Geoff's right. He moves like an ice floe, hmm?" Carter's voice was warm, fond. "I don't doubt he's having guilt. Do you want us to back off, or do you think it would cause more problems?"

Like an ice floe. Ha. His mother would say like molasses in January. "No, just the opposite. I want to help him expand his comfort zone."

"Perfect, because the night we spent together at the

house was delicious. I ached the next morning."

"Yeah." He nodded, wistful. That had been quite a night. He didn't really have words for everything he'd been feeling, everything he'd seen. He just grinned and shrugged. "Yeah. Amazing. We need to do it again soon."

Really soon.

Like tonight at his place.

"I concur. What are our hard and soft limits, between the two of us?" Carter held his gaze, the look serious. "And I mean between you and me as lovers and us as couples."

"Those are the big questions." This was the real meat of their discussion, wasn't it? Anything—everything between them would affect their boys one way or another. They had to set the example, present a united front. He looked down at the beer in his hand, breaking eye contact because trying to think under the weight of Carter's gaze was too hard.

One thing Saul knew for sure; he and Geoff were able to be genuinely, deeply in love with more than one person. Geoff even more than he was. Troy was not, though that didn't mean it wouldn't change or grow over time. He was learning from all of them that love was complicated.

He honestly didn't know about Carter, and he wondered if Carter knew the answer yet either. But they'd get to the two of them in a minute. There was one thing he was sure about.

"Everything for me comes down to taking care of our boys." Especially whatever limits—or not—that they set for each other. "I think the floggers and the bondage, those things... I honestly can't imagine a scenario where I would need that kind of submission from Geoff. I think there's a hard line there unless the boys make a specific request." At least for now, maybe forever.

"That's fair enough. I have the inkling that might get

incredibly overwhelming for Troy, and for Geoff as well, if I'm honest." Carter opened his menu, and that was the first sign of nerves Saul had seen. "I know that my boy is curious to top Troy. Possibly even eager."

He believed that. He opened his menu, too, looking over the burgers. "That's a conversation they should have, then. I'm not going to tell Troy who he can or can't fuck, but that probably shouldn't be an in-the-moment decision for them either."

"That's why we're having it now, right? Does Troy want Geoff?" Carter put the menu down, eyes on him again. "I think that there is no way that Troy will be able to give in without you telling him he can submit to Geoff."

"Does he want to have sex with Geoff? I think so. Does he want to submit is another question, and I'm not sure we should answer that for either of them. It's fine with me if he does, just as it's fine with me that he submits to you. If Geoff wants that, I think Geoff needs to be Dom enough to negotiate that with Troy himself, with or without us present. Of course I'll make it clear to Troy how I feel."

"That's fair enough. It'll be interesting to watch, won't it?" Carter smiled at the server as he came over. "Hey there. I'd like an order of fried mozzarella sticks and onion rings, please."

He laughed. "I'll have a cheddar burger, medium, and a defibrillator for the old man."

The server laughed and winked at him. "There's one on the wall by the bar. I'll be back, guys."

He waited until the guy was a few feet away. "Everything about them is interesting to watch, don't you think?"

"I've been watching them a long time, so yes. I find them —and you—fascinating."

"I appreciate how direct you are." Saul winked at Carter

and took a sip of his beer. "You want to talk about us. About our boundaries? I guess that means you have thoughts?"

"I have questions, more than anything, but yes. I'd like to talk about us." Carter's lip curled up in a wicked, playful smile. "I'd like to find out what wickedness we can devise together."

"You mean like naked, three-legged house cleaning or like a real scene?" He gave Carter his best casual smile and kept his real curiosity to himself. Questions? What kind of questions? Because he had questions too. Like what happened after that searing kiss? What did Carter's skin feel like? What did the Dom look like all blissed-out?

He sipped his beer again. These weren't questions he should be asking himself in public.

"I believe 'yes' is the answer. I would happily do a scene together with the boys. I want to spend some time naked with you, experiencing all the ways we can get each other off."

Oh fuck. He was so in. "Well, Mr. Lee, that sounds thoroughly enjoyable." He chuckled and put his empty beer glass down. "I need to talk to Troy about what he'll allow in a scene with others around. We haven't gotten to that yet. I honestly don't have any idea."

He'd love to show Troy off. Show Carter and Geoff how beautiful his boy could be, how pure Troy's submission was. But he understood that Troy might have reservations, and if so, he'd respect them.

Ha. Of course he would. Like he had a choice. He wondered if Troy had figured out yet how much control a sub really had.

That didn't mean he wouldn't stress how goddamn lovely Troy would be, how hot it would be. How Carter and Geoff would watch and wish they were him.

He wasn't above a little self-serving seduction. He was a Dom after all.

"Honestly, I think the hardest part is going to be staying in tune with them if we're distracted. I'm not implying we shouldn't enjoy ourselves, but it might be challenging at first. I was thinking of telling them that safewords can be used any time. Like if Troy thinks Geoff is moving too fast, or maybe Geoff doesn't feel comfortable with something we're doing, you know? A safeword from either of them should stop all of us."

"Absolutely. I wouldn't have it any other way. I believe that we acknowledge—especially during scenes—whether someone has a particular need. Geoff doesn't always tell me what he tells Troy; I would tell you different things than I tell Geoff, you know?"

Exactly. Saul nodded. "Also, with four of us, it's easy to think you said something to someone that maybe you didn't. So, in-scene or not, even if we're just fooling around, I think the boys need to know their words will be respected."

He was relieved that he and Carter were so similar in their approaches to the details. He'd always felt details and clarity were important.

"And we'll have to be honest with one another, hmm? Trust in each other."

"No question. That's key." The server came by with their food and set it down, leaving them ketchup and two fresh drafts too. He didn't recall ordering a second, but he wasn't about to argue. "I'm an open book."

"I'm not."

The urge to roll his eyes and snap, "no shit," was huge. "I know. Why not? I'm not judgy." He reached over and stole one of Carter's onion rings.

"I suppose—" Carter used his mozzarella stick to buy time to think. "Damn, that's hot!"

He chewed his onion ring, focus glued to Carter. He'd allow the distraction, give Carter a second to breathe, but he wanted an answer. "Careful. Don't burn your mouth. I want a taste later."

"Yes, a burned tongue is no one's friend." Carter chuckled, the sound tickled as hell. "And I suppose it's my nature, mostly. A few hard lessons learned in a few hard ways."

He heard that, but times changed. He'd been lucky and he knew it. Luckier than Troy too. "So when I find you hard to read, I should feel free to call you on it?"

"Go ahead. I'll try not to grump." Suddenly Carter stared into him. "It might be nice to have a friend that is willing to call me out."

Jesus. Surely Carter had friends. "I'm willing. And listen, same here, man. That's how we do better, right?"

"It's how we learn. Questions and mistakes."

Yeah. It was. He'd have to see how well it went over the first time he called Carter on something. He had a feeling that "how we learn" wouldn't be the Dom's first reaction.

"Look at us. We're so well adjusted." He laughed and picked up his burger. Emma called him on shit all the time. But this was different. He'd try to remember that.

"Totally. I'm adjustment man." Carter managed to keep a straight face for about two heartbeats.

"Yeah, okay, Fort Knox." He took a big bite of his burger and hummed. "Mmm. Not bad for ski lodge food."

"Right? I love the onion rings. I spoil myself every fourth ski."

That was so Carter it was almost predictable. "Every fourth ski. Precisely? What, do you write it on a calendar?"

Screw that. He was having them every ski. He worked off enough calories.

"I don't have to. I just remember." Carter winked at him. "My mind is the strongest thing about me."

"Maybe. I saw Geoff's stripes." He winked back at Carter. He'd approved of that work. Carter was smart though. Sharp. He was dying to watch the man work; he knew he could learn something.

"I'm proud of the way he wears the cane, his stripes. I used to worry about laying them in between his ink, but I have that down."

"That would make me proud for sure." He'd wanted Carter to teach him how to use the cane properly, but after the other night... "I'm thinking Troy and I need to explore dialing things down in the pain department, not up."

Troy looked lovely in stripes, and there was no way he could give it up entirely, because he knew what he needed too. He'd just have to ask Troy to give him that gift sometimes. Troy responded beautifully to the deep work. He'd rarely been as proud of Troy as he'd been that night.

"Yeah? Can I ask what's up? You hear that so rarely."

"Well, I had asked him to really concentrate on the line between what he needed and what he was willing to take. Kind of exactly what you were talking about before with him and Geoff, right? I don't feel like he's been given a lot of opportunity to just explore what really does it for him."

He leaned back from his burger and sipped his beer. "I was pretty much just working out, some heavy, thudding repetition with two floggers, and that was as far as we got. He called a safeword when I went for a real blow."

Troy might object to this conversation; some of it was very personal, but frankly he hadn't had a sounding board on Troy yet and he needed one. He knew Carter would keep his confidence.

"Interesting! So he's been accepting the pain because he thought he should?"

"I don't actually know. I don't know if that was what happened to work for him that night, or if that is what Troy really needs yet, you know? I think I should…" He looked at Carter. Why not get his friend's take on it? Why not ask for some advice? "What do you think about trying sensation work? Long sessions, heavy bondage, sensory dep?"

"I think you two have some amazing things to try." Carter dipped his cheese stick in the marinara. "Seriously, explore everything. I bet Troy finds out things about himself that he doesn't even know to wonder about."

"What do you think about a service weekend? Can you guys get two days off at the same time? Or is that kind of impossible? Naked boys on their knees for forty-eight hours while you and I get pampered and have our way with one another?" Saul laughed. He was only half joking about the last part though. "Massages, meals served, baths drawn, hot drinks in the hot tub… I doubt Troy's ever had to sustain his submission that long."

"After the holidays, sure. Although, I don't know…You know, your boy served a long time and never got more than a 'thank you, boy' for it. It'll be Geoff that ends up biting someone and having a temper tantrum." Carter shrugged one shoulder expressively. "Regardless, I'm in."

"You're right, you know. He's all yoga 'ohm' and everything." Something to think about anyway. "What's Geoff's biggest challenge?"

"He gets lost in his art, in organizing things for our community. I make sure he focuses on me, so that he starts focusing on himself."

That sounded exactly like what he'd expected. Right brained, mother hen, didn't like to look too deep. "He's a good boy. He's also a good friend."

"He's the best friend a man could have. Your boy comes in neck and neck on that front. Troy is the most loyal, reliable, decent man I've ever known."

"Yep." Troy was a lot more than that too. "He...he loves me. In every way imaginable. I'm not bragging, I'm... humbled. Stunned. I just—" He suddenly felt young and stupid again. At first, he didn't like feeling that way around the guys, but lately it was more of a good feeling. That they accepted him for all of who he was. "How many people get to say that?"

"Not very fucking many, my friend. Congratulations."

He gave Carter a quirky smile, just going with the feeling. "I'm ridiculously lucky." *Dork. No more beer for you.*

"We are."

Saul loved that about Carter, how he could put so much truth in so few words.

"Right. We." He leaned forward and touched Carter's arm just briefly. "We are lucky."

"We are." They sat in silence for a minute, before Carter asked, "Do you know what the surprise is?"

"No idea. But they're clearly up to something big if you are supposed to keep me out all day long. Do you?" He gave Carter a toothy grin.

"I know that Geoff brought boxes that Troy had stored at our place."

"Boxes? That sounds like more than a fancy dinner." Boxes. That Troy was hiding from him as a surprise? Boxes. Did Troy have a project? "Oh."

Oh wow. Troy definitely had a project.

"There are a couple of things I asked for in the bedroom,

and I know he said he had a design, but he never showed me. You don't think—I mean I only asked for, like, two things, but what else could it be?"

Holy crap this would be a really good night.

"I don't know. I know he needed help, and that he's been whispering with Geoff. You know how things grow with them." Carter winked over at him. "Should I be desperately jealous?"

"Well, let's think about this. Troy took the time to design something, conspired with Geoff, then bought a bunch of stuff and hid it at your house so I wouldn't see it. And he needs help setting it up. I think the answer might be... yes."

Damn. He might be jealous of himself.

"Yeah. You're going to be fucking sore in the morning. I'll take Troy's shift at the diner tomorrow, if you want." Carter was a good man, one hell of a friend, and an understanding Dom.

"Thanks, I think we'll both appreciate that. And we will owe you one." He was sore already. Maybe his arms would match his legs by morning.

Or even better, his dick.

"So how long are you supposed to keep me out?"

"They're going to text, but they were talking about meeting for pizza for supper? I'm not sure they knew."

"Ooh, Pizza. Good thing we exercised and didn't eat onion rings today." He leaned toward Carter, grinning. "So do we have to stay here or is it safe to go back to your place and make out... I mean soak in the hot tub?"

"Oh, you are a smart man." Carter's eyes lit up, damn near sparkling. "I like it. Hell, if you're an orgasm or two up on Troy, you'll last longer."

"See? You're looking out for my well-being." Hell, he was

twenty-five. He was already the fucking energizer bunny. He waved the server over and got the check.

"What's my part of the bill, man?" Carter pulled out an ancient wallet and Saul expected to see it fall apart instead of unfold.

"Less than the lift ticket you bought me. Put your wallet away before it disintegrates." He waved Carter off the check and put cash in the folder.

"Do not mock the wallet, kid. It's way older than you are."

"It must have a story if you're still carrying it around and risking losing your credit cards." Saul pushed back his chair and stood up, feeling the stretch in his hamstrings. "Oh. Ow."

"Ask Troy for stretches, man. He's always got something. Until then? I'll bubble your ass 'til you're melty."

Oh, melty in a tub with Carter sounded so good.

"I know a few. Troy's got me doing his practice with him now most days. But he'll know some targeted ones, I bet." They practiced together was really more the truth. Troy didn't twist his arm; Saul enjoyed both the exercise and the quiet time together. "It's weird. I kind of love it."

"Troy swears it saved his life. He can do things with his body that I can't even fathom." They headed to pick up their equipment.

"Mhm. I can just about tie him in knots. Keeps life interesting, for sure." But for Saul it was more about his mental game. He'd never really thought much about meditation or quieting his thoughts, and Troy still had a hell of a time leading him through things sometimes, but it was getting easier, and he was learning. And he kind of thought he was more in tune, a little sharper, like he could read people better. Especially his sub.

He probably should have been colder as they packed up Carter's truck, but the thought of some one-on-one with Carter was keeping him warm.

"Geoff tried, but he hated it—the quiet, the stillness—he damn near lost his mind."

"I can't think of a better reason to make him do it." He hopped in the truck, laughing. "That sounded just like Troy."

"Yeah, yeah. You didn't have to put up with both him and Troy bending your ear about it."

"I can see how it wouldn't be Geoff's thing. He's pretty high strung. You have your hands full without Troy schooling you on the 'restorative benefits' of yoga."

Saul glanced around the parking lot and not seeing people around, he caught Carter by the back of the neck and hauled him into a hard kiss.

He loved how Carter met him, opened to him, and then took his mouth in turns. The man tasted like beer and onions and smelled like sweat and man. Crazy masculine, totally confident. Carter was as sexy as they came.

Carter eased back, the line of the man's cock evident and stiff in his jeans. "Let's take this to the house."

"You're driving." He settled into his seat and pulled on his seat belt. "I go where you go."

"I like the sound of that." Carter started up the SUV and got the heater going. "I like it a lot."

"Cool." He was good with it too. Carter was even confident about driving. It was nice to just let down his guard, just be a guy. He hadn't been on equal footing with a close friend in ages, let alone a friend with benefits. He hunkered down into his seat and watched the scenery go by.

———

THE TEXT from Geoff came in about seven, waking both Saul and Carter up from a nap. They'd dozed off, tangled up together on Carter's couch in front of the big fireplace, and even the idea of pizza wasn't entirely convincing Saul that he should move.

"Maybe we should tell them to bring us takeout." He leaned into Carter, yawning.

"You don't want to see what your boy's been up to?" Carter stretched, moving under him, muscles rippling. "That'll hurt his feelings, now."

"You know I do. I'm just comfy." He kissed Carter's chest and forced himself to sit up. "Pepperoni does sound good."

"Sausage and green olives for me, thanks." Carter pulled him back down and hugged him hard. "You're warm."

"Mmm. You're not helping." He wasn't above admitting that those arms felt good though. He could be happy right here for a while.

"I know." Carter didn't sound terribly worried or sorry, if Saul was honest.

"I'm glad we got a nap. I don't want to be tired for Troy's surprise." He needed to be sharp, because he knew he and Troy would want to try it out right away. He wouldn't let Troy down after all that work and planning for the world.

"Well, we're meeting them there in twenty, so I suppose I need to get my shit together." Carter sighed dramatically, playful as hell.

He grinned and huffed a soft laugh against Carter's neck. "Good thing we already showered."

"No shit, otherwise we'd be smelling like tomcats." Yeah, they'd had fun—and Carter had proven that old Doms had some tricks up their sleeves.

"Okay." He pushed up and levered himself off the couch. "Let's find our clothes, old man." His were... shit, mostly by the front door, he'd bet. They'd teased and played with each other the entire drive home, so by the time they pulled into the drive, they had been lit up.

He shuffled off to find his clothes and dragged them back to get dressed by the fire where it was warmer. "Are we going to be late?" Damn. Troy and Geoff would give them such shit.

"Yeah. I'll have them go ahead and order." Carter pulled on his boots.

He shook his head and grabbed up his coat, pulling it on and heading for the door. "I'll text Troy from the truck. Come on, you. Get your keys."

"Look at you moving." Carter stood and snagged his keys and wallet. "Grab my coat."

He scooped Carter's coat up off the floor and helped his new lover on with it. If there was any question earlier, it was sure official now. He had more than just a little crush on the man.

"Thank you. Come on. Let's get you to the church on time. I wouldn't want to fuck up your night." Carter patted his ass, squeezed it a bit.

"You couldn't." He was looking forward to it way too much. He'd take the teasing. He pulled Carter out the door and into the SUV.

They headed into town, the city already beginning to be dressed for the holidays. Thanksgiving was just a couple of weekends away now, and he was looking forward to the party, to hanging out with Geoff and cooking, to gearing up for his winter job. He started humming "White Christmas" as Carter parked the car.

"They're sitting by the window." Carter smiled and the expression on his face as he looked at the boys was adoring.

Saul knew it would seem strange to some, but he loved

everything about this new relationship. From the supportive, affectionate vibe when he and Carter were together, to his understanding and his feelings for Geoff that grew deeper every day.

And Troy, of course. He was only starting to appreciate the different ways his boy kept them all honest. Troy was everyone's barometer.

"Softie," Saul teased, though he liked the view just as much. He caught Carter up from behind and gave his lover a squeeze. "Let's go in."

"You got it. How can the pizza smell so good when I ate my weight in fried goodness?" Carter got them in, and the smell of garlic and bread was amazing.

"Because it's pizza." He grinned as Geoff stood up and waved them over, and they made their way to their boys, weaving around the other tables. "Hey there. You guys look handsome. Mind if we join you?"

Troy looked amazing, actually—he was all cowboyed up with his white shirt and soft brown leather vest, cheeks warm with excitement. "Hey, sailor. You want a beer?"

He pulled out a chair for Carter and then one for himself. "I would. Is it date night? You look great." *Like, can't-take-my-eyes-off-you great.*

Like, he wanted to take that Texan dancing in Denver this weekend after truck shopping great.

"Thank you, Sir." Troy beamed at him, and he swore his boy bounced. Actually bounced. "How was your day?"

"It was fantastic. The old man is a better skier than I am though. I'm a little sore from trying to keep up." He stretched his back and exaggerated a pained look on his face for Carter's benefit.

"Uh-huh. Right. Work on his hamstrings, Troy. Maybe

you can lean him over the bed." Carter had the smile of a demon.

Saul wanted to laugh, but instead, he gave Troy the eye. "Or maybe not."

"I bet I can figure a way to ease your aches, Sir." Butter wouldn't melt in his boy's mouth.

"You think so? If you're a good boy, I'll let you try tonight."

Geoff leaned back in his chair. "Jesus, Carter. Turn a fire hose on them, will you? We're about to eat."

Saul winked at Troy and cracked up.

"Don't be jealous, boy," Carter muttered. "I know full well that you had Troy on his knees for you today. He's the only one of us that hasn't shot yet."

"Yes, Sir." Geoff lowered his eyes and blushed a dark pink. Even the boy's ears were burning. "Wait. You too?"

"That's a beautiful color on your boy." Saul winked at Carter.

"Isn't it?" Carter held Geoff's eyes, that wicked smile never wavering. "Did you have a lovely day, boy?"

"Yes, Sir. Troy and I got some work done. We talked about the Thanksgiving menu too." He watched the way Geoff glanced up at Carter, the look sweet and submissive. "It was nice to spend time together. It felt good."

"That doesn't surprise me at all. We're family." Carter leaned back in his chair. "I assume I'm doing the turkey and ham?"

And macaroni and cheese and Brussels sprouts, and pumpkin pie... well, that was Saul's mom's house anyway. He wondered what goodness these guys got up to.

"Will you have time with work, Sir?"

Carter laughed. "You two will do most of the rest of the work. I just want the credit for the major bit."

"Right. Hey, everyone! Carter put the turkey in the oven." Troy winked at Carter, and he got the idea this was a joke as old as time.

"Yep. Those two hooligans can do the rest." Carter's grin lit up the room. "I bet Doc lets you borrow Ben."

Geoff nodded. "I'd love to have him. He needs some time with friends." Geoff looked at Saul. "Do not give him a knife though. He'll cut his fingers off or something."

Saul laughed. "Gotcha. He can stir something. Set the table."

"There you go. Usually it's Troy and me, but we're going to work just fine together."

"I get to be a hooligan while my boy works. Go figure."

Geoff gave him a smoldering look. "We'll make it fun. We can take sanity breaks."

He glanced at Troy, who was on his phone, typing away. Texting? Who on earth would he be texting?

"You're not working, I hope." Though it was possible, since neither he nor Carter had been at the diner all day.

"Answering a few texts and adding something to the grocery list." Troy winked at him. "Both bosses played hooky today."

"I'm glad you can get away with that once in a while." Two big pizzas landed on the table in front of them and beer for him and Carter. "We had onion rings earlier. It's a good thing we got some exercise in today."

He'd have a slice, but Saul was thinking he better go easy if he planned to work with Troy tonight. He'd already decided he was just going to sip his beer. He didn't want to ruin the surprise Troy had worked so hard on. He already knew Troy had the day off tomorrow, but Troy didn't. He'd pull that out of his sleeve later. Or let Carter do it. "Pepperoni!"

"And sausage and olive. They're good to us, man." Carter grabbed a piece of pepperoni and put it on Geoff's plate, before getting a sausage slice for Troy.

"Did I tell you guys I'm getting seasonal work? I got a job renting and maintaining ski equipment and snowboards. The next time we're at Jack Frost, I'll ski free. It starts right after Thanksgiving." Hard work outdoors a lot of the day, but he was looking forward to it.

"No shit? You should meet a ton of people. I have a couple of clients that work up there and they love it." Geoff grinned at him. "You'll need to eat a ton more food working like that."

"Right? I did it last winter, too, so I have some idea of what I'm in for. I was in good shape by the time we opened the shop last spring. Right now, it's three long-ass days a week—twelve-hour shifts. But then it's four days off." He looked at Troy. "If that works for you."

"Yes, Sir." Troy gave him a nod, a smile. "Most weeks, we'll have at least two days off together."

He reached over and squeezed Troy's wrist. "Perfect. And then I can plan all kinds of shenanigans for the other two." He was actually hoping for some crossover with Geoff and Carter too. "Emma and I are closing the bike shop up next week. She and her new girlfriend are flying to Hawaii to work there for the winter."

"Oh wow. Why didn't I get that idea twenty years ago..." Troy sighed dramatically. "I could have landed in the islands, but no..."

Geoff snorted. "No, you got stuck here in the land of cold winters and hot men. Bummer."

"Tragic." Saul gnawed on the crust of his pizza. "Are we taking some of this home for a midnight snack?"

"If you'd like." Troy leaned close, whispered, "I'm eating

light this evening."

He'd noticed, and he was glad he'd already made the same choice. He gave Troy a nod, the whisper made him tingle with anticipation, and he was feeling ready to go home. "Did you bring Geoff in your truck, or are we all headed back to our place?"

"We're going home, Master. Geoff is going home with his Sir. We have plans."

"Do we?" He loved the way Troy said that, a little daring without being disrespectful. "I'm looking forward to finding out what they are." He had an inkling, of course, but he had no idea what he was actually going home to. "Shall we, then?"

"Please. Please, Sir." His boy was almost vibrating.

"I'm ready." He pushed back from the table. "I'm going to take my boy home, guys. Carter, thank you for hauling me off today. I really had a great time."

"Anytime. I had a ball." Carter offered him a smile as Geoff put half of the leftover slices in one box.

"You're still good for tomorrow? I'll make sure Troy owes you one." He picked up the box from Geoff and handed it to Troy. "Keys, boy. I'm driving."

Troy handed the keys without a single murmur.

"I got it. I want a report tomorrow. Have a blast." Carter winked at him. "Geoff and I are going to share dessert."

"Ooh. Enjoy it. I bet mine will be delicious, just fewer calories. Night, Geoff. Carter. Let's go, boy." He shouldered Troy toward the door. "Where'd you park?"

"Right next to the building." Troy offered him a smile that warmed him to the bone, even with the frosty air.

"You have a surprise for me?" He smiled back, playing into Troy's mood, Troy's excitement.

"Yes, Sir. I can't wait for you to see it. I can't wait."

They climbed into Troy's truck, and Saul leaned close. "I can't wait either." He took a light tease of a kiss, denying Troy the longer one his boy's lips were begging for, and started the truck. "Patience."

"I've been patient for weeks, Master. I can wait 'til we get home."

"Good boy. Did you have a good day with Geoff?" He didn't waste any time heading home.

"I did. We worked hard, but we had a lot of fun, a few good talks." Troy looked out the window, attention on the streetlights.

He watched Troy out of the corner of his eye as he drove, wondering what was happening in that head. "A few good talks" wasn't something he wanted to ask more about right now because this was their night, his and his boy's, and he didn't want either of them distracted. But he and Carter had had a good talk too. He'd ask tomorrow, over coffee and breakfast maybe.

The drive went by quickly, and he grinned at Troy as he parked the truck. "We're home."

Troy beamed at him and took his hand, squeezing it. "Are you ready?"

"So ready. I've been ready since the second I saw you tonight. Everything about you is turning me on, baby."

God, look at that smile. It lit up the cab of the truck. "I love you. Come in, and I'll show you what I've done."

He lived for that smile; he really did. He wanted to see it on Troy's face every day, and he was willing to put in the time to make it happen. He slid out of the truck and handed Troy back the keys as he followed his boy inside.

The house was clean, but the smell of sawdust permeated the air. Troy locked up, put the keys down, and then took his hand and led him upstairs.

The bedroom door was open, a spotlight shining down on Troy's present. His boy had created a—he wasn't even sure what to name it. There was a frame with bars and leather cuffs, with multiple places to bind and support his boy. On top of that, there was a padded spanking bench, pegs for his tools, ankle cuffs, spreader bars. One side was even a huge St Andrew's cross. It was a work of art, of passion, and of love.

He stared at it until he realized he was squeezing Troy's fingers so hard he might hurt the boy. Then he let go, went right to the apparatus, and walked a slow circle around it, taking in not just the features but the quality of the work.

"Boy." Damn. His boy planned this for him. For them. There was no way Troy couldn't hear the emotion in his voice. "This is...stunning. Incredible."

"Thank you, Master. I wanted to offer you something one-of-a-kind. Something special."

"I feel special." He went to Troy and pulled his boy close. "It's the best gift I've ever gotten, next to you." He took Troy's mouth in a heavy kiss.

Troy moaned and opened for him, hands wrapping around his sides. His boy was ramped up, groaning into his mouth.

Saul was buzzing, too, and he let the kiss actually feed the part of him that needed to find focus. He intended to make good use of his gift tonight. He took Troy's head in both hands and muscled his boy up against the cross, mentally filtering out any thought that wasn't entirely about this moment.

The wood was sanded smooth, the height perfect, but what was better was the whimper that tore from his boy.

He raked in a deep breath when he finally broke the kiss, gaze glued to Troy's as he started to unbutton the boy's shirt. "I want to know what you're most eager to try first." He untucked the shirt and finished off the last two buttons. "What turns you on, boy?"

"The cross, the bench. I wanted to fulfill your fantasies." Troy let him push the shirt down, basically trapping his wrists.

"Mine?" He took the gift at face value and let it be about him. He wanted his boy to wear his stripes, but not yet. He'd work up to that. First, he wanted to see his boy over the bench. He wrapped the shirt around one hand, keeping Troy's wrists pinned, and leaned their hips together, rocking gently, giving the boy something to feel. "I know your words, yellow and red, and I expect you to use them. I'll be very disappointed if you should, and you don't."

"Yes, Master. I hear you." Troy groaned softly, lips brushing against his ear. "And yes. Your fantasies. This is my fantasy, right now."

"Mmm. You're mine, then." Saul let his boy go and went to look the bench over. "Get those boots off. Don't waste time."

"Yes, Master." Troy shot him the most wicked, naughty look as he sat on the end of the bed and tugged.

He discovered sturdy looking eye-bolts in all the right places, a wicked grin of his own pushing at his cheeks. "That's my only rule for you tonight, by the way. Use your words when you need them. You can say anything you like; come or not as you please. If you choose to follow orders. you'll be rewarded. If not, I'll deal with you appropriately. Doesn't so much matter to me. I'm getting my flogger out either way."

He glanced over at the bed. "Are you done yet, boy, or what?"

"Feet are bare, Master. Jeans are off." Troy came right to

him, sex pouring off him, happiness radiating from every extremity. When Troy got close, he took one of Saul's hands, bringing it around to the flat base of a plug filling Troy's ass. Troy's whisper was sandpaper rough. "This is a gift for you from Geoff, Sir."

Naughty, wonderful Geoff. "Oh, that's nice." That explained the boy's glow at dinner, didn't it? He jostled the plug, pressed it deeper, gave the base a turn. "Geoff is a good Dom, and a naughty boy. I can't wait to snitch on you both to Carter."

"I think he was looking forward to that." Troy gave him a dazed, happy look. "Master."

No doubt. But he wasn't interested in talking about Geoff right now.

"Boy." He looked Troy over, frankly admiring. He loved that he was fully dressed, and his boy was standing there naked for him, waiting, half-blissed out before they'd even really begun. He took another kiss, a slow one that hinted at the fire burning in his belly and the emotion in his chest. "You're beautiful. On the bench, head down the incline. I want that ass high."

God, just giving that order gave him goose bumps.

Fuck, yeah.

Like Troy, he was already a little high with the anticipation.

Saul didn't supervise directly, though he had an ear out for the boy as he picked out cuffs and leather straps and eyed the thuddy floggers that his boy had enjoyed so much the other night.

Troy draped himself over the bench, unmarked ass offered up like a sacrifice. He'd never seen Troy quite like this—red head down, white ass up, dark ink like a map. Talk about fantasies.

He smiled and gave the plug a pat, then sat on the floor in front of Troy to put the boy's cuffs on. The ritual was the same for him whether Troy was standing or... even more submissive. Saul stroked his hands over one wrist, then took his time putting that cuff on before moving to the other. "I really should be more grateful to Geoff."

Troy met his eyes, and he was transfixed by the happy, dazed desire in his boy's gaze. "Yeah?"

"Yes. Not only did he help you put all of this together today for my benefit, but that plug looks hot with your ass nicely presented for me, and I'm sure he knew I would be pleased." He threaded a strap through the D-rings in the cuffs and adjusted it under the bench, limiting Troy's movement. "Get comfy; ankles next and then I'm tightening this."

He kissed Troy, which did nothing to change that lovely, dazed expression, and then got up to get the ankle cuffs.

"I feel like a kid on Christmas morning." Troy shifted, hips rubbing from side to side, and then he arched and stretched.

Saul set the ankle cuffs down and ran a hand over one of Troy's perfect, pale ass cheeks. "You look more like a naughty boy on Christmas Eve." He hauled back and dealt Troy a smack, hand carefully curved to maximize the sound and minimize the sting.

That earned him a little moan, and Troy spread a little wider.

Yeah. "That's my boy." He bent and fastened the cuffs on his boy's ankles with the same care as he had the wrists— more in fact, since Troy couldn't see what he was doing. "Settle and tell me when you're comfortable."

Troy pushed down into the supple leather, the rich

chocolate brown a lovely contrast to Troy's skin. "It's perfect."

"It is, isn't it?" He didn't warn Troy before he gently worked the boy's balls free so they hung against the back of the bench, in plain view—and plain danger too. Or at least that was what he wanted Troy to think.

He hadn't had such good a view of Troy's guiche piercings before. Saul thought about fishing that lovely cock free as well but decided to leave it so the boy could rub off against the leather if he wanted to.

His boy flushed dark, but it was the hum that proved that Troy appreciated his efforts. The hum and the way that pierced sac tried to draw up.

Saul hummed back and cinched the straps, binding his boy's wrists and ankles down tight. That was hot as fuck, but the best part was still coming. He started touching, running his hands over his boy's inked skin, tracing the triskelion patterns that covered nearly every inch of his boy's body. "You're gorgeous. And you're mine. Every inch. Every nerve. Every thought you have tonight is mine."

"All of me," Troy agreed. Goose bumps popped up under his fingers, and he smoothed them away. "I need you like air, Sir."

"Good boy." He cleared his throat, shaking his head as his own arousal crept into his voice. He pulled down the pair of floggers that Troy enjoyed so much and swung them gently where his boy could see them. "A warm-up for me and little reward for you, boy. For thinking of me, for all this work. And then I'll ask for something for me."

There was a whispered "yes, Sir," and Troy shivered in anticipation. He closed his eyes for a second, breathing this in.

Their first time using this setup, the first time exploring

their new playground. Like a lot of things in life, in general and with Troy, they'd never get the first time back. He cleared his mind, determined to pay attention, to remember all of it.

He swung the floggers in the air, testing his arms, his range of motion. "Just light for practice." He twirled his wrists, checking distance and angle and aim, the falls of his floggers falling gently on his boy's pale ass.

The rhythm was steady and simple, and Troy's backside began to pink. It was hard to judge how Troy was doing from this angle, so before he really started to work, he cheated and moved the falls, letting them tap and thud against the base of his boy's plug.

"Master..." Troy tightened his ass and wiggled.

Troy was just fine.

"Breathe. Real work now." He started swinging, hand over hand, setting a rhythm to anchor them both and help Troy find that space again. He let himself get lost in the rhythm and the work, feeling his muscles warm and his breathing grow deep and even. His mind was clear and his focus on his boy, whose ass was turning a lovely warm color. Troy breathed with every other blow, panting heavily and offering up heady noises.

He slowed his blows finally, not really clear on how long it had been, but he knew, like he knew his own name, that Troy was fine. Better than fine. He dropped his floggers next to the bench and moved in behind Troy, groaning softly as his hands settled on the boy's hips and the bulge in his blue jeans pressed hard against Troy's plug.

Troy grunted and fought to get contact, to rock into him. "Oh fuck, you're hot."

He leaned back a little, just enough to frustrate Troy and pretended to be all business, when he was feeling anything but. He could take his boy right here, and he would one day, but not tonight. He needed his boy on that cross. "How are your hands, boy?"

"My hands? Master? They're bound."

"Yes, boy." Hopefully Troy's fingers weren't as numb as the boy's mind. He moved around to check them for himself. "I wondered if they were tingling. Going numb? Wiggle your fingers."

"Oh. Duh." Troy actually giggled, the sound young and goofy. "I'm good. All good. Ten fingers, ten toes."

"One red ass, one woody." He took a kiss and let it get heated but cut it short, making sure to leave Troy hungry.

Troy tried to reach for him, the motion instinctual. "Lord have mercy, you make me dizzy."

Saul laughed. "Take deeper breaths." He stood up, scooping up one of his floggers as he walked around the bench. "I neglected something, didn't I?"

He hadn't forgotten. How could he forget the best part? He just needed to make sure Troy was with him before he moved on. He moved around behind his boy again, and rocked the flogger lightly, letting the falls brush over Troy's exposed sac and slide over the piercings.

"Sweet fuck!"

He loved making Troy lose control, loved that wild sound.

"That means 'do that again, please, Sir,' right?" He did it again, only with just a hair more purpose.

"Fuck. Yes, Sir. Please." Troy bowed like someone pulled a string on his spine.

Okay, now it was fucking hot in here. He paused to yank his shirt off over his head and tossed it into a corner.

Better. Now he could enjoy the show.

He went back to work, giving Troy's balls a gentle

flogging, hyperaware of Troy's signals. They begged and pleaded, asking for more.

Saul had given Troy blanket permission over orgasms, so he watched and listened, letting his boy's reactions settle into his balls and make him ache. He enjoyed the buzz and appreciated that his afternoon with Carter had smoothed out his edges and made him patient.

"Beautiful boy. Needy boy. Talk to me." Patient, maybe. But fuck, his voice was rough.

"God, I need you. I'm on fire already." The words were simple but so hungry.

"You'll have me, but not yet, boy. I need something from you first." He dropped the flogger again and loosened the straps binding Troy's feet and hands down but left the cuffs on. "Let's get you on your feet."

"Yes, Sir." Troy rolled himself up, graceful and stable, even if he swayed a bit. "Oh, I was worried I'd get too light-headed, but we're good."

He'd been worried, too, and just to be sure, he took his boy by the shoulders and looked Troy in the eyes. "You're sure?"

Troy held his gaze, eyes clear. "I may be a little giddy, Master, but that's excitement, happiness. Joy."

He knew Troy was happy in general, but this look was new. The pure joy was new. "Such a good boy." He gave Troy a quick kiss and then sat on the bed to take off his shoes. "Hang up my floggers and settle facing the cross, please."

"Yes, Master." The excitement poured off his boy, wave after wave of it. Troy put the floggers away, the action graceful, almost reverent.

Oh. Look at that.

He was surprised at how much the sight of his boy handling his floggers turned him on. He loved it. "On second thought, boy, pick up the long-handled flogger with the braided handle and present it to me." He set his shoes and socks aside and stepped toward the cross.

There was precious little that was more beautiful than his boy on his knees, flogger held up to him. It made him breathless for a second, and his chest ached, his heart pounding in his ears. He'd really had no idea before he met Troy that it was possibly to love someone this much.

He swallowed and forced a deep breath, willing his hands not to shake as he took the flogger from his boy. "Thank you, my own. Please stand and go face the cross."

"Yes, Master." Troy stood at the cross, the light pouring down on him. Such a sight.

Saul stepped up behind Troy and kissed his neck. "You must have known, when you built this, when you put the light where it is, how you would look."

"Geoff did the lights, Master, full disclosure. He said this was good."

"He was right." He hung his flogger over Troy's shoulder and slid his hands up one arm, lifting it to lock his boy's wrist in place. "What does it feel like? Do you like it?"

"I feel ten feet tall and bulletproof. I feel like I could come a dozen times. I feel like I've pleased you."

"You have. I'm more than pleased, and you and I aren't finished yet tonight, either of us." He moved to the other arm and did the same, locking the cuff to the cross. "I don't know about a dozen times, but we could try for a couple." He cupped one red, warm ass cheek in his hand.

Troy's laugh slid down Saul's spine, sweet and electric, as Troy pushed into his touch.

He grinned and bent to deal with his boy's feet, then stood and slid his flogger off Troy's shoulder, letting the falls brush over his boy's back. "I'm looking forward to this."

"Yes, Master. God, I feel like my whole body is lit up, you know?"

"I do." He felt powerful. Troy had given him everything, and he felt strong. Adored. Loved.

He knew he had to be careful not to let too much of that exhilaration into his arm, keeping control was part of this gig. Part of his responsibility. Control over Troy, but control over himself as well. He reached around to feel Troy's prick; he craved the intimate touch and hoped it would ground him. He got a firm grip on Troy's shaft and stroked down to the tip, rolling his boy's Prince Albert under his thumb.

Troy's head fell back, muscles going taut all over the lean body. Jesus, that was pretty. Troy's prick swelled in his hand, the ring going slick with need.

"Boy."

Troy didn't buck or beg, so Saul didn't press their luck and let the boy hold back if he wanted to. Instead, he stepped away and sent the heavy flogger swooping through the air, testing the weight. Much more gently, he tested the distance, too, the ends of his flogger falling lightly on Troy's shoulders.

His fingers were twitchy, adrenaline pumping already, and Saul knew this was what he needed to settle. But he also knew that Troy had called a safeword the last time they worked together. He didn't want to be hesitant, but he didn't want to yank Troy's headspace away either.

"We're still working to understand what you really need but know that this is one of the things that I need from you. Know that you please me, that this will satisfy me. Breathe and use your words if you need them. You're mine, remember. I insist we keep you whole. That's more important to me than anything else."

"I'm yours, Master. I've never been so spread and

bound." Troy didn't sound worried or panicked. No, what Saul heard was a wonder, an amazement that belonged to him and him alone.

Never.

It was hard to believe that there was a time when he felt intimidated by the ghost of a Dom he'd never met, one that Troy had seemed to miss so intensely. But he wasn't intimidated anymore. Not at all. He'd earned his place, worked for Troy's love, and this moment belonged to the two of them.

"Starting easy, but it won't stay that way." Only long enough for him to know for sure where the hard blows would land. He brought the flogger down once on each shoulder, with a long breath in between.

Troy took the blows without moving, without complaint. It fascinated him—the way that Troy could sink into silence.

Saul stepped up and looked at the marks, which were light but would show him where he landed. The placement looked pretty good; a little higher and little farther right on the one side would be better, but they were safe and a lovely hint of what was to come.

"Breathe." He stepped back into place, rolled his wrist, then laid down four more blows, harder, louder, raising red marks he could just make out under the ink.

The only response Troy gave him was when the strong fingers wrapped around the chains holding his cuffs, the sound a whisper of music.

"So quiet." He liked to hear his boy, and he might, eventually, but his boy deserved this journey too. Those blows were for Troy, the next ones were for him. "Steady. Breathe."

He dealt out six solid strokes with the full strength of his arm, three to each shoulder. He stopped there, though he could have managed more, to have a look at his work, listen to Troy, get a deep breath. He didn't need more; he needed Troy.

He wasn't sure his boy was with him, still and silent, not even sure Troy was breathing.

Saul reached around and flattened a hand across his boy's belly. He decided not to say anything. He just took an exaggerated, deep breath, let it out slowly, then did it again. Sure enough, his boy followed him, sucking in the next breath with him, exhaling with a shivery sigh.

There. Troy was right there.

"Good boy," he said softly and took a look at Troy's back. His stripes were angry and red in some spots, deeper and obviously more painful in others. He moaned without meaning to, the ache so intense he wasn't sure he could stand it anymore. He dropped his flogger next to the cross and gripped the base of Troy's plug, giving it a light tug as a warning and then pulling it free.

Troy grunted softly, ass pushed out like his boy was following the plug. It was a substantial toy, and he let himself imagine Geoff working it inside, making his boy ache.

"Pretty. Feels good, I know." He wasn't expecting an answer.

He took the toy to the bathroom, ditched his jeans, and dug out a rubber, hissing as he rolled it on. Damn, he'd felt fairly patient until he touched himself. He looked Troy over hungrily, focused on the way the lighting showed off his boy's stripes.

Troy was shifting restlessly, hips rocking, moving in the beam of light.

"I'm here, boy. Right here." He moved up close again and dropped his voice to a whisper. "Right here."

"Master. I'm so empty. Help me, please."

He grinned. His boy was so deep it was both hot and completely adorable. "I've got what you need, boy." *And then some*. Troy was plenty ready for him, so he wasn't subtle. He lined up, took his boy by the hips, and with a rough moan, eased himself inside.

"Yes." It wasn't a cry or a plea, but something that sounded utterly satisfied.

"Yeah," Saul agreed. Fuck, it was about time. He was on fire. "You feel so good." He shifted his hands, finding a good spot to dig in his fingers and hold on.

"Need you." Troy tried to find the give in the chains, the spot where he could fuck himself on Saul's cock.

"What's the rush, boy? You've waited this long." He rocked into Troy with a groan. He knew damn well what the rush was; he felt it too. "Your back... you wear my stripes so... well. Fuck." He took his boy, driving deep. The stripes would need care. He always enjoyed that part, and they'd get there. This was too sweet to focus on anything else.

"Waited and waited." Troy's body gripped him, milked him fiercely. Pushy, desperate boy.

The way Troy fit on the cross was just perfect and it stretched his boy just right, showing off muscle and bone, stripes and ink. He shifted his weight, taking a wider stance, and hauled back on Troy's hips as he thrust, making their bodies bump together over and over.

Every thrust, Troy rocked and bucked against him, and when Saul pegged Troy's gland, his boy cried out for him.

"Oh, I like hearing you." He tried for that spot again. Forget floating, he wanted to send his boy rocketing into space.

"There!" Troy's word split the air like a hatchet. "Sweet fuck. Right there."

"Got you." The only word to describe how Saul felt at the sound of that shout was joy. He never felt more elated than when he could make Troy give in and lose it. His balls pulled up and his cock swelled. "Gonna make you come so hard for me."

And he was going to follow his boy right off the cliff.

"Yes. Yes. God yes." His boy was babbling now, and his body held him almost painfully tight as Troy fought to find their pleasure.

Jesus, Troy made his eyes cross. "Fuck...fuck." He rocked against his boy hard, pinning Troy's chest against the cross, hips grinding.

Troy's wild pleas cut off suddenly, and the scent of spunk was sharp on the air.

Every nerve lit up as Troy contracted around him. "Yes!" His hips sped frantically as his thrusts grew shallow and his orgasm raged through him. Saul gulped in a breath and shot hard, forehead falling against his boy's neck.

"God..." That husky whisper made him smile. "You like your present, hmm?"

He didn't move; he couldn't yet. "I love it." He sucked in another breath. "I love you." *Come on muscles, let's go.*

"Love you." Troy stretched, that motion gripping his prick, making him gasp.

"Jesus." He pressed his palms against Troy's hips and tugged himself free. "I just...you need to...I'll... hang on." Shit, he couldn't even get words out that made any sense. Saul walked a little stiffly to the bathroom to quickly clean up, feeling every second of his day of skiing now and knew he was tired. That was good work. He took two Advil and hurried back to his boy, not wanting to leave Troy alone and bound for more than a minute.

Troy was resting one cheek against his arm, humming

softly, swaying in his bonds. That was a happy boy right there, and he couldn't be more proud or feel more honored or more in love. Troy's contentment, the stripes, his boy's spent cock hanging loose and relaxed, made Saul breathe deep and his chest puff up. "You're stunning."

Better than you deserve, Saul. You smug bastard.

Saul grinned and moved around in front of the cross, looking at Troy through the various support bars on the other side of the structure. It was time to move the boy, but he didn't want to do anything too suddenly and risk destroying the lovely headspace Troy was in. "I need to look after your back, boy. Are you ready to come down from there?"

"Mmm... Yes, Sir. This is comfortable, but it's time." Troy smiled at him, licked his lips. "I'm dry as a bone."

"I hear that." Now that Troy said it, he was too. "Feet first." He moved slowly, just the way they'd begun. He started with a hand on his boy's hip and kept contact as he freed Troy's feet, then made his way up again, following the length of one arm to start on the cuffs binding Troy's hands.

He kept his body pressed against Troy's, offering his boy something to support himself with, and when that one arm was free, Troy took the opportunity to lean.

Leaning on him had to sting with all that raw skin on his boy's back. He considered the options, obviously one bound hand too late, deciding the bed was just a few steps away and they could make it. Rookie mistake, and he rolled his eyes at himself, but he wouldn't make it again.

"I'm going to get this arm down and put it over my shoulders. I need you to make it to the bed, okay? Then we'll relax."

"I can stand up, Master. I was just taking advantage." Troy kissed his jaw, the touch a bit sloppy, completely sweet.

That made him smile. "Naughty." He was kidding this time. Troy had been good as gold and damn well knew it. He freed Troy's hand, and they moved to the bed where he helped his boy sit, then went for water and his kit.

Troy turned on some music, something low and sensual, throbbing in the background. His boy had fallen in love with the idea of playlists and had one for every situation.

"Oh, nice. Good idea, boy." He sat with Troy, handed off a bottle of water and set two more down on the nightstand with his kit. He opened the last bottle for himself and chugged it, almost finishing it in one long gulp.

Troy had finished his first bottle and was drinking on his second by the time he came up for air. "Good, huh?"

His sweet boy was flying.

"Good, yes." If he gentled the boy along, it could last all night. Maybe even the next day. Saul finished off that first bottle and picked up his kit. "You'll have some chores tomorrow. Bondage furniture that needs to be cleaned thoroughly. And my floggers and cuffs too. After breakfast, of course." He'd keep Troy busy and focused. Let the boy enjoy that high as long as possible.

"Oh Master..." Troy sounded so disappointed, and his shoulders tightened. "Tomorrow's my day on at the diner."

He leaned close to Troy and whispered, "I know one of the owners. He offered to take your shift."

"Oh..." He felt Troy's smile against his cheek, and his boy relaxed. "Thank you, Master. Thank you so much."

He took Troy's hand and gave it a squeeze. "Thank Master Carter. He's given us a gift, don't you think? You'll return the favor for him sometime."

"Yes, Master." Troy chuckled softly. "I have absolutely no doubt."

"Mhm. I can't wait to see that." Like, really. "Do you need a bio break before I see to those stripes?"

"I'd better. You know me, I get to where my teeth are floating, and I just don't want to move." Troy chuckled at his own joke and padded off to the en suite.

This almost-giddy Troy was adorable and knowing he had taken his boy there made Saul so proud it ached.

He got up to turn the spotlight off over Troy's masterpiece but lingered a second, running a hand over the cross. Damn. This was it, right? This was the dream. Flogger in one hand, boy in chains, this was his fucking fantasy come to life.

He stepped back and turned the light off, putting that part of his evening to rest.

Troy came to him, smelling of toothpaste. "On my belly, Master?"

He nodded and led his boy back to bed by the hand. "Did you get a look at them?"

"I tried, but I only got a glance. I can feel them." Troy stole a quick kiss.

Oh, that was a good idea. He took a longer one, holding his boy by the nape, and left them both breathless. He admired the slightly dazed look in his boy's eyes before pointing to the bed.

"Master..." There was sweet grin on Troy's face as he settled.

"I know. I love you too." He sat close and turned a critical eye to Troy's back. The stripes were his, but the next hour or so belonged to his boy. Aftercare was necessary, of course, to keep Troy healthy, but he knew emotionally that kind of healing was necessary for him too.

"Are they pretty?" Troy asked, words muffled in his arm. "Your marks?"

"They're…" Pretty? "Astonishing. Marvelous." Humbling, in a way. That his boy loved him that much. He swallowed and got to work. Some of the welts were raw and could take more than a few days to heal up.

There was something deeply satisfying about Troy's sounds as he worked. His boy held nothing back, offered himself up without a single worry, with no hesitation.

They didn't talk, though they were communicating just fine. He worked for a long time, carefully and gently, until he was satisfied that Troy could rest comfortably. By the time he was done, he was tired. Exhausted even, but in the best way.

Saul closed up his kit and picked up his water bottle, finishing up what was left in it. "Are you still awake, boy?" It was hard to tell. Troy had been so still and quiet the last little while.

"Yes, Master." But only the slightest bit, he thought.

"Sleep as long as you need. Don't feel like you have to haul yourself out of bed to make breakfast or anything. You've earned a lazy morning. We both have." With Troy safe and comfortable, Saul went back to the bathroom to wash up and brush his teeth. He made sure the heat would stay up overnight so Troy would be warm enough not to need blankets, and then he climbed into bed with his boy.

Troy immediately moved to drape over him, murmuring softly. His boy was hot against him, boneless and heavy, the soft curls tickling his chest.

He curled one hand around Troy's bicep and tangled the other in his boy's red curls. "Thank you, boy. I love you. Sleep well."

He didn't need a response. The way Troy was holding him, trusting him, said it all. He knew.

8

————

Carter wasn't exactly sure why Geoff was so quiet after seeing Troy, but he could sit with silence easily. His boy would talk to him soon.

He sat on his recliner, watching Geoff putter around.

It had been a lovely day—between playing on the slopes and playing with Saul, he was relaxed, ready to focus on the brightest light in the universe.

His Geoff had caught his eye from the very first second, and he'd never looked away. Geoff had been his from the get-go, no question.

People could bullshit about love at first sight being nonsense all they wanted. Fuck that.

He'd known from first sight.

Geoff disappeared into the kitchen, and not long after, he heard the whistle of the kettle. Geoff's decision to bring him a cup of tea instead of a nightcap was telling enough, but when his boy knelt at his feet, he knew they had some work to do tonight.

Carter cupped Geoff's cheek, letting himself see his boy —the swirling emotions in his eyes, the lines beside Geoff's lashes from laughing, the lines beside his mouth from worrying. There was a bit of something in Geoff's hair from whatever construction they'd been up to, and Carter brushed it away.

Some of what he saw was familiar, reminiscent of the way Geoff looked after a tattoo session with Troy. But it wasn't the same; there was less intensity but more confusion. Geoff sighed and leaned into his hand, and those eyes slid closed so he couldn't read them anymore.

"I'm trying, Sir." In typical Geoff fashion, the boy launched into their conversation mid-thought so that Carter was starting at a disadvantage. Except he wasn't, because this was something he'd dealt with dozens upon dozens of times before. "But I think I need help."

"I'm right here." And he would help, if in no other way than listening and absorbing the worry and fear and proving that he was with Geoff on the other end.

Geoff nodded and rested against his knee. "I'm here with you, but I keep thinking about him. Troy. I'm having trouble... We had a great day. So much fun. We were working together, but he was very submissive anyway and it felt so natural. Just easy. I liked that. But now I can't... I don't know how to let it go."

"How to let what go, boy?" He imagined he knew the answer—how to flip that switch between sub and Dom—but he wanted to be sure, to hear the truths in Geoff's voice.

He'd learned his lesson in that.

"How to let that go." Geoff sighed, probably frustrated that Carter hadn't just jumped in and clarified things, and tried again to answer. "How to go from that to this. How to shift from thinking about Troy as my sub. To clear that out and think about just you, about being yours. To put one thing down and pick up the other." Geoff started out speaking carefully, but once the ball was rolling, he grew more confident.

Carter's immediate reaction was to insist that all of Geoff was his regardless, but that wasn't going to help, so he went with, "I don't think it's immediate, boy. You're making a huge change in your world view."

Geoff sat up and looked at him. "That's okay? You're not displeased? I'm sorry. I really am trying, Sir."

Silly man. Geoff had never—never—displeased him, no matter the roles they played, but this was where he could allow his boy to lean hard. "That is more than okay, and I'm proud of you. I love you, and I see how hard you're trying. Talk to me."

"Okay." Geoff took a deep breath and visibly relaxed. "Okay. Thank you, Sir. I love you. I just feel like I'm learning to walk again. I want to. I hope I can. It's just more confusing than I thought it would be. It's not as simple as just being one thing with him and another with you, is it? It's all me, and I'm yours, so it's all yours."

"Brilliant boy." He leaned down and kissed Geoff in reward. God, his Geoff was so self-aware, so in the know when he allowed it to happen. "Exactly so. We're together in this, in all things, and there is not a bit of you that does not belong in my heart, hmm?"

"No, Sir. I'm yours, body and soul. Thing is, though, it's like I'm standing on Jell-O. It's shifty. When you're around, it's easy, but you weren't today." Geoff shook his head. "So many decisions."

"Yes. I think maybe it would work better if we were all together the next few times. I'd like to be there for you, and I can't imagine Saul not wanting the same for Troy." They'd already committed to that anyway, so it was a simple thing to offer.

Geoff nodded and shifted to kneeling again, working his knees apart. "Thank you, Sir. That feels right. Much better." The boy's hands slid over Saul's thighs, and Geoff smiled up at him.

"I want to hear about your day, boy. Tell me everything." He wasn't asking because experiencing this through Geoff was hot and exciting. Nope. Not a bit. He reached out and brushed Geoff's hair back, to mute his smile a bit.

"Well, it started with a lot of heavy lifting. The lumber in our garage and the chains and leather and all. We loaded up his truck and drove it all over there and unloaded it." Geoff's thumbs dragged up the inside of his thighs. "We worked up a little bit of a sweat."

"A bit? I'm sorry I missed that. I do love to watch you move." And there was no doubt of that. "Did it turn out?"

Geoff's eyes went wide. "Did you see his plans? He built an incline spanking bench with a leather seat, while I put up a rack with pegs for all of Master Saul's tools, and then we built this freestanding... *thing*. It's got a couple of bars and is covered in rings for tie downs and a cross on one side with chains." Geoff's fingers got dangerously close to getting the boy in trouble. "And then we put in a spotlight."

"A spotlight?" Oh, the voyeur in him came to life with that thought, even as he waited to see if Geoff would push too far.

"Yes, Sir. Right over top. Troy put it on a dimmer so Master Saul can set it however he wants. It's amazing. Imagine Troy chained to the cross, all of his ink under that spotlight? Makes me shiver. Master Saul is so lucky." Geoff's hand ghosted over Carter's crotch and tugged gently on the top button of his blue jeans.

"Pushy boy..." He chuckled softly, tapping Geoff's nose with a gentle finger. "Is that for you?" he teased.

"Yes, Sir." Geoff caught his eye. "Let me love you a little."

"I will. I expect to hear all of your story though. Don't get distracted."

"Sorry, Sir." Geoff tried to look contrite but wasn't terribly convincing. "We took a break for a late lunch before cleaning up. Troy made grilled cheese and soup, and crunchy croutons. It was so good. We ate by the fire in the living room and watched a little TV. *Cupcake Wars.* So sexy." His boy was just messing with him now.

Carter laughed and caught Geoff up, kissing his boy hard enough to steal that teasing smile. "You're going to end up over my lap, boy, with a rosy ass."

"Oh, God. Then wait until I tell you about the Shop Vac. I sucked up so much sawdust." Geoff winked at him.

"Little shit." He drew Geoff into his arms, getting a hug. "I'll Shop Vac you."

His fingers knew exactly where to tickle his boy, and soon they were both howling with laughter, Geoff's tension dissolved.

"Stop! Jesus..." Geoff giggled and squirmed, trying to get a breath. "Please, Sir."

He backed off, letting his boy relax against him, reach for his center again. He stroked along Geoff's back, bringing them back together. The jokes hid worry, and he knew that, but he needed to hear the parts that Geoff would replay again and again.

Geoff leaned hard and settled, and he could tell right away that the anxiety was gone. After a quiet moment, Geoff shrugged, shoulders rolling against him. "I don't even know whose idea it was. It should have been mine. Maybe it was, but honestly I'm not sure." Words just started to flow, right off the top of his boy's head without thought or censure, and he knew this was the important bit.

"We were talking. Troy was telling me how long he'd been planning this, how excited he was for Master Saul to see it and use it. And then he thanked me. All I said was you're welcome, and that it felt good that he wanted my help, that he trusted me with something so important, and then I... oh. I guess maybe I did start it. I kissed him."

Sweet boy. What he would give to have been a fly on the wall. "And he liked it."

"Yeah, he did. And I did. And we just made out for a while. It was nice. Slow, you know? Just..." Geoff blushed and sighed. "Romantic, I guess. Not crazy and hot like the last time, which was great by the way, but this was... different. It was just us."

"It was the same for me with Saul. No hurry, no stress—just two men together." After they took that first edge off anyway. It had been romantic—surprisingly so—and the orgasms had come in waves.

That got him a smile. "It feels good, doesn't it? They feel good."

"They do. Saul is very energetic." And young. It was one hell of an ego boost.

"Energetic." Geoff laughed. "Troy's blow jobs are like church. And he doesn't seem to have a gag reflex."

He chuckled. Good. They needed to share this. "Lucky. And you like them slow and deep. You must have been in heaven."

"Oh, yes, Sir. When Troy gives you one, I plan to watch very closely. He's magic." Geoff shifted in his lap and looked at him. "And he wouldn't let me return the favor. He was saving it for Saul. For their scene. How hot is that?"

Blistering. Saul had to be over the fucking moon. "He's a good boy. We're so goddamn lucky."

"We're lucky with boyfriends, Sir. I'm lucky with you."

Geoff tucked fingers into his waistband and tugged. "What do you need, tonight?"

"You. Come to bed, and we'll remind each other how lucky we are. I promised Saul I'd open tomorrow and let Troy have an extra day."

"Oh!" Geoff hopped up. "So sweet, Sir."

"I bet he'll need to sleep in, wouldn't you think?" He imagined Saul was going to tear Troy's ass up.

"Very late." Geoff pulled him toward the stairs. "And if we drop by after you're done at the diner tomorrow, I bet he'll have stripes to show us. We could bring dinner, and Saul could give you a tour of Troy's masterpiece."

"You call over tomorrow, hmm? Make sure Saul agrees. I'd love to." Geoff had the best ideas when he had something to be passionate about.

"Yes, Sir. I will." Geoff stopped by the bedroom door to let him go in first, a quirky little gesture that his boy had done for him as long as he could remember.

And just like every night, he stopped to kiss his boy on the forehead. They did this, even if they were livid, even if they were both in tears.

They weren't either tonight though. Tonight, they were communicating well. Thankfully Geoff had gotten all those thoughts together without a paddling because he really did have to work tomorrow. Geoff followed him in and started undressing, folding everything before dropping it in the hamper—another one of Geoff's quirky habits that he just let happen and never really questioned.

"I love you." Carter sat with a soft groan. Right. Keeping up with the kid was hard work.

"I love you, too, Master." Geoff knelt in front of him and helped get his shoes off. "You're sore, huh? First day back on skis."

"You know me well, boy. I'm not as young as I want to be."

Geoff folded his socks, the boy's smile gentle, sweet. "You never will be if you don't keep trying, Sir."

"Indeed, my love. That's true." And he could keep trying, for all of them.

"It is. Lots of people to think about now, Sir. Well, not right now. Right now, it's just you and me." Geoff worked his shirt off and slid warm hands over his chest.

"Yes." And there was nowhere else he'd rather be—right here with his boy, happy and warm and in their bed.

Geoff knelt and opened his jeans, then quietly worked them over his hips, down and off. "Troy and I did talk about one other thing today, Sir." The boy's voice was soft, but the words were sure, confident, and their eye contact was steady. "We agreed that neither of us wants to serve more than one Master. We have plenty of room for friends and lovers, plenty of room to play and even scene together if we talk about it first, but in the end, we only belong to one man."

"Yes, and you belong to me, balls to bones." That was why he'd let Troy swing in the breeze all those years, wasn't it? Because he had his boy, and if the choice had to be made, Geoff would always win.

"I do. It's not even something that has to be said anymore, is it, Master? I like saying it—that I love you, that I'm yours. But we know, whether it's said or not." Geoff leaned in and kissed his belly.

"It's a fact." He stroked one hand over Geoff's head. "But it's good to hear." He never wanted his boy to think he couldn't tell the truth, share himself.

Geoff kissed the inside of each of his thighs, nudging them open, and then nuzzled right in, tongue circling under his sac.

"Damn..." All the times Geoff had done this for him, and it never failed to make him dizzy.

"Mhm." Geoff shouldered under one knee, urging him farther back on the bed until he could plant his feet flat. "I'm yours, Master," Geoff said between long drags up his shaft with a hot tongue. "My pleasure is your pleasure." His boy's clever tongue dove through his slit and the head of his prick slipped right into Geoff's mouth.

He rewarded his boy with a deep, heartfelt groan, letting Geoff hear his need, hear what his boy was doing to him.

His boy took time, long strokes followed by slow circles around the head, fingers rolling and tugging his balls. He knew Geoff. All of it was meant to make him burn, to drive him slowly out of his mind. Geoff knew him too. His boy knew it would work, knew that he could no more resist that mouth than he could resist the need to breathe.

His boy hummed at him and offered up deep, hungry sounds as the attention grew more intense. Fingers gripped the base of his cock and held him steady so Geoff could control the angle as he slid down his boy's throat.

"Jesus. Boy." His glutes were hard as rocks, and his entire body shook like he'd taken earthquake pills.

Geoff pulled up suddenly and sucked on his own middle finger, eyes burning, and by the time Carter found the wit to protest, that finger was pressing against his hole, and his cock disappeared deep into his boy's throat again.

He roared, that sweet fucking pressure in him, around him, more than he could take. He arched up, bucking hard into Geoff as he shot, the world shattering into a thousand pieces.

Geoff hummed and fussed and let him come down slow, with nuzzles and kisses and lazy, warm fingers tracing circles on his skin.

"Boy." Carter put everything he was into that one word —his thanks, his pleasure, his love, his soul.

"My Master." His boy curled up beside him and kissed him, returning all of it. He drew Geoff close, holding him so tight that their hearts beat in time. His boy sighed and settled. "It's good to be home."

"It is. Always. We've made a place that's ours." He kissed Geoff's forehead. "You good, boy?"

"Yes, Sir. Are you sore? Do you need some Advil or anything? You should sleep."

"I'm good." He would take a handful in the morning. "Love you. Make sure my alarm is set?"

"Will do, Sir. Close your eyes. I love you." Geoff kissed his chest and snuggled close, but he knew that once he was asleep, his boy would put water on his nightstand and set his alarm, put all the stray clothing in the hamper and whatever other little chores came to mind before climbing back in bed.

Geoff was good to him.

It was his life's calling to return the favor.

9

Thanksgiving was Geoff's favorite holiday. He and Carter had been hosting dinner since Carter had brought him here all those years ago. In the early days before they had found a group and really solidified their chosen family, it'd started as more of an open house kind of thing and all kinds of people came: coworkers, clients, friends, pretty much anyone that was orphaned for the holiday that year.

That eventually got too big, and then it became invitation only for a while, though the guests changed and the attendance was more sporadic. But in the last six or seven years, it had been the same group of men for the most part. This group was their family, their chosen family, and apart from his Master, who earned his gratitude daily even after all these years, this group was what he was most grateful for, and what he wanted to celebrate.

He and Saul weren't Troy when it came to cooking, but everything was made with love. The four of them had discussed a menu, Troy froze a couple of things for them ahead of time and the rest he and Saul had made together yesterday, while their men held down the diner.

And that was who was with him in the kitchen now. They worked together like lovers, Master and Sub roles aside, with an ease of friendship that Geoff hadn't experienced with anyone but Troy in twenty years.

"Bird is done!" Saul was peering into the oven, grinning. "Oh my God, it looks so good. I'm going to pull it out to rest. You want to put the sweet potato thing in? Troy says it needs about half an hour at three seventy-five."

Carter had gotten out of bed at some ungodly hour to put the turkey in and then gone to the diner to get them set up for the day. His Master and Troy were there now and would be home shortly, once they knew the staff was all in place and the diner was in full swing.

"On it." Geoff let Saul lift the turkey but hovered with oven mitts in hand in case Saul needed a last-minute assist. He should have known better; Saul could probably lift three of him.

The doorbell rang. Thanksgiving Day "dinner" was a come-when-you-want and stay-as long–as-you-want kind of day, very casual, and he knew who that would be. Doc had been an early bird since way back; the Dom liked to sit and watch football on Carter's big TV.

"I got the sweet potatoes," Saul said with a laugh.

"Thanks." He dropped a kiss on Saul's cheek and headed for the door.

Doc and Ben were standing there, little Ben all smiles in a way he rarely saw, both men's arms full of bags and containers.

"Hey!" He smiled back. "So good to see you both! Come on in, Sir. Ben." Once the door was closed against the cold air, he took everything Doc was carrying. "What did you bring? Master Carter and Troy will be home soon." Carter would start a fire and probably join Doc for football.

"We have a chocolate pie, artichoke dip and crackers, and six bottles of wine." Ben was almost bouncing. "How can I help?"

Doc looked at his sub with a fond, happy look, and that amazed Geoff. He couldn't wait to tell his Master.

Saul wandered out with a dish towel in his hands. "Doc. Ben. Happy Thanksgiving."

"Did Troy put you to work, boy?" Doc grinned and winked at Saul.

Saul's hands rested on Geoff's shoulders, and he caught himself leaning into the touch. "I'm supervising this troublemaker."

He rolled his eyes. "Ben, honey. Give that stuff to Master Saul and get your Master settled with football. Then come on in the kitchen."

Ben hesitated for a second, but Saul laughed and took Ben's food. "Go on. Look after your Master and then come help."

Hadn't he just said that?

"Yes, Sir." Ben relaxed and took Doc's arm, and they headed into the living room.

"I guess you have the magic touch."

Saul snorted as they put the food down. "Just authority. You're not a switch today, you know."

Damn. That was true. This group didn't know about their foursome yet, did they? How had he not even thought about that until now?

"Is it weird?" Saul asked. "We can keep everything quiet until we've all talked."

"No, not weird." But the question worried him a little. "Do you want to keep things quiet?"

Saul shrugged at him. "Do you?"

That was interesting. He knew damn well Saul would never have shrugged at Troy. Or answered a question with a question. Probably not with Carter either.

Geoff liked the way Saul trusted and let his guard down when they were together. "No. I love my new family."

"Me too." Whatever uncertainty Saul had been feeling visibly disappeared, and the look on the Dom's face changed completely. Geoff yelped in surprise as Saul backed him into the fridge and kissed him. "Breathe. Your Master will be home soon."

Oh, that was good. The kiss for sure but also the gentle reminder about where his head should be. Right. Carter would be home soon. His Master would be tired and hungry, maybe want a quick shower. Probably Troy, too, but Troy was Saul's to look after today. He didn't need to worry about that. "Thank you, Sir."

"You're a good boy, Geoff. Let's deal with the food before our men get home." Saul's smile was so young, so sweet and affectionate it made his heart ache a little.

"Uh...I'm h-here to help." Little Ben was white as a sheet, eyes wide. "What can I do?"

His eyes went wide, and he looked at Saul feeling a little panicked. *Shit.* Shit, was Carter going to be mad? They didn't even get to ask Troy. But Saul didn't flinch, didn't pull away suddenly or anything. Saul actually gave him another quick kiss and just smiled at Ben.

"Come on in, Ben. What did you want to do with your pie? Does it need to go in the fridge?"

Wait. Wasn't Saul going to say anything?

"Y-yes, Sir. It's covered in whipped cream." Ben looked to Geoff with huge eyes, but when Saul cleared his throat softly, Ben grabbed the pie and brought it to the fridge.

Saul held out a hand, pulled him clear, and opened the fridge door for Ben. "When do most people show, Geoff?"

"Well..." God, this was awkward. "Uh. Master Matt and Kris will probably be next. Maybe an hour or so, after Master Carter and Troy get here for sure. Master David and Travis will show up pretty much right before dinner because they stop at Travis's mom's place first."

"Sounds good." Saul closed the fridge door and looked at Ben. "Does your Master need coffee or anything? Something to snack on?"

"I don't know. I should ask, right, Geoff? It's our first Thanksgiving all together. I want it to be perfect."

This he knew. "There's a bowl by the microwave with some nuts in it, Doc loves those. And then ask him if he'd like a beer. He'll tell you he wants coffee for now. He'll want the beer once everyone else gets here." He winked at Ben. "That way he won't know I clued you in."

"Oh. Thank you." Little Ben hugged him spontaneously, which he'd only ever seen happen with Troy.

He returned the hug, genuinely pleased. "Today will be perfect, don't you worry. Doc is already in his element over there watching football, and you know there's nothing he likes better than good food and good company."

He and Saul watched Ben scurry off with the nuts.

Saul opened the oven door and checked the sweet potatoes. "Is Ben a little different than the last time I saw him?"

"I think so, yes. He'll confess everything to Troy, and Troy will tell us tonight." Ben thought Troy was magical.

"Back when Troy was recovering from heart surgery, Ben was around a lot. You remember? Ben looked up to him back then, and I think they're closer now. He's a sweet kid. I don't know a lot about him, but it seems like he needs friends, and Troy is very patient with him."

Geoff leaned on the counter. He had to ask. "You didn't explain about us."

"Nope. I don't owe any sub that isn't mine an explanation for my behavior. I didn't want him to think we were hiding something, but if he doesn't ask what he wants to know, then he'll find out soon enough what's going on, won't he?" Saul winked at him.

Geoff crossed his arms, interested in that statement. "So, you wouldn't owe me an explanation for something like this?"

"Of course I would. You're mine. Not in the same way that Troy is mine, but you are."

"Oh." A flood of heat crashed through him, warming him through to the bone.

"Master was so pleased." Ben snuck back in and poured a cup of coffee. "Thank you, Geoff."

"You're welcome." He really wanted to finish that conversation with Saul. But then again, he wondered what really needed to be said. Saul was sure, and he liked it.

Saul gave his shoulder a pat. "What's next? Set the table maybe?"

"We—" The doorbell rang. "—should open the door."

Saul laughed. "After you."

It was early, but he'd bet it was Matt and Kris. Either that or Carter had left his key. He reached for the door and opened it up to find his Master and Troy standing there grinning. "We're home!"

Carter looked so happy. A little tired maybe, but he just loved that smile. "I'm so glad." He pulled Carter inside and Troy went right to Saul.

"Hey, boy. How are you?" Carter kissed him before he got to answer. Didn't that make his knees weak?

Good. So good. Even better now.

He leaned into Carter and let his master's kiss and musky scent settle him. Carter cupped the back of his head, holding them together, the kiss going on and on, long enough that he lost track of the world.

It felt so good knowing Carter had missed him, even after just a morning apart. His master's greeting just made his favorite holiday that much better.

"Good to be home, boy."

"What can I do?" Troy asked, and Carter rumbled.

"We have to be back at the diner in fourteen hours, Troy. You can sit, right, Saul?"

"You can sit," Saul agreed easily. "Geoff and I are having fun—Ben is here and the other subs will be along to help. Our bag is up in the guest room if you want to shower or change. If not, Doc is watching football."

Geoff had to grin as Saul caught Troy's sleeve. "Yes, I mean it. Enjoy the day. I've got all weekend to sleep in. You don't."

"You both should go upstairs and bathe," Geoff suggested. "We should have endless hot water."

Carter looked at Saul with a raised eyebrow, and Geoff didn't miss the look that passed between them. Saul gave Carter a nod, and he just hid a grin because he wasn't sure at all that Troy was following that silent conversation.

"Go on, boy. Upstairs with Master Carter to clean up."

"Are you sure, Master? I know there's so much work I'm leaving you with..."

"I got this, Saul. Thank you. We'll be back." Then Carter simply wrapped one arm around Troy and walked him upstairs.

Saul chuckled and looked at him. "I get the feeling Troy is in for a surprise." A warm hand slid over Geoff's ass and moved him back toward the kitchen.

"Right? He's going to just stand and blink." Geoff almost envied him.

"They need a little time alone. You got yours with Troy without Carter around. They've got a little speed bump to get over."

"I know." He sighed because he knew Saul heard the "but" whether he'd said it or not.

"Troy and Carter are working all weekend." Saul pointed that out so casually that he almost didn't pick up on what the Dom was actually telling him.

"They are." A little frisson of excitement caught him. "Tattoos aren't huge Christmas gifts, you know."

"Sounds like you've got some time off, then. Can I take you out in my new truck?" Saul pulled the sweet potatoes out of the oven.

"Oh, I'd like that, very much." He had free time, although he intended to help at the diner when the guys needed him.

"Saturday's going to be hell at the diner, so I was going to suggest we see if we could be useful. I mean, I know he's not cooking, but Troy used to come home wiped out on Saturdays when it wasn't a holiday."

"Yeah." Actually, Troy might be cooking this weekend, who knew? They might be that busy.

"We're staying all weekend, so we'll find time."

"You're a good man." Geoff reached out and took Saul's hand.

"I-Uh. Pardon me?" Little Ben said. "I'm sorry, but a timer went off?"

"Thank you, boy. I did just take the sweet potatoes out."

Saul took a couple of steps toward Ben. "Come in. Come on, over with Geoff a minute."

"Y—yes, Sir." Poor Ben looked positively terrified.

"He doesn't bite, Ben." Geoff smiled at his nervous little friend. "Troy's upstairs with Carter."

Ben looked at him sharply. "They are?"

"Ben. We're a quad now. It's not just me and Troy or Geoff and Carter anymore. We're together." Saul spoke gently to Ben, slowly. "We're a foursome. And it's not a secret. It's just new."

"Oh. Oh thank God." Ben grabbed his hand and squeezed. "I was so scared, because you're my friends."

"I thought at first you were just curious, but I could see how you'd be worried."

"You know that he was the first person to be good to me. I couldn't lie to him." Ben was calming, one breath at a time.

"I can appreciate that. But he'll tell you the same thing." Saul was good with Ben, holding the boy's hands and being sure to make eye contact. "It's still new, we're all working it out, but it's very real. I promise."

"Congratulations, Sir! That's super cool, and you must be *really* tired."

Saul laughed. What a great sound, so free and young. "So far I'm all right, boy. But thank you for your concern. Why don't you ask Geoff what you can do to help?"

"Point me and shoot me, Geoff. I like helping."

Geoff grinned and put Ben to work cleaning vegetables, and soon Kris and Mike were there and the kitchen was filling up with laughter and joy.

"Smells good in here, boy." He felt Carter's arm snake around his waist, and he leaned back, breathing deeper. Everything was just right now.

"Thank you, Sir. I've had a lot of help."

"We're just waiting on David and Travis, hmm?" Carter nuzzled his temple. "Happy Thanksgiving, boy."

"They'll be along. They always scoot in just in time for dinner." He sighed and turned to face his Master. "Happy Thanksgiving, Sir. Your turkey came out perfect. Everything good with Troy?"

"You should have seen his face, love. It was priceless."

"Oh. I wish I'd seen it. Did you send him back to Saul?" *Did you get what you needed? Did Troy? Can I have a kiss?*

"I did. He needed his Master, and I needed my boy. Kiss me." Carter's hand was huge and solid on his ass.

"Yes, Sir. Please." He went up on his toes and got the kiss he wanted, giving Carter his whole self, reassured by the connection.

Carter kissed him like there was no tomorrow, like they didn't have company. Like he was everything Carter needed.

He hadn't doubted, not really. He was glad for Troy and Carter to have some time together, but this still felt good. He'd never had a doubt about Carter, not once ever in all their years together, and his Master had always kissed him like this. It made his skin tingle, made it hard to breathe.

Soft laughter slowly made its way into his consciousness. "Good day at work, Carter?" Doc asked.

"Very good."

"I've been here a while, enjoying your TV. I didn't realize until I saw Troy that you were back from the diner. It's good to see you. Happy Thanksgiving." Doc stuck out a hand to shake, but he knew as soon as Carter took it, Doc would pull his master in for a hug.

As sure as night followed day, Doc hugged his master tight. "It's going to be a lovely holiday, my friend."

"You have a new arrangement to celebrate, I understand? Or is Ben telling tales?"

Geoff jumped in quickly. "Ben's telling the truth, Sir."

Kris looked up, eyebrows raised. "Arrangement?"

Carter took it right in stride, thank God. "Troy and Saul have joined me and Geoff as a committed quad."

"What? Geoff! That's so exciting!" Travis pulled him into a hug. "Congrats!"

He couldn't smile any broader if he tried.

"Indeed. Congratulations to you all." Doc gave Carter a clap on the shoulder that sent his master forward a step.

"And dude! Troy! You were a sleeper unit, weren't you?" Kris goosed Troy from his wheelchair.

"Hardly." Saul caught Troy, laughing and pretending to hold the boy back from going after Kris.

"Oh, I get it. It's really your fault, isn't it?" Matt stuck Saul with an elbow. "Young, progressive, full of ideas."

"Insatiable libido." Carter crossed his arms.

Matt laughed. "Oh, nice. Looking to make it six?"

"No." Saul chimed in immediately, sounding stern but grinning broadly, making it hard to take the Dom too seriously. "Anyway, I hear Kris keeps you plenty occupied."

"He does. You keep your hands to yourself, Junior." Matt scowled at Saul, and everyone laughed.

Kris flexed, and they all—to a man—stopped and stared, admiring the hardest body any of them had ever seen.

"Damn." No surprise Saul would say something first. "No promises, man. Six is starting to sound good after all."

"No chance." Matt put possessive hands on Kris, staring them down. "He's mine, every single inch."

Kris groaned softly, leaning back toward his Master. "Yes, Sir."

Saul gave Matt's shoulder a squeeze. "He certainly is."

Geoff leaned into Carter again. It wasn't that long ago that Kris had been buried under PTSD, and look at him now. He and Matt were, well, back to who they were before Kris's deployment, before his injuries. They were happy and they both looked great.

"Doorbell!" Ben called out, like they hadn't all heard it. The kid was too damn cute.

"That's David and Travis. Saul, can you organize folks and get the table set? And then we'll sit." Geoff went to answer the door.

"You got it," Saul called after him.

The guys arrived with a huge pie from Travis's mom, a roast, and a gallon of cider. "We're here!"

"Yay!" Geoff laughed and hugged Travis, but he did the lowered-eyes thing for David because that was what David liked. "Happy Thanksgiving, Sir. Come in. Dinner's almost ready."

Doc came out and shook David's hand. "Football's on. Hello, boy."

Travis beamed like a sub who'd had some wine at his mother's house. "Hello, Sir."

David and Doc headed for the TV, and Geoff pulled Travis into the kitchen. He didn't hesitate for one second to take four cookies off the plate they'd brought and tuck them away on top of the fridge. He did it every single year. "I always steal those. Your mom makes the best cookies."

"She sends them just for you." Travis kissed his cheek. "Happy turkey day."

"Aw she's the sweetest. I'll write her a note. It's a very happy turkey day, Travis. Look around. You'll see what I mean."

"Table is set, Geoff. What's next?"

"Open the wine? And can you send Carter back in here to carve this bird?"

"On it. Ben, pick a couple of bottles of Doc's wine and

put them on the table for me?" Saul disappeared again with Ben on his heels.

"We're informal today?"

He blinked at Travis. "Oh! Oh, no, honey. Master Saul and I have been cooking and setting up dinner for two days together. I just forgot. But thank you for reminding me what company I'm keeping." He'd gotten everyone else right, sheesh.

"No criticism. Just seeing where I need to be. I'm a little tipsy; I don't need to be in trouble."

"I know, Trav. We're kind of formal and not. Going with the moment. No worries. Enjoy your buzz." He returned Trav's kiss on the cheek.

"Boys."

Geoff blushed when Carter came in, even though he wasn't doing anything naughty.

"Master Carter!" Trav ran over for his hug, a sweet, goofy puppy dog of a man.

Carter's eyes went wide, and Geoff made a little drinking gesture at his master. So cute. He let Trav cling a minute and then interrupted. "Let Master go, Trav; he needs to carve the bird."

Travis laughed and hopped away. "Oh. Sorry. You just give the best hugs, Master Carter. Happy Thanksgiving!"

Carter swatted Travis gently. "Go take drink orders, boy."

"I'm on it!"

"I got your carving set out, Sir." He took a deep breath, enjoying being alone in the kitchen with his master for a minute. "And the platter is next to the sink."

"You good, boy?" The words sounded casual, but he knew better.

"I love this. You know I love this, and it's even better this year. Saul's great." This part was a little hectic, getting everything and everyone to the table, but it was a kind of hectic he knew how to handle. He slipped into Carter's arms. "*Keep it light. It doesn't matter if something needs five more minutes. No one is judging.* I know. I can hear you in my head."

"So lucky, to have me out there and in here, hmm? Thank you for all the work you do for this. You let me have a family Thanksgiving." Carter kissed the top of his head.

And that was really all he needed. If Carter was happy, he was happy. Those words, the thanks and the praise, lit him up inside. "You're welcome, Master. I love you." He gave Carter a hug and then got out of his master's way so Carter could carve.

Trav came in to make drinks, and Ben came in to carry sides.

"Guess what, Geoff honey. Troy dozed off in Kris's lap." Trav was all chuckles. "It's so adorable. Master Saul is snapping pictures."

Oh, man. That was awesome. "You wore him out, Master."

"You know our Troy; he falls asleep whenever he gets warm and comfortable," Carter shot back.

"Right. I'm sure that's all it is." Surely it had nothing to do with Carter and Troy showering together. "Of course."

He had to go peek. Had to. Possibly take a picture of his own. He crept out to the great room, and sure enough, Kris held Troy like he was precious, one hand gently sliding over Troy's spine.

That was the sweetest thing ever. He smiled at Kris and went to Saul, who was leaning against the mantel, looking on. "How adorable is that?"

Saul took his hand. "He's happy. He can relax."

"Don't you feel bad having to wake him for dinner?"

"No. He's been looking forward to those sweet potatoes and the turkey all week. You and Kris can wake him if you like. I'll go see if Carter needs help."

"Oh. No, Master Saul, that's—"

"We've got it, boy. We won't burn down your kitchen."

"...Okay?" He watched Saul go, blinking after him.

Doc and Matt went, too, followed by Dave, leaving all the subs there, grinning at each other.

"He looks happy, hmm?" Kris kept petting. "He's finally gained some weight."

"Master Saul's good for him, good to him. He's really getting what he needs." Troy was happy. Maybe for the first time in as long as they'd known one another.

"I'm so glad. Who wants to wake him?" Kris asked.

"Geoff should," Little Ben whispered.

"I can do that." He smiled at Ben and then knelt next to Troy and leaned in to kiss his lover awake. "Dinnertime, honey." He pressed light kisses to Troy's forehead and cheek, finally landing one square on the lips.

"Mmm..." Troy's smile was like the sunshine coming out. "Everything smells so good." Those stunning green eyes opened, and Geoff could see himself reflected in them.

"Thank you. Are you ready to eat? You've got Kris pinned."

He caught Ben whispering to Travis but let it be. Travis hadn't been there for the big confession about their new relationship in the kitchen earlier so that kiss must have seemed pretty shocking.

"I'm good," Kris protested gently. "Hungry, but good."

"He's mobile. I've ridden on his lap before." Didn't Troy sound wicked?

Geoff snorted. "Yeah? Was it good for you, Kris?"

"Would you expect anything less from Troy?"

"Okay, jokers." Travis stepped up behind Kris's chair and started pushing Kris and Troy toward the dinner table.

"Come on, Ben. I need help." He took Ben's hand and pulled the kid into the kitchen where he found Carter, Saul, Doc, and David chatting over cocktails and wine. Matt was ducking out, probably to help Kris in the dining room.

"Masters. With all due respect, please get out of my kitchen."

"Naughty." Saul laughed. "Gonna take that one over my knee later."

Carter snorted. "Only if we all get to watch."

There was a lot of laughter as the men left the kitchen. He just rolled his eyes and looked at Ben. "Sometimes you have to push a little."

Ben had already picked up the rolls and another bottle of wine to take to the table but paused long enough to wink at Geoff. "Sometimes, yeah."

He blinked at Ben's back as the boy left the kitchen and grinned widely. How wonderful was that? Their baby was growing up.

You go, Little Ben.

He looked around the kitchen and discovered almost nothing left to be done. The Doms had already taken the turkey to the table, all the veggies, various potatoes, and even the cranberry and the gravy, and there were only two of the six bottles of wine Doc and Ben brought left sitting on the counter.

He just kept on smiling because he knew Carter must have asked them all to help, to save him a little work. That gesture might seem small to some, but with this crowd, it wasn't, and it was appreciated.

He was grateful. That was what today was about, wasn't it? And he had even more than usual to be thankful for today. He listened to the joyful voices of his large family in the other room, heard Saul's voice and Troy's answering laughter, and it was all he could do not to burst into tears. Big, sloppy, happy tears.

He breathed it all in deep, filled a pitcher with ice water, and headed out to the dining room.

10

Troy sat in the back of the diner, cigarette in his hand. He hadn't lit it, not yet, but he wanted to.

He just needed the energy to grab one of the lighters the cooks stashed out here.

The time between Thanksgiving and Christmas was fabulous for business, but he was pulling doubles to make up for the time off around Christmas, and he was fixin' to lose his ever-loving mind.

"Boss! Troy? You back here?" Jimmy ducked around the corner, a thick, dark ponytail swinging over one shoulder. "Davis sent me to find you. Fryer's down, Boss. Are you smoking again?"

"Not yet. And if you rat me out, I'll set your ass on fire. Let me fiddle with it. It's grumpy." Sort of like him. He put the cancer stick in his pocket and headed in, doing his damnedest not to stomp.

Davis was in the weeds. Nothing the cook hadn't handled before, but like Troy, days on end of it was starting to wear on him. "Goddamn thing won't hold temp, and I have orders backing up." Davis stuck two plates in the window. "Forty-seven!"

"Did y'all check the breaker? That one's..." He opened the breaker box and flipped it back on. "It's back. You need to not overload that one, Davis. It's tricky."

"Uh-huh. I need to get orders out on time, too, man." Davis didn't even look at him, and both hands were busy. "Let me know when that's hot again."

"You got my chicken fingers, Davis?" Elle was a new-hire, and she was the best thing to happen to Christmas at the diner.

"No, ma'am." Davis set a little plate with two star-shaped pancakes on it in the window. "That's to keep the little guy happy. It'll be up soon."

Elle laughed. "Creative. Cross your fingers. Thanks."

Troy got a wok down and got it full of oil and heating. "We'll get you caught up. I'm going to tell everyone fried anything is slow for now." He was replacing that breaker, dammit.

Davis nodded. "Thanks. I'm under water a little. I think my eyeballs are floating." Two more plates went up. "Forty-four!"

He left Davis for a second to ask Angela to spread the word, and his phone buzzed in his pocket on his way back to the kitchen.

I know you're busy. Carter says come soak in the hot tub after closing. Love you.

He shot back a heart and grabbed an apron. "Go pee, man. I'll spell you."

Davis was amazing, but he'd been cooking in this kitchen for twenty years. He had this.

"Now? I can wait until—"

"I'm good. Go ahead." Troy stepped in.

"Right. Thanks, man. Back in a few." Davis stepped around him and disappeared toward the back.

He started cooking and singing, slinging hash and flipping burgers. The specials were macaroni and cheese and green chile chicken soup, and that eased up the pressure on the kitchen significantly.

Davis came back—smelling like a cigarette, dammit— pulled on a clean apron and started backing him up, dishing out and sorting orders, and with Jimmy restocking for them, things were moving smoothly in no time. Smooth enough he could have left the kitchen. But he didn't.

"Is there a manager I can talk to?"

"Uh. Boss?" Davis tapped his shoulder and pointed, and he turned his head to find Geoff standing there.

"Nope. No management here." He winked at Geoff, plated a chicken burger, and headed over. "Hey, you. How goes?"

"Fine." He felt Geoff's eyes on him, looking him over. "Are you okay? Carter and I came down to check on you after all I got was a heart."

"Blew that damn breaker again, and Davis was in the weeds. Been a day, but we're managing, I think." Maybe.

"Yeah?" Geoff reached for him, tucked two fingers into his shirt pocket, and pulled out the cigarette.

Shit marthy.

"I didn't smoke it." He'd just loved on it a little bit. Mostly.

"I can see that. What about the rest of the pack?"

"Troy, what's going on?" Carter came storming over. "Front of the house needs you. Take that apron off. You're not a cook anymore."

Geoff looked at Troy and hid the cigarette in his own

pocket. "Davis was in the weeds, but Troy was just telling me that they'd caught up."

Troy opened his mouth to snap back, but he just shut it and headed to the front without a word. Goddamn it. He'd gotten them caught back up; wasn't that part of his job?

He was going to grab the rest of that pack and smoke them, one after another after another.

"Boss? I need ones, please." Elle offered him a warm smile, one that promised that she wasn't pissed at him.

"I'm on it."

"Thanks." Elle handed him two twenties to change.

He took the twenties and headed for the safe, passing Carter and Davis along the way. "I'll get someone in to replace the breaker on Monday. You'll have to make it work until then. You can keep Jimmy; I'll put someone else on the dishes."

Troy thought that he'd just cancel with the guys tonight. Saul could go. He wanted to curl up and just be. He started to go get the change, but had to send one of the kids to bus tables, then checked in with Geoff. "Did you want a sandwich or something?"

Geoff brushed his cheek with warm fingers. "No, thank you. I'm holding out for dinner. What can I do?"

Give me my cigarette? "I'd love a hug real quick where Carter can't see..."

"Come on." Geoff stepped into the office and held the door for him. "Carter's tired, and he's stressed. He's not good at not being here when it's busy, so he's been itchy all day."

"I'm doing a good job. I am." Was he whining? He thought he was whining.

"Of course you are, honey." Geoff closed the office door, pulled him into a hug, and rubbed his back. "It's not you. Carter's still adjusting to not being the only one in charge."

God, he needed this—just a little reassurance, a little care. He hid his face, just for a second, and inhaled the scent of his Geoff.

Geoff didn't move at all, just let him rest. "You've got this. You two should make some time to sit down and talk soon before you both lose it."

"After the holidays. We'll have time then." At least he hoped so. They'd stay a little busy through ski season, but spring would be dead...

"Sure you want to wait that long?" Geoff let him go and straightened his shirt, smoothing it over his shoulders. "Smoking isn't a good answer."

"I didn't. I just needed to." It would calm him down in a second. Hell, just having the cigarette in his pocket helped. "You know how it is."

"I do. I also know you have better ways of getting what you need." Geoff put his cigarette back in his shirt pocket. "But I'm not going make that choice for you. Or judge."

"I love you too." He kissed Geoff's cheek. "I'm fixin' to sit down and cry, you know? I got to get back out there before my partner comes hunting me."

With a stick.

"You do. And I'm here to help, so just tell me what I can do. Other than keep Carter off your back." Geoff grinned.

"I don't suppose you're going to arrange supper?" Maybe he could drive up the hill to see them. Maybe.

"Saul and I are already on it. Dinner, hot tub, and alcoholic drinks. And no need for a designated driver."

"Oh..." So tempting. So fucking tempting. "That sounds like heaven."

"Boss?" Davis sounded stressed.

Troy put the change for Elle in Geoff's hands. "Gotta go,

honey. Give that to Elle, please?" He headed out at a run to put out another fire. Hopefully not a literal one.

He was relieved to find that Carter wasn't in the kitchen. He grabbed an apron and dug in again, daring Carter to say something about it. The best thing he could do was keep the food coming out, consistent and hot. Elle had the front of house, and better than that, Carter had it.

Geoff was around, running food and checking on Jimmy. The only one not around was Saul, which wasn't that strange, really. Saul didn't have a history there, didn't have twenty-plus years invested in the place the way he and the others did.

Saul would just make him cook French toast.

The thought had him laughing, the sound ringing through the kitchen.

"What's funny, Boss?"

"French toast."

Davis looked confused. "Shit, did I miss an order? I didn't see it."

"No. No, man. I just got to thinking. Don't mind me. I'm just losing my mind a little." And thinking about his Master because Saul eased him.

"I hear that. I can't believe this is my life until Christmas!" Davis joined him laughing and flipped a handful of burgers.

"Trial by fire, my friend. Trial by friggin' fire." He cracked up, building a club sandwich. He was thinking chili for Monday special.

"Thanks for being so cool about helping me catch up, Boss. I was starting to lose my shit. You're damn useful in here."

"No worries." Honestly, he didn't mind cooking. He was quick and consistent, and that was what diner cooking meant. He was trying to do that in the front of the house, but he wasn't as successful.

Maybe an hour later, Elle popped into the window. "Troy, Davis. Carter's closing up. We have some tables finishing but no new orders."

"Woo. Yes." Davis shifted from cooking mode into cleaning-up mode just like that.

"Good deal." He set the dishwashers to work and went to check setup for tomorrow, making sure the guys had everything they needed.

"Geoff's helping Elle set up for tomorrow up front." Carter leaned in the doorway, arms crossed. "You okay?"

I don't know, am I? "Been a wild and woolly day."

"Saturdays are tough. I shouldn't have tried to take time off. We'll just have to overlap more this month."

"I'm sorry. I can close up." *Dammit.* Dammit, he wasn't okay at all. He had been trying so hard to do this right, especially with leaving the twenty-third to head to Saul's momma's. *Motherfucker.*

"Not a chance. We'll do it together, which is what we should have done to begin with today. December is always busy as hell; I just wasn't thinking."

Troy glanced over, heart pounding hard. He didn't know what to say. He wanted to say everything. He wanted to scream, he wanted to push into Carter's arms, but he found himself utterly fucking frozen.

Carter's focus was on him, staring hard. "Why don't we go sit in the office for a minute?"

He nodded and closed the walk-in door. The office was three steps away. Three long goddamn steps.

Carter moved in behind him and spoke softly against his neck. "Okay, boy. I've got you. Go."

"Yes, Sir." And that was what he needed. Just a breath and he could walk into the office, knowing Carter had him.

Carter followed him, shut the door quietly behind them, and pulled him in, settling knowing arms around him Saul was confidence and strength; Carter was solid experience. "I'm sorry I snapped at you when we arrived."

He wanted to explain, to tell Carter that he'd been doing what he thought was right, but Carter knew that, so what came out was, "Thank you."

He leaned into Carter, inhaled deeply, and forced himself to relax and soak up the comfort Carter offered.

"Everyone agrees that you cleared a backup and got orders moving smoothly—Ella, Davis, even Jimmy—and that's your job. You've been working your ass off, putting in a lot of hours. I don't want you to feel like you have to earn time off with Saul and his family, so we need to figure this out."

"I know it's a hassle. I'm sorry. It's a shit time of year to take a few days off, but Master Saul says his family are excited to meet me. How often does that happen?"

"Hopefully just this one time in your life, right? Next time, you'll know them." Carter laughed softly. "It's the right time of year to take time off to be with family, Troy; we're just not all lucky enough to have it. I hope you're excited to meet them, too, and I want you to enjoy them. I told Saul you'd have the week, and I expected you both back in time for dinner at the house on New Year's Eve."

"What if—" *What if they hate me? What if they look at me and go, you're twenty years older than my son?*

"Hmm. Yes. What if?" Carter led him over to a small beat-up couch that had been there longer than he had.

They sat together, both of them, like they'd done a hundred times. God, he was tired down to his bones.

"What did Saul have to say about all your what-ifs?"

"Why on earth would I tell him?" The question shocked him enough that he answered without thinking.

Carter turned slowly and looked at him, dark eyes serious. "Why on earth would you not? He's your lover, your Dom. How could you keep such a thing from him? How can he help if he doesn't know?"

"I'm not going to stress him out over my shit, not with heading home over the holidays." Hopefully, it wouldn't matter. Maybe it wouldn't. It could be fine. "It's not his fault I'm old."

With a bad ticker.

"Troy, are you listening to yourself? You're not going to stress Saul out with your problems? What is the matter with you? Would you expect Geoff not to talk to me?"

He looked at Carter, eyebrows up in his hairline. "I'm damn near his mother's age, and we all know it. Even still, he's so excited, so pleased to bring me home. I won't mess that up for him. I can't."

"Those are Saul's people. That's who raised him, and he doesn't care about your age. Do you want to go? Do you want to meet his family?"

"Of course." Why wouldn't he? Maybe because his family was either dead or hated him? Fuck that. Love meant sucking it up and giving Saul all he had. "I just worry. I shouldn't have said anything."

Not to Carter, anyway. Geoff would understand that. As much as Doms said they wanted all your emotional shit, they really didn't. That was a shit-ton of weight. He'd been watching this happen for years with the men in their circle of friends.

"Stop that." Carter leaned in and gave him a quick kiss.

"I understand the worry, Troy. I don't think Saul would be all that shocked to hear it. But that's up to you."

"I just want this to be all he needs. It's just been a few years since I had any family but y'all." He took Carter's hand, touching the thick, square fingers. "I've spent Christmas with y'all for a long time."

Carter smiled and looked at their hands. "Yes. True. But you know Geoff doesn't—I wouldn't call it celebrating Christmas. More like hiding from it. We'll miss you, and we appreciated Saul's invitation, but one of us has to be at the diner."

"I know. I'm sorry. I appreciate you being understanding. I've said that, right?"

"We want you to enjoy your new family." Carter stood up and pulled him to his feet. "This is a good thing, Troy. You're lucky."

"I know." That part he knew, without question. He was the luckiest son of a bitch he knew. "I know that with all my heart."

It was time to close up.

———

TROY WASN'T sure how he'd ended up sitting in Carter and Geoff's front room, really. He'd intended to go home, curl up, and pout, but he was here, showered, wrapped in a huge robe, and resting between Carter and Saul.

"Honestly, Carter, we need a new coffee maker. That one just gives me fits, and it gets worse every time I use it." Geoff put a mug of hot coffee in Troy's hands and kissed his forehead. "Here you go, honey. Just like you like it."

"Thank you." That decided it—he'd send an amazing coffee maker for Christmas. "You spoil me."

"Not really. You just smelled like a grill and needed a shower."

Saul snorted and hooked an arm around his back. "You guys are a tough act to follow."

Troy didn't even know what that was supposed to mean, but the warm weight was so welcome, so right.

Carter, though, he just grinned. "That's us. The opening act."

Geoff rolled his eyes. "Saul made dinner, guys. It's warming in the oven. Who's hungry?"

"You made supper, Master?" Oh, that rocked. "I am starving. I'm glad I didn't cancel."

"I did. Lasagna. I had all this time on my hands because Carter said he didn't need me at the diner."

Carter sighed. "We were fine. And no one was letting you cancel, boy."

Saul got up. "Come on Geoff, let's get dinner on the table. They'll come running when they smell it."

"Running is a bit of a stretch, but I'm ready." Troy offered Saul a thankful smile. God, he did love lasagna.

Geoff took Saul's hand, and they went into the kitchen. Carter looked at him. "I didn't know Saul could cook."

"He does a decent job. He likes to experiment." Fast? God no, but the food was good. Mostly.

"Experiment, huh?" Carter laughed. "Come on. Let's go see if we get food poisoning."

"I heard that!" Saul set a big dish on a trivet on the table. "Mom's recipe. Didn't mess with it at all. You can't, because it's perfect just like it is."

Geoff brought out wine and a big basket of garlic bread, and Saul sat a plate down in front of him.

"Thank you, Sir." He actually teared up, but he stopped

that shit in its tracks. No. He wasn't that tired. He was just being a moron.

"You're welcome, baby. I want to know what you think." Saul made himself a plate and sat with Troy, smiling as Geoff filled his wineglass. "Thanks."

"I think it smells great." And he hadn't had to make it. It was going to be amazing.

Carter sat down and dug right in. "Oh. Yeah, that tastes like a momma's recipe." Geoff put a big hunk of garlic bread on Carter's plate. "Sit down, boy. Eat."

"Yes, Sir." Geoff kissed Carter first though. "Mmm. Garlic."

Saul laughed but was watching *him*.

He took a big bite, the sauce and cheese and garlic just about perfect. He didn't say a word; he just took another bite.

"That works." He got a big smile and then Saul dug in too.

"Nothing better than comfort food on a cold night." Carter looked to be really enjoying dinner. The plate Geoff had made was empty already. "Troy had a hell of a day, Saul. But I've been thinking it's time to do what everyone else does around here this time of year and hire some seasonal help. What do you think, Troy? Another server to free up Elle when you're on, and a backup chef for Davis when I am? And then we just don't either of us get Saturdays until mid-January."

"I think if we have the budget, it'll help our sanity." He took a sip of his wine, then met Carter's eyes. "Somehow this was supposed to give us more time off, and we're both working our asses off, and we're never together. I love working with you."

Hopefully, that sounded ironic and not pitiful.

Carter raised a glass to him and took a sip, mulling it over. "So we need to fix this. Because you're right. I wanted to work with you too. Should we hire a manager? Are we at that point? Financially, with both of us invested, it's less of a strain on either one of us, so maybe we could swing it. Then we could pull off something that at least functions more like a normal nine-to-five."

"I don't want to break us, but...we need an answer. Our food costs are good; our overhead is reasonable. I like the staff."

"I'd like for Troy to not have another day like today." Saul leaned forward and looked between them. "If Geoff and I get a say here. The point of taking Troy out of the kitchen, as I understood it, was to make sure he didn't have this stress anymore. It's not good for him. It's not good for anybody."

Carter nodded and leaned back, the Dom's body language saying more than words. "You're right, Saul. That was the intention. That and to give Troy a stake in something he'd put so much sweat into."

"I tried to do a good job, Carter. I'm just...I'm fucking tired." Like down in his bones. He held Carter's gaze. "But I can do this. I have your back."

"Troy... Carter?" Geoff put a hand on Carter's arm, and Carter took it and kissed it to soothe the boy, then reached across the table to Troy.

"Troy. You don't have anything to prove to me. You've been doing an amazing job. I know damn well you can handle anything. The question isn't whether you can; it's whether you should have to."

"And you shouldn't." Saul sounded adamant about that.

Geoff sighed. "No, honey. You shouldn't have to."

"We'll figure this out." Carter squeezed his hand, and the touch was a comfort. "We're smarter than we look."

"Well, thank God for that." Troy winked over, and that horrible tension began to back off.

"I don't know. Some of us look pretty damn brilliant." Saul stretched up tall and smiled.

"You did manage a decent dinner at least." Geoff took another bite and swallowed it with a sip of wine.

"It's amazing." He started eating, reminding himself that he was hungry. "Better than French toast."

"Ha. No. Nothing is better than your French toast, not even my mom's lasagna." Saul kissed his cheek. "Don't tell her I said that. Man, she is looking forward to meeting you."

"Good. I hope she's pleased when she sees me." He wanted that approval for his Master. "I've never met the parents before."

"Mom has seen pictures, baby. It's not like you're going to be some great shock. We text every day."

"Don't you have like a hundred siblings too?"

Saul laughed. "Just three. They're all older, and they all have kids. All of them. Abner and his wife Jesse have three boys, Sandy and her husband Oliver have twin girls in kindergarten, and Alexa and her boyfriend Wes have a brand-new baby girl. Well, I guess she's not brand new; she's gonna be a year soon."

"Jesus, that's not meet the parents, that's more like meet the Reynolds horde." Geoff laughed, winking at Troy.

"Right? It sounds like a busy, festive time." And he was scared to death. Excited too. Totally wigged out.

"I wish you guys could come. I mean, I get it, but I'd love my whole family to be there." Saul smiled at Geoff and Carter.

"One of us needs to be in town. I'm not sure that's ever going to change no matter how Troy and I work things out."

"It's okay, sweetie." Geoff shrugged at Saul. "You and Troy deserve this. It's not my favorite holiday anyway. And we'll see you for New Year's Eve, right?"

"Of course. Carter made me promise." Saul laughed.

"We'll have a kiss at midnight for the ages," Carter murmured.

"That's something to think about, isn't it? Now I'm really looking forward to it." Saul grabbed another hunk of garlic bread and took a big bite.

Troy loved that—the enthusiasm, the joy, the life in his Master. It made him shiver and ache, deep down.

Geoff put his fork down on a totally clean plate. "I was thinking maybe you'd like some New Year's ink, Troy. We should talk when you get back."

"We should—all of us." Troy's skin didn't just belong to him anymore. Maybe it never had.

Saul took his hand under the table. This was really something he and Saul needed to discuss again; they just hadn't had a chance yet. "Let's talk after the holidays."

Geoff looked between them curiously. "Okay. Sure. Sounds good."

Troy took a deep breath and let himself lean. "I love you, Master."

"I love you too. You do sound tired, boy. I brought a bag so we could crash here, or I can take you home. Your choice."

"Either way, you can sleep in, Troy. I'm on tomorrow, and Elle will be in. We'll be fine." Carter finished off the last of the wine.

"Can we snuggle on the sofa, all of us?" He wanted to sit in a puppy pile and luxuriate in men and skin and comfort.

"He has the best ideas." Geoff got right up and started clearing the table, and Carter was about half a second behind.

"Mhm. I'll help."

Saul didn't offer to help, and his Master kissed him so hard he wasn't going to be any help to anyone either. He blinked up, clinging to his lover's shoulders.

"Please." He didn't even know what he asked for, only that he knew his Master would give it to him.

"Come on. They'll catch up." Saul stood and pulled him up out of his chair, never breaking contact as they made their way out to the couch.

Saul sat in the corner of the big sectional, drawing him down and holding him. He melted in, the world becoming small.

Carter joined them a short while later and stoked up the fire, and Geoff shut off most of the lights to let the glow warm them too.

Geoff sat in Carter's lap, drawing Troy's legs over to tangle with his. Troy sighed, Saul's heartbeat in his ear.

"It means something that just hanging out is so easy, I think," Saul offered, tangling fingers with Carter and resting them on Troy's knee. "And I don't mean simple necessarily, but easygoing. Relaxed."

"And Carter says I think too much." Geoff laughed softly.

"No, I said you overthink everything. There's a difference."

"I love being home here too." How many people had that? Two homes? Two families?

"I always feel a little decadent here too. With the hot tub and the fireplace and everything?" Saul kissed Troy's hair. "I mean, I came from an apartment that I shared with four guys before I moved in with Troy. This is like a palace by comparison."

"I remember that," Carter said, his voice soft, low. "We were in a tiny apartment for a few years, hmm? A one-bedroom while we saved for this. The kitchen didn't even have a real fridge."

"You could brush your teeth while sitting on the toilet." Geoff chuckled. "I didn't mind it though. I didn't need room. I just needed you."

Oh that made Troy so happy. That was why he loved them both so much. They proved that forever was real.

"Charmer." Carter kissed Geoff without the slightest concern for anyone else in the room, and Troy understood what Saul meant by easy but not simple. That was their moment, but it was hard not to want to be a part of it.

Saul tightened an arm around him. "Our boyfriends are hot, huh?"

"Blistering." He couldn't have looked away, and right now, he didn't have to. He could admire.

Stare.

Let himself get aroused, his cock filling.

"Mhm." Saul kissed his neck, then slid a hand into his robe and teased his nipple, circling fingers around it and rolling his piercing under a heavy thumb.

"Master." Heat began to build from his chest, sliding down to meet the arousal in the pit of his belly.

Geoff moaned softly, resting his forehead against Carter's, and both men smiled.

"You want them?" Carter asked softly, and Troy knew Geoff wasn't going to say no.

Saul whispered in his ear. "They're looking at you, boy."

"Who wouldn't look?" Carter murmured. "He's stunning.

Pierced and inked, built like a brick shithouse—our Troy is sex on a stick."

The words made him blush, and he twisted to hide his hot cheeks against Saul.

Saul let him be, stroking fingers through his hair, the other hand still working his hardware. "You're beautiful. I've told you so, many times."

"May I, honey?" Geoff shifted over, fingers hovering over the belt holding his robe closed.

He nodded and licked his lips. He felt beautiful, desired, lovely. "Please."

Geoff pulled the belt free, and then there were hands all over him, relieving him of the robe altogether. Carter tugged Saul's sweater off, so when Troy relaxed back again, it was his skin on Saul's. Saul held him and sighed, and Carter stole his master's breath with a kiss.

Geoff's fingers joined Saul's in playing Troy like a guitar, tugging and twisting his nipple rings, Geoff watching his reactions like a hawk.

Saul moaned for Carter, the sound vibrating through Troy, and he felt his master's cock grow thick against his hip. Carter took Geoff by the back of the neck and steered Geoff's mouth down to Troy's chest.

"Mmm. Yes, Sir." Geoff sucked one nipple in between hungry lips.

He would have bucked Geoff off if it hadn't been for Saul's hands, steel bands around his hips. His eyes flew open, and a crazy sound slipped from him as his nipple went painfully hard.

"Damn." Carter stared at him, tongue sliding along white teeth. "I'm going to kiss you, boy."

It wasn't much warning, but it wasn't like he was going to say no either. Carter leaned over Geoff's back and took a light taste. "Lovely." The second move was stronger, deeper, Carter's tongue diving between his lips.

Saul moaned, and Troy opened then, knowing his Master was watching, was appreciating this. Carter's kiss stole his breath, the hungry touches of that slick tongue somehow matching Geoff's suction.

Saul rocked under him, hard length looking for friction, and he wasn't sure whose fingers caught him low behind the balls, nudging and rolling his piercings.

Troy arched his back, his eyes rolling up as his ass dragged along Saul's need. He heard Carter's rough chuckle before his lips were taken again.

"Geoff. Boy." Saul's voice was low and dry. "Run upstairs to my duffel and grab the little bright yellow bag for me?"

"Yes, Sir."

"Leave your clothes in our room while you're at it." Carter gave the order still hovering only half an inch from Troy's lips. "It's only fair after all."

Troy hummed softly. Geoff was lovely to look at but even better to feel. "Thank you, Sir."

"My pleasure. Absolutely." Carter looked over his head at Saul. "Are we getting a show?"

"Hopefully with full audience participation. What do you think, boy?" Saul caught his earlobe and sucked on it.

"I'm yours, Master." He was all in and being loved on. He was happy to follow Saul's lead.

Saul shifted Troy slightly to undo his jeans, and Carter took over, working around Troy to slide them the rest of the way off. "Why don't you help Master Carter with his clothes, Troy?"

"It would be my pleasure, Sir." He unfastened Carter's shirt slowly, luxuriating in it, remembering Thanksgiving Day, the pleasure of baring Master Carter's body to his eyes.

Carter stayed still and just watched him, focus going from his fingers to his face and back again. "Are you feeling better?"

"I'm feeling connected to y'all. I'm warm, happy, glad to be home with all y'all." That was better.

"We're happy to have you here, both of you. I'm feeling good, looking forward to the rest of our evening. This is special, I'm learning more and more just how much." Carter let him slide the shirt off, exposing smooth shoulders and a healthy crop of slightly graying chest hair.

Troy leaned forward and kissed Carter's nipple as he reached down to open Carter's belt. Master Saul was a fire behind him, Carter was filling his senses in front of him, and he was over the moon.

"Oh, look at you all." Geoff dropped the little bag on the coffee table and stopped close behind Carter, running hands around to Carter's chest. "Master."

Carter drew in a shaky breath, the only slip Troy had seen so far in the Dom's composure. Saul on the other hand, was all over his back with hot fingers and a hotter tongue, not pretending at all that he wasn't into everything.

Troy opened Carter's jeans, moaning softly at the musk and heat he found there. He eased Carter's boxers down, daring to steal a lick at the tip of that heavy cock as he did.

That made Carter hiss and rock back into Geoff. Saul leaned right over his head and kissed Carter, threading fingers into Carter's hair.

"God, I love watching you guys kiss." Troy looked up and caught Geoff's hand snaking around Carter's cock. He licked at fingers and shaft, teasing all of them before he sucked a little mark on Geoff's thumb.

One of them broke off the kiss. It was hard to tell whether it was Carter or Saul, but both of them sucked in deep breaths. Saul reached for him and pulled him to his feet, then turned him and took a kiss from him as well.

Troy stepped close, rubbing up along his Master's thigh, Saul's heavy cock a brand on his belly.

"Want you, boy." Saul nuzzled at his neck, fingers sliding over his shoulders. "And I know Master Carter wants to see, don't you, Carter?"

"Fuck yes." Carter's voice was a low growl. "I do like a good show, don't I, boy?"

"Yes, Master. You love to watch." Geoff was panting softly, and Troy could feel their attention on him.

Saul's hands slid down his spine and cupped his ass. "You want to ride, boy? For starters?" Saul let him go and sat on the couch, legs spread and cock standing out thick and proud.

"It's what I was made to do, riding." Some things you never forgot, and Master Saul made sure he got some good practice.

"Eager." Saul grinned and pointed to Geoff, who was digging a rubber and lube out of Saul's little pouch.

"Just being of service, Sir." Geoff didn't even blush, just pressed them into Troy's hand. Carter chuckled darkly, and Geoff bit gently into his shoulder.

Troy circled Saul's cock, jacking his Master with slow, steady strokes, up and down, nice and easy. He knew just where to touch, how to make his lover need.

Saul drew in a deep breath, eyes locked on his like there was no one else in the room, nothing else his Master cared to see. There were other hands on him, Geoff's probably, warm fingers stroking over his back, tracing patterns in his shoulders, but Saul only had eyes for him just then.

"Yours, Master." His Master was the center of the world, his touchstone. Troy leaned down, sucking the tip of Saul's thick prick, tugging until he got a taste of that heady pleasure.

"Mine. Ah. Fuck." Saul groaned and one hand tangled in his hair.

Carter grunted and sat close on the couch, close enough to touch, and pulled Geoff down with him, the two of them watching.

Troy gave himself over, letting Saul move him, push him down on that needy cock, letting his Master use him.

"You said he loved sucking, boy." Carter's words sounded dark, wanton.

"Yes, Sir. You can't fake that."

"No." Saul grunted softly. "My boy doesn't fake anything." Saul kept him there a bit, moving slow and deep, making them both feel it.

"Sir, can I—"

"No." Carter cut Geoff off instantly.

"But if Saul—"

"Boy." Carter's tone was a warning.

Geoff sighed. "Fuck."

"Boy!" Carter barked, and Geoff whimpered.

"Sorry. I'm sorry, Sir."

Saul either didn't care to focus on them or was ignoring the exchange, but Troy knew what Geoff wanted, and Saul must have too.

Troy's job and joy was to focus on his Master, to suck and pull and moan and adore Saul's cock.

"Want you now, boy." Saul stopped him eventually, cupping a hand under his chin and pulling away.

He released Saul with a soft whimper, caught between missing the wonderful comfort of Saul in his mouth and knowing Saul was fixin' to fuck him into next week. "Master."

Saul licked his lips and pulled him up. "Geoff, take the lube from my boy and slick him up for me." Saul kissed him, tongue gliding along his lips.

"S...Sir?"

Carter hummed. "Don't make Master Saul ask you twice, boy."

Geoff whimpered softly as Saul arranged him, kneeling with his knees outside his Master's. Saul drew him down into a kiss, spreading his legs so wide he was totally exposed.

"Thank you, Sir." Geoff took the lube, but it seemed like ages before Geoff touched him. Trembling hands cupped his ass and spread him even farther, and it wasn't fingers that slicked his hole but a hot, hungry tongue.

His eyes flew open, and he cried out into his Master's mouth. Saul grinned at him, the expression wicked, but Troy couldn't even begin to hide the flood of need that took him.

"Jesus, Saul." Carter shifted even closer, leaning in to take a searing hot kiss from Troy, moaning into his mouth.

All Troy could do was feel. He was nothing but sensation and heat. He held onto his Master, the only solid thing in the world.

In the blur, he felt Geoff's tongue replaced by cool slippery fingers pushing inside him, twisting and sinking deeper.

"That's enough, Geoff." Saul's tone was low, his voice quiet. "Thank you."

"My pleasure, Sir. He's so beautiful."

Troy could hear Geoff and Carter speaking softly but couldn't make out what they were saying.

"Troy," Saul whispered. "Come on, baby. I need you."

He would have answered, but that was more than he

had. He rose up and waited, trembling as Saul lined up, the hot tip kissing his hole.

Then he sank down, taking his Master in.

"God. Yes." Saul's eyes closed, head tilting back, hips rolling up under him. "You feel so good."

Yes. Yes, he felt awake, like every nerve was lit and ready for him to move. He rocked his hips, intent on driving them both mad.

Saul's fingers caught him by the hips as they moved together, and those blue eyes caught him again, drilling holes as deep as his soul. "That's it, yes. Fuck."

Nothing felt better than this—being present and happy and so full he swore he could feel Saul's cock when he swallowed.

"Geoff." Saul didn't get a chance to say anything else before Geoff kissed him, but his master didn't waste the opportunity and took Geoff by the scruff, returning the kiss, turning it heavy and hard. Carter grunted, making more room for Geoff between them, one hand lazily stroking himself as he watched.

Troy kept moving, letting himself imagine sucking that heavy prick while Saul drove inside him, stretching him, taking him.

Saul and Geoff parted, both of them panting and a hungry grunt on Saul's lips. His master pushed Geoff down between them and Geoff groaned and tasted the head of his prick.

"Oh. Hell, yeah." Carter seemed to approve.

"Pr-pretty." Troy just managed to choke the word out when Saul jerked him down, tilted him just so, and lit him up. "Master!"

"My boy." Saul rocked him, needy prick rubbing him just right again and again.

"Go on, boy." Carter's raspy order cut through the fog. "Take him deep."

Troy's sharp scream surprised him, and he shot, his entire body shorting out with pulse after pulse of pleasure. He fell back, Carter's strong hand catching him and keeping him where he belonged.

"Troy!" His master's fingers dug into his hips and Saul bucked up a couple of times before letting out a wild cry, cock jerking and pulsing inside him.

Geoff pulled off him with a pop and a shout of his own, but Troy couldn't focus on that. Saul was pulling him down, asking for a kiss.

He gave it, slow and sloppy, his world spinning in lazy arcs as Saul tasted him.

"Mmm. Love you." Saul's kiss was just as lazy—gentle and satisfied. "Such a good boy."

"Love." That was the best he had. Love. All his love.

"Check out our men," Saul whispered. "They're gorgeous." Carter had Geoff bent over the arm of the sofa and neither of them seemed to hear. They were so lost in each other.

He rested against Saul's chest, watching with eyes that kept trying to close.

Carter's face twisted and he let out a low grunt, eyes closing as he came—the most subdued sort of nirvana Troy had ever seen.

"Thank you, Sir. Thank you." Geoff was totally lost and babbling, making Saul chuckle.

Troy hummed, snuggling into Saul. The best part about this whole thing was hearing Geoff and Carter love each other and not be hurt.

Their lovers tumbled onto the couch beside them, and

Carter rested his head on Saul's shoulder with Geoff in his lap.

"Damn."

"Uh-huh." Saul nodded. "You two are so beautiful together."

Geoff smiled at them. "You guys are fu—really hot."

Carter laughed, but weakly. "Good catch."

Troy turned his face and got Carter's lips in a soft, gentle kiss. Carter buzzed his lips, tickling him and making him chuckle. "You two are beautiful." He winked. "Really fucking beautiful."

Geoff cracked up, shoulders shaking against his lips.

Saul sighed. "I am boneless. I have no bones. We don't have to move yet, do we?"

"Stay. Please. I'm so happy." Troy was fixin' to float away.

"Mmm. Me, too, boy." Saul tucked him tighter.

"I can't tell you what a great relief it is to finally hear you say that, Troy." Carter took his hand and held it. "I... really don't have words."

Geoff slipped his hand over both of theirs. "I think those were pretty good ones, Sir."

"Yes. Love y'all." Hells bells, wasn't this something. His family all right here.

Right here in front of the fire, warm and relaxed. Nobody was going anywhere for a while. Not if he could help it.

11

———

"Do you think they'll make it to the airport tomorrow, Master?"

Carter looked at his boy. "They'll make it."

"What if they don't though?"

"Then they'll come here, and Troy can help at the cafe." Easy peasy. "Are all the presents wrapped for them?"

He sort of hoped Geoff said no. Geoff needed his ass warmed before Troy and Saul got here, and he wanted a reason.

"Yes, Sir. He'll be all right, won't he? With Saul's family? I think he's nervous."

Troy was nervous? "You're not worried, are you?"

"Of course I am! He's always with us for Christmas. He's going to be—" Geoff bit those pretty lips together and looked at him with wide eyes.

Carter waited for Geoff to finish. He prayed that the visit went well, or he was going to have three shattered lovers and only two he could beat it out of.

Geoff sighed, looking defeated. "I know. He's with Saul. He's happy. But I still want him here. I'm worried they won't like him, or they'll think he's too old, or too... weird. I want him here where I can keep him safe."

"Saul invited us, remember? We just can't swing it without a manager, but Saul wanted us there." He wasn't sure how Geoff would handle a full-on Christmas extravaganza.

"Oh, I know. Maybe it's just as well." Geoff leaned on him, pressing that worried head into his chest.

He held on, rocking his lover for a second. Not too long, because Geoff didn't need to wallow. It wasn't good for him, and Troy sure as fuck didn't either. "That's enough, boy. You're going to make yourself sick."

"You're right. Sorry, Sir. I should go start some coffee and put some snacks out, right? I'll... I'll go do that."

"Come here." He had put Geoff over his knee for twenty years and twenty years from now, he'd still be doing it, heating his boy's ass and reminding Geoff where he belonged. Carter didn't tease, didn't hesitate. He laid down one hard smack after another, pushing it, because Geoff was wearing jeans.

It took eight or ten good ones before the boy relaxed, bending over his thighs and curling the fingers of one hand around his ankle. "Thank you, Sir. Thank you." He'd lost count by the time his boy let out a soft sob and finally gave over.

"There we are." He changed to rubbing, patting, just keeping his boy buzzing, out of his head. His hand was warm, just the barest bit swollen. Lord, he'd needed that.

Geoff hung there, humming to him softly, riding the endorphins. It was a good sign that the boy settled so readily; it meant Geoff's anxiety over Troy was still plenty manageable and not something likely to return tonight. "Mmm. Good to me."

"I love you, boy. Giving you what you need is my honor." Always had been. Always would be. He kept touching, drawing lazy circles on Geoff's backside.

He listened to Geoff's breathing, felt his boy's heartbeat steady and even against him. Not fifteen minutes ago, Geoff was spinning out, and look at his boy now. If that didn't make a man feel needed, nothing ever could.

Geoff pushed up and slid off his legs to kneel beside him. The lines of worry in the boy's face were gone, replaced with a goofy little smile, as if the boy were drunk. Geoff would lose that look in a few minutes, but he loved it while it lasted. "What can I do for you, Master?"

"You can remember that I'm here, watching your fine ass, knowing it's lit up." The guys would know too; they'd see it.

"Yes, Sir. I'll carry it all night. I'm yours." Geoff shifted, the boy's eyes closing for a second, and he knew Geoff had done that on purpose. To feel it. To feel him.

"Balls to bones." Carter let his pride show in his voice, his love.

He saw lights coming up the drive. Perfect timing. The rest of his family was on their way.

"May I please go get the door, Sir? Does Troy still have his key? They should have keys, don't you think?"

He reached in his pocket and held out two key rings with keys dangling on them. "You read my mind."

Geoff's smile was brighter than Christmas. His boy hauled himself up with a soft grunt and kissed him. "I love you."

He patted Geoff's ass, making his boy gasp. "Love you, boy. Answer the door."

"Yes, Sir."

Carter watched him go, listening to the little sounds as his boy straightened himself up for company.

"Hey, you guys! Oh, I've missed you. Come in."

"Hi, Geoff." Saul kissed Geoff before stepping around the boy, smiling as their eyes met. "Hey, old man!"

"I'll show you old man, kid." He grabbed Saul and kissed him. "You two all ready to fly out?"

"Yep. First thing tomorrow. Looks like we're going to get lucky; there's supposed to be a break in the snow. Mom says there's tons on the ground there. Like over two feet."

"We're going from one pile to another." Troy looked drawn, but he offered Carter a smile as he put a metric shit-ton of presents under the tree.

Saul gave him a meaningful look and a shake of the head while Troy's back was turned and mouthed, "Nervous."

"Oh, honey. Let me help you with those." Geoff rushed over to help Troy set the presents down, the little hitch in his boy's gait impossible to hide.

Saul raised one eyebrow, and Carter had to grin. He did love the way a well-spanked boy moved.

"Nice," Saul said quietly, grinning back at him. "I should have made some time to do the same."

"You'll have an opportunity this evening, if you need it. It'll give him something to think about on the plane." Carter believed strongly that a sub needed something to focus on besides his worries.

Saul nodded. "We'll see. Part of me wonders if this time he needs to work through this on his own, you know?"

Carter didn't know about that. Troy had reason to be scared, but then again, Saul knew his parents. He hoped to God that Saul was right.

Saul squeezed his shoulder like the kid read his mind.

"I'm just wondering. How Troy holds up tonight will make the answer clearer. Beer?"

"Eggnog?"

"No kidding? Sounds great." Saul followed him into the kitchen.

"There's leaded and unleaded. I'm assuming you want the grownup version?" He grabbed four glasses. "You ready to see your mom?"

"Leaded please. And yeah, I'm excited. It's been a while, and I can't wait for her to meet Troy." Unlike Troy, Saul seemed completely relaxed about the visit. Confident, like always, like only a twenty-something could be.

"Excellent. Maybe your mother could come out here and see your shop." Geoff was weirdly good with parents.

"Oh, that's a neat idea. I never thought of flying her out here. I've just always been the one who traveled. I should ask her. Maybe when it's warmer in the summer. She'd love the mountains." Saul took the cup of eggnog and sipped it, shivering. "Ooh. Good stuff. Thank you. Troy! Eggnog!"

When Troy didn't answer, Carter peeked out, finding the boys wrapped up in each other. He waved Saul over to see.

"Look at them. They're adorable." Saul sighed. "I do feel bad, taking Troy away from you for the holiday. He's going to miss you both. I will, too, but he—it's different. Is Geoff okay?"

"Geoff has bad Christmas shit. Troy deserves lights and noise and music."

"Troy will get plenty of all of that. I hope he's not overwhelmed. Or... well, he will be overwhelmed, because we're a lot of company." Saul laughed. "I hope it's not too much is all. Is there anything I can do for Geoff?"

Carter hadn't been able to in twenty-plus years, and it would burn his ass if Saul could. The simple fact was, though, if Saul could help find Geoff joy in Christmas, Carter would take the hit to his ego. "Honestly, I have no idea."

Saul nodded. "Okay. I'll just keep my eyes open." Saul leaned against the kitchen counter and looked at him, head tilted a little. "What about you? Are you okay? I know you'll be working your ass off, but we'll miss you."

"I'll be fine. I'm going to sit for Geoff, let him work on my sleeve." He only did it twice a year—Christmas and his birthday.

"I know you'll be fine; that wasn't what I was asking. It's so easy to just focus on your sub instead of yourself, isn't it?"

"Of course." Carter sounded a little like Doc. Just a little.

"Oh, fine. Don't talk to me." Saul's smile made the comment playful instead of annoyed. The kid stepped into his personal space, right up toe to toe with him. "I'll be patient. I believe I've fallen for you, Carter Lee. Every stubborn, stoic, overbearing inch of you."

"I'm going to miss you both this week, kid." He held Saul's gaze. "If we can't get away next year, you'll have to stay here with your Colorado family."

"That's fair." Saul brushed his cheek with the back of one hand. "We can alternate. That's what my sister and her husband do. But then we'll miss Thanksgiving, so be careful what you wish for." Saul winked.

"You'd miss Troy, man." He wasn't losing his partner for Thanksgiving.

Saul laughed. "Damn. You are stone cold. Looks like Mom keeps Christmas."

Carter grinned at him. "After that shower this year? I have something to fight for."

"I think I can say for certain you won't have to wait for Thanksgiving to do that again." Saul looked over his shoulder. "Should we go see if they need us? Not that they look like they do."

"We can. Or we can drink our eggnog and admire. I'm easy."

Saul shifted to stand beside him instead of in front, and did just that, sipped the eggnog and watched the boys. "I want to do a scene. After the holidays, you know? A real one. I want to watch you work. I want you to see Troy—he's so beautiful it hurts."

Oh. The thought of that—them working together for a goal—made his mouth dry. "I would love that. We can plan it together."

"It's a deal." Saul took his hand, tangled their fingers. "A long scene, slow build, lots of real submissive head work maybe. That'll give you something to think about while we're gone."

He nodded, but his lips curled in a smile. Oh, the texts he intended to send while they were gone. He was going to drive Saul crazy.

Saul was watching Troy carefully and seemed to be fighting an urge to go over there, so when Troy sat up and stretched, it seemed like as good a cue as any to check in on their boys. "They're alive."

He kept hold of Saul's hand and led him over, the warmth of the fire growing stronger with each step. His eyes were for Geoff, and it felt amazing, the relaxation in his boy's face. "Feel better, boy?"

"Yes, Sir. Thank you so much for letting us... have that." Geoff tucked up against him, arms around his waist.

He kissed Geoff's temple. Giving Geoff what he needed was his only focus. "You're welcome, boy. Merry Christmas, Troy."

Oh. Well, he might get an answer when Saul was done swallowing Troy's tonsils.

"Good idea." He crooked one finger at Geoff. "C'mere, boy. Kiss me like you mean it."

"Yes, Sir!" Geoff tossed an arm over his neck and pulled him down, locking lips like the boy had suddenly turned Top on him. Someone was feeling better, had given Troy something he needed and was buzzed from it.

Geoff leaned on him, and the kiss grew sweeter as his boy relaxed. He cupped a hand over Geoff's ass and got a gratifying moan in response.

"Master Carter wished you a Merry Christmas, boy. In case you didn't hear him."

Carter loved that fuzzy, melty look in Troy's eyes.

"Merry Christmas, Sir." Troy lifted his chin and offered his mouth. He took that offer as well as the sweet, swollen lips.

"Ooh." Geoff ducked around them, and Saul laughed.

"Yeah, yeah. Come here." Saul playfully caught Geoff up in one arm and dipped him over, making the boy squeak before planting a kiss on Geoff's lips.

"We're glad you two are here," Carter said, not just to Troy, but to all of them.

Saul pulled Geoff upright again. "We were just saying that in the car. This house feels like home when we're all together. It's easy to relax."

Saul handed Troy the glass of eggnog. "Try this."

"Are you trying to get me drunk, Sir, or just lube me up?" Troy took the glass and drank deep.

"Well, if it works, great, but I really just wanted you to try it. It's so good. Did you make it, Carter?"

"Geoff did. I'm thinking about making an eggnog pie as a special next year."

"He says that every Christmas, Master," Troy whispered.

Saul glanced at Carter and winked. "Good luck with that."

"If someone would just get behind me here..." Carter reached over and goosed Troy.

"I'll do it." Saul raised his hand. "Pick me!"

They all cracked up, a pile of happy men, tickling and playing together, and it was...amazing. Natural. Normal.

"I need more eggnog. Christmas movie? Popcorn? Come on, Geoff." Saul whisked Geoff off to the kitchen, leaving Carter there with Troy. He had a hard time believing that was accidental.

Carter looked at the curly mass of red hair on Troy's head and lifted one fine curl off the boy's forehead. It was hard to believe now that Troy had shaved himself bald all those years. In some ways that felt like a lifetime ago. "Thank you for helping Geoff."

"I love him." Simple as that. "I love you."

Carter's chest clenched, the words echoing through his fucking soul.

Troy was watching him, but he waited to speak until he could breathe again, cradling the boy's cheek in his palm. "I... I didn't realize how much I needed to hear you say that. I love you too."

"I know." Troy leaned into his hand, trusting him to hold on, hold him.

He was good for every bit of that trust. That was a promise he could make. "Is it wrong for me to tell you that I'm jealous of your other family?"

"No. Next year, we can stay home with my family. Master Saul will understand."

Carter wasn't sure that was totally true, but that would have to be between Saul and Troy.

"We'll see how next year plays out. Right now, I want you to enjoy them. They love Saul. That's quite a thing for this group. You should see what that looks like, enjoy it."

"My plan is to keep my head down and my mouth shut, right? Just take my cues from my master."

"Oh, Troy. No, love. You're not going to be Saul's boy there. You'll be his lover. His partner. Be yourself."

Troy smiled at Carter as if to say, poor, poor silly man. "I'll always be his boy. It'll just be a secret."

He laughed. Always was quite a concept. "You make me happy. Good boy."

"Thank you, Sir." Troy leaned close. "I can call home? If I need you?"

Oh, sweet baby. "You can call home any time, even if you don't." Carter couldn't imagine going a week without hearing from Troy, but he hoped the boy didn't actually need to for any other reason than missing home. He wondered if Saul really knew what a tall order this was for their Troy.

"Good deal. I'll want to hear y'all's voices. Seriously. I'm heading to Yankee-land on purpose."

"I heard that!" Saul and Geoff were headed back with a giant bowl of popcorn and cups for everyone.

"Troy was just asking if it would be appropriate to call us."

"Of course! We can't go a whole week without talking to you guys. You call any time you want, with or without me, baby. No worries."

Troy grinned at Carter, green eyes all lit up. "I love popcorn."

God. It felt like Saul came along out of nowhere and somehow took ten years off all of them. Especially Troy. "Sit. You and Geoff can find us a movie."

"I've got the remote!" Geoff plopped on the couch, and Saul set the bowl down on the coffee table.

"Are we going to open presents tonight, y'all? I want Geoff to have his for Christmas morning."

Oh lord, what had Troy done?

"You want to do that now? Works for me." Saul sat on the other side of Troy.

"I... Christmas morning?" Geoff looked more than a little uncertain.

Carter looked at the three of them sitting there and sighed. "You haven't left me any room."

"There's always room." Troy stood. "I'll play Santa. You sit with Geoff."

"You're the skinniest Santa I've ever seen." He took Troy's seat, and Geoff curled into him.

"Excuse me. I think I've fattened him up a little," Saul protested.

Geoff made a disgusted sound. "Don't listen to them, honey. You're perfect."

"Ho ho ho. No presents for you, Saul." Troy brought Geoff a huge box, and Carter a flat, small one.

"You either. It'll be under Mom's tree. Ha."

"Troy! What is in this box?" Geoff's eyes were huge.

"Your Christmas present." Troy looked like he was about to explode.

"Open it, boy. Before Troy passes out." He flipped his box over in his fingers. Tie? Gift card?

Geoff ripped open the paper. "Whoa." The boy slid to the floor with the box and kept ripping like a four-year-old, revealing what Carter thought was meant to be a coffee maker, but it looked very fancy. "Whoa! Oh my God, Troy. This is amazing!"

"Merry Christmas." Troy grinned, kneeling down with Geoff. "It can do anything you want. Push-button."

He opened the box he held, finding a gift certificate for one hand-designed bondage rack. Troy glanced up at him, winked.

"Ho, ho, ho."

"Troy. Thank you." He reached for Troy but could only reach the boy's shoulder, which he gave a squeeze. "This is amazing. I can't wait."

Geoff glanced over, but his boy was pulling out foam and instructions, totally focused on his present. Saul and Troy both beamed at him.

Saul gave his knee a pat. "A gift that keeps on giving. Trust me, I know."

Geoff wasn't paying them any attention. "I can't wait to throw out that piece of sh...tuff in the kitchen. Oh! It has a grinder on top and everything!"

"It's very generous. Thank you." Carter grabbed Saul and kissed him, because he could.

Saul accepted the kiss, smiling against his lips. "Thank Troy. The gifts were both his idea. I'm more of a thought-that-counts guy. I'm hopeless with presents."

"I like thoughts. Honestly. You two have made Geoff very happy."

"With any luck, you'll be a happy camper too. Fancy coffee to drink while Geoff is tied to your custom apparatus." Saul winked. "Geoff was very happy, anyway. I know it. Troy knows it. And you know it too. This is just holiday distraction. Just fun."

"We all deserve a little of that, don't we?" Carter laughed as Geoff discovered something else the coffee maker could do, his boy squealing.

"Yes. We do." He liked the fond way Saul looked at Geoff,

with so much more than the heat he knew was under the Dom's skin. Protective, affectionate—there was something to knowing that Geoff had more than just him to lean on now. Carter tried not to feel guilty about feeling like Saul and Troy lifted a little weight from his shoulders. It was good that he wasn't Geoff's sole source of support anymore.

He didn't need much himself, but he liked knowing Saul was in his corner, that he could say things to Saul he didn't want to burden his boy with. Add to that the fact that Troy had his back professionally, would be there for him and the diner? He was solid.

"Thank you, Sir!" Geoff untangled from a hug with Troy and popped up off the floor, landing in Saul's lap. "I love it. So much to play with. I almost want to have the group here for brunch instead of in the evening one weekend so I can show it off."

"You're welcome, boy. Name the time, we'll be here." Saul accepted a quick kiss from Geoff. "You need help taking that into the kitchen?"

"Probably." Geoff turned to Carter. "Master! Did you see what they got us?"

Carter laughed. Us, huh? How long before Geoff would even let him push buttons?

"I did, boy. Did you see this?" Carter handed Geoff the note from Troy, his voice going dark. "I'd say for us, but really it's for me."

Geoff read, his eyes going wide. "Oh...Wow."

He loved the looks in Geoff's and Troy's eyes—both lit up and dancing and then, boom, Geoff was on Troy's lips, kissing him hard.

Saul laughed and stood up. "Let me get the coffee maker into the kitchen. You can supervise these hooligans." Saul scooped up the coffee-maker box like it weighed nothing.

"So good to us, and I can say thank you the right way, love."

Troy groaned for Geoff and pulled them tighter together.

Carter rolled his eyes and snapped his fingers at them. "All right, break it up, you two. It's not bedtime yet, and we have popcorn to eat."

"Popcorn!" Saul trotted back into the room and sank into the couch. "Who picked a movie?"

He was going to invest in a huge sectional. One with two recliners on either side. Oh, or one with enough sections to fuck on...

"Porn?" Geoff climbed up next to him.

"No." Saul snorted.

Geoff made a face. "Since when are you a prude?"

"I'm not. I just want to actually see the end. And I'm adding to your stripes count for that question. You're welcome, Carter." Saul crossed his arms, looking smug.

"Can he do that?" Geoff asked, moving to sit in Troy's lap, his boy radiating laughter, pleasure, pure joy. "Master?"

"He just did, didn't he?" He'd take it too. "Oh. Hi." Carter dropped an arm over Saul's shoulders as the kid got comfy and close.

"Troy's busy." Saul handed him the remote. "Age before beauty?"

"Then this thing is mine and I'm keeping it."

He listened to Saul laugh and looked over at his boys cuddled together on the couch. A holiday movie, a little eggnog, presents—it didn't matter that it wasn't Christmas Day. It was a Merry Christmas all the same.

12

"Are you all visiting for the holidays?"

The lady standing next to Troy while he waited for the bags so Saul could wave down his brother looked like she could use a little merry. She had a fierce frown, a long pointy nose, and reminded him markedly of Mrs. Feezel from third grade.

"Yes, ma'am."

Didn't they have heat in the airport? Even Denver had figured out heat.

"Troy!"

He looked over his shoulder to find Saul smiling and waving at him. Even from this distance, he could tell the taller, bearded man beside his lover was family. They had the same walk, the same blond hair, and sure enough as they got closer, he recognized those same eyes. Older, more weathered, but just the same.

"Found him! Abner, this is my partner, Troy Finch."

Abner offered a handful of thick, callused fingers. "Troy. Very good to meet you."

"Pleased to meet you, sir. I'm just waiting on the bags,

and then we'll be good to go. Thank you for coming to fetch us." Troy smiled and tried to look like he knew what the hell he was doing.

"My pleasure. And my mother said I had to." Abner laughed, the sound deeper than Saul's, but the cadence was also the same. So strange.

"Abner! Oh, hey, that's yours." Saul moved in beside him, pointing.

"Got it." He grabbed his bag, then glimpsed Saul's, so he got both. "We're good to go." The 'Master' was implied.

"I got this one." Abner took Saul's bag from him. "Okay, guys, this way."

Saul took his hand as they fell in behind Abner and held tight. "It's only about a half-hour drive."

"Hope you guys brought your long johns." A set of sliding doors opened and a gust of icy air hit them as they headed out into the parking garage. Abner picked up the pace.

Saul gasped. "Jesus. Merry Christmas. It can't be much colder than Boulder, but it feels colder."

"You guys have a lot of snow?"

"Not quite as much as y'all. Eighty-eight inches a year." Enough. Plenty enough. Troy knew they got another couple feet on top of them.

"How many do you have now?"

"I guess there's about a foot on the ground. It's cold there too." Saul let go of his hand and ran ahead. "Is this the new truck?"

"Yep. My new baby." Abner's "new baby" was a new model Honda Ridgeline, and the guy started it up remotely.

"I like it. Troy just helped me pick mine out. I got a Silverado."

"Nice. Hop in. I got that, Troy." Abner slid Saul's suitcase in the back under the hardcover.

"Thank you, sir. Sweet ride." Saul's was prettier, no question.

"Thanks."

Saul opened the back door. "You can hop in the front, Troy. Better view."

"No. No, Sir. You ought to be able to visit with your brother." Troy could sit and visit with anyone, but Saul hadn't been home in a while.

Saul raised an eyebrow but didn't get into it with him, just traded places and climbed into the front. "Thanks."

"Mom's got meatballs in the Crock-pot."

Saul twisted in the seat to look at Abner. "The big ones for subs?"

"You know it."

"Yes! One of Mom's specialties, Troy. Meatball subs."

"I've never ever met a meatball I didn't like, and meatball subs are amazing." Troy grinned at Abner in the rearview mirror.

Abner nodded. "A food guy. Mom's gonna love you."

Saul turned and winked at Troy. "Troy is an amazing cook too. I bet she ropes him into helping."

"Well, she's not getting much help from Sandy or Lexi."

"What? Not even Lexi?"

"Lexi can't get away from the baby. And Wes is useless." Abner snorted.

"Shit, is he really?"

Abner shrugged at Saul. "There might be hope. I think he's just terrified."

Saul laughed. "Yeah, okay. Because you were never terrified?"

Abner grinned. "Gee, I can't remember."

"Well, I've been a cook for twenty-some odd years. I'm more than happy to get to work." Maybe even eager. Cooking he understood, and not being useless he loved.

"You offer, Mom will put you to work. So, you're a chef, Troy?"

"No, sir. I'm a short-order cook, which means I'm fast, consistent, and I take orders with the best of them."

Abner laughed. "That'll work."

"Troy is actually half owner of the diner where he *used* to be a full-time short-order cook. But I'm learning that twenty years of doing anything means it's part of you forever."

"True enough. I'm doing the math, here, Troy. Twenty years as a short-order cook makes you what, forty? At least?"

"Abner." Saul sighed.

"Relax. It's just a question, Saul."

"I'll be forty-five next month." He wasn't going to apologize for something he couldn't change.

"That works for you? My brother's not too much of an idiot?" Abner joked.

Saul shook his head. "Seriously?"

"He's one of the brightest guys I know. I reckon I'll keep him." He wasn't hearing any shit against his lover, big brother or not.

Abner nodded and turned a corner. "We all know Saul's bright. You're the first man he's brought home to say so."

"Just a question, my ass."

Abner shot Saul a grin.

"Then I'm the first one that loved him." That worked for him, balls to bones.

Saul sat up straighter in the front seat. "Happy?"

"Hey, now," Abner protested. "I needed to know who I was bringing home to meet my mother."

"Excuse me? You don't trust me to make that call?"

"After Peter? No. Nope. I don't. Or Kyle? Oh! Or that guy with the ponytail that sang all the time... uh—"

"Ian." Saul rolled his eyes and sighed.

"Right. Ian. What the hell was that?"

"Okay, okay. Point taken."

Abner laughed, and Saul punched his brother in the arm. "You see what I put up with, Troy?"

"Yes, Sir." Good lord, Saul had dated a shit-ton of men. Not that he'd have brought either of the ones he'd loved home. Or Geoff and Carter. Oh, he needed to text the guys. "How far are y'all from the airport?"

"Almost there. Another ten minutes maybe."

"Awesome. I'm starving." Did Saul just bounce in his seat?

First he texted Geoff. *Made it home. S is bouncing. O.o Miss y'all.*

Don't forget to give the staff the turkeys, boss. Then Carter.

Carter answered first. *I'm not your boss. I did remember the turkeys. Glad you're there safe, make sure you come home safe too.*

Yes, boss. Someone cleaned out the fryer?

Boy. I will text your Master.

He's busy. Be nice.

I'm NOT your boss. Davis is on it. We're going to be fine. How's it going?

He was thinking about how to answer that question when Geoff's text came in too. *YAY! You're there? I miss you already. Are the Yankees being nice to you? Is Saul happy to be home? Are you okay? I love you!*

In the car. He's bouncy. I'm fine. I love you too. Dork.

Then to Carter he sent, *I'm solid.*

And, just to tease, *Boss.*

It was sort of fun, needling the bear from here.

Brat! Carter fired back, and then added, *You've got this. I'm taking Geoff to work with me when he doesn't have a client. Just to keep him busy. Idle hands and all.*

He could always ink his name on your butt cheek. He held back his laugh, because he sure as shit didn't want to explain.

Oh. My hand has a date with your tattooed butt cheek when you get back, boy. I think I'll start keeping track while you're gone.

Geoff chimed in a second later. *Are you texting Carter? You should see the look on his face... wow.*

"Almost there. Everybody made it this year, Saul. First time in forever. I think you guys might be sleeping on the rollout."

"On the rollout?" Saul sounded horrified.

Abner shrugged. "You're the youngest, even if your boyfriend isn't."

"Damn."

I may be getting us a hotel room, he sent to Geoff before reminding Carter that his ass and dick were the only non-inked bits he had.

Uh-oh. That sounds bad.

The next text was from Saul. *Holiday Inn?*

I'll make a reservation. He glanced up and grinned.

Abner pulled down a long driveway and parked alongside four or five other vehicles. Every light was on, the big white house glowing with warm light and surrounded by snow. There were a couple of crooked snowmen in the yard with hats on, scarves around their necks, black charcoal eyes, and carrot noses.

"We're here!" Saul bounced out of the truck like he'd been ejected.

He hit reserve on the hotel room and then slipped out himself. "Go on in. I'll grab our bags."

God, his lover looked like a teenager, so dear and eager and wonderful.

"Leave them for now, Troy. Come on." Saul took his hand, tugging him toward the house. "You have to meet Mom."

The front door opened long before they got there, and an older woman hovered in the doorway, with two little girls dressed exactly alike peeking around her legs. "I'm sorry, boys, there's no vacancy."

"I'll sleep in the bathtub." Saul jogged the last few steps and gathered the woman up in a bear hug. She was a tiny thing in leggings and a floral tunic, and the tips of her gray bob were dyed bright blue.

"It's so good to see you!" She let Saul hug her, but then leaned back and studied her son's face. "You've been eating. You look good."

Saul smiled at her. "Troy's been feeding me. Mom, this is Troy."

She extracted herself from Saul and smiled at him with Saul's eyes, her expression strangely affectionate for someone he'd never met. "Troy. I've heard so much about you. Welcome."

"Thank you, ma'am. I appreciate the invite." He held out one hand, offering her a smile. "Merry Christmas."

"Please call me Kathleen. Or Mom, whatever you're comfortable with." She took his hand but didn't shake it so much as hold it. "Merry Christmas to you. May I hug you? I'm really better with a hug than a handshake."

"Yes, ma'am. Of course." He walked right into her arms. You had to love a woman willing to give hugs to strange cowboys.

"Oh, you're a good hugger. I approve." She let him go, and just as Saul had, she took him by the hand and pulled him inside.

"Uncle Saul!" Both little girls glommed onto Saul who crouched down to kiss them. Abner stepped around all of them, gave Kathleen a quick kiss and disappeared deeper into the house.

"Come on in the kitchen, Troy. It's the best room in the house."

"Yes, ma'am. It usually is, in my experience." The house was cozy, warm, and looked like Christmas had exploded in it. He approved. He didn't do classy.

"Saul said you liked to cook."

"Grandma, can I have some cocoa?" A handsome boy not quite shoulder height with dark hair and dark eyes stepped out from behind the kitchen island.

"This is Brant, Abner's oldest. And he actually knows how to ask politely."

"Can I *please* have some cocoa?" Brant looked at Troy. "Are you Uncle Saul's friend?"

"Yes, sir. I am." He held out his hand. "Troy. Pleased to meet you."

Brant shook his hand. "Grandma said you're a cowboy."

"I am, yessir." That was the very core of what he was, deeper than DNA.

"He was a rodeo cowboy, Brant." Saul bumped shoulders with Troy, sounding proud.

"No way, really? How cool!"

"Really really. I rode roughstock, mostly bulls." Troy wasn't sure he could do it again, get on a bull. Maybe, but probably not.

"You must have great stories."

"Come help me with the cocoa, sweetheart, and let Uncle Saul and Uncle Troy get settled."

"Later?" Brant whispered and winked at him before hurrying over to the stove.

Uncle Troy, huh? Well, that was sweet as all get-out.

He waited until they were alone before he whispered, "I booked us a hotel room for the duration."

He swallowed the Sir.

Saul tangled their fingers and squeezed briefly. "You smile and nod. I'll handle breaking the news."

"Is that my baby brother?" A woman as tiny as her mother walked into the kitchen with a baby perched on one arm.

"Nope!"

"Haha. You're funny. Hey, *Small*. About time you got here."

"Really?" Saul rolled his eyes at the ancient nickname but kissed her anyway. "Lexi, this is Troy."

"Troy, the illustrated man? I've heard about you. You're brave, coming here for a holiday." Lexi hefted the baby on her hip. "And this is Mia."

"She's beautiful, aren't you, honey? You look just like your momma."

The little one looked at Troy, and he winked at her, making her coo and burble. Babies loved him. It was a thing.

"Oh, you're so hired. Why didn't you tell me your new man was good with babies?"

"I didn't actually know." Saul grinned at him. "Must be the red hair. Everybody loves a ginger."

"Okay." Kathleen laughed as the kitchen filled with other kids wanting cocoa. "Have some meatballs, guys, and then go sit by the fire and meet everybody else. There's too many bodies in my kitchen."

"Mmm. Meatballs." Saul went to the Crock-pot and pulled the lid off. "Oh. It's good to be home."

"I'll hold the little one so you can make your plate, Miss Lexi," he offered. He held his arms open, and Mia launched herself like she knew he'd catch her.

"Whoa, Mia." Lexi laughed. "Are you sure, Troy? You've been traveling. You must be hungry." She lingered for a second the way mothers do, making sure everyone was okay.

"I'll be right here, I promise. I know it's tough to juggle babies and eat." God knew he'd heard that about a million times. It was funny; they said that cowboys were good for taking care of critters and making babies, and he didn't do either.

He was plenty good for Saul though.

"Saul said I would like you." Lexi winked at him and Saul handed her a sub already made up. "I feel spoiled. You two need to come home more often."

"Who else needs one?" Saul started putting food together for Abner and then loaded up a couple of plates for the crew in the living room that Troy hadn't met yet, leaving him in the kitchen with Mia and Kathleen, and a whole lot of quiet.

"Oh. Better." Kathleen looked at Troy. "You okay over there?"

"Yes, ma'am. Right as rain." The little one was asleep, which worked nice for him.

"We're a close family, but Saul warned me we'd better not scare you off." Kathleen laughed, as if that was a silly idea. "Honestly. Look at you and that baby. You just earned your place here."

"It would take a lot to scare me off, ma'am. She's a doll baby." Man, Geoff would be riding his ass right now.

"Yes she is." Kathleen came closer. "You need to eat

something. Let me take her for you so you can try my meatballs. I know you were a cook forever, but maybe they'll pass muster."

"They smell like heaven. Honest to God." He'd eat those meatballs if they were turds in tomato sauce.

"Mhm. Try them. The kids ask me to make them every year, so I must be doing something right." Kathleen took Mia from him, and the baby stayed asleep, zonked right out on her shoulder.

Kathleen's fingers brushed his wrist, and it wasn't accidental, she tapped a finger against his ink. "I know what this means, you know." She looked at him, blue eyes keeping him still for a minute. "I know who my son is. And I know how he feels about you."

"I—" Shit. Fuck a doodle goddamn do. Okay, breathe and answer the woman, even though what he wanted to do was—*go outside and have a cigarette*—run for the hotel. This was Saul's momma, for fuck's sake. "I wouldn't hurt him for love or money."

She reached over and gave his cheek a pat. "Good boy."

"Yes, ma'am." He stood and got himself some meatballs and bread, leaning against the counter to snack. The food was delicious, and he hummed, just letting himself enjoy it while resolutely not thinking about the idea that Saul had told Kathleen about their relationship.

Nope. Not thinking at all. Not even a little.

"He looks happy. That's all I want for him, so thank you. He's struggled with that. I'm glad to meet you finally." Kathleen gave him room, puttering around the kitchen doing things one-handed while Mia slept.

"What can I do to help?" If she didn't have anything, he'd work on dishes.

"Well, let's see. Tonight I need to make a couple of pies.

And I thought I'd make some muffins for everyone for the morning. What's your favorite pie?"

"Cherry, but I've never met a pie I didn't like. What kind of muffins?" He didn't even offer to make pie crust. You didn't offer to make crust in a woman's house.

"Blueberry for Abner's crew and banana chocolate chip for Lexi and Saul. Simple enough."

"Yes, ma'am. You want me on that?" He could make a muffin. "Or I can just start helping with dishes."

Kathleen grinned at him. "Let my kids do the dishes. From what I hear, you can be trusted with breakfast. Pantry's over there."

"Yes, ma'am. Blueberry and banana chocolate chip. I'm on it." The pantry had everything but the milk, eggs, and fruit, so he could do this.

"You just help yourself to whatever, and if you can't find something let me know."

Lexi came in to drop off dishes and take Mia, reporting that Saul sent apologies, but was buried in kids and playing a board game. Kathleen seemed pleased to hear that and cleared the island, getting to work on her pie crusts.

He whipped up the blueberry first, making sure to work fast and clean. He fully intended to give Miss Kathleen no reason to change her mind about him, and Saul felt comfortable leaving him, so that was good.

He couldn't wrap his mind around a momma that knew. Hell, his daddy had told him to commit suicide for being gay. Geoff and Carter neither one had a lick of family. He didn't know how to think on this.

"Those look good, Troy," Kathleen murmured. "So you like owning a restaurant?"

"Yes, ma'am. Very much. It suits me." And it was

obviously something he wanted to do, because he sure wasn't starting yoga teacher training.

The kitchen had a double oven and Kathleen set them both to preheat. "I bet it's a lot of work, but I guess it's about what you're built for, right? My Mark was a firefighter. Abner is a firefighter. Saul wasn't built for that."

"No, ma'am. He's never mentioned wanting to do that." His Master liked to fix things, to work with his hands, and he liked to go fast. Troy thought he enjoyed the management part of his job, too, honestly. Saul didn't bitch about work, much.

He didn't think he had twenty years ago, either, if he were honest.

"Nope, never. Sandy is an attorney. She tried to get Saul to come work for her one summer during college. She thought he should try getting a law degree to go with his environmental thing. She tried to tell him there'd be good money in it, and he told her he didn't need good money." Kathleen laughed. "Saul might have made a decent lawyer, but he's never had that kind of drive. You were pretty driven before the cook job, I bet. You'd have to be to ride bulls, I would think."

"It was what I was good at, and it was fun, so that's what I did. I loved it." He was never going to be Arnie though. He knew that; so did Arnie. He would have only been a decent local rider, no one important.

The short-order cook of the rodeo.

He damn near choked on sudden laughter.

"Dare I ask what's so funny? Are you trying to picture Saul in a business suit?" Kathleen stretched her first pie crust into a ceramic pie plate. "Does he even own anything but shorts and jeans?"

"Ski pants and sweaters. He loves the heavy sweaters."

Kathleen nodded like she knew. "Always has. Do you like the cold weather?"

"I like the seasons. I miss springtime in Texas, but I love the mountains. It gets harder as I get older." *No. Shit. Don't say that. Dammit.* "You ought to come visit, ma'am. We have a guest room."

"Oh, I know all about getting older in this cold weather. It can be awful. Why Abner had to move this far north, I have no idea." She stopped kneading her dough for a second and looked at him. "Saul's never invited me to come visit, you know. I might just take you up on that."

"Well, you're more than welcome. Anytime. We have a great condo with one hell of a view." Bad Saul! Lord have mercy.

"He said he likes living with you. And he told me you helped him buy a truck? First serious relationship, first home, first car, you're turning him into a respectable young man, you know. That's one advantage of loving an older man, I guess." Kathleen dragged the other pie plate over, this one was shallower. "And there are advantages to loving a younger one, too, I suppose. Hm?"

"I couldn't say, ma'am. The partner I had before Saul passed away. I guess you could say I'm a long-term kind of guy."

"I know how that feels." Kathleen reached over and rested her hand on his for a second and then gave it a pat. "Ready to put those muffins in the oven?"

"Yes, ma'am. They're good to go." He got them in and set a timer on his phone, before he started cleaning up.

Kathleen got to work on her filling. The deep-dish pie was going to be apple and the shallow one she set aside along with a bag of frozen cherries that needed to thaw.

"Cherry was Mark's favorite too. I knew there was a reason I liked you. That, and you are very neat when you bake."

"Thank you, ma'am. Clean as you go, right? It makes for a nicer life." And a happy lover, a happy business partner, a happy Master.

"Okay. I smell trouble." Saul came into the kitchen all smiles, bringing along a totally different energy. "Well, muffins maybe. And trouble."

"Mostly just muffins." Troy was actually being perfectly good, and he knew it.

"I wasn't talking about you. I was talking about her." Saul put an arm around Kathleen.

"Well. No pie for you," Kathleen teased.

"Oh. That's a credible threat."

"Troy has been excellent company while you've been playing Uncle." Kathleen leaned on Saul a little, and Saul held her up easily.

"They're all getting to be like, little people. For real. The twins are funny."

"They are. And those boys keep me on my toes." She patted Saul's stomach. "Go on and relax, both of you. I'll take it from here."

"Are you sure? I don't want to desert you." Or leave the kitchen where he felt comfortable.

"I'm sure, dear. Go on out and meet the rest of the crew. Take a cup of coffee with you."

"Oh, coffee. Good idea." Saul went and pulled two mugs from a cabinet.

Troy went to the fridge. "What do you want us to use in our coffee, ma'am?"

"There's everything you can imagine in there, dear. Flavored things, cream, milk... the kids can't agree on anything. But I stock it all because everyone deserves their coffee how they like it, right?"

"Yes, ma'am." He pulled out sweet Italian creamer for Saul and doctored one of the mugs. "Would you like a cup, Miss Kathleen?"

"No, thank you. No caffeine for me after lunch. I'll never sleep."

Saul brought the carafe over to pour. "Mom turns in early and is up with the sun. She gets her caffeine in early."

Kathleen nodded. "I do my yoga with the sunrise."

"Troy practiced twice a day before I met him, Mom. He's got me doing it with him now."

"All the wisest people do."

Troy chuckled softly. He wasn't sure about that, but his daily practice helped him center, helped his soul when he couldn't find another way. Of course, he was finding his soul needed help less and less these days.

Saul hooked an arm through his. "You have to see Abner's Christmas tree. It's huge."

"Yeah?" He'd never put one up, because he'd always worked, and Geoff and Carter had decorated. And he had fairy lights in the courtyard, didn't he? "Lead the way."

Saul pulled him into a large living room full of family members and children he hadn't met yet. At one end of the room were windows looking out at the snowy backyard, on the long wall was a tall fireplace with a fire roaring in it, and off to the left of that, a Christmas tree that had to be eight or nine feet tall.

"The angel on the top of the tree is Mom's. When she moved in with Abner, she gave him most of her ornaments and stuff, so a lot of these are things I grew up with." The angel was in a white-and-gold robe and held a gold lyre in one arm and a book in the other.

"Oh, that's something else. I'll have to get a picture of you by the tree." Geoff and Carter would love that.

The tree looked beautiful—years of ornaments and love and history. Family.

God, he would sell his soul for a cigarette. Right now.

Saul took his hand and held it gently. He knew his master could sense something was up, but Saul didn't ask questions. Saul wouldn't do that in all this company.

"I made that one in third grade." Saul pointed to a yellowing Santa made of cotton balls and felt. "I can't believe it hasn't disintegrated by now."

"Oh, look at that!" Troy grinned, just imagining little Saul dipping cotton balls in glue. God, how adorable. "I'm going to have to ask your momma for pictures."

Saul rolled his eyes. "Oh, no. Don't do that. She has albums of them, and she'll happily show them to you."

"Did someone say pictures? And were you ever going to say hello to me?"

"Hello, Sandy." Saul smiled and hugged her. She looked over Saul's shoulder at him. "Are you Troy? How did I not know you were a ginger? You're very handsome."

"Sandy." Saul laughed though. "Geez."

"Yes, ma'am. I've been a carrot top my whole life." He held out his hand. "Pleased to meet you, ma'am."

What a huge mass of folks. Troy loved it. It was like going to a party where you really didn't know anyone, but everyone was willing to make friends.

If parts of it hurt, that belonged to him, and he had no intention of sharing that with Saul. That was none of his Master's; that belonged to him.

Sandy shook with him, strong and confident like the lawyer Kathleen said she was. "Very good to meet you. Okay, both of you smile." Sandy pulled out her phone. "I'll text it to you, Saul."

"Oh. Cool." Saul tugged him closer to the tree and put an arm around him. "Smile, baby."

"Yes, Sir." He winked over and smiled for the camera, leaning into his lover. He wanted proof of this.

Sandy took a bunch of pictures and then started texting. "You guys are adorable together. I'm sending them right now. I have to show Mom. Mom! Mommy, look at this picture!" Sandy took off for the kitchen.

"Oh, boy." Saul's phone started chiming. "Let's see."

It was them. His Master looked relaxed and happy and so young. "Look at you!"

"We look great. Can I send this to Carter and Geoff?"

"You should. They'd be tickled." The guys would love that. "Do you mind if I take one of you by the tree?"

Saul's eyes caught his, all that blue sparking in the lights from the tree. "I don't mind." Saul tucked the phone away and stood by the tree again, smiling. "Good here?"

"Yes, Sir. That's perfect." He zoomed in and took his picture, and the results worked for him.

God, he was a lucky son of a bitch, wasn't he?

Saul pulled his phone out again, thumbs tapping on the screen. "Let me send the one of us to our guys and then I'll get one of you too. May I?"

"Sure, if you want." Troy felt his cheeks heating as he saw that Saul had a half dozen texts from Carter. Ass.

"Okay, move on over there." Saul didn't take the picture right away though. His master just stood there smiling at him, head tilted.

"Ma—you okay?" *Dammit.*

"I'm perfect. Part of me just can't believe you're here, that you're putting yourself through all this craziness for me."

"I must love you." Troy grinned and winked. "Everyone's been nice as all get-out, honestly."

"I love you too. Smile." Saul lifted the phone and took a couple of shots, then stepped a little closer. "How about we socialize for another hour or so, and then I'll say we're tired from the flight, and we can go get a beer or something? We can call a Lyft. Everyone wants to play in the snow tomorrow. We can come back for that."

"Did you tell your momma about the hotel?"

"No. Not yet. Trust me on this. It's better we just play it like this is what we'd intended all along." Saul smiled at him and kissed him. Just a peck, but right in front of—

"Uncle Saul!" The little boy standing there crossed his arms, looking stern. Adorable but stern.

Saul winked at Troy, looking mischievous, then leaned down to look at the boy. "Hey, Benji. What's up?"

"Uncle Saul, the mistletoe is over there." Benji pointed to the little tuft of greenery hanging from the ceiling near the fireplace. "That's where you kiss people."

"Right, Uncle Saul. Don't you know that?" Troy rolled his eyes dramatically, teasing Saul with all he had.

Saul made a goofy face. "Well, color me embarrassed. Thanks for setting me straight on that, little man." His master scooped up the kid, dragging him over to the mistletoe and blew a big raspberry on the back of Benji's neck.

"Uncle Saul!"

"Better?" Saul grinned, all teeth.

"That's not where you do it, baby brother." Abner marched over, lifted Benji up and did the same on the boy's tummy, making Benji giggle and squirm.

"Man, I can't do anything right tonight." Saul laughed and winked at Troy.

"I believe that's the down-side of being the baby brother." Troy chuckled, hiding his smile in his coffee cup.

"Are you the baby too?" Abner asked, and Troy shook his head.

"No, sir. I'm just me." He wasn't going to explain about his baby sister or anything else.

Saul jumped right in, teasing Abner. "He's older than you, Ab. He might pull rank around here. Plus, Mom likes him."

"Oh, good! Troy can be the responsible one this week, then. I'm off the hook!" Abner's laugh was deep and filled the room.

Troy chuckled, but he nodded and played along. "I'm good at that. Just let me know what you need."

"Good man." Abner hauled Benji up on his shoulder and marched off. "Bedtime for you, son."

As if that were a cue, kids and parents disappeared from the room, and suddenly, it was just Lexi and her boyfriend, and them.

"Ooh. Seats." Saul claimed a spot on the couch and patted the cushions. "Quick, Troy. Before they get back."

"I can see why they tease you." He sat next to Saul, swallowing his sigh. Oh man, he was sore. Part jet lag, part stress, he had no doubt.

"Yeah? You're no better than the rest of them." Saul leaned on him with a sigh. "I don't know where I put my coffee."

"I see it." Lexi's boyfriend popped right up and brought it over.

"Hey. Thanks, Wes."

"Least I can do. When you're not around, I'm the one they all pick on."

Lexi laughed. "It's true. My poor Wesley."

"I'm the newest, or at least I was. You're screwed, Troy, my man."

"Story of my life."

"You're the newest, and I'm the youngest. Damn." Saul shook his head and sipped his coffee.

"Troy, your muffins came out beautifully." Kathleen came in and took a seat near the fire. "Oh, it's good to get off my feet."

"Thank you, ma'am. You just holler if there's anything you need me to do at all."

"I will do that. You can count on it. Dinners are challenging with this crew."

"Hey, Mom. We're going to get a ride to our hotel in a few minutes. We're beat."

"To—" Kathleen looked at Saul, then at Troy. "Oh. Sure, sweetheart. I understand. You'll be back in the morning?"

"That's the plan. I hear there's muffins and some snow to play in with the kids."

"There is. And Troy's already provided breakfast, so we're in good shape." Kathleen winked at him. "I expect you two to rest. I'm going to keep Troy busy tomorrow."

"No worries, Mom." Saul looked at him. "Get us a ride, please?" His Master's tone was clear, the "boy" implied.

"Yes, Sir." He pulled up his app and got things going.

"Wes, honey, can't you run them to their hotel?" Lexi asked. "It'll save them some pennies."

"Oh, well. Sure, I guess so." Wes stood up. "Happy to."

Saul waved a hand. "You don't have to do that, Wes, but thank you."

"No worries. It's cold out and who knows how long it will take Lyft to get here. I'll just warm the truck up." Wes stepped right past them.

Kathleen chuckled. "He needs some air, I guess."

Saul stood up and kissed Kathleen on the cheek. "It's good to be here, Mom."

"It's so good to have you both. Sleep well. Good night, Troy."

Troy smiled at Kathleen, hugged her carefully. "See you in the morning, ma'am."

"That you will. We'll have a good time tomorrow. It was lovely chatting with you. Thanks for your help."

"Night, Mom."

Saul led him from the room. Abner had left their suitcases in the hall, and Saul handed him his coat. "Ready?"

"Yes, Sir." Troy shrugged on his coat and grabbed the bags.

His master smiled at him and let him deal with both bags as they trudged out to Wes's Jeep. "Not quite the sweet ride Abner's got, but it'll get us all out of the house." Wes laughed, helping Troy get the suitcases into the tiny space that served as a trunk.

"Oh man. I've always wanted one of these. A soft-top CJ7 was my dream vehicle when I was a kid, and they're damn popular back home for four-wheeling on the mountains."

"Nice. I have a soft top, but it's no good in the snow." Wes tilted the front seat forward for him so he could get in the back. "If we have time, I'll let you drive it off-road later in the week. Fun as hell in the snow."

"Oh, I bet. I'd go for that." Troy grinned, feeling a little wicked. "I can drive like a bitch."

Wes tore out of the driveway, spitting up snow from the back tires. "You're on, man. If we can't tomorrow, we'll do it Christmas Eve."

Saul laughed. "Can I come? I'll even sit in the back seat."

"If you're a good boy," Wes teased. "We even have a car seat."

Troy barked out a laugh. He could just see that, couldn't he?

Saul snorted. "Cute. I know who I'm going after with snowballs tomorrow."

"Oh excellent. Now I don't have to go easy on the runt of the litter."

Saul punched Wes in the arm.

"Ow!" Wes laughed. "That's cheating, trying to damage my throwing arm."

Troy began to laugh, tickled as all get-out. Thank God his Saul had this. It made his heart happy.

"How did you guys get away with the hotel thing? We tried but it didn't fly. Like, at all."

Saul grinned. "Well, let's see. No grandkids, the gay thing, oh, and Troy is an old man."

"Ancient. Practically one foot in the grave."

"He's had health issues. He needs quiet and rest." Saul laughed softly.

Wes snorted. "It's the grandkids, isn't it?"

"You know what it really is? I'm her baby."

"I think it's because your man is a big ol' brown-noser and made muffins five minutes after walking in the door."

Saul nodded. "There's that."

"Whatever works, right?"

"Is this you guys? Holiday Inn, right?" Wes pulled into the lot and right up to the front doors.

"That's us. Thanks for the ride, Wes."

"Thanks for needing one!" Wes hopped out and let Troy out of the back seat.

"See you in the morning, sir. Thanks." Troy grabbed the bags. "I'll go on and check us in."

"Thanks, baby."

He left Wes and Saul chatting, and by the time Saul came in from the cold, he had room keys.

"Sorry to make you wait." Saul came over and grabbed a suitcase. "You want to head upstairs and stay there? Head up and then go get a drink?"

"Let's go get our stuff put down, and we can decide?" He might could use a beer.

"Sounds good to me." Saul hit the call button on the elevator and the doors opened immediately. "Are you okay? Are you tired?"

"I'm okay. Tomorrow will be tough, right? Waking up two hours earlier than normal?" Of course, Saul had been running up to work the mountain, and he was built to be up at the crack of dawn, so maybe not.

"Oh, I hadn't even thought about that. You want me to take you to bed two hours earlier too?" Saul waggled narrow eyebrows at him.

"I don't know, Master..." he shot back, teasing terribly. "I am really old..."

"Right. Downright geriatric. I better just let you sleep, huh?" They got off the elevator and headed down the hall toward their room.

"I might have to jack myself off just to get to sleep." He dared to pinch Saul's ass.

"Ah! Oh, you're a naughty boy. I might forbid it." Saul stepped aside so he could open the door.

"Jacking myself? I haven't done that since you said my cock was yours." He got the keycard in and waited for the green light.

"What? Really? I didn't think you'd taken me that seriously." Saul followed him inside.

"You're my Master. I listen to you."

Saul stepped close and touched a hand to his face. "Thank you, boy. You make me proud."

He turned his face and kissed the palm, his cheeks hot. He was a dipshit, wasn't he? He needed to remember that, while he was always Saul's boy, Saul still wanted to just be a normal couple a lot of the time. Saul's expectations weren't Arnie's. "Thank you, Sir. Did you want to go get a beer?"

"Yes and no. What time is it? We said we'd be back for breakfast, and I really don't want us to be exhausted tomorrow. Maybe we could just watch a movie." Saul kissed his warm cheek, smiling.

"Works for me. It was good to meet your momma." Troy took a hug and then got to work hanging up shirts.

"She liked you right away. I knew she would." Saul dug out toiletries and took them to the bathroom. "I think she might have liked you even before she met you."

He smiled, but he hoped he was making a decent impression. He wanted to be welcome so Saul could bring him up.

"Are you okay? I know my family can be a lot of company, but I think they're good people mostly."

"They're lovely. Really. Your mom is a charmer."

"Still. This is way better than the rollout in the living room, though, right?" Saul came up behind him, snaked an arm around his chest and kissed the back of his neck.

He let his head fall forward. "Yes, Sir. It's a little quieter too."

He felt himself begin to relax, to ease.

"It's hard, right? I can't call you boy... it's strange." His Master just stood there with him, breathing, connecting.

Right, but your momma sure knows what I am. "I love the way they care for you. It's sweet as all get-out."

"I'm lucky. I sometimes wish I lived closer, but then I

remember that I like my lifestyle, and it's easier to manage not in my mother's back pocket. Airplanes exist for a reason, right?"

"Yes, Sir. You'd miss the Rockies." Hell, Saul would miss him.

"I would. Not to worry, I know where my home is." Saul started rubbing his shoulders, working out the little knots and kinks from the day.

"Oh." Goose bumps broke out all over his body, and he let his head fall forward.

"Come sit." Saul steered him to the edge of the bed and climbed up behind him, hands settling in to rub his shoulders again. "What do you think Carter and Geoff are up to?"

"Carter is making apps for tomorrow, listening to the Eagles, and dancing around naked. Geoff had a client tonight." He knew the guys, all the way.

"Carter dances naked?" Saul laughed gently and went after a knot near his shoulder blade. "What are we doing here?"

"O-only when he's alone." He arched, his nipples going tight and hard like Saul had shocked him.

"I'm not even going to ask how you know that. And naked in the kitchen? Ew." Saul hummed at him. "Hot spot right here, baby."

"Electric." And he wouldn't tattle on Geoff for love or money. Saul would just have to wonder.

"I think I got it. But I'm going to get you a massage when we get home. Is this flying? Stress?" Saul sat beside him on the end of the bed and bumped shoulders with him. "Tomorrow you can throw snowballs at me. You'll feel much better."

He bet his bottom dollar he'd be in the kitchen helping

Kathleen, but he didn't argue, he just leaned into his Saul. "What are y'all's Christmas Eve traditions?"

"Well, let's see. We do our big meal Christmas Day, so we usually take it easy. Mom gives everyone—everyone, so be warned—Christmas pajamas. And then we watch movies and eat popcorn and play board games and just hang out. Even Mom. She finishes all the cooking and the prep work for Christmas Day ahead of time so she can join in."

"Board games and popcorn sounds perfect." He usually spent Christmas Eve with Carter and Geoff. They did appetizers and watched bad porn, usually with Doc.

"Abner will try to get you to play Monopoly. Say no. And play Scrabble with Mom at your own risk."

"Good to know. I'll just avoid that altogether. Surely one of the kids wants to play Candyland." He managed to keep his smile hidden. "Maybe Don't Break the Ice."

Saul nodded, looked dead serious. "You're wise, boy. Chutes and Ladders is a hit. War. Crazy Eights."

"I'll stay at the kiddy table. Crazy Eights is my jam."

Saul took his hand and stroked long fingers over the back. "I love you. Even if you belong at the kiddy table."

"I love you." He swallowed the Master and turned his hand over. "Do you want a shower before we find a movie?"

He could totally text Carter.

"You know, that sounds like a great idea. You pick the movie." Saul hopped up. "I'll be back in a few."

"I'll be right here." He stripped down, found a movie, and then texted home. *Survived night 1. His moms super dear.*

Geoff texted back first. *Did u get a hotel?*

Yeah. Yay. Lots of kiddos.

Oh so much better. Yay.

It's a coup to get along with your mother in law, boy. He could sense the calm in Carter's text and recognized it. The more Geoff needed, the steadier Carter would be right through until New Year's.

It is. They're great people. Honestly. It's like a...TV show. S told her that I'm his sub. And that wasn't odd. Nope. Not at all.

Geoff fired back immediately with a bunch of exclamation points.

That's one I haven't heard before. But S knows his mother, I guess.

Did he tell her about us too??

Dunno. Didn't ask. I froze. He was just going to pretend it hadn't happened.

You okay, boy?

Fine. Wondering what life would have been like if his family had been...not suicidal? Not full of death? Not homicidal homophobes that hated him? Not his family. There was something comforting with Carter and Geoff because they were alone, too, at a time when the whole world was about family. Saul couldn't understand that, and he sure as shit never wanted Saul to. Never. Still, it hurt a little. Just a little.

Troy hadn't seen his father since Arnie had died twenty years ago, and God knew that had ended badly. Most things that ended with a shotgun in your face were bad.

Geoff shot back with, *God how embarrassing is that?*

Boy. He wasn't clear whether that was meant for him or Geoff.

Sorry, Sir.

I was talking to Troy. I'll deal with you later.

Oh. Him. Damn.

Troy changed the subject. *How are the apps going? I made muffins.*

Stuffed mushrooms are done, Geoff's weird cheeseball thing is done, I decided to try some spicy shrimp that turned out very well, and I also made caramel popcorn. I think we'll do three or four more and call it done. Muffins are an excellent way to ingratiate yourself, boy. Well done.

My weird cheeseball thing that Sir eats most of before any of us get any.

I want spiced pecans. I'll make us some for NYE. The parties could be epic, and he was looking forward to having Saul this year.

Perfect. We miss you, boy.

I miss y'all. Bad. And it made him feel like a piece of shit, because everyone here was so nice, and Saul was so happy. Still, he'd spent twenty Christmases with them. More than Saul even remembered.

God, he wanted to go home.

I'll send pics 2morrow. It should be a great day.

Sounds great. Family is a good thing, boy. Let them love you too.

There were ten thousand thoughts in his heart, none of which he could let himself think or feel. He just wasn't going to deal with any of this, good or bad. Nice thing he was damn good at just not dealing, one way or the other. *Love y'all. Night.*

He turned off his phone and pulled out his yoga mat. This was the place where peace happened. Solomon's words were in his ear:

This is why we practice, to embrace emptiness and just breathe.

His body moved before his brain even noticed he'd begun.

13

Geoff knew it was Christmas Day. He didn't care. It was barely dawn and he had his sketch pad out, working on the next bit of his Master's sleeve. He'd been thinking about this piece since Thanksgiving, when he discovered that Saul was born in April and was an Aries, a fire sign.

It was interesting that fire was the element that had been missing, the element that ultimately bound the four of them together.

He wove the elements into each other on paper: his air swirling Carter's water into a funnel, but he didn't like that, so he'd tried starting with Troy's earth. He'd get it. He just needed to focus and not think so damn hard. And then he'd have to run it by Carter, of course.

Oh. What if he started with water and fire?

He started sketching madly.

"Coffee, boy?" The words were soft, low, twining into his thoughts.

He sat up from where he'd been drawing, stretched out on the living room floor, and shifted to his knees. "Sir. I'll do that. You're up so early."

"No, love." A mug was held out to him. "Merry Christmas."

"Thank you, Sir." He took it and sniffed it, knowing it was the good stuff, made in the brand new coffee maker from Troy and Saul. "I'm sorry, Sir. I didn't mean to wake you. I just had an idea and I wanted to sketch it. I couldn't stay in bed."

"You're fine, boy. I'll be on the sofa." Carter kissed him and then wandered off to wrap up in a huge fuzzy blanket, coffee in one hand, book in the other.

He watched his master for a minute just to make sure and then burrowed back under his own blanket and got back to work as the sun rose higher.

It must have taken him a while to finish because when Geoff looked up again, the sun was full out. He'd used up a few pages with trial and error, exploring. But he'd finally hit on something and spent time developing one idea in particular.

He left his sketchbook open and set it down next to his master. "Would you like some more coffee, Sir? That one, the orb, is my favorite." It had all the elements circling inside, kind of like the yin and yang only instead of just two swirls, there were four. He wanted to do it in color, but he wasn't sure what Carter would think.

"I would please." Carter was almost finished with his book, and Geoff knew what a gift it was to have quiet time to indulge. He put the book down and picked up the sketchbook. "There's an open container of half and half in there."

"Thank you." He left Carter to look. His master would look at the orb, and the two or three things he'd played with before it as well. They usually settled on a final design together.

He was absurdly gleeful as he got them both refills, deciding that the joy of Christmas was making coffee with their new coffee maker. He'd text the guys and tell them so later.

"See anything you like?" He handed his master a mug and sat down, sneaking his toes under Carter's blanket.

"I do. I'd like us all to have this one." Carter pointed to the orb. "But our Troy doesn't have room."

"Well... he does. But we'd have to get Master Saul's permission." Geoff winked at his master.

"Indeed. You going to stick it on his ass cheek?" Carter's eyes danced, teasing the hell out of him.

"That, or the head of his penis." He grinned wide. He was actually thinking the side of Troy's neck, but this was more fun.

Carter winced and cupped his cock. "Oh man, you are wicked."

He laughed and pushed the blanket off Carter's arm, then smoothed his fingers over the skin, tracing his previous work and stopping over a bare patch. "Maybe here?"

Carter looked down, looked at the sketch, then looked at his arm again. He loved this, how Carter paid attention, focused. "I like it. It fits well."

He nodded. "I think so. Tucked right in here." He sketched the outline on Carter's arm, picturing the lines, scaling it to size in his head, tracing the design with his finger.

It was a good thing he'd apprenticed young in tattoo artistry because he didn't know what else he would do if he didn't have it. He could sketch, he liked to draw, but he wasn't into seeing anything he'd done up on a wall somewhere.

There was something about ink and skin that clicked for

him, even if Carter had had to save him from the man who'd taught him everything, his first Master.

Well, it wasn't like Carter had to. Lots of people had had the opportunity, Geoff thought, if they'd wanted to. If they'd cared to. But they hadn't. Carter didn't have to; he'd chosen to.

And Geoff's whole life changed after that. That's what this segment was about right here, the path through the fog that ran up the outside of Carter's arm. Geoff traced it, remembering the day he'd inked it and everything he'd been feeling. Christmas, many years ago. Too many to count.

Too many to think about. No thinking. Breakfast.

"Are you hungry, Sir?"

"Mmm...I can be." Carter shivered at his touch. "I remember that Christmas. It's been a while. So many good years together."

Geoff glanced up and met Carter's eyes because he was safe there. His master was right. There were many, many good years. Plenty to overshadow a few bad days. "Yes, Sir. I'm lucky."

"We are." That was that—simple and true. All the worries in the world, and his Master never once let him believe that he wasn't treasured, beloved.

He dragged his finger higher on Carter's arm to trace the length of chain looped in a heart-shaped knot around the letter "G", then higher still to the tree, whose trunk and canopy was a flogger and whose roots spelled out "SIR".

That was one of his favorites, partly because it had been their longest session together, and partly because he'd woven in the term of respect so carefully that you could miss it unless you knew it was there.

"Love you, boy. You going to let yourself work on me

today?" Carter always asked, and it was rare that he wasn't able to let his sorrow and anger go so he could say yes to his Master.

"Yes, Sir. I want to give you that orb. We might not finish it. We might have to do the color another day, but I want... I want our guys to see it." He sighed. "I miss them. Can you tell them to stay next year, Sir? Make them stay here with us."

"That's their call, boy." Carter understood though. Geoff knew. Troy and Saul needed to be with them.

"Is it? Aren't there four of us now? You'd get a say if I wanted to go somewhere, right?" He understood that this year had been planned, and Troy wanted Saul to be happy. But it should be a discussion; he was convinced of that. Saul had his tradition, and that was fine, but Troy had one too. Troy's Christmas was with them. "You can't tear a family in half without discussing it."

"Fair enough." Carter reached for his hand, stroking the palm. "I miss them."

"Troy especially." He missed Saul, too, but Troy he didn't have to explain to. Troy would just sit with him and know, even in a way Carter couldn't. His master tried, and it was enough, but it wasn't what Troy knew.

Troy hurt with him—hurt for him, almost—and it made everything better.

Poor Carter. He took a breath and found a smile. "Okay. Food, and then ink. Yes?" He kissed Carter's forehead. "Do you need more coffee?"

"You get the coffee; I'll warm up the cranberry bread that Troy left for us."

"Great." He pulled Carter up off the couch and kept hold of his master's hand all the way to the kitchen. "I almost forgot he left us bread."

Geoff started Carter's coffee and dragged his phone off the kitchen counter to text Troy.

New coffee maker is making the holiday way better, but I miss you.

Miss you. So much. I'm thinking about you.

Geoff sighed, trying to figure out if knowing that made him feel better or worse. *Ready to come home yet?*

Yes. I wish you were here. They're good people, but...y'all are my people.

Geoff knew what he wanted. He knew it was selfish, but he wanted it anyway.

We'll explain to Saul for next year, right? He'll understand. Maybe you can get a sooner flight?

"Troy says he's ready to come home."

"This is new. He's scared. Of course he is. But it sounds like they're being kind to him, hmm?" Carter didn't sound worried. How could he not be worried?

He shrugged. "I guess. He says they're good people."

"Maybe we should let him try to enjoy himself and relax a little, and not keep asking if he wants to come home."

Geoff snorted. "Maybe." Maybe not.

"Saul invited us next year." Carter dropped that like a turd in the punch bowl.

He froze reaching for his coffee mug. "I know. The last time we talked about this you gave me a spanking. Someone has to be here for the diner; you said so. You want to go now?"

"I don't know. Troy and I would have to have a manager we could trust, and we haven't even decided if we can swing that." Carter shrugged. "I want today to be ours though. How often do I have a whole day with you and me and nothing else? It's a gift."

Geoff moved into Carter's arms. "It is. I'm just...me. And

today is Christmas. And I can't help worrying about Troy. I should be focusing on you, I know. I want to."

Carter held him, lips soft on the top of his head. "You should call them and tell them merry Christmas."

"I haven't wished anyone a merry Christmas in forever. I'm the Grinch." The phrase even felt strange to say. "Is the bread warm yet?"

"It is. Go drink your coffee. I'll meet you in the living room."

"Yes, Sir." He pulled his cup off the coffee maker and doctored it up, then went and sat on the couch to wait for Carter. He wondered why it couldn't at least be snowing. He did want to get Carter to the shop though. He leaned over and picked up his sketchbook, looking at the four elements swirling around in the orb.

Four. Together. It was strange how fast that had become important to him. Maybe because he'd loved Troy all this time, and how could he not love someone like Saul who made Troy feel whole and special.

Carter brought him a plate of bread and plopped down beside him. "Ta-da!"

Okay. He had to smile at that. "Woo!" He leaned over to kiss Carter's cheek and snag a piece of Troy's bread. "Cheers?"

"Absolutely." Carter kissed him happily.

"Oh, it's so good." Geoff hummed and chewed, enjoying every bite. "I'm so glad he left it for us. Coffee and breakfast was easy, huh? Troy is good to us."

"He is. He wanted to make sure you were well taken care of."

"I know. But he didn't have to worry about that, I'm yours. I'll always be well taken care of."

"Exceptional answer, boy." Carter lifted his fingers up and kissed them.

"Thank you, Sir." Carter seemed unusually sentimental today, and he wasn't sure why. His master had been a little fixated on age lately, one of the strange truths that came with Saul as a lover and a partner. And he also thought maybe Carter might be missing their men more than his master had expected to.

Whatever it was, his master was right, they didn't get a day to themselves all that often. So would it really be that hard to put his anxiety aside and just be present for Carter? Wasn't that his job? To keep his focus on his master?

Geoff smiled at Carter and combed fingers through his master's hair. "You are so handsome."

Carter blinked, looking honestly surprised and pleased. "Thank you."

"You're welcome. What do you want to do for dinner tonight, Sir? After your ink? Do you want me to cook? Do you want to go out?"

"I have everything set up for us. It'll take a few minutes in the oven; that's all." Oh, wasn't his Master pleased with himself?

"You do?" Carter must have brought food home from the diner. "Thank you, Sir! I'll give you a shoulder rub after. Or we could go walk through the lights at the Civic Area and have some cocoa."

"I'd love to take a walk after we eat. We'll taunt Troy and Saul with selfies of our beauty."

He laughed. "And your ink. We have to show off your ink." Which they needed to get dressed for so they could go, right? He stuffed a big bite of the bread into his mouth.

Carter chuckled at him. "Eager fingers. They wait all year to get hold of me."

"They do. I can't wait. As usual." Geoff knew Carter wasn't really an ink guy. Carter appreciated ink on other people, and Geoff knew his master genuinely thought he was talented, but he'd had to slowly convince Carter to try one.

That first time had been a great experience, and they'd had lots of good ones since. But he only got to do it twice a year at most—a Christmas gift and a birthday gift—so it was special.

"Kiss me, boy." Carter's command was immediate and quiet.

Oh. Love. "Yes, Sir." He pressed his lips to Carter's without hesitation, skin tingling at the order.

Carter held his head, keeping them close, their connection strong as it had ever been, maybe stronger.

"Mm." Geoff leaned into Carter's hands and tucked his fingers into his master's shirt, the connection so easy and so necessary. "Love you. Always, always. Right?"

"Always, always. Right." Carter took another quick kiss. "Let's go make me beautiful."

He was sure his smile had taken over his whole face. "Yes, Sir!" He pulled Carter off the couch and let his master chase him the stairs.

14

Saul reclined on the couch next to Troy, legs stretched out, feet up and ankles crossed. Everyone looked about the same, in various states of food coma. Abner was asleep, and Wes's eyes were closed, Mia lying flat on his chest. The only one that didn't seem tired was Mom, who never overate as a rule. She was sipping tea in her chair by the fireplace and reading a book.

His boy was leaning on him, and he held Troy's hand in his lap as he half-watched *The Muppet Christmas Carol*, which was on to entertain the kids.

The hotel had turned out to be a blessing in disguise; they got to hang out all day and leave when he or Troy had enough and go recharge their batteries for the next day. He thought Troy had started to relax a little. His boy was certainly getting along well with Mom, which was great.

Troy had been helpful and friendly. The kids liked him, and the family were being good. Even Abner seemed to like him. He was having fun, but something was just a little off. Troy wasn't quite himself, not even at the hotel.

He picked up Troy's hand and kissed the back of it. "Tired, baby?"

"I'm okay. Dinner was nice, wasn't it?" Troy smiled for him, cheeks going the barest bit pink.

"So good. I am so full. Mom's roast was perfect as usual, and her potatoes. Did you make the rolls? They tasted like yours." He kept his voice low to match the energy in the room. Sandy and Oliver were talking quietly, too, on the opposite couch, but he could hardly hear them.

"Guilty." That pleased his boy, he could tell. "Did you have a good morning?"

"I had an amazing morning. It's so good having you here. It means a lot to me, to Mom... It just made the whole day better." Saul carded fingers through his hair. "How about you?"

"I'm glad I could help. I wanted to." Troy relaxed under his touch, and it served to show Saul how tense his boy had been.

"How long has it been since you took a vacation? Like, went anywhere but Boulder?"

"I've gone camping a lot." Oh, that was a non-answer answer.

He remembered that conversation. Troy didn't sleep in the woods alone. The longest Troy had been camping were the two nights they went together. "So, you haven't been away from home for any length of time in over twenty years. Pretty much since your drive to Boulder after Arnie died."

That was a fact, not a question. And it explained a piece of why Troy was so tense. They'd been here three days and they had what, five more?

"It's hard to explain, but yeah, basically. I spent seven years on the road, not having anywhere that was mine. Now I do."

That made a lot of sense. Maybe more than Troy thought it did. "You don't have to explain, baby. It was just a question."

How could he keep Troy here until New Years? The boy would keep it together for him, he knew. Troy would do anything he asked. But that wasn't fair. And he didn't want to think about the cost to Troy. It wasn't like he brought a flogger with him, or would use it if he had.

His phone buzzed and he pulled it out of his pocket to find a picture of Carter and Geoff and one of Carter's Christmas ink. "Hey, look." He held the phone where Troy could see it.

Troy smiled, reaching out to make the image of the ink bigger. "Ah, it must be Christmas. I was worried it wouldn't happen."

"You were? Why? Don't they do this every Christmas?"

"No. Some years, Geoff can't. Carter wants his focus totally. Sometimes Geoff needs to just be sad."

"Why?" Why on earth would Christmas be sad? Geoff had Carter.

"Geoff's parents and little brother died in a house fire Christmas day. He was seventeen, and they rescued him, but..." Troy shrugged, the motion weirdly vulnerable, like his boy was trying to protect his heart. "Us old men, we're covered in scars, right? Bulls, fires, beatings, gunshots. It used to be more common, I think?"

"Jesus. That's horrible." He squeezed Troy's fingers, not wanting to bring his boy down. He was glad to know, though, and to understand why this holiday was so hard for Geoff. It would help him help the boy in the future. "Well, they don't look sad to me, either of them. And that sphere thing is beautiful."

"It is." Troy leaned on him with a sigh.

Saul pulled his phone back and texted Carter. *Great ink! Looks like you guys are having a decent day. Can you do me a favor? Give us an excuse to come back to Boulder day after tomorrow.*

Geoff, the diner, anything. He couldn't make Troy stay five more days. They could compromise. They'd come and Troy had been amazing.

Is everything all right? Are you okay? That was their Carter.

We're fine. We had a great Christmas, and everybody likes Troy a lot. But he just can't relax. I'm doing what I can, but it's not enough.

He wanted to be enough; he felt like he was failing Troy because he couldn't be. But Troy wasn't happy here, whether his boy admitted it or not. Saul could feel it.

He tried not to be disappointed, reminding himself that he'd had high expectations and that wasn't Troy's fault. Change didn't happen quickly for his boy. Troy needed time to adjust to Saul's family.

I'm a little... I think I expected too much of him. Saul was feeling young and stupid again, and he knew it wouldn't be the last time. *I don't want Troy to feel guilty, though. I need your help.*

One more day. They'd enjoy tomorrow, then Carter would bail him out, and he'd think things through more carefully next time.

I'm always willing, man. Sucks for you. I'm sorry.

I'm good. I just want him to be. Thanks.

He flipped back to the picture of Carter's ink and showed it to Troy again. "Are you going to want more ink soon, baby?"

"I'm running out of room, but if Geoff says so." Troy winked at him, playing with him.

"If Geoff says so, huh?" He huffed, teasing right back. "Naughty."

"Yup. We'll have to get his permission." Troy's smile was purely wicked.

He nuzzled Troy's ear and whispered, "You're getting a spanking tonight, boy."

"Promises, promises." Troy shivered, though, and Saul felt his boy relax. "Looks like we got more snow at home, huh?"

"Hard to tell. It felt like a lot when we left." Troy was probably right though. "You want to try some snow biking when we get home? It's really fun."

"God yes. I've never tried that, but I want to. We should take the snowmobiles out too." Troy's grin made the corners of his eyes crinkle up.

He loved how Troy was game for stuff like that. His men all loved to complain about how old they were, but he rarely paid it any attention. It never stopped Troy from trying something new if it sounded fun. And it always seemed like they had something to teach each other. "That I have never done. Carter has snowmobiles? I bet I could get us rentals up at the resort too."

"He has two; I have two. Mine are kept on a little trailer. Carter keeps his in the shed and we just drive them out. It's a big joke, because Geoff won't go, so we both have an extra."

"Why do you have two? Couldn't decide which color matched your ink better?" He poked Troy in the ribs gently.

"I bought them from a cook that was having a baby. He needed to sell them."

Saul just laughed. That was so Troy. "I love you, you goon. You want some coffee? Or are you ready to head back to the hotel?"

"I could use a cup of coffee, sure. You think your

momma wants to play cards or something?" Troy was trying, so hard.

He couldn't ask any more than that of anyone. Saul nodded, giving Troy a smile. "I bet she would. She likes gin and spades. Come on. I'll make her tea, and you make us coffee."

His mom's head turned as they got up. "Oh. Saul, sweetheart—"

"Some more tea?"

"Oh, you're good to your old mother." Mom smiled at him. She had such an approving smile. He liked to make her proud.

"Troy thought you might like to play some cards."

She lit up a little. "I'd love to Troy. Just a hand or two."

Troy grinned over. "I do love a card game, ma'am."

"I like him, son. You can keep him."

He didn't think he and Troy had ever played a single hand of cards outside of camping. But they had other games to keep them busy, plenty of them.

"Thanks, Mom!" He hustled Troy into the kitchen. "Hear that? Mom says you're mine."

"Mothers know best."

"Suck up."

Troy looked at him, one copper eyebrow going up. "Any way I can get it."

"Naughty." He was feeling a little naughty, too, and kissed his boy, tangling tongues with Troy right there in the middle of his mother's kitchen.

"Boys, be good." Mom swatted his ass on the way by.

He blinked and broke off the kiss, eyes going wide. "Mom! You're supposed to be waiting for your tea in your rocker like a good little old lady!" He could joke all he liked, but he felt himself blush all the same.

"We're playing cards. That happens at the table. Tea, boys."

"Yes, ma'am," Troy said as he winked over.

"Yes, ma'am," Saul repeated but with a slightly different inflection, shook his head, and went to fill the kettle while Troy made their coffee.

That wink and Troy's complete lack of embarrassment made him wonder if Troy had baited him into that on purpose. He'd be mad, except kissing his boy in Mom's kitchen had been pretty damn satisfying, even if he had gotten a swat.

"Still drinking the lemon, Mom?"

"Chamomile tonight, please."

Saul put the lemon away. "So difficult."

"That's me. Demanding old woman."

Did Troy just chuckle?

Someone was in trouble. Again. Still. Tonight at the hotel would be fun.

"What are we playing, *old woman*?"

"Gin. I don't want you to have to think too hard."

He laughed. "Thanks."

"You should take Troy over to the university tomorrow to see the campus."

"Maybe. I'd have to borrow a car and maybe ask Troy to drive. Honestly, he's better in the snow than I am."

"The Texan?" Mom was on a roll.

"Hey. I'm like a Coloradoan now. Partly."

"Mom's teasing because I didn't bother to get a driver's license until two years ago." Saul filled his mom's mug with hot water and brought it to the table.

She reached over and patted his hand. "It's okay, son. You were a late bloomer."

He sighed. "I rode my bike everywhere!"

He caught Troy texting. Oh, little shit.

Saul wanted to remind Troy that technically, the phone was his and he could take it and read everything. But he didn't. "How's the weather looking, baby?" The "baby" should have been "boy", but even though she knew, he just couldn't do it in front of his mother.

"Snowy." Troy slipped the phone in his pocket and then handed him his coffee, leaning in to whisper. "I just couldn't imagine anyone calling you a late-bloomer."

Saul grinned. Yeah, he wasn't a late anything. But his mom didn't need to know that. He was her youngest, and he was perfect, of course. "Crazy. It's a big snow year, I guess. Thanks for the coffee."

Saul took it and sat down. His butt hadn't been in the chair two seconds before Mom was dealing.

Two seconds after that his phone was blowing up.

"What the—sorry, Mom. My phone's going nuts." He pulled his phone out to look at it.

Late bloomer? Srsly?

God master. What does that make Troy?

Well fucked?

LOL

I will spank you both. Yes, he meant Carter too. Troy was well-fucked, though, if he did say so himself.

Bwahahahahahaha! Geoff was begging for it. *Troy says he's getting it tonite. Give him ours.*

Master Carter will dole them out for me, no doubt. He grinned and added. *Hard.*

"Son, we're playing cards. You can visit with your friends later."

Oh my God, was he just schooled by his mother in front of his sub?

"Sorry, Mom." He texted one last time. *MOS gtg.*

Seriously. Was he twelve? He turned the sound off on his phone and stuffed it in his pocket.

Troy was laughing at him behind that coffee cup. He knew it. He probably deserved it. He didn't have to admit that to Troy though.

Mom dealt out the first hand, and he looked at it, trying to remember how to play. Not that it mattered because Mom was going to win anyway. And if she didn't, Troy would. So really there wasn't much need to worry about rules.

"So how did the two of you meet again, Troy? Saul told me, but I've forgotten."

He raised an eyebrow at his mother because that was a lie. She forgot nothing. She just wanted to hear Troy's side of the story to see if they matched. Or maybe to see if he left out anything juicy—which if he had, Troy wouldn't enlighten her. His boy was pretty private.

"We met at the diner, ma'am. He fixed my boss's bike."

Wow. He didn't realize Troy was quite that private. He'd told Mom a shitload more than that.

"I wrecked his boss's bike first. Then I fixed it and brought it to the diner for him."

"I raised you right."

He'd made a bad turn and been riding recklessly. He could have really injured Carter if the hit had been more direct, so fixing the bike was the very least he could do. He repeated some of what he'd already told his mom for Troy's benefit.

"The diner was insanely busy, and Troy brought out my breakfast so it wouldn't get cold in the window. He looked at me with those incredible green eyes and that was it. I was hooked. I wanted to take him out."

Troy snorted. "He left out the part where I made him French toast a dozen times to seduce him."

"Seduce me? Flirt maybe. I don't think you knew what to do with me when you got me." He winked at Troy, putting all the love he had into a smile.

Mom laughed happily and laid her cards down. "Gin."

"Man, talk about distract and attack. Impressive, ma'am."

Mom exchanged a knowing look with Troy. Saul would have lost whether he was distracted or not. But he was distracted, thinking about how adorable it was that Troy had just told his mother that the French toast was a form of seduction.

If that was really true, it had totally worked. And it would be just like a sub to be that sneaky, too, to let Saul think it was all his idea. His brilliant boy.

He remembered that—French toast in different shapes, lunches delivered at the bike shop, even now at the ski shop. A constant seduction, every day.

"Shall we play one more, gentlemen?" Mom picked up the cards and started shuffling.

"If she is calling us gentlemen we'd better not say no. I mean, how often does that happen?" Saul sat back in his chair and sipped his coffee.

"I'd be a fool to refuse her." Troy picked up his cards. "This time, I'll pay attention."

"Sounds like a challenge," Mom said, winking at him.

He picked up his cards and looked at them. They weren't that bad, actually. Maybe if he focused he could win a hand.

"Who are you dating these days, Mom?" Two could play at her game, right?

"Is that polite? Asking your mother if she is dating?"

"I didn't ask if, I asked who." Saul gave her a sidelong look.

"Really. The impertinence. His name is Roy, and he's a banker in town. Nice man. About to retire."

"A banker. Very nice." Troy looked at his cards, then nodded to her. "Does he have a family too?"

"He has a son. Just the one, but local. John works with Abner at the firehouse. Roy and I met at a pancake breakfast there."

"Mmm. Breakfast." Saul laughed, putting the card he'd just picked up in his hand and discarding another.

"I see that this is genetic. Breakfast as a way to y'all's hearts."

"Total coincidence." His mother said that at the exact same time he did, and he gaped at her. "Or, maybe not."

They started cracking up, giggling like kids. He loved how easily his mother laughed. It was one of the things he missed most after moving away.

To his utter shock—and pleasure—Troy was right with them, happy laughter filling the air.

He wanted to bottle this moment. Just seal it up in a jar so the next time he was missing Mom he could open it up and live it again.

Wow. That sounded like something Carter would say. He missed Carter and Geoff. He wished they'd come. It would have been complicated, but he'd have had everyone in the same place.

"Ah, that was fun." Mom sighed and put her cards down. "Gin. I think I should turn in."

"I'll get us a ride to the hotel," Troy murmured, and Mom shook her head.

"Take my car, boys. I know where you are."

Saul stood up and kissed her cheek. "Thanks for a great Christmas, Mom. And for kicking my butt yet again at Gin."

"It was a perfect day, no small thanks to your Troy."

Mom stepped around the table and gave Troy a hug. "I know you lost your mom a long time ago, honey, but you have family now."

"Thank you." Troy kissed her forehead. "Go get some rest, lady."

Wait. Wait, what? How did she know?

"Thank you, Troy. Good night, boys."

Saul watched his mom go, then put the cards away and picked up her tea mug and his empty coffee mug and put them in the sink. "Did you tell her about your mom?"

Troy set to washing them up, nodding once. "She asked. Was I not supposed to?"

"You can tell her anything you want. I was just curious. She's easy to talk to, isn't she? She's a good listener." He wanted to be that way for his men.

"She's very kind. She's a lot like you."

"That's quite a compliment. But if that's true, then I'm more like her." He stepped up behind Troy at the sink and kissed his boy's neck. "Time to go to the hotel."

"Yes, Sir." Troy leaned for a second. "It's time to rest for a while. Be...us for a while."

He nodded. He needed that too: contact, connection. "Be us." He grinned and went to get Mom's keys. "I owe you a few swats."

"I don't know what you're talking about." But nothing could hide the sudden lightness in Troy's step, the eagerness.

Since moving to Boulder, he'd had a number of conversations with other Doms about wants versus needs. A boy's needs had to be understood by their Dom, but the Dom wasn't responsible for the why of it, why the boy needed these things, any more than Troy was responsible for why Saul, as a Dom needed what he needed. But that didn't stop him from being curious.

The bounce in Troy's step, knowing that they would both have their needs met tonight, made no logical sense to him at all. He was grateful for it, grateful every day that this was a mutual arrangement, that he didn't need to ask for forgiveness for being who he was. But he was always curious why his boy needed in the first place.

It wasn't a question he knew how to ask. Troy might not know for one thing, or it might be painful, or just impossible for his boy to put into words. That kind of discussion went beyond intimacy, into a space that was deeply private. He supposed he'd never know unless Troy chose to share it with him.

But he knew Troy loved him, and that love went deep. That, his boy had more than words for. Troy showed him all the time, and never more than these past few days.

"I found her keys. I'll start it up." Saul grabbed his coat and headed out.

"Good deal." Troy headed to the laundry room where their gloves and hats were drying out. Saul knew his boy would stop on the way to speak to everyone, shake hands, and give hugs. Troy had made everyone easy around them, even if the boy was stressed out.

Mom drove a Ford sedan that looked like it hadn't left the driveway since it started snowing in Syracuse. He found the snow brush in the trunk after pushing off several inches of snow with his hands and got the rest of the car cleared off. He wondered if he should drive or ask Troy to.

By the time Troy joined him, he'd decided screw it, he could drive. He climbed into the driver's seat and moved the seat back what felt like three feet. "Jesus, Mom is short."

"I bet you said that the first time you drove my car too."

"Possibly. But not out loud." He grinned at Troy and pulled out, the car fishtailing as he turned out of the driveway. "Whoa."

"Careful, now. Don't break us before you get me to the hotel." Troy was fighting the laughter for all he was worth.

"Shut up. I don't think Mom has driven this in a while; there's ice on the tires. I bet Abner drives her around, or her new boyfriend. What was his name? Roy?" The roads were slippery but deserted, and he managed to stay in his lane.

"Yeah. She was pleased to tell you, hmm? About him." At least Troy wasn't holding on for dear life.

"She was. Abner had mentioned she was seeing someone, so I sort of knew, but I wanted to let her tell me. Ab knows her son pretty well; he called John "dependable". That's a huge compliment coming from him." Abner's priorities had always been simple. Show up. Do what you say you're going to do. Don't be an asshole. That was pretty much it.

"Abner is a guy I would hire, if he needed a job." It was hard to tell if Troy was joking or not, especially since he actually had to watch the road.

"Well, you could count on him showing up at least." He turned a corner at a traffic light. "Almost there. Which is good because this car is shit in the snow."

"Do we need to get her tires? Does she need chains?"

"No. This is perfect. She just won't drive. She doesn't need to."

"Okay, if you're sure. I don't want her driving on shitty tires." There was something incredibly sweet and sad and wonderful about the worry and care in Troy's voice.

"Thank you, baby." Mom liked Troy, genuinely. She was happy that they were happy. "If it worries you, we could get her some snow tires tomorrow. You're allowed to be worried; you've been officially adopted, I think."

"I'll check them when we wake up. I want to make sure."

They slid into the parking lot, Troy laughing as they skidded to a stop. "Do it again!"

He hadn't hit anything, right? All good. He dropped his tone and looked over at Troy. "Watch it, boy. You're on my time now."

"Good." Oh, daring boy. Someone needed his attention badly. "I'm all yours."

"Yes. You are." He got out of the car and locked it up, moving quickly and expecting his boy would follow him all the way to their room.

In fact, Troy damn near crawled up his ass he was following so close. Eager.

That was perfect. Just the little boost Saul needed. He could feel his shoulders square up and his confidence building as they neared the room. He keyed in and stepped aside to let Troy go in first, giving the boy's ass a swat as Troy passed him.

Troy made it as far as the bed. Excitement and need was painted on his boy's posture. "You have a good Christmas?"

"Yes. I had an amazing day. But I'm hoping for at least one more gift." He took Troy's chin in his fingers and searching those lovely green eyes. "What do you say, boy?"

"Anything you want, Master." Troy didn't hold anything back at all, offering all that need without a hint of shame.

He nodded and kissed his boy, quick and hard, leaving them both wanting more. "Everything off, please. Don't rush." They both needed to breathe a minute.

Troy worked off his boots, baring his feet before he stripped easily without hurrying. All that amazing ink appeared first, Geoff's signature clear. Then Troy opened his belt buckle, exposing hip and cock and thigh.

He watched without moving until Troy had placed everything in a pile. "Very nice, boy." His fingers itched to touch, but he made himself wait another minute and pulled a zippered pouch out of a dresser drawer. He sat it on the bed and took out Troy's cuffs.

"How was your Christmas?" The question wasn't meant to distract but to help Troy focus on something. Saul put the cuffs on slowly as ever, fingers caressing and soothing whenever they touched Troy's skin.

"There are a dozen answers to that question, Master—from good to funny to shocking to painful. I'm glad to be here with you."

He gave his boy a smile as he finished with the cuffs. "I've been really happy to have you here, boy. I know some of this isn't easy for you, and I'm grateful that you're doing it anyway. I love you for that."

He caught one of Troy's nipples and rolled it in his fingers, letting the piercing tug as it may.

Troy's eyelids went heavy, and those lips parted, tongue flicking out to wet them.

Saul took his shirt off and added it to Troy's pile, then reached into the bag on the bed and found the clamps he'd brought. He'd had to think about quiet toys for traveling. He knew they'd need something, but the hard-hitting tools were out of the question with his family around. These weren't meant to be torturous, but they'd be hard for his boy to ignore.

"You're beautiful." He studied Troy's eyes, his boy's cheekbones and those hungry lips. "I'm proud of you."

He rolled that nipple again, prepping it for the clamp. Figuring out where to place it with the hardware.

"Proud of me?" Troy was in the space between focused and unfocused, between his mind and his body.

"Always. This week especially. You've done nothing but think of me." He fastened one clamp in place gently, then released it and let it bite.

"Oh!" Troy blinked, that gentle fog disappearing, focus on him.

"There you are. Good boy." He took Troy's other nipple in his fingers. "Hopefully these are a good surprise. I had to find some new tools for us for this trip. We'll figure out if they're not your thing, I'm sure."

"Not my thing? I-I'll let you know." Right. Troy wasn't going to have to tell him anything.

And he hadn't heard any complaints so far.

He set the second clamp in place, releasing this one gently as well. "Breathe, remember."

"Yes, Sir." Troy sucked in a breath, teeth sinking in his bottom lip. "Breathing."

That pretty cock was lifting, filling to diamond hard.

He swallowed, his boy's reaction everything he was hoping for. He was half-hard himself, his balls aching with wanting Troy, but he made himself wait—made them both wait.

"Mmm. Gosh, I don't know. How are you feeling about my clamps, boy? It's...hard to tell." He grinned and gave the short chain between the clamps a very gentle tug, testing his boy out.

"Oh..." Troy suddenly grew taller, straighter. "Oh fuck me, it's so much better..."

"Yeah. It is." He kept pressure on the chain and took another kiss, this one deeper than before. He had Troy's attention; there wasn't any need to hurry now. He teased his boy's lips open with his tongue, hungry for Troy's submission.

Troy shivered, pushing into the kiss, proving to him how much his boy needed this, wanted his domination.

He hooked a hand behind Troy's neck and held his boy in place, sweeping his tongue through his boy's mouth, forcing Troy's tongue out of the way. He could taste the tension between them. It was so real, so intense.

He got his other hand around one perfect ass cheek and pulled them together until he could feel his boy's cock pressing into his hip. Troy's bound hands were caught between them, Troy's fingertips dragging on his chest. The sweet prick leaked against him, his boy only keeping his hips in control because Saul held him so tight.

Saul slid a hand to Troy's shoulder, pushing the boy down. He dragged his cock out of his jeans, the touch of his own fingers making him moan. "Want you, boy."

He wanted a lot—his boy's mouth, Troy's ass—and he planned to have it all.

"Everything, Master." Troy grabbed one of his thighs, tugging him close, before that burning suction enclosed him, threatening to steal his control. God, his boy was too good at this.

"Fuck." He threaded both hands into Troy's hair, fighting the urge to just shove gracelessly into that hot mouth. Not because Troy couldn't take it; his boy could and would if he wanted it, but because it was so much better to let Troy work.

Bright green eyes stared up at him, the look hungry, desperate, and happy. No one had ever looked at him like that. Ever.

It made him breathless, made his chest ache. Saul raked in a deep breath as pride and love flooded through him, and his shoulders relaxed, muscles he hadn't realized were tense letting go. He must have been more worried about his boy than he'd known. "So good. Love you."

Troy's bound hands found his balls, cradling him carefully as his entire prick was engulfed. Troy swallowed around him, throat closing around the tip of his cock.

Jesus. His eyes crossed, and it was all he could do not to let Troy have him, lose himself and let the boy push him past sense. He arched over Troy's head and felt more than heard his own growl.

"Good boy. That's enough." He wasn't sure how he got the order out through the thickness in his throat.

Troy whimpered, swallowing again and again as his boy set him free, inch by agonizing inch.

He rocked back on his heels, tugging himself the rest of the way out with a grunt. He held Troy at arm's length for a second to get a breath, his boy looking ready to take him back whenever he wanted.

"On the bed, boy. I want to see that ass nice and high."

There was a soft moan, a whispered, "Master," but his boy crawled up on the bed, head down, ass up as he'd ordered.

"No shouting now; we have neighbors." He gave Troy's ass a good smack using his palm, slightly quieter, but he couldn't say for sure it wouldn't be heard in the hall.

Oh well.

Troy stilled for a moment, stiffened, and then his boy spread those thighs for him, shoulders sinking deeper into the sheets.

"Oh, good boy. That's lovely." Saul braced one knee on the bed to get a better angle and dealt out a dozen or so more, wanting to see the pink in those cheeks, to make the body beg for him. He swore he could see as Troy gave himself over, leaning into his blows, offering him one moan after another. The sweet skin began to heat, grow rosy and hot.

"Mmm. Mine." He finished undressing, toeing off his shoes and dropping his jeans, then took his time with a condom and digging out lube. His focus was on his boy, watching the little show on the bed. His boy could never be still, not once Troy was out of his head. "My beautiful boy."

"Yours. Yours, Master. I needed this, so bad. I ached for it. You. Your will."

His will.

Saul nodded and climbed up on the bed, nudging his boy toward the headboard, letting himself focus on his own need now, his own desire for Troy. He intended to claim every bit of his right as Dom. Take everything he needed from his boy.

He grabbed the lube and slicked his prick but didn't take time to ready the boy, instead pressing in close, guiding himself, pushing inside Troy with maddening restraint.

"Fuck." The thousands of lines of ink on his boy's back seemed to swim, to shift as Troy's muscles rippled. Saul felt the answering caresses around his cock, his boy encouraging him in deeper.

He nodded again, not that Troy could see, and gave one ass cheek another good smack before he started to move, rocking deep even as his body ached to go at his boy hard, determined to keep control a little longer.

Troy groaned, meeting every single thrust, fraying at his control. His boy couldn't stay still, inside and out, working his prick.

"Damn, boy." Maybe it was the moment but suddenly he didn't know why he was trying so hard. Troy wanted this as badly as he did. He exhaled and let go, grasping and digging into Troy's hips as he drove forward, hammering into his boy.

"Yes!" The exclamation was a whisper, but he heard it ringing out, loud and clear. "Harder, Master, please. Want to feel you all fucking day tomorrow."

"Yeah." Saul growled, the sound rumbling in his chest and echoing in his own ears. He reached for Troy's shoulder and hooked his fingers there for more leverage, pounding into his boy hard. He focused on the pressure building in him and trusted Troy could manage.

"Fuck!"

That wasn't a whisper. His boy was feeling it.

Saul grinned against Troy's shoulder, his need pulling his lips away from his teeth. His world went white-hot as Troy squeezed him, milking his cock.

Troy was making him work and he loved it. He slammed in again and again and started to vibrate, to tremble against Troy's back as his orgasm built to bursting. He was trying to hold out. He knew exactly what he wanted.

"Gonna make you come, boy. Want to feel you." He let Troy have his weight and snaked his other hand under Troy's chest, finding the chain attached to his boy's clamps and giving it a solid tug.

Troy went still, body clamping around him like a fist, so he pulled once more, hard, and his boy bucked, slamming back against Saul as he shot.

Troy went so tight around him it made him gasp, made his balls draw up hard, and he had to move. He rocked hard against his boy, sending Troy flat into the mattress, and thrust until his boy finally relaxed enough to let him shoot.

His vision tunneled, and all the air seemed to leave the room as his orgasm flooded through him, making him shake and moan.

Troy panted underneath him, breathing hard, trembling the barest bit.

Saul waited until the roaring in his ears eased off before he dared to move, groaning as his spent cock slipped from inside his boy. He hung over Troy, placing gentle kisses on his boy's shoulders and spine, watching and listening for what Troy needed now that he could think again.

"Good boy," he offered, testing, his voice rough and dry.

"Exceptional Master," Troy shot back.

So sweet. He couldn't love Troy any more than he did right now. "Thank you, boy. Can't have one without the other, hm?" He slid down to the bed and rolled Troy over. The clamps needed to come off, and that was going to be a little jarring. Better now than let the boy get too settled.

Troy blinked over at him, a soft, quiet smile on his face.

He smiled back and brushed a lock of hair off his boy's forehead, the red curls dark with sweat. Troy was beautiful —floaty and hormone-drunk—a look he would never get enough of.

"I need to take these off, okay? They'll burn after but not for long." They'd be sensitive tomorrow, though, something else for the boy to think about. Saul didn't give Troy time to answer, just dropped his fingers to each of the clamps and released them at the same time.

Troy grunted, spent cock jerking, a bit more spunk leaking out.

His smile turned knowing. He wouldn't forget how much his boy liked the clamps, or how quickly they got Troy's attention. He smoothed his hand over each one, soothing the angry nerves as the blood rushed back in. "That's done. Just breathe."

Troy nodded, rolling into his arms and offering him a soft kiss. "Thank you. I needed that, more than you know."

He'd known; it was his job to know. But there wasn't any reason to argue the point. "I did too. In more ways than I could explain if I wanted to."

Troy melted against him, warm and cuddly, lips velvet against his collarbone, his jaw.

God, this was so much better. He still didn't think he should make Troy stay in Syracuse much longer, but tomorrow would be okay. Easier. Hopefully Troy would be more relaxed, and they'd go home on a high note.

"Love you, boy. More than words." He pulled Troy tighter, dropping a kiss in those red curls.

"Merry Christmas, Master." Troy took a deep breath and just crashed against him, his boy sound asleep.

"Merry Christmas." One of his favorites. They'd made some good memories. He let his eyes close, knowing he'd drift off just as quickly, and every bit as satisfied.

15

"Was Saul mad when you told him you wouldn't make something up for him?" Geoff looked around at all the people in the airport, wondering where everyone was going. Somewhere warm, he hoped. That's what he'd do if he could go somewhere this time of year. Somewhere with sun and a pool.

"Coffee, babe." Carter handed him his grande Caramel Brûlée Latte and he smiled at it. Starbucks was the only good thing about having to wait for a delayed flight from Syracuse.

"They should be landing any minute now, right?"

"If they haven't already. One of them will text me. Relax, they're home now."

He was glad the guys were home, but he wasn't relaxed. What if Saul was mad? What if Troy was upset?

"So, was he mad? What did he end up telling Troy?"

"The truth, I hope. Which is what I encouraged him to do. The only thing he was mad about, I think, was that he had to step out onto a cold porch to talk to me about it on the phone." Carter sipped his own coffee. "Some things should not be discussed over text, no matter what the kid says."

Carter did have a point. Saul could probably compose an entire novel by text. So weird.

"You think they'll still want to have dinner? You think they'll be in the mood?"

"Boy, I swear to God if we weren't in an airport, I'd have you over my knee. For the last time, relax. Don't make me regret letting you have sugar."

"And caffeine." He gave Carter a wide grin.

Carter looked smug. "It's decaf."

"Ah!" He pouted. That wasn't fair.

"I know, but trust me. I know you. You'll be making coffee tonight." Carter winked at him, not being the slightest bit ashamed.

"I hate it when you're right. Oh. Wait. You're always right." He made sure his tone was dry as the desert.

"Yep. The absolute rightest." Carter's lip only quirked a little bit.

Their phones went off at the same time and the text from Saul read, *Getting our bags, can't believe you waited for us, thank you! Troy is hungry. I'm starving. See you in a few. xo*

The "xo" was everything. He wanted a few of both.

He beamed at Carter. "They're home!"

"I know." The words were a little rough, but the expression on Carter's face was eagerness, hunger.

It was more than a few, but finally Saul and Troy did appear, walking toward them at a pretty good clip. Saul waved before they were close enough for it to be polite to shout hello. Geoff waved back, but truthfully he was watching Troy.

Troy came right to him and hugged him, holding on tight. "God, I missed y'all. So much."

"Hey." He held on just as tight, feeling like he could finally get a deep breath. "I'm really glad you're home safe. I can't wait to hear all about it."

"In a bit." Saul had an arm around Carter's waist. "It was a long trip. Thank you so much for dealing with the delay and everything; the weather in Syracuse was crazy."

"No problem."

Jesus, he'd been so worried and in his own head that he hadn't seen Carter's stress until it started to ease.

So much for putting his Master's needs before his own. He'd make up for it.

"Come here." Saul looped an arm around Geoff and pulled him in, the hug every bit as genuine as Troy's. "We missed you both. We have lots to talk about."

"Looking forward to it." *I want to hear that you're not leaving us for Christmas next year.*

Saul glanced over at Troy and Carter, who were talking so quietly Geoff couldn't hear.

"You guys ready?" Saul took his hand. It felt sweet and kind of protective. "I sure am."

"Yes. I'm going to feed you and then..." He glanced at Saul. "Take you home with us?"

Saul nodded. "Perfect. Troy needs that."

Troy, huh? "Well, we're all concerned about what Troy needs, Sir."

Saul rolled those blue eyes. "Me too. I need to regroup a little. And you're going to keep that between us for now."

"You know it. We all need each other tonight." Carter and Geoff had a surprise for the guys at the house. Their Christmas present.

Geoff and Troy got the bags in the bed of Carter's truck and then climbed into the back seat. As the truck started to move, Geoff put an arm out, Troy leaned right into him, and just that easy they were curled around each other and snuggling. Let the Doms have the front; this was way better.

"How's the diner been? Crazy?" He heard Saul ask Carter but didn't have any inclination to join in the conversation.

"Can I kiss you hello?" Troy asked, already nuzzling his jaw, humming softly.

"I almost forgot we're allowed to do that." He stole the moment and kissed Troy, their lips touching a little tentatively at first, like they were remembering how this worked between them.

Troy smiled, a soft sigh pressing into his lips. "Home."

Then Troy began whispering, "Home, home, home," dropping kisses on him between each word.

"I know," he whispered back. "Where you belong. Both of you. With us." *Don't leave again. I know I can't ask, but I want to.*

Troy nodded and climbed into his lap, moaning for him, and Carter growled.

"You two be good. We're going for supper."

"We're really good, Sir. Promise." He grinned against Troy's cheek.

"Super good." Troy's laughter was sweet and warm and so necessary.

"Boys, do I have to pull down the armrest to separate you?" Saul sounded amused. "Or should we just toss you both into the snow?"

"You're not helping things, Saul."

"No. I guess not. But I wasn't really trying."

"Don't make them pull over, right?" Troy nuzzled the corner of his mouth, tongue flicking out to tease him.

"Right." He turned his head and tangled his tongue with

Troy's, coaxing his lover into another kiss. Troy was so familiar, even their kiss felt like home.

He could hear his Master laughing, but it didn't matter. He was warm, and it was getting dark, and Troy and Saul were home.

"Okay, you guys. We're here." They were resting, totally innocently, but somehow time had passed, and he hadn't noticed.

"Troy. I think we... Troy, wake up." Geoff drew his thumb over Troy's cheek.

"Should we just leave them here, Carter? Let them follow if they decide to wake up?" Saul opened the door, and the dome light came on, making Geoff squint.

"I'm awake. Where did you pick for supper? My Master's starving."

Saul laughed. "Don't worry about me, boy. Master Carter's got us covered."

Geoff helped Troy off his lap, and watched as Troy slid out the door and right into Saul's arms. So graceful.

"Worrying about you is my job, Master."

"You're a good boy. And it's a relief to hear that name again."

Geoff smiled, threading his fingers with Carter's. "Feeling better?"

"I am." Carter squeezed his fingers, holding on tight. "You?"

"Much. We're a family again." Geoff took a deep breath and nodded, letting Carter lead them away from the truck. "Way better."

"Good. We are and the diner is closed until the second. We are lucky men."

"And the New Year's party to look forward to, right?" Next to Thanksgiving, Geoff loved their New Year's Eve

Party. Sometimes they had a theme, sometimes they planned games or someone would do a scene, sometimes the Doms just hung out in the hot tub and the subs snuggled by the fire… he wasn't sure what Carter had in mind for this year yet. Usually they talked about it right after Christmas, but Saul and Troy had thrown them off their schedule a bit.

"God yes. The best way to start the year—surrounded by family." Carter looked happy, relaxed now. "Everyone's excited, I think."

"Ben called me asking about Doc." Doc never made it to midnight. "He wanted to know if they could stay the night again. I told him I had to talk to you. I was thinking Saul and Troy would stay in our room with us. Or I guess we could all take a day and clean out that back room. Put a bed in there."

"Uh-huh. I vote they stay with us in our new big boy bed." It made sense. After all, that was what they'd done for Christmas—a huge custom bed for four that had places to bind two subs at the same time.

"That's a unanimous vote then. They're going to love it." He already loved it. Though sleeping in it without them felt a little lonely. But this was step one in his plan to convince Carter to ask them to move in.

Carter would ask one day. Hopefully one day not too long from now.

Saul jogged past them all to open the door, the huge smile making Saul look even younger. "After you."

The steakhouse was quiet, not too busy, and smelled like heaven. Someone was celebrating having his family home.

"Mmm. Oh, man. It smells so good in here. Good choice, Carter." Saul was pleased too. Geoff liked that. "Big steak, boy?"

"You mean you don't want poached chicken and steamed veg, Master?" Troy teased.

"What's the matter, Troy?" Carter shot back. "Did you eat a meal already?"

Geoff bit his lip. Listen to Carter be all Dom over Saul.

"He sure doesn't sound like he wants to eat, does he?" Saul winked at Carter, but the look was warmer.

"If I started eating more than once a day, we have to blame Saul. It was on his order."

"He was too skinny."

Saul just put it flat out there, and there really wasn't any arguing. Geoff wouldn't argue anyway; Troy looked amazing. More amazing all the time.

"He's gorgeous." Carter looked at Troy, then at Geoff. The expression in his Master's eyes burned him down to the bone. "We're damn lucky men, Saul."

"No question."

God, he blushed hard all over, feeling his ears turn pink. Even his shoulders felt warm. "Sir."

"Table for four?"

Saved by the host. He took a deep breath to cool off as they were seated and opened the menu to hide behind a little.

"What are you having, Geoff?" Troy's voice slid over his nerves, soothing him. "The steak smells so good..."

He glanced at Troy and smiled. "I don't know. You? The steak does smell good, but look at these pasta dishes. Oh, man." Fettuccine Alfredo. Mmm. So good. "They have shrimp."

"Yeah? I want..." Troy chuckled. "Everything. I want one of everything."

"When did you turn into me?" Saul laughed too. "I'm having a steak, and a skewer of shrimp with it, and mashed potatoes for the table. And wine. I don't care if you have to roll me out of here. You probably will."

Geoff just wanted everyone to get home. They could sleep if everyone was in food coma. He could live with that. He just wanted them all to sleep together, under one roof, in one bed.

"I think I'm going to get a... God, I don't know." Troy leaned back and shook his head, eyes rolling dramatically. "I'll just go with cheesecake."

Everyone laughed at Troy, but Carter laughed the loudest. "Such a difficult decision. You could go really crazy and have coffee with it."

Saul leaned across the table toward Troy. "Cheesecake sounds good. I'll have a bite of that too. You can feed it to me."

Oh so pretty.

He had to admire, but it was Carter who growled. "We'll order a whole cake to feed to each other at home. Order your boy a steak, Saul."

Geoff watched Saul glance over at Carter and then grin into the menu.

"Sure thing, pumpkin."

Geoff decided he'd get in trouble if he laughed at that one, so he hid it behind his hand.

Carter snorted and leaned over, whispering something in Saul's ear that made the other Dom blush.

Saul coughed lightly, not looking away from the menu. "New York Strip for Troy, I think."

Geoff enjoyed the look on his master's face, just a little smug.

"Okay," Troy whispered behind the menu. "That was sorta cool."

"Right?" he whispered back, doing his best not to giggle as he set his menu down.

Saul's voice floated over. "Naughty."

The server came over, and they ordered food, which changed the dynamic slightly and the subject along with it, but he wasn't going to forget that moment any time soon.

When the food arrived, there was steak and pasta and veggies and potatoes. He and Saul both got shrimp too. None of them were leaving there hungry for sure.

Troy was sharing stories, making everyone laugh, and every few minutes, one of Troy's hands snuck under the table to touch him, stroke his thigh.

I'm here, honey.

Geoff understood. Home for Troy wasn't Boulder or Texas or Syracuse or really anywhere else. Troy's home had been with Arnie and following the rodeo around and then with him and with Carter. Troy hadn't been away from home in over twenty years.

And he hadn't had to miss Troy even for a day in all that time.

He returned the touches when he could, squeezed Troy's fingers if they lingered long enough. Every touch, every sigh made Troy smile, relaxing more and more.

They were in a corner, protected from view from most of the restaurant, so it didn't surprise him when Troy dared to kiss his cheek.

He blushed again; it seemed to be his lot tonight. "How's your steak, honey?" Implied in that question was a longer conversation that included, "I missed you," and "I love you," and he knew that Troy heard it.

"Exceptional. Want a bite? I'll share."

"Yes, please. You should try my pasta. It's luscious." He twirled up a big bite for Troy on his fork.

Troy cut him a generous bite, and they exchanged forks.

"What?" Carter asked. "You're not going to feed him?"

"No, Sir. We're adults." He beamed at Carter.

Carter rolled his eyes, and Geoff knew he'd be over Carter's lap for a few playful swats if they were home. "That you are, *boys*."

But they weren't home yet, were they? He could get away with a little fun. He elbowed Troy. "The steak is seasoned just perfect."

"I thought so. I do love a steak. I just don't think about ordering them often."

"Well, you need your energy more these days to keep up with your Dom." Saul was young, but Carter had nothing but respect and that was enough for Geoff. Plus, Geoff and Saul had become friends. Real friends, he thought.

He remembered the first time Saul joined their Sunday group, when everyone tried to tease Saul about being a baby Dom. Saul made sure that didn't last long, impressing everyone out of the gate. Saul and Troy had a conversation, and within what seemed like minutes, Troy was on his knees. Nobody thought of Saul as green after that.

"I do, but it works. I think he might keep me." Troy glanced at Saul, and they stared at each other for a second. The love just glowed.

"Consider yourself kept."

Damn. The possessive tone in Saul's answer made little hairs on the back of Geoff's neck stand up.

Me too, please.

A whole cheesecake in a box landed on the table next to Troy, and Carter nodded to the server. "Perfect. Thank you. May we have our check as well, please?"

"I have it right here."

The server set it down in front of Carter, but Saul reached across Carter and snatched it. "Got it!"

"Butthead," Carter shot back, trying for it.

Troy leaned against Geoff, whispering softly, "I'm so glad I don't have to worry about that part anymore, love."

Love.

Every time Troy said that, his heart jumped and pounded. He wondered if it would always do that. He thought maybe it would; it still did for Carter. He reached out and traced Troy's bottom lip with one finger.

"Nope. We can just let them duke it out and sit here smiling at each other."

"Works for me." Troy brushed his fingertip with a barely there kiss. "God, I missed y'all. It was nice to meet all of Saul's people, but I am so glad to be home."

"We have a surprise for you at home." He grinned at Troy. "A big surprise. And Carter spent some time working on ideas for the gift you're going to build him. With help from me, of course."

"Yeah? Excellent. I'll start working on it after the first of the year. I can't wait to see what all y'all thought about." Troy waggled his fingers in front of his face. "I'm good with my hands."

"Boys, we're ready. Come on." Carter pulled out Geoff's chair.

Sweet and in a hurry. So cute. He couldn't remember the last time Carter was this eager to get home. Geoff popped up out of his chair and pulled on his coat. "Love you." He gave his master a wink as they headed out the door.

He felt someone grab his ass on the way out the door and looked over his shoulder to fuss at Carter, finding Saul right there instead.

Saul looked right at him. "Looking forward to seeing that tonight."

"Oh." Okay. He liked that idea.

Carter nodded. "Won't be too long a drive."

Saul rubbed his hands together. "Hot tub?"

"Maybe. We might have something better."

"Better than the hot tub?"

"Yeah, the new coffee pot." Geoff climbed into the back with Troy.

"Ha! I'm glad you like it so much."

"He adores it, and I'm making use of it myself." Carter grinned at him through the rearview.

"When I let him." He drew his fingers through Troy's hair, wrapping a curl around one finger and giving it a light tug.

Troy leaned in, moving right into him. "More kisses, please?"

"Hm. I don't know if I brought enough with me," he teased Troy, hovering close but not offering a kiss. "You have to share, you know. Other people might want a couple."

"I've been saving them up for years and years." Troy swooped in and kissed him hard.

"Mm!" His surprised squawk was muted by the kiss, and he grabbed at Troy's coat for balance. Troy was everywhere he could see, everything he could hear, and he returned the kiss eagerly, wanting a taste of whatever Troy had for him.

"They're being naughty again, Carter. We're going to have to watch them in the back seat."

"Let them. If I weren't driving, I'd be naughty too."

"Aren't we supposed to be setting a good example?" Saul laughed softly. "I missed you too."

Carter's chuckle was low, and Geoff could hear the

hunger in the sound. "Maybe after three or four days, it'll be more of a low roar again, hmm?"

"Maybe. We're on vacation. Even I might be a little worn out by then."

He giggled against Troy's lips; he couldn't help it. The banter in the front seat just made him happy. "I think they like each other a little," he whispered to Troy.

"I'm so glad. This is..." Troy shrugged, grinned sheepishly. "I don't have the words."

Troy didn't need them; he knew exactly. "Me neither, but yeah. It's right. It's what it should be."

"Keep your clothes on, boys. We're getting close to home." Carter took a corner hard, and Saul laughed.

"If we live that long."

"I've driven with you, Master Saul." Geoff rolled his eyes. "In the snow. You don't have much talking room."

"Touché. But I'm going to remember that, boy."

"Oops?" He winked at Troy.

Troy leaned in, lips at his ear. "He has an amazing hand. I didn't know..."

"Didn't know...what, honey?" Geoff smoothed a hand over Troy's shoulder.

"How amazing a simple spanking could be. How satisfying it is."

Geoff grinned wide. It was one of Carter's go-tos for when he was anxious and unsettled, and he loved it. "Simple, right? And there's nothing like that skin-to-skin connection." That's what was so wonderful about it. A quick, uncomplicated connection. Floggers and other toys were great, too, but... it was different. "Arnie wasn't a spanker, huh?"

"No. He used a belt, and he could be slappy, but this was different."

He winced inwardly but made sure it didn't show. A belt wasn't love, but maybe none of that mattered anymore. Saul was love.

"Totally different. It's fun discovering something new, isn't it?" It didn't happen that often with him and Carter anymore, but sometimes things happened by surprise, or Carter would want to try something out. He liked those moments, even when they discovered they didn't work for them. Fresh was fun.

"Yeah. Just wait until I make Carter his Christmas present. You two can play."

Us two. Maybe four.

"I can't wait."

"All right, gentlemen. We're home." Carter turned up the driveway, truck rolling over the snow like it wasn't there, and parked next to Saul's brand-spanking-new truck, which had been sitting there since they took the guys to the airport.

"I'll grab our bags. Master." Troy grinned over at Geoff and winked. "I may have to do a load of laundry in the morning."

"Geoff, you'll help Troy. Right? Just put the bags in the guest room, boy." Saul took Carter's hand. "We're staying the night."

"Of course I will." He wanted to show Saul and Troy the bed. "Can I..."

"Just the guest room and then down to sit on the sofa, boy." Ah, Carter wanted to wait.

Saul pulled Carter inside, and Geoff and Troy got the suitcases. "So were you happy to come home early?" He held the door with his back and let Troy go in ahead of him.

"I was. They were so nice, but I was ready for y'all and my mountains and real life." Troy sat one of the suitcases down. "Mostly y'all."

He nodded. "Saul was ready too. He told Carter you guys needed to come home and he was going to change your flights." He set the other suitcase beside Troy's and looked into Troy's bright green eyes. "I missed you, but the rest wasn't too bad this year."

"Good. I worried. Carter's ink is amazing. I love it." Troy pushed right into his arms. "I love y'all."

"I worried also, and we love you." He held Troy until he worried that Saul and Carter would be looking for them. "Our masters are probably waiting, huh?"

"They're making out, I bet, and we're missing it."

"Too pretty to miss. Come on."

Troy grabbed his hand and tugged, suddenly lit with excitement. "Let's go."

"Shh. Sh."

Geoff slowed Troy down, and they crept down the stairs and into the living room, finding exactly what they'd expected—maybe better—Saul and Carter making out, standing in front of the fireplace. Carter had his fingers in Saul's hair and Saul's hands rested low on Carter's hips.

"See?" he whispered. "Pretty."

"Gorgeous." Troy sounded stunned, pleased, wanton, and one of his hands slid around Geoff's waist.

"Should we worry about the boys?" Saul looked right into Carter's eyes, the emotion between them obvious even from across the room.

"No. They're standing right over there." Carter grinned at Saul, and neither of them so much as glanced in Geoff and Troy's direction.

"Naughty. They might need to worry about us."

"I'm not worried. Are you, Geoff?" Troy was husky, the words pure sex.

"Nope." He took Troy's hand, moving toward their masters. "I'm actually very turned on."

Saul did look over then, right at him. "Maybe we can have the cheesecake for breakfast."

"Or tomorrow for dessert," Carter murmured, one arm held open to them. "Come here, boys."

"Hey," Saul said softly as Geoff got close.

"Hello, Sir."

He and Troy were pulled in, their four heads pressed together like points on a compass, quietly breathing each other in.

Geoff felt that last bit of tension ease, and he could see it, too, in all his lovers' faces.

Carter leaned toward him. "Do you think we should give them their Christmas present finally, boy?"

Oh, he was so ready. He started smiling, the grin so big it pulled at the corners of his lips.

"I think he's ready." Troy's lips brushed Geoff's cheek.

"Must be a pony. Look how excited he is." Saul chuckled.

"Mmm. Not a pony." Carter straightened up. "Bigger."

"Bigger than a pony?"

"Yes. Huge. And it's upstairs." Geoff got behind Troy and pushed his lover toward the stairs.

"Should we be scared?" Saul asked. "Troy, you know them. Should we be terrified?"

Troy giggled, the sound soft and shockingly young. "Totally. Geoff's a prankster, remember."

"You know us, too, I think, Saul." Carter herded Saul along as well and they climbed the steps laughing and poking at each other.

"Wait. Wait a sec." Geoff covered Troy's eyes and looked at Carter.

"Oh. I got Saul." Carter covered Saul's eyes. "Don't peek, or I'll spank you."

Saul snorted. "Yeah? Good luck with that."

"Where are we going, Geoff?" Troy wasn't the least bit tense.

"Right... in here." He steered Troy into the master bedroom and waited for Carter. "On three?"

"It's your show, boy."

"Good. One, two, three." He let go of Troy's eyes but didn't look at the bed that he and Carter had carefully made up that morning. He was watching Troy. He wanted to see the reaction.

"Whoa."

That was Saul.

"No way." Saul was gaping. "That's the biggest bed I've ever seen."

"Oh Geoff. It's for all of us." Troy looked stunned. "All four of us."

Saul took two running steps and dove, landing on his back in the middle the bed, arms and legs spread wide. "Check this out!" Saul laughed, grinning like a fiend. "Come on, you guys!"

Troy kissed him, sweet and slow and then Troy went to Carter and lifted his face for a kiss. "Thank you."

"You're welcome."

Carter kissed Troy, and it was so pretty. Geoff let them have their moment. He crawled up on the bed beside Saul, who rolled right up on top of him.

"I love it. It's the perfect gift. Thank you."

"You're welcome." He barely got the words out before Saul kissed him, one hot hand sliding up under his shirt.

He moaned and leaned into the touch, opening for

Saul's exploring tongue. This wasn't soft and yielding like Troy, but curious and hungry, burning hot.

"Did you see the tie-downs?"

Saul broke off their kiss abruptly. "Did Carter just say tie-downs?"

"Two sets, for two subs." He beamed at Saul, although he missed that kiss already. "Want to see?"

"Is that a real question?"

Both Carter and Troy started laughing, Carter leading Troy over to show Saul the sturdy hooks, hidden by decorative bits of molding.

"Damn. I do like a tricky bed, don't I, boy?" Saul winked at Troy.

"You do, Master." Troy looked unsure, looking toward the bed, then toward Carter.

Carter brushed Troy's cheek with the back of one hand. "Go ahead, it's yours too. Ours."

Geoff held out a hand. "Come on, honey."

"Wow." Troy crawled into the bed, moving right into his arms. "Our bed, huh?"

"Ours. I'm hoping the two of you spend a lot of time in it."

"Boy." Carter was giving him a look.

"Sorry. Sir."

"What Geoff means is that you should consider yourselves welcome here any time."

Troy grinned at Geoff, pressed their foreheads together. "This means we can spend the night together more often. New Year's Eve."

"New Year's for sure. Any time. It feels pretty empty just the two of us."

"I think I like what Geoff said before. About us spending

a lot of time in it." He heard Saul laugh, but Troy was so close right now, stretched out with him. He was distracted.

"Bunch of one-track minds." Carter sighed. "All entirely too clothed."

"We can fix that." Saul started tugging on Carter's shirt.

"We can." Carter's voice was getting rough, and he knew that tone. Geoff could see his Master working Troy's shirt off.

"Definitely." Geoff reached down and loosened his jeans, playing a little tug of war with Saul and getting one arm free before he pushed the jeans down over his hips. Saul growled so he helped finish with the shirt first, then wiggled free of his jeans, which Saul took and tossed off the foot of the bed.

"Damn, you're pretty." Saul ran one hand down along his chest, tracing his ink. "You going to decorate me too? You going to leave your mark on me?"

"Can I?" God, he'd love that. "Carter wants you to have one to match his."

"I'd like that. You'll have to be careful with me. It'll be my first time."

"I'm always careful." Oh, his ink and no one else's? Perfect.

"You can handle it, babe."

Geoff smiled at Carter calling Saul "babe."

"If you say so." Saul seemed to like it too. "I trust you."

Geoff nodded, daring to lean in and brush his lips against Saul's, the little spark of electricity enough to make his eyes cross.

"Mmm. I'll take that." Saul cupped a hand behind his head and kissed him again, those hips still covered in denim scraping against Geoff's prick.

Behind him somewhere, Troy moaned.

He wanted to know, but he didn't want to disturb the kiss, the way Saul took his lips was too good to look away.

Carter moved in behind him on the bed, he didn't need to look to know those hands or the musky scent of his Master. Troy was on Saul's other side, working those jeans down over Saul's lean hips.

"This bed is amazing." Saul whispered to him and reached back for Troy.

"Merry Christmas." The last of the words were gasps because his Master's fingers found his nipples and tugged.

Saul rolled and coaxed Troy in between them, and Geoff reached for the other sub. "Yeah. Hey, honey."

One of Carter's hands landed solid on his ass, and he pressed into it, even as he tried to get closer to Troy.

"Hey." Troy leaned in, stealing a happy kiss, fingers in his hair. Troy tugged carefully, not enough to hurt, but enough to tingle.

Carter's lips touched Geoff's shoulder and his master's fingers, slid over his hip, lighting his skin on fire. He shivered, anticipating what would come next as those fingers pushed under his balls. "Sir..."

Troy leaned back into Saul's arms, putting a little space between them.

"Geoff's been anxious for you to share this with us." Carter's fingers circled and stroked and tugged his balls, making it hard to concentrate on the other two.

"What do you think, boy? We can't have Geoff anxious, can we?" Saul's voice was teasing, playful.

"No, Sir. How can I help?"

God, Troy was so sweet, so needy, and unbearably fucking obedient.

"Why don't you see how he tastes? Try his nipples."

"Mmm. He'll like that." Carter gave his balls another tug

and made him moan.

"That would be my pleasure." Troy held Geoff's gaze as he spoke, the connection only breaking when Troy got too close.

Jesus, Troy was the hottest thing ever. Geoff hissed as Troy drew a hot tongue across one of his nipples. It was all he could do not to swear. "God."

Saul and Carter exchanged a kiss over his head.

Troy focused on his left one—soft suction was interspersed with sharp, tiny little bites. Maddening. Troy was driving him crazy.

There were hands on him everywhere, and a moan from deep in his gut forced its way up and out. Carter's hands, maybe Troy's, maybe Saul's... he just couldn't tell. "Fuck, guys."

The chuckle was Saul's, the soft "tsk" in his ear was Carter.

The "oops" was totally Troy.

Troy hissed after that, and he looked down to watch Saul twisting Troy's nipple piercings. Fuck, that had to sting. Maybe he should ask Carter if he could get them too.

Troy looked like he was into it, like he was right there, focused on Saul's touch.

Carter was rocking, thick cock rubbing hard against him, and he arched back, wanting.

"Pretty little slut. You want my cock?" Oh. Carter was on fire, was playing up for Saul.

"Yes, Sir. Want you inside me. Please, Sir." He wanted his master hot, and if Carter wanted to put on a show, he was all in. "Please!"

"Good boy." Carter's fingers pressed into his hole, hot and slick.

Finally. Fuck, that felt so good. He sighed and shifted his leg to give Carter more room.

"Nice. What do you think, boy? Isn't Geoff stunning?" Saul's voice was low.

"Perfect. He's perfect." Troy's voice was shredded, raw and rough with emotion. "Master..."

"You want him, boy? You want Geoff to have you? Let Master Carter drive?"

His eyes crossed, just the suggestion making him groan.

Troy whimpered softly. "I want y'all. God help me, I love all y'all."

"We've got you, boy. You'll have all of us. Give your master your mouth."

"Fuck, yeah. Come on, Troy."

Carter shifted and Saul slid up to the headboard, someone's fingers sheathed Geoff's cock in latex.

"Oh, God." They were going to let him have Troy. "Troy. Is this okay? Are you okay?" Saul knew Troy's safewords, right?

"Please, honey. I've wanted so long."

That was all Troy got out before he took Saul's cock in his mouth.

Carter groaned. "I want to feel that mouth again. Not now. Now I need my boy."

"Please, Sir." God, he was aching. He wanted... everything. Troy, his Master. He was so close. The waiting was killing him.

"Breathe, boys." Carter took him by the hips and whispered in his ear so soft he was sure only he could hear. "Go on, love. He's yours."

"Mine...?" He'd dreamed, fanaticized even, but he'd never dared imagine this would be real. He hadn't been inside another man since he was too young and stupid to understand what it meant.

"Take him." Saul's order was incredibly both gentle and firm at the same time.

"Love you." Geoff meant all of them, but especially hoped Troy heard him. He lined up and pushed in, gasping as Troy stretched around the head of his aching cock. "Oh. Oh, fuck."

Saul cried out, eyes wide. "Fuck, Troy's good. He likes it. Take him. Now."

"Yes, Sir." He looked up at Saul, but Master Saul's eyes weren't on him. He only had a second to register that Saul had been talking to Carter when his master took him hard, forcing him deep into Troy.

He shouted and the room erupted in sound—grunts and moans and rough gasps. He tried to find his own rhythm, but it was impossible. He belonged to his master, and Carter had all the control. He bent over Troy's back, watching the ink—his work—twist and stretch and bend as Troy moved under him.

Geoff couldn't breathe; he couldn't focus. All he could do was move and feel. And hear Carter urging him on. Saul's hands were holding Troy's head and he glanced up to find those blue eyes laser focused over his head, watching his Master. So hot.

Carter shifted and Geoff gasped as every nerve started to buzz. "Again. Fuck, please, Master." Geoff really had no idea if he'd managed to say that out loud.

"That's one, beautiful boy." He'd complain, but then Carter pegged his ass again, slamming into him and making him shake. The pressure on Geoff's gland sent lights flashing behind his eyes.

"Oh God. Sir! Troy!"

"Fuck!" Saul shouted suddenly, drawing Geoff's focus. Saul's head rolled back to rest against the headboard and

Geoff watched as Saul went still for a second and then rocked up off the mattress and into Troy's mouth. "Good boy."

Jesus, Saul looked shattered.

"Make him come, boy." Carter pulled some weight off him, and suddenly he was able to move. The order wasn't even necessary; as soon as Geoff had room, he drove into Troy hard, trying to push Troy higher while fighting for focus as he rocked back onto Carter's cock after every thrust.

"Troy. Fuck, come on, honey. Let me feel you."

"Geoff!" Troy was sobbing, asshole gripping his cock, working him wildly. "Please, help me."

Carter's voice sounded in his ear. "You're making him wild, boy. Making him lose his mind."

Help?

Geoff had a second of panic, not understanding what Troy was asking and he glanced up at Saul. Saul mouthed, "Touch him", calm as could be and gave him a wink.

Oh.

"I've got you." Geoff slid a hand over Troy's hip. Troy's cock was hot and strained into his fingers, and he pushed his thumb through the slit, working it against the piercing there.

He felt the weight of his touch ripple all through Troy's body. The sweet ass grabbed his dick, milking him almost painfully as spunk sprayed over his fingers.

Geoff's gasp got stuck in his throat so that he managed little more a strangled sound and rocked back against his master.

Carter growled and dove into him, pinning him against Troy again. Geoff saw stars as he came and dropped his head to Troy's back, holding on, offering everything he had left to his master. Carter took it, slamming into him and making his oversensitive body scream. He needed to give this to his Master, take what Carter needed to give him.

"Let him have it, stud." He wasn't sure when Saul had moved out from under Troy, but Carter's rough pants and grunts were cut off suddenly, muffled by what sounded like a deep kiss.

He swore he could feel Carter's cock swell inside him, stretching his hole and making him gasp and then his master was filling him, marking him deep inside.

The kiss broke off and Carter gulped in a breath, mumbling, "Good boy," to him. The words from his master filled him, making him happy. Making him proud.

Saul flopped back on the bed and whispered to Troy, offering gentle kisses and running a hand over Troy's brow and through the sub's hair.

Everything was so sensitive; it didn't matter who moved, it made him shudder. It was almost too intense. "Sir..."

"Shh. I have you, boy." Carter's voice was soft, and suddenly he was pulled away from Troy, wrapped in his blanket and cocooned. "I have you."

"Yes, Sir. Love you." He leaned into his master hard, letting the heavy blanket along with Carter's warmth and words settle him. "Troy's okay?"

Saul answered him. "He is. Troy's just perfect, Geoff. He's floating, feeling good. Aren't you, boy?"

"Mmhmm. Good, Sir." He'd never heard Troy sound like that, oddly distant, happy.

"Mmm. See that, boy? You made him fly."

He knew it wasn't all him, it was all of them, but he smiled anyway. He loved seeing Troy in Saul's arms, being solidly with his own master and all of them together. He was over the moon.

That was the way to break in a bed.

16

Carter woke up with Geoff on his right side, still wrapped tight in his blanket. Saul was on his left, sprawled out and exposed.

As for Troy?

He smelled cinnamon rolls and coffee, heard the sounds of barely-there humming and someone doing laundry.

Now his question was, stay up here with these lovers or go downstairs with that lover?

"Mmm. Cinnamon?" Saul stretched out long and then rolled up and tucked an arm over his middle. "Oh. You're not Troy."

"I'm not." He leaned in and took his kiss. "Good morning. He's downstairs."

"Good morning. I'm not disappointed." Saul gave him another. "This is awesome, waking up with you."

"It is. Merry Christmas." His holiday was really starting now.

"Merry Christmas." Saul looked over him at Geoff. "Is he still out? He doesn't look like he moved at all."

"He's resting, soul-deep. He was stressing. Now he can

breathe." Geoff needed his family to be together, good or bad.

"Troy too. But he doesn't need rest; he needs what he's doing right now."

Carter nodded. Taking care of them, feeding them.

"How about you? Not stressed at all, huh?" He heard the gentle teasing in Saul's tone, but it was softened even further by the fingers combing through his hair.

"To quote your boy, I'm as happy as a pig in shit." He did love his Troy-isms. "Hell, there's nothing to be stressed about right now, is there?" They were all there, Troy was making breakfast, and they were naked.

"Not right now, nope." Saul let it go at that, but those bright blue eyes held his. "You're a handsome guy, did you know that?"

Carter fluttered his eyelashes outrageously. "Who, moi?"

He knew he wasn't butt ugly, but he'd never made anyone goo-goo eyed.

"Of course. It wouldn't be worth saying that to your sleeping sub, would it?" Saul smiled at him. "Should we get up and have some of that fancy coffee?"

"We should. When did Troy get up?" He turned to Geoff, making sure his boy was swaddled but able to get out at will.

"I don't know exactly. Early. Twenty years of getting up at 4:00 a.m. is just in his bones now." Saul sat up, scratching sleep out of that mop of hair. "He doesn't sleep in unless I give him a reason to. Or an order."

"And then he wiggles and hums and reads, hmm?" He slipped out of bed and grabbed two of the soft robes Geoff had chosen. He was tickled shitless to see that Troy had grabbed one for himself.

"Makes me insane. Me, I like to sleep late when I can. So

I don't make it an order often." Saul took a robe from him and slid it on. "Oh, this is nice. Thanks."

"Geoff chose them. They're soft and warm, and we'll need them this winter."

"I suppose we will." Saul followed him down the stairs so closely it was a wonder they didn't trip on each other. As they made their way into the kitchen, Saul put an arm around his waist. "Boy? I smell something delicious."

"Cinnamon rolls and bacon. Coffee?" Troy went to Saul, offering his lips.

"Mmm." Saul gathered Troy close like he was precious, kissed the boy like it was as essential as breath. "I like bacon."

"Master." Troy melted against Saul with a quiet little sigh. "Good morning."

"It is a good morning, isn't it?" Saul gave Troy another quick peck." Give Master Carter a kiss and then get us some coffee, please." Saul went to the stove and peeked in at the cinnamon rolls. Carter appreciated the way Saul set the tone for the day right away, giving Troy clear expectations.

"Master Carter." Troy came to him, raising up on tiptoe, brushing their lips together. Carter placed his hands on Troy's hips, leaning down so that the brush became a real, solid connection. Troy hummed softly, tongue sliding on his lips, hot enough to make him shiver.

Saul laughed softly. "Maybe the boy wants you for breakfast."

Wasn't that a lovely thought? He chuckled, though, and let Troy off the hook. "I'm available, but don't you need your coffee?"

"I do. Such a sacrifice. You're good to me." Saul leaned against the counter, grinning. "Troy can get a taste of you for dessert tonight."

"I'll take you up on that. I've missed your boy's mouth." He rubbed the lips in question, and Troy sucked his finger in. Goddamn.

"Sorry, you'll have to wait for next Thanksgiving." Saul teased, not even trying to break them up. "Geoff though..."

"Geoff could write odes. He says—" Christ, Troy was working him like a goddamn hoover. "He says there's no one better."

"In my scientific opinion, I would have to agree." Saul stepped up behind Troy and slipped a hand into the robe where it opened at Troy's chest. He had an imagination; he could guess what Saul had done to make Troy gasp and let go of his finger. "Coffee, boy."

"Yes, Master." Troy winked at him, wicked as hell, before heading to make their coffees.

"It's like a magic button, eh, Saul?"

"Hasn't let me down yet." Saul took Carter's arm and led him out to the living room. "Should we have a fire? Or did you think maybe we were going somewhere today?"

"I hoped to enjoy each other, relax." They could watch movies, chat, eat. "I'll start the fire. I brought a shit-ton of wood up."

"We were hoping the same. I'll help. Show me how you do this fire thing. I'm good with a campfire, but my brother's picky about how you set up in his fireplace."

"It's simple. I should have gone with Troy's gas fireplace, but I was stubborn."

"Nah. This is way more manly. What's a fire if you don't put in some effort? You can convert it when you're old."

One of the mugs hit the counter in the kitchen with a definite click.

Oh, he was the authority in Troy-kitchen-ese. Someone had hit a nerve.

Saul sighed and looked toward the kitchen, then gave Carter a shrug. "I'm in trouble no matter what I say next, aren't I?"

"Just let it go. Actions are important." Carter kept his voice low. "This is all new. This whole holiday. He's trying hard, right?"

"He's doing great. I couldn't ask for more. And I've learned a lot, too, to be honest. About him, about what's reasonable especially, about needs."

"Yeah? Excellent. That part is exciting as hell." He missed it, but only rarely. There was something wonderful about knowing you had forever.

"It is." Saul nodded thoughtfully. "Even when you know you've made mistakes."

"We all make mistakes, man. We're human." That was easy. Perfection caused ulcers.

"I know. And it's not like he's in pieces over it. It's just a fact, so I'm not beating myself up. Much." Saul winked at him. "I thought the new machine Troy bought you made a fast brew?"

"Yeah. Maybe he's poisoning it."

"I was pulling out the cinnamon rolls before they burned." Troy handed them each a coffee. "If I was going to poison you, I'd do it at work."

He snorted. "Ah, yes. Too obvious here, I suppose. I'll watch my back."

"I guess I'm safe then." Saul took a sip from the mug Troy handed him.

"Possibly." Troy rolled his eyes and gave Saul a quick kiss on the cheek. "Should I go wake Geoff? The rolls need ten to cool."

"Carter? Should we let Geoff sleep or wake him?"

"You can wake him, Troy. Just be gentle. And don't let

him pull you back into bed. It's one of his favorite tricks."

Saul laughed. "You speak from experience, I take it?"

"He can be very... persuasive."

Troy was almost bouncing on the way up to the bedroom.

Saul tilted his head. "There's no way Troy's going to resist, is there?"

"Not a chance."

Geoff was madly in love, and Troy was happy to snuggle in.

"I can look the other way for a while. They need it. And there's bacon. There might even be a fire eventually."

"Don't make me swat you." He had to chuckle, though, and he headed out to get some logs. "Grab some of that newspaper, you butthead."

"Swat me. I'd like to see you try it."

It was bitter cold out, and he could smell the snow coming. Carter's bathrobe wasn't helping at all, he worried his testicles might never drop again. Oh, fuck a duck. Good thing they had no plans. He might sit on Saul and use him to warm up all his parts.

"Jesus Christ!" He guessed Saul had regrets about coming to hold open the door for him. "Get in here. It's fucking frigid."

"No shit. Almost too cold to snow." His nipples were so hard they were about to slice through his robe.

Saul hustled him in and closed the door, giggling. "I won't tell Geoff the cold is making you swear."

What? Carter stopped short and then he made the connection, his own laughter bursting out of him. "Oh, man. I have to tell you; that's a rule for my boy. I make it approximately an hour into opening at the diner before I am tearing somebody up."

Saul's jaw dropped. "Oh man. I was so impressed with that principle. You've shattered your pristine image."

"Oh good. It's hard to be pristine with your lover." He wanted to have a friend, a lover, a partner that knew him.

"I'm decidedly not pristine myself." Saul wadded up newspaper while he set the logs in the fireplace. "So why the rule? Just something to keep Geoff on his toes? Or is there a reason?"

"I prefer it in a scene, especially in a public scene. It's a matter of respect." He got everything set up, put in the starter and the paper. "And it gives him an easy way to ask for a spanking without asking, no matter where we are."

"I knew I was going to learn from you." Saul was sincere, and brushed fingers down his arm, making sure he knew it.

Well, damn. That heated him, all the way to the core, and he hid the blush in the nascent fire. "We're going to learn from each other a lot."

He'd never hoped for a lover who was a Dominant too. He hadn't known it could happen, but it had, and it was amazing.

"I hope so. And it's kind of wild knowing we'll have to figure out some things together, right? About them." Saul slid a hand down his back and cupped one ass cheek. "About us."

"About us." He liked the sound of that. He didn't remember the last time someone besides his boy touched him so easily.

"Come on, Old Man. Let's steal cinnamon rolls and then I'll tell you a secret." Saul flashed a flirty grin at him that made the kid really look like a kid.

"Ooh..." Secrets? He was all over shared secrets. He wrapped his arm around Saul's waist and led him toward the kitchen. "Do you want glaze on them?"

"Is that even a debate? Who doesn't want glaze on them? And don't say you. I don't know if I can take another shock after the swearing thing." Saul took his coffee cup and started making refills.

He snorted, grabbed the powdered sugar and the milk, and started making his glaze. "I love the sweet stuff. You know that."

"I do. The important question, though, is how do you take your coffee? I should know this."

"Cream and sugar, please." Every little thing they learned about each other made it better, richer, and he found himself a little overwhelmed by the simple question.

"Cream and sugar." Saul went to the fridge and pulled out the cream. "I like those flavored things when they're available, or just some cream if not. Troy buys me this yummy creamer."

Saul set his mug down on the counter next to their breakfast. "Oh man. Those look so good."

"He's one hell of a cook." Hell, Troy was one hell of a man. "He couldn't cook at all when I hired him, but it didn't take him two weeks before he was on the line." God, Troy had been a baby, so scared, so shaken—this little red-headed sub with huge green eyes and bruises covering him, buckles in his shaking hands. Christ.

"That sounds like the man I know. Totally capable." Saul looked thoughtful for a second, then smiled and picked up a plate. "Come on, let's sit. I don't think we'll see the boys for a while yet, and I did promise you a secret."

"Let's sit by the fire." He wanted to be able to touch, but he also needed a blanket for his legs. Normally he'd just run up and grab bottoms, but he wanted to allow the boys their morning.

Saul set everything down on the coffee table and eagerly

dug a fork into one of the rolls. "Mmm. Oh, I picked the right sub. So good."

Carter nodded, but his mouth was full. Troy had perfected this recipe about ten years ago and it was so, so good. Geoff had wanted more cinnamon, Carter didn't care for raisins, and all those changes had made the current incarnation sweet.

He had to wonder what Saul would bring to it.

"So. Ready?" Saul glanced over, then leaned forward and picked up his coffee. He looked for a minute like maybe he was going to hide in his cup, but Saul finished that sip and caught Carter's eye, grinning. "I have never been fucked. I'm a totally kinky and confident virgin."

Oh, that made his balls draw up, and he forced himself to not groan. "Lucky for you, I can not only keep your secret, I'm totally interested in helping you experience a nice, long fuck."

Saul's grin changed into a shy smile and his lover blushed a deep pink but still managed to hold his gaze. "I've never been interested, honestly, but I've been thinking about you a lot lately. You get me. I think you understand what it needs to be. And I'm curious. I want to know."

"I do understand." And he understood that this would be theirs, something between lovers, something they could share. "We'll have to make a day that's ours."

He had no doubt he could make it good. None.

Saul nodded, offering a little more honesty. A little more for him. "That's what I want. I want you. To myself." Saul cleared his throat and reached for another bite of breakfast. "And that should be easy enough. We just offer them a day to themselves. Tell them to go out and have some fun."

"Troy will want Geoff to help build my Christmas

present. Hell, the boys would love a regular day to just be together. They like to snuggle."

"Perfect." Saul gave him a hot look. "They can build here, and we can fuck at our place. I like it."

"I do too." He reached out, slid his hand in the robe, and cupped Saul's balls, rolling them nice and easy. "We'll take our time."

Saul sighed and leaned in to kiss him. "Bed's not as big, but there's a gas fireplace."

Butthead. "Well, you know Troy. He's old." He pushed in and brought their lips together.

"Mhm." Saul laughed into the kiss, then moaned when Carter gave his lover's balls a little tug. "You play dirty."

Saul had no idea. "Never."

He stroked the line of skin behind Saul's sac, pushing nice and firm, making Saul feel it.

Saul's hips rolled back, giving him more room, and Saul's hands pushed into his robe, fingers finding his nipples and rolling them in warm fingers.

"Jesus." Saul's fingers were fucking magic, the pressure making his eyes cross. Carter was just going to have to give as much back. He used his nail this time, dragging it across the little strip again.

Saul gasped, eyes going wide. "Fuck, Carter."

The moan didn't come from Saul this time, but it was very familiar.

"Shh. They'll hear you."

"I know, but *fuck*."

Saul pulled away enough to look at him. "Naughty boys."

"They are." He stroked again, then gave Saul a wink. "You think we should go punish them?"

"See?" Troy didn't even bother to whisper that time.

Saul swallowed, stifling what he knew should have been a moan. "Yes. Should we let them eat something first? My boy's a bear when his blood sugar is low."

"Absolutely." Carter grinned, then threw his head back. "You two better get your asses down here, *tout suite!*"

Saul laughed into his sleeve at the thunder of footsteps in the stairwell. When their subs came into view, though, Saul's face changed entirely. "Knees."

Geoff and Troy hit their knees right away, and if that wasn't proof enough they were feeling guilty, nothing was.

Carter waited long enough that both boys looked uncomfortable. "What did I tell you, boy?"

"Don't let him pull you into bed."

"It's not like you to disobey, boy. Did you tell Geoff what Master Carter said?"

"He did. It's not all his fault." Geoff was almost stammering.

"Was I talking to you, boy?" Saul looked at him, a little hint of amusement in the lift of his lover's eyebrow.

Geoff sighed. "No, Sir."

Troy just nodded. "He was warm. I dozed off a second."

"I don't know, Carter. They're almost too adorable to punish. Almost. Go get breakfast and coffee, and Master Carter and I will discuss what to do with you both." Saul gave them a wave. "And bring the bacon out with you when you come back."

Troy stood and held out a hand to Geoff. "I made cinnamon rolls for us."

"Did you put raisins in them?" Oh, his boy was *cruising*.

Troy giggled softly. "Come on, turkey."

"God, I love them." Saul watched them go, then stood up and straightened the robe Carter had done a nice job of mussing up. "So, they both need to settle. Thoughts?"

"What works best for your boy? Mine loves a light spanking, a blindfold, sometimes I drape him over the arm of the couch even and go about my day." That one made his boy crazy, because Geoff felt exposed and vulnerable.

"Troy can kneel all day long without blinking. He needs a little stimulation. Something that interrupts his Zen. I have this great set of nipple clamps he's into. I could pull those out. I've never tried a blindfold with him, so I don't know how he'd feel about that. New things can be great, like those clamps. Wow. But I'm always worried I'll hit a nerve. Arnie did some damage."

He tried not to wince, but he did. He'd been Arnie's best friend, but it had been years before Troy, and they'd come to the lifestyle separately. He'd had no idea until years after Arnie's death that it had been rough when Geoff had come to him. "I didn't know, man, about Arnie. I met Troy after Arnie died."

"No, I know that. It's just a fact. It's something you should know about. We haven't run into anything all that traumatic yet, but it's always possible. I will tell you that punishments aren't a thing with Troy. They don't work; they're pointless. He's a perfect sub. So I just keep him off-balance, make him work to focus. More discipline kind of stuff."

That made sense because, honestly, the spankings were proof to Geoff that he cared enough to discipline, that he knew Geoff needed. "The clamps were a success, though? Excellent."

"He loved them. And they did the trick."

The boys arrived quietly with their food and coffee and the plate of bacon. Saul reached right down and grabbed a piece.

"No touching, boys." Saul practically inhaled the bacon.

Carter wasn't sure Saul had even chewed it. "And you can speak to us if you need to but not to each other. What are your safewords, Geoff?"

"Red and yellow, Sir..." Geoff looked at Carter, wide-eyed, and he just smiled.

"And yours, Troy?" he asked.

"Red and yellow." Troy was beginning to frown.

"Not to worry, boy." Saul cupped a hand under Troy's chin. "I just need to know because if Geoff uses one of his words and Master Carter is in the bathroom, I better know what's up. Right?"

"Yes, Sir." Troy leaned close, whispering just loud enough that he could hear. "Can I sit in your lap? Please?"

God, so sweet. His boy was way more of an active challenge, thank God.

"Yes..." Saul drew the word out curiously, settled back down on the couch, and held his arms out.

"I'm sorry." Troy curled in and held Saul for a long minute. "Thank you, Master."

Carter sipped his coffee and watched them together, paying attention to how Saul took care of Troy, speaking softly but firmly.

"We're not angry, either of us. But I think I made my expectations clear this morning, and Master Carter did warn you. Geoff is quite the temptation, isn't he? We've got a couple of days off still. You and Geoff will get time, lots of it. I promise."

"It's so hard to tell him no now that I can say yes."

Carter gave his boy a look. "This would be a perfect time to apologize."

"Oh. Yes, Sir. I'm sorry I didn't listen when Troy told me what you'd said. And I'm sorry I made it hard for you to do what you'd been told, Troy. But Sir—" Geoff blinked and stopped talking. "Sorry."

God, that was adorable. Utterly. It had been so long since he'd had his boy off-kilter.

He pointed to the plate. "Bacon, boy."

Geoff picked it up and held it out to him without a word.

"Can you bring that over here next?"

"Are you planning on chewing this time?" he teased.

"Shut up." Saul took a piece off the plate. "Go ahead, Troy, if you want some."

"No thank you, Sir." Troy hid in his coffee, stealing bites of cinnamon roll.

The temptation to tell Troy to stop pouting was huge.

"All right." Saul kissed Troy on the cheek and patted the boy's ass. "Back to your knees. Finish your breakfast."

Once Troy was settled, Saul stood up. "Remember what I said. No touching, no talking. Stay right where you are. We'll be back." Saul headed for the stairs.

Carter followed, figuring the cue was for him. They made it to the bedroom before he started grinning.

Saul shut the bedroom door and laughed softly. "Oh boy. Okay, I'm thinking pants. I also think we should crank the fire up a notch and maybe the heat so they can be nice and naked for a while."

"Lord, your boy can *pout* like nothing going." It was adorable as hell. He grabbed his pajama pants and tugged them on.

"Right? I used to think he was playing me, but no, he just pouts. And it does no good at all to tell him not to. He needs a win. He needs a 'good boy'. That's the only thing that works. So I need to give him a way to earn that." Saul dug up some sweatpants and pulled them on, then tossed a zippered bag on the bed and pulled out cuffs and what had to be those clamps.

"And Geoff babbles. It's cute. He didn't seem all that sorry to me, though." Saul laughed again.

"No, because he'll do it again." He went to his toy chest and found a pair of cuffs and a blindfold. The biggest punishment he could give was to not let Geoff see Troy.

"Guess I should bring my Kindle down with me. Should be a long, relaxing morning." Saul scooped up his toys, looking like a Dom and not a kid now. So weird. "After you."

"Exactly what I wanted. We can always watch TV." He was easy, really. He just craved time with them all together.

"TV. I haven't done that in forever. Maybe we should binge something" They chatted as they made their way back to the living room, and Saul went straight to Troy.

"Boy." Carter slipped the blindfold on right away without explanation, knowing it would frustrate Geoff more than anything else. He got a whimper in response. "Serving side by side can be distracting, boy. I want you focused."

"Yes, Sir."

He could hear Saul speaking to Troy but couldn't make out what was being said. Saul had Troy standing and was taking time and care putting on the boy's cuffs.

All that loving attention, and Troy was still pouting.

He rolled his eyes and put a hand under Geoff's elbow. "Come on, boy. Over my knees." He carefully led Geoff over to the couch.

Geoff was already beginning to relax. He knew the drill, and this was coming home.

The house was still a bit chilly, so he let Geoff keep the robe but as soon as his boy settled, he flipped it up to expose Geoff's bare backside. He smoothed his hand over the skin, warming them both first, then set about pinking his boy's pale skin with several measured swats.

The sound caught his lovers' attention, and he knew both Saul and Troy were watching, but he kept his focus right where it belonged.

His boy had asked for him; it was Carter's pleasure to indulge him. No one showed his hand up so well as his Geoff.

Geoff moaned for him—a long, lovely sound as his boy relaxed, all the tension disappearing.

"Oh, good boy. Very nice, Carter." Saul's voice was soft, and the praise for both of them sincere.

"Isn't he lovely?" He stroked Geoff's nicely warmed skin. He looked over to Saul and Troy, curious as hell whether Saul's boy had stopped pouting.

Troy's robe was over the arm of the couch and the boy stood in front of Saul in cuffs and nothing else, focus on Geoff. Carter didn't see a pout. He wasn't sure exactly what he was seeing, but it wasn't pouting.

"Hold this, boy." Saul slipped one clamp into Troy's hands, and teased a nipple, rolling it and tugging on the piercing.

"Master..." Troy's expression softened, but the boy's prick began to fill as those nipples went hard as diamonds.

Saul didn't reply; he just nodded to Troy and eased the first clamp into place. "Don't forget to breathe, boy."

"Breathe..." Troy rippled, lips dropping open.

Hmm...definitely not pouting now. Very nice.

Saul took the other clamp from Troy's fingers and fixed that one on just as gently. The motion seemed incongruous with how intensely Saul and Troy were staring into each other's eyes. "That's my boy. Are you chilly? Why don't you kneel a little closer to the fire, and I'll give you your robe back."

Saul didn't wait for an answer. He simply lowered Troy down where he wanted him, careful to make sure the boy was stable, comfortable, warm.

When Saul met Carter's eyes, Carter nodded, making sure his approval showed. He swore he saw Saul's shoulders square up. Pride looked good on his lover.

Saul grabbed more bacon and sat on the couch next to him and Geoff. "That ass sure is pretty."

"Isn't it?" Carter tapped it again, just a little hard, making Geoff wiggle. "He pinks beautifully."

Saul smoothed a hand over one of Geoff's warmed cheeks and then gave it a little love tap. "I think Troy would benefit from a light tug on that chain every so often. Just saying."

"Ah. That might be arranged." Carter reached out, tugging the chain connecting the clamps with a long, steady pull. "I'll have your mouth tonight, pretty boy."

Troy licked his lips and nodded.

"The 'yes, Sir' was implied. I'll vouch." Saul chuckled and picked up his coffee.

"S-sorry, Sir. Master."

Saul took a sip of coffee and leaned down, feeding the coffee to his boy. "Damn, that's hot."

Geoff whimpered softly and wiggled on his thighs, begging another swat, which he gave, plus a couple more, for good measure.

Saul finished whispering with Troy and settled into the couch again. "That's fascinating. How long do you usually let your boy just hang out there? Would you like a warm-up on your coffee? Troy would be happy to get it for you."

"He's good for a bit. If he needs more and is light-headed, I can lay him down over my legs with his head on the armrest. He can stay there for hours." He grabbed his coffee cup. "Boy, I need another cup." Then he winked over at Saul. "And I want to watch your pretty ass all the way."

"Leave the robe, love. And take my cup too. Let me know right away if you can't manage it with the cuffs on." Saul looked at Carter. "It's the best ass I've ever seen. Also very spankable, I've discovered."

"Have you? Clever man." He admired as Troy walked away. "Does he respond well?"

That was something he'd love to see, Troy reddened and needy.

"Very well. It wasn't over my knee, but we'll try that soon. It got him all hot and bothered though. I enjoyed it too. I liked the little sting in my fingers and the feel of his skin getting hot."

Carter was sure Saul wasn't trying to sound seductive with that last bit. Maybe the kid didn't notice his voice dropped into that register.

"It's incredibly intimate, I think. Skin-on-skin, immediate." He popped Geoff again, proving how immediate it was.

Geoff grunted softly. "Love you, Master."

"I don't think I've ever seen your boy sit still so long." Saul handed him a piece of bacon.

"He's perfect like this." Relaxed and easy, focused— Carter reached down to check his boy, who kissed his fingers.

"Coffee, Masters." Troy appeared like smoke.

"Thank you, boy." Saul took one mug and handed it to Carter, then took the other and gave Troy's chain a slow but firm tug. "How do these feel?"

Troy moaned, the pretty cock bobbing. "G-good. Master.

Good."

"So sexy. Boy, I wish you could see this."

Geoff wiggled in his lap. "If that's your wish, Master, you could take off my blindfold so I could see. I'd like to see, Sir."

"Oh, my brilliant boy." He started laughing, because Geoff never ceased to make him happy. Laughing and warming Geoff's butt with steady swats to remind his boy who was the Master here.

"You've got a live one there." Saul stood up and moved Troy back to his spot, helped him kneel, and draped him with the robe again. It was maddening that Carter couldn't hear the things Saul kept whispering to the boy.

"I do. He keeps me busy. And happy." He scooted closer to Saul when he sat and shifted Geoff so his boy could rest on the arm of the sofa.

"Both good things." Saul leaned against his shoulder, coffee in hand, and sighed. "I have to go back to work on the mountain next week, so I'm planning on enjoying the hell out of these few days we have together."

"We all have to get back to real life. I understand." Hell, he was so glad Troy was home, was able to come back to work. Carter liked knowing when he had his men around him.

"Did you know that Emma and I are trying to buy the bike shop? We're going to make an offer on it in the spring. The owner doesn't even live in Boulder anymore. If we can manage that, I can take a lot of the winter off next year."

"Whoa. Yeah? I think you two would be great at that. You've been running it anyway, right?" All four of them would own their own businesses then. There was something deeply satisfying about that.

"We have been. All we do is call the owner and tell him

what we're up to or ask if we can spend money on something. Emma's been doing the ordering without checking with him for a couple of years; we just discuss things between us. I think he'd be happy to get out from under it. And I don't really want to do anything else. I love it there."

"You can tell. If you need help with reports or something, let me know. We can help."

Saul's head tilted to smile at him. "Yeah? Thanks. We might. I appreciate that." Saul snuggled a little closer. "So, what's on Netflix?"

"Let's find out." They were having one hell of a day.

He'd been ready for his lovers to all be home.

17

Geoff's tattoo shop was technically still closed for the holidays, but he was there and setting up all the same. Saul had asked to get inked before their New Year's Eve party so it would be healed up enough to show off to the other Doms.

That was a compliment, and Geoff felt great about it. But he was also nervous. He was never nervous before he got to work, and he'd been obsessing all morning, trying to understand what was going on with him.

Nervous, obsessive, anxious. That was a hell of a cocktail. He should be more settled; he and Troy had served their masters all day yesterday, but he was struggling, and he was pretty sure Carter had noticed.

Geoff had inked Troy for so long that it had turned into something comforting and sensual, so it wasn't inking a lover that had him going. He inked Carter a couple of times a year and that didn't make him nervous, so it wasn't inking a Dom either.

There was something about Saul.

Whatever it was, he'd better figure it out before Saul and Troy got there.

Carter watched him with serious eyes, expression unreadable. Geoff was considering kicking him.

There was absolutely no need to check his equipment, he did that before he'd closed up shop for the break, but he did it anyway. He needed to keep his hands busy so his mind could work.

He glanced at Carter again and sighed. "If you've got nothing else to do, you could find a playlist that Saul would like and cue it up for me."

Carter shot him a look as he stood to go to the old-school iPod he had connected to a Bose speaker. "I'll put you over my knee, boy."

Promises, promises.

"Thank you for your help, Sir. It's Saul's first tattoo. Did you know that?"

"I did. That means you'll have done Troy's first, my first, and his first. That's special."

"Yep." Okay, that was cool. He hadn't thought about that. "What if he doesn't... I mean, he asked so he really wants it, right? He's not just being nice to me. Right?"

"Boy, ink is forever. You're under his skin, and tonight, you'll make it permanent."

"Under his skin. I like that." He was ready for permanent. "Forever is good. He'll be ours forever."

"I think he already is." Carter came right to him, hauled him up into a hard, wild kiss.

Oh, hello. His fingers scrabbled up Carter's arms, looking for somewhere to hold on. *Yeah. Love you, too, honey.* He returned the kiss with interest, pulling on his lover's shoulders.

Carter knew just how to make his eyes cross, how to make his worries shatter into a thousand pieces.

"Knock-knock?" Oh, Saul was here.

"I don't think they hear you." And Troy too.

"Hell no. I wouldn't want to hear me either."

Troy cracked up, and that made him giggle against Carter's lips.

"Little tattoo artist, little tattoo artist, let us come in." The sound of this petite cowboy faking his 'wolf' voice had him tickled half to death.

"Or I'll huff and I'll puff and Troy will blow your master again."

Geoff pushed back from Carter, breaking the kiss and laughing. "I don't know if you can take that again, Sir."

Carter chuckled, gave him a buss on the lips. "It'll be fun as fuck to try though."

"Well, Saul and I will be busy for a while so..." He winked at Carter. "I mean, I don't have any objections."

Saul laughed. "I'm getting needles and you're getting a blow job? Somehow this doesn't seem fair. Although I think Troy is a little hoarse today."

They both looked to Saul, and Geoff felt his eyebrow lift even as he saw Carter's go up. Then Carter asked, "Hoarse you have a cold or hoarse you had something long down your throat last night?"

"My boy is perfectly healthy." Saul put an arm around Troy. "He enjoyed your enthusiasm, Carter. Didn't you, boy?"

"Yes, Master." Troy grinned, wicked and teasing. "Tickled my tonsils."

"I aim to please." Carter's voice was dry as dust, and that was all he could take. Geoff started howling with laughter, clinging to Carter to keep his feet.

"All right, you jokers." Carter shook his head, gave him a swat, then looked at Saul. "You sure this is the guy you want doing your ink?"

"I'm sure." Saul came over to them. "I've seen his work."

That sobered him up a little. "You're sure? Because if you're having any second thoughts—"

Saul gave him a level look. "I'm not having second thoughts."

"And I'd understand if Troy had reservations. You're—"

"Boy? Any reservations?" Saul didn't so much as twitch, blue eyes staying steady on his.

"There's no one on earth better. I've given him all my skin. I trust him with yours."

He took a deep breath, thinking he should feel better, less nervous. But he really didn't. "Okay."

Saul took his hands. "I trust you. I love you. This is going to be awesome." Saul kissed him softly and smiled.

"Oh." Oh, that was good to hear. "I love you too."

He tried another breath, feeling much better.

"I'm excited." Saul tossed Troy his coat. "Where do you want me?"

"Just sit on the chair. Did you decide where you want it?" Geoff stole a kiss from Troy on his way to the coat rack.

"Hey, love." Troy's face was easy, relaxed, and the trust honored him.

"Troy and I were thinking either my chest or my forearm. I kind of like my chest." Saul tugged his T-shirt off and sat.

"Chest," Carter agreed.

"It's a good chest," Geoff concurred.

"Do I get to shave him?" Troy sounded altogether too excited.

Geoff snorted. "Go for it. But it's not going to be that satisfying; he's baby smooth already."

Saul rolled his eyes, but Geoff figured he deserved the dig after all the old man jokes.

"Still, I can sneak in a little nipple play while I'm doing it." Troy was high as a kite. Maybe not physically, but either way.

"Naughty." Saul's smile took any hint of reprimand out of the word.

"Come here." Geoff handed Troy the razor and a towel. "You shave. I'll get my Sharpie."

"I'm on it." Troy managed to arrange Saul perfectly, and he got his stencil blown up about thirty percent so he could transfer it.

"Oh look, Carter. Mine's going to be bigger than yours." Saul gave Carter a toothy grin that cracked Geoff up.

He shook his head. "Doms."

"Mmhmm..." Troy smiled and dragged the razor around Saul's chest, flicking a nipple every chance he got.

Saul snorted. "You only have to shave where the ink is going to go, boy."

"Are you sure?" Troy laughed and cleaned Saul up, careful to get all the soap off. "It's going to be so pretty, Master. You're going to love it."

"I know I will. I love the one Carter has. I'll have to talk to Geoff about where he can put yours."

Oh. Saul was going to let him. "I was hoping we'd be able to talk about that. But today is about you, Sir."

Saul nodded. "I think I'm ready."

"Good. I think I am too." He winked at Saul. "Scoot, Troy."

"You got it."

"Come sit on my lap, Troy. You can tell me what's got you so revved."

As if Carter didn't know damn well.

Saul took his hand, and it was warm and steady. "All right, boy. Give me your best first-timer speech."

"It's going to burn. Remember to breathe, let me know if you need to stop, and for God's sake, if you are about to sneeze, warn me." Geoff kissed Saul's cheek. "We'll start with the outline and then you can decide whether you want to keep on with the color."

Saul gave him a nod, let go of his hand, and settled back in the chair. "Breathe. I can do that. I remind Troy all the time."

"It feels like someone scratching a sunburn—not pleasant, but not deadly." Geoff made sure the transfer worked for him, touching up the lines with his Sharpie, then handed Saul a mirror. "You like the placement?"

Saul smiled into the mirror and those blue eyes lit up bright and happy. "Perfect. Troy is right. I'm gonna love it."

"You are." If there was anything he knew, he knew that he could lay down some ink. "I'm going to start with one line, let you get a feel for it."

"I'm all yours."

"Ours," Carter corrected.

"Mmm, no. For the next few hours, I'm Geoff's." Saul winked at him.

"Then I'll take Troy. Just for the next few hours." Carter's laughter filled the room.

Geoff rolled his eyes. "One line. Deep breath in and then let it go."

As soon as Saul exhaled, he laid down his line, keeping it short and easy. Lots of Doms didn't handle the burn.

Saul tensed visibly for a second and then laughed,

letting it out. "Jesus, I think the buildup was worse than the real thing." He could see Saul relax back into the chair. "I'm good. Let's go for it."

"Good deal. Remember, breathe, and let me know if you need to move. Troy, turn the music up. I love this song."

"Yes, sir!"

"Oh, me too." Saul made a show of taking a deep breath, lay back on the headrest, and closed his eyes.

The outline went down like a dream, and they broke for coffee and to give Saul a break, although Geoff had to admit, Saul was a trooper.

"You want to keep on and finish, or are you ready to call it off and do color another day?"

"No, I definitely want to finish." Saul was looking at the outline in the mirror. The Dom's eyes were bright, and his voice was full of wonder. "I should finish it. Right, Troy?"

"You should finish it, Master. You're flying."

Geoff grinned at Troy, because Troy got it.

Saul caught Troy up and kissed him heavily, one hand ghosting over Troy's fly. "I am."

"Geoff is magic." Troy whimpered, hips rolling toward Saul's touch. "Master, please. I'm so hard."

"Has Carter been teasing you, boy?" Saul backed away from Troy, headed for the chair.

"Yes, Master."

"His nips are sensitive after the clamps. It's amazing."

Geoff chuckled softly, whispered, "Carter's so not helping."

"He's a Dom. Help is kind of a relative concept." Saul winked and settled back. "Personally, I feel amazing."

"Good. I'll do my best to keep the endorphins flowing. Colors the same as Carter's?"

"Just the same." Saul nodded. "I like that they'll be

identical. I want Troy's to be the same too. Who's going to do yours?"

"I'll do it on my leg." It would make it easy. The real question was where to ink Troy. Butt cheek? Cock? Scalp?

"Yeah? Cool. That's totally hot, you know. I'm so going to be here for that." Saul kissed him suddenly, sure fingers curling behind his neck. Geoff sank into Saul's side, careful not to touch the fresh ink, his hand landing gently on Saul's fly.

"Mmm. Save it. We can all play tonight." Saul let him go. "I'm going to ask your Master if I can have you."

"Yes, Sir. Thank you." His ball sac tightened, and he sucked in a long cleansing breath. Right now, he had good work to do.

He snapped on a new pair of gloves. "You ready, Sir?"

Troy moaned, and they both shook their heads. Then Saul smiled at him. "I am."

"All right then. Let's do this." He spared Saul a smile and then he got back to work, finishing off the ink that would mark them all as family.

———

WANT to find out how Saul & Troy & Carter & Geoff's story ends? Download Making the Rules, Book 3 in the series, now!

If you enjoyed Making a Mark,
move on to Book 3 right now!

Making the Rules
The Triskelion, Book 3

The rules keep changing as Saul and Troy and their good
friends and lovers Geoff and Carter are figuring out how
they all fit together in their evolving relationship. Subs Geoff
and Troy test the limits of both their friendship and their
Doms' patience as they discover new things about each
other, and Doms Carter and Saul wrestle with how to be the
men their subs need and become lovers in their own right.

As they all push boundaries trying to decide how to move
forward, Troy begins to feel like he's constantly one step
behind, and he's having trouble keeping up with everyone
else. He's already unsure how much more change he can
accept, so when a tragedy strikes, it threatens to completely
overwhelm him.

Geoff, Carter, and Saul all come together to help Troy cope,
and to figure out what he needs. But what they all soon
discover is they have to understand what they each desire,
and that making the rules is all about that balance.

FIND OUT MORE
or Buy on Amazon

Interested in learning more about BA's cowboys and Jodi's gentlemen? Want free fiction and news? Join our newsletters!

What's Up with Jodi
http://bit.ly/whatsupjodi

Spurs and Shifters
https://lp.constantcontact.com/su/A9CRUzp/baandjulia

ABOUT JODI

JODI takes herself way too seriously and has been known to randomly break out in song. Her men are imperfect but genuine, stubborn but likable, often kinky, and frequently their own worst enemies. They are characters you can't help but fall in love with while they stumble along the path to their happily ever after. For those looking to get on her good side, Jodi's addictions include nonfat lattes, Malbec and tequila any way you pour it.

Website: jodipayne.net
Newsletter: http://bit.ly/whatsupjodi
All Jodi's Social Links: linktr.ee/jodipayne

Hey, y'all!

We want to thank you for giving Making a Mark a try and we hope you enjoyed the story. If you can spare a few minutes to post a review at the eBook website where you made your purchase, we'd very much appreciate it!

Don't forget to "like" our Facebook pages and groups to keep up with all the news--new releases, sales announcements, giveaways, sneak peeks-- and of course the rodeo pictures, coffee memes and just general fun. We'd love to have all y'all!

Yeehaw and thanks for reading!

BA & Jodi

ABOUT BA

Texan to the bone and an unrepentant Daddy's Girl, BA Tortuga spends her days with her basset hounds, getting tattooed, texting her grandbabies, and eating Mexican food. When she's not doing that, she's writing. She spends her days off watching rodeo, knitting and surfing Pinterest in the name of research. BA's personal saviors include her wife, Julia Talbot, her best friends, and coffee. Lots of coffee. Really good coffee.

Having written everything from fist-fighting rednecks to hard-core cowboys to werewolves, BA does her damnedest to tell the stories of her heart, which was raised in Northeast Texas, but has heard the call of the high desert and lives in the Sandias. With books ranging from hard-hitting GLBT romance, to fiery ménages, to the most traditional of love stories, BA refuses to be pigeon-holed by anyone but the voices in her head.

BA loves to talk to her readers and can be found at http://batortuga.com/ and her newsletter signup link is http://bit.ly/BAJulianews

AVAILABLE FROM JODI & BA

The Cowboy and the Dom Trilogy

First Rodeo, Book One

Razor's Edge, Book Two

No Ghosts, Book Three

The Soldier and the Angel, a Cowboy and Dom Novel

Sin Deep, a Cowboy and Dom Novel

East Meets Westerns

(single titles)

Wrecked

Window Dressing

Flying Blind

Special Delivery, A Wrecked Holiday Novel

Temptation Ranch

The Higher Elevation Series

Heart of a Cowboy

Land of Enchantment

Keeping Promises

Bigger Than Us

The Triskelion Series

Breaking the Rules

Making a Mark

Making the Rules

Les's Bar Series

Just Dex

Hide Bound

The Lone Star Series

Tending Tyler

Roped In

The Collaborations Series

Refraction

Syncopation

Puzzles Series

Cryptic